Empire of Wolves

Jonathan Blanks

Copyright © 2024 by Jonathan Blanks

Hardcover ISBN: 979-8-9908503-0-9

Paperback ISBN: 979-8-9908503-1-6

Ebook - EPUB ISBN: 979-8-9908503-2-3

All rights reserved.

No portion of this book may be reproduced in any form without written permission from the publisher or author, except as permitted by U.S. copyright law.

Contents

Prologue - Cecil	1
1. Gabriel	10
2. Lesley	23
3. Gabriel	32
4. Gabriel	38
5. Lesley	48
6. Lesley	57
7. Gabriel	71
8. Gabriel	79
9. Gabriel	92
10. Lesley	104
11. Gabriel	119
12. Gabriel	134
13. Gabriel	161

14. Lesley	172
15. Lesley	179
16. Lesley	189
17. Gabriel	200
18. Lesley	216
19. Gabriel	231
20. Lesley	245
21. Gabriel	254
22. Lesley	267
23. Lesley	276
24. Gabriel	293
25. Gabriel	303
26. Lesley	316
27. Gabriel	324
28. Lesley	335
29. Gabriel	343
Epilogue - Gabriel	359
Epilogue - Lesley	363

Prologue – Cecil

5000 Year Ago

The sun sank beneath the horizon, its gentle rays painted the deserted city with a soft, warm glow; a fearless band of warriors emerged from the shadows, their hearts filled with inescapable purpose. Clad in intricately adorned leather armor and adorned with wolf pelts that fluttered in the evening breeze, they forged ahead with an air of determination etched upon their faces. Cecil, a man of massive stature, possesses raven-black hair and piercing blue eyes, a striking combination that exudes a commanding presence.

The once-thriving city was a desolate ruin, a ghost of its former self. The group moved through the silence, their footsteps echoing emptily. Anxiety clawed at Cecil's chest as he stood amid the remnants of a place he once called home. The sight of the devastation stoked the flames of his fury even further, a tainted conflagration that burned relentlessly within his soul. With a sweeping gaze, Cecil surveyed his surroundings and pointed towards a grand fortress, a newly built marvel of magical engineering , dominating the city's center. Inside, he believed, resided his target: the former ruler of the realm.

The sword's pommel, decorated with a meticulously crafted wolf's head, gleamed with icy white eyes, mirroring Cecil's menacing gaze. Along the rain guard, a crest depicted a one-eyed wolf, surrounded by a circle of soaring ravens, adding a touch of mystique and power to the weapon's design. Vivid ice-white runes lined both sides of the sword, emanating a radiant glow.

As the warriors approached the formidable fortress, an ethereal aura of elemental power emanated from them—fire, wind, water, and lightning. Their unwavering strength and resilience shone like radiant beacons, creating a tapestry of steadfast determination. With a thunderous battle cry, they marched through the narrow streets, their footsteps resonating with an indomitable energy. They had come to fight, but their enemy proved elusive, leaving them in a state of anticipation and readiness.

A sudden ear piercing crack drew the formidable warrior's eyes, capturing the spectacle of a monumental rift in the celestial realm. It was a swirling vortex of darkness and energy, with jagged edges that seemed to pulsate with an otherworldly power. Through a tear in space-time, an ominous gateway unfurled, revealing a realm immersed in absolute darkness. This malevolent domain was under the sway of dark forces, where Oblivion reigned unchallenged.

Their eyes were locked on the ethereal rift in the fabric of reality. Gleaming swords, ablaze with fervent flames, exuded an atmosphere of limitless power. The warriors braced themselves, anticipating the moment of their glorious purpose. The warriors were united under the leadership of a warrior, whose blade emanated a profound blue fire that danced along its length, captivating all who beheld it. With determination, the warriors chanted the name of their leader in unison: Cecil.

From the rift's sinister depths, a legion of winged imps materialized, resembling ominous bats as they swarmed forth, driven by a malevolent purpose. The expanding rift posed an imminent threat, poised to engulf everything in its perilous path. Cecil felt his spirit being tugged away by an unknown force he clung to the understanding that Sol, his god of light, was the sole entity tethering it to his, and his warriors, body, a glimmer of hope amidst the encroaching darkness.

Cecil and his warriors came face to face with the beings of pure darkness. Their skin was so dark that it swallowed all light, and their eyes were a warm orange, with teeth and claws that had a starry pattern. In the heart of the night, the imp-like creatures moved, and their presence sucked the colors from their environment. Blades clashed with monstrous claws, creating a symphony of violence as shadow and light collided in a deadly dance.

Amidst the turmoil of battle, he fearlessly entered the fray, cleaving through the relentless swarm of imps that surrounded him. Drawing upon his innermost strength and unleashing his fury, he transformed into a radiant blaze of glory as his razor-sharp blades sliced through the shadowy flesh of his enemies. The blood and carnage satiated him, igniting a primal lust within his heart.

A second wave of warriors entered the fray, overwhelming their opponents with superior skill. Some of them roared like thunder, and their thunderous blows struck with the power of lightning. Some possess the extraordinary ability to harness the fury of gale-force winds, unleashing a destructive force upon their enemies.

Moreover, a chosen few are gifted with the remarkable power to transform into monstrous beasts, resembling men in shape but possessing incredible strength and agility. They bite, tear and rip through the flesh of their darkling adversaries with relentless determination. However, the reinforcements were not enough to save the day. In the fierce conflict, the warriors fell one by one, leaving Cecil as the sole survivor. In the blazing embrace of ethereal blue flames, Cecil was unable to indulge in the luxury of grieving for his fallen comrades. Instead, he acknowledged and respected the tranquil peace they had found in the luminous embrace of Valhalla's light.

In the midst of the relentless onslaught of shadow beasts, Cecil's resolve proved unwavering. He forcefully advanced, cleaving through the horde with each strike of his blade, cutting a path straight into the keep. Though their sharp claws tore at his flesh, he refused to falter, pressing on with every strike. Deeper into the keep, he ventured, one beast at a time, until the once dense horde dwindled, leaving the hallways free from their menacing presence.

At the conclusion of the long and winding corridor, an imposing set of double doors awaited. Two Void-infused warriors, former comrades he once called brothers, stood guard. Their black armor bore a familiar emblem, a one eyed wolf encircled by a murder of ravens. Their warm-colored eyes narrowed as they raised their weapons and charged at Cecil.

With all his strength, Cecil fought defensively, outmaneuvering the two Void-infused knights in agility and sword play. Cecil sliced one's throat, splattering its black blood on the wall. He then stabbed the other, pinning him to the wall, and the orange light in his eyes faded as he slumped down.

As Cecil stepped over their motionless forms, an enigmatic energy, slipping free from their lifeless bodies, seeped into his own. A surge of pity welled up within him, mingled with a sense of gratitude as their departed souls nourished his inner flames, strengthening him. With a powerful kick, he forced open the massive double doors, revealing a solitary warrior inside.

Upon a throne of ebony wood and stone, The Void King sat, his form encased in black plate mail that mirrored the dark flesh of the creatures around him. An aura of darkness radiated from his body, absorbing the surrounding colors. Adorning his shoulder was a crest that displayed a remarkable image - a solitary-eyed wolf encircled by ravens gracefully soaring overhead. This identical crest was also present on Cecil's runic sword.

Suspended behind the formidable Void King, a colossal Crystal emanated a soft radiance, its gentle shimmer casting an ethereal glow. As if filled with immeasurable energy, it resonated with a subtle hum, enchanting all who beheld its majestic presence.

In a moment of calculated contemplation, Cecil traced his fingers along the keenly honed edge of his blade, aware that the opportune moment to strike down the king, his king, had finally arrived. In this act of retaliation for the fallen, he sought the ultimate glory and vindication.

The Void King eyes glowed a smoldering orange beneath his ornate plate mail helmet ordained with a crown of pure shadow. He wielded a massive two-handed sword that looked impossible to wield. In a single, powerful motion, the Void King grasped the sword with one hand and effortlessly lifted it to rest upon his shoulder. With a narrowed gaze, he leaped from his simple throne. The glistening blade descended, slicing downward in a decisive strike.

Cecil evaded the colossal blade, retaliating with a slash of his own. However, the two-handed sword, an immovable force, intercepted Cecil's bastard sword, blocking its advance. Their steel rang out as they clashed against each other, sending sparks flying. Their energies clashed without physical form, creating a storm of arcane power that threatened to tear the world apart.

In the aftermath of a grueling battle, Cecil's labored breathing reflected the overpowering influence of the Void King's dark magic. As a sense of defeat loomed, a flicker of optimism emerged. Sol's radiant light bathed Cecil's mind, dispelling the encroaching darkness and revealing a vision of a majestic tree reaching towards the heavens, ablaze with luminous light. This divine encounter ignited an idea within the warrior.

Delving into his pocket, he retrieved a small, unpolished teal stone and a seedling, harboring hope for a potential turning point. Cecil held the stone and the seedling in his hand and closed his eyes. He concentrated all of his energy on the items, and with a surge of power. They began to be illuminated in a bright teal light, the seedling blazing with its own pure white flame.

In a surge of fury, the Void King's roar echoed through the air as he unleashed a torrent of dark energy toward the warrior. Protected by an energy field emanating from the stone, the warrior's eyes gleamed with determination as he emerged. A triumphant smile graced his lips as he charged at the Void King. With one mighty swing of his sword, the warrior harnessed the stone's power and focused it through the blade. The resulting blow left the Void King reeling from its devastating impact.

As the Void King's dark sorcery waned, he staggered backward. Sensing the vulnerability, Cecil unleashed a flurry of relentless strikes, fueled by the burning passion within. The Void King's feeble attempts to retaliate were no match for Cecil's indomitable ferocity, leaving his defenses shattered.

In a critical move, Cecil drove his sword into the Void King's chest, driving him down onto his large wooden throne. The blade pierced through the king's body and into the wood, pinning him in place with the long bastard sword.

The Void King let out a bellow and a blood-curdling screech. Black blood flowed from his wounds and teeth. It was thick with a translucent star-like pattern, but he showed no signs of weakening as he thrashed in pain. The wood of the throne warped and sprouted wild growth until it became more tree-like, wrapping its vines around the struggling king, holding him in place.

Tearing at the veins that bound him to the throne, The Void King struggled to free himself. The veins grew faster than he could tear them apart, but he managed to free a hand and began to pull the blade from his chest.

In his euphoric moment, Cecil's disquieting realization dawned upon him. Contrary to his expectations, the Void King's demise was not as final as he had believed. The malevolent entity continued to exist, posing an imminent threat.

Cecil drove the sword into the back of the throne, whispering a prayer as he touched the hilt. The wolf eyes embedded on the hilt and runes began to glow with blue flames, causing the Void King to screech in pain, burning him from within.

A surge of dark energy burst through a tear in the sky, consuming all light and empowering the Void King. With brute force, the Void King began to tear through the wooden roots faster than they could grow. His body slid over the sword, but the roots persisted, rooting him in place.

In the throne room, a colossal boulder crashed through the ceiling, knocking the warrior off his feet amidst a shower of falling debris. The boulder then unfurled, revealing itself to be an enormous, hulking creature composed of pure darkness. Its mouth was filled with star-shaped teeth, and its eyes shone with a faint, eerie glow.

Cecil engaged the beast in a fierce hand-to-hand combat, his fists ablaze with blue energy. Despite his valiant efforts, the beast's immense strength proved overwhelming. Realizing that brute force alone would not be enough to defeat it, Cecil resolved to use his wits and cunning to gain an advantage.

In a cautious dance, Cecil circled the colossal beast, maintaining a safe distance from its formidable reach. The creature's ebony hide concealed shadows, and its fiery orange eyes emanated an eerie glow. With deliberate movements, Cecil traversed around the beast, his unwavering gaze fixed upon it. Despite the beast's deafening roar, the warrior remained undeterred, patiently awaiting an opportune moment to strike.

In a sudden turn of events, the beast launched a ferocious charge upon Cecil. With nimble reflexes, Cecil evaded the attack and unleashed a torrent of powerful punches in retaliation. However, the beast pivoted and lashed its tail with immense force, sending Cecil crashing into a nearby wall with a resounding thud. Despite the impact, Cecil regained his composure, rolling out of the way to avoid a successive onslaught from the beast. In a swift counter-offensive, Cecil unleashed an explosive energy blast, catching the beast off guard and forcing it to stumble backward.

In a swift move, Cecil seized the opportune moment to strike once more, unleashing a potent punch that connected solidly with the beast's head. A roar of agony erupted from the beast as flames engulfed its wound, causing it to collapse onto the ground in defeat. Standing tall over his vanquished foe, Cecil glared defiantly at the Void King. Despite his struggles to rise, the Void King's maniacal laughter echoed through the air.

From his back, the king unfurled a pair of dark wings. Dark waves of violet and green energy pushed Cecil back, causing him to slide across the ground. Crashing through the ceiling came three more hulking beasts, followed by a swarm of flying creatures that descended, hissing and growling.

With a clear sense of purpose, Cecil beseeched the sun god, Sol, in prayer. In the hushed silence of his closed eyes, a luminous blue flame engulfed him, granting him an otherworldly aura. He surged forward and wrested the wolf hilt sword from the grasp of the Void King. In a powerful and decisive strike, he plunged his fist deep into the gaping wound of his opponent.

In response to Cecil's formidable strike, the Void King emitted an anguished cry. From his chest, roots and tendrils erupted, eerily illuminated by a piercing white light, starkly showcasing the devastation wrought upon the creature.

Once more, Cecil offered a fervent prayer. He then hovered momentarily before propelling himself skyward with explosive force. In his wake, he left a trail of brilliant blue light, annihilating the nearby dark creatures as he soared upward, breaking through the ceiling and heading directly toward the massive rift.

From the innumerable rifts, an incessant swarm of adversaries emerged, forming a tempestuous onslaught. Immense creatures descended from the sky, resembling fiery meteors; their impact pulverized the earth and annihilated countless warriors. The extraordinary abilities and energies of these warriors proved futile against the overwhelming might of this formidable force.

In the midst of a swirling tempest of malevolent creatures, Cecil soared high into the sky. His majestic sword crackled with brilliant streaks of blue flame as it sliced through the air, igniting each winged beast into a fiery ball. With unrelenting determination, Cecil navigated his way through the menacing creatures, aiming to reach the rift in reality. Evading those he could not defeat and skillfully avoiding the colossal falling creatures, he drew closer to the rift. The radiant power of light surged through his veins, growing more intense and scorching as the world around him faded into a muted grayscale.

The darkness spread throughout the land below, transforming it into an embodiment of the void. Lush green fields turned barren and blackened, while the once clear blue sky became a tumultuous mass of dark clouds. The air was thick with the smell of sulfur and decay, and the distant echoes of screams and battle clashed.

Despite the overwhelming sense of despair, Cecil knew he must act. He raised his hand, and a blinding light surrounded him. With a sudden burst, the light shot from his hand into the sky.

For miles, the light traveled until it reached the edge of the darkness, where it hung—a radiant beacon of hope—defying the encroaching tendrils.

With a profound inhalation, Cecil focused the entirety of his energy upon the stone. In this solemn moment, he bid a heartfelt farewell to his brothers, harboring a fervent hope that their paths would cross once more within the hallowed halls of Valhalla. The light within it intensified until it exploded outward in a thunderous roar, consuming the rift and the warrior.

Chapter One

Gabriel

Bright light filtered through the narrow gaps of the bedroom window, it illuminated Gabriel's face. Stirring from his sleep, he opened his eyes only to shield them from the blinding glare. Taking a moment to collect his thoughts and steady his breathing, he prepared to embrace the day. With a resolute gesture, he tossed the blankets aside, exposing himself to the crisp morning air that swept in through the partially open window. The cool breeze sent shivers down his skin, awakening his senses.

With a fluid gesture, he rolled out of bed, elongating his limbs and raking his fingers through his disheveled, short, black hair. To invite more natural light, Gabriel slid open the blinds. From his third-story attic, he surveyed the neighborhood— Greenfield, a conventional suburban area characterized by its tranquility and peacefulness. Rows of white houses with russet-hued roofs formed a uniform pattern.

Gabriel always checked the view, even though it was always the same until yesterday. In the distance, he saw a construction crew breaking ground. It was another expansion to his little corner of the world. Gabriel was hopeful that there would be some better stores in the next couple of years.

He threw on some plain clothing, blue jeans, and a t-shirt that read 'GPD', where Gabriel had been a police officer for the better half of a decade. He took pride in protecting and serving. Granting him a purpose in life, a reason to live beyond his sister Lesley.

Homemade art pieces littered the dresser and shelves all around the room. They ranged from hand macaroni art to some more refined work of art. One piece depicted a woman shrouded in dark shaded colors. Another one of Lesley, his sister, rode a rocking unicorn. His eyes lingered on an old family portrait of them with their parents.

As he exited the room, he placed a hand on a sheathed bastard sword hanging on the wall. On its hilt was a crest depicting a one-eyed wolf with a circle of ravens soaring overhead. The ritual always seemed to make him feel a little more at ease.

The doorway went into a spiral set of stairs that led from his attic bedroom all the way down to the basement. He walked down past the second level and straight to the first level where he entered the kitchen. There he found his little sister standing at the kitchen island, in the middle of the kitchen, eating from a bowl of blueberries.

Gabriel's gaze lingered on the small scar gracing her cheek and ear. While most people would overlook it, it was impossible for him to ignore its presence. Her silken black hair flows down to the middle of her back. Her eyes are a couple of jeweled sapphires. She wore a long checkered red and black skirt with a black top with red trim, solid black stockings and black shoes. A standard school uniform with a gold emblem Griffin on the front.

"I see you are ready for school for once." Gabriel said, referring to her school uniform.

"Ha ha." She said with a slight indifferent shrug. She gestured to the bowel containing fresh berries still damp from being washed.

Gabriel opened the refrigerator and took out a container of Greek yogurt. He opened it and put a handful of berries into the yogurt. He stood on the opposite side of the island.

Gabriel noticed Lesley roll her eyes, but he decided not to say anything. He didn't want to start an unnecessary argument so early in the morning.

They ate in silence for a few moments. The ticking of the clock was loud. A strange tension built.

"How has school been going for you, any new drama?" Gabriel asked with a forced casual grin, breaking the silence.

Lesley shrugs again, "No. No drama." They ate for a few more minutes, the air between them growing more awkward by the moment.

"No drama? But there was something?"

"Yes, classes and homework," With a sneer, Lesley halted her movements to gaze at Gabriel. "I should get going." She picked up her bag. From the basement, a loud crash of metal on stone had rung out. The sound of metal gym plates had hit the equipment and floor. "What the hell was that?"

Gabriel narrowed his eyes and grimaced, unconvinced that Lesley had not tossed something where it did not belong. Lesley enjoyed using their home gym but was not very good at keeping it tidy. "You have to put the plates back on the rack when you are finished or they could fall and break something."

"I didn't even go down there today."

"Well the crash from the basement says otherwise."

"Are you going to assume that it was me, without even considering the possibility that there is a larger issue? Maybe you misplaced something and forgot about it."

"It's ok to use the equipment. But put the stuff away correctly."

"Wow. Can you please stop with the third degree?" Lesley slammed down berries back into the bowl. A couple slammed on the side, fruit juice smeared into the side of the bowl. "I like you better when you don't assume things."

Gabriel sighed, looking down at the bowl of blueberries. He had failed to avoid the argument, and it had even started over something so trivial. He knew he was wrong but he couldn't bring himself to apologize. "I'll take care of it." He said after a pause. "You should get going before you're late."

With a snarky tone and a roll of her eyes, Lesley retorts, "As if I haven't made that clear already."

Gabriel nodded, with a clenched jaw, looking into his breakfast as he listened to her walk away, the sound of her school shoes clacking on the hardwood floor. Gabriel felt her fury in the way her footsteps scraped against the hardwood floor, grating on his nerves. As the front door swung open and slammed shut, an eerie tranquility engulfed him.

Gabriel stood there, eating blueberries and yogurt. He had felt lost, as though he had no idea where he had gone wrong. He stood there for a few more minutes, still thinking to himself that she was growing up too fast, but was still a child.

He shook his head, correcting himself. "Grown up too fast," he grimaced with mixed emotions. With wide eyes, he shook his head in indecision. Her birthday had arrived, but he was conflicted about taking action, if any. He pulled out his phone and searched for birthday gift ideas before doom scrolling through news headlines.

As he scrolled through his phone, he saw a news headline that read, 'Incompetent Construction Crew Found and Destroyed Ancient Artifacts.' Gabriel clicked on the link, but then heard a loud bang and a clatter of what sounded like metal on metal, the sound of more gym equipment crashing. He began to feel guilty for accusing Lesley, as this sounded like a bigger mess than she could have caused from negligence. Gabriel sighed, and set his phone down on the counter.

"This can't be good." Gabriel removed a kitchen knife from its block, flipped it around into a reverse grip, and ran down the spiral staircase with a few graceful strides. He heard a sudden painful groan, then continued walking down the stairs.

At the bottom of the stairs, he saw a strange woman on her knees, writhing in pain. She wore white, tattered clothes—a sleeveless top and puffed-out pants that tucked into her boots. Her white clothes were dirty and torn, with tattered and frayed fringes.

Gabriel saw his gym equipment and weights strewn about in disarray, making it seem like an explosion had gone off. A woman sat in the middle of the mess. Gabriel stared in shock for a moment before announcing himself.

"Greenfield police department." If she heard him, she made no movement to acknowledge it. Gabriel realized she was either injured or intoxicated. "Are you okay, miss? What happened down here?"

The mysterious woman shifted her gaze to Gabriel, her stern features and fluid movements a stark contrast to the intensity of her emerald eyes, which bore into his soul. She stood up, unstable and fatigued, and took a moment to study Gabriel before relaxing her posture. "I mean you no harm, Guardsman," she said as she glanced around the room. "Where am I?"

"Guardsmen? I'm not a guard, I'm a cop. You are breaking and entering my home. Who are you and how did you get in here?"

She let out a soft chuckle, the sound causing her to wince and rub her sore ribs. "Breaking and entering?" she said, her tone tinged with amusement. "That description isn't too far off, I suppose."

She scanned her surroundings once more. "The last thing I recall is that I was losing ground with Viktor. Then I was…" Her voice trailed off as she stared at him for a brief moment. "Identify yourself," she demanded, her tone exuding authority.

Gabriel's brow furrowed as he took in the sudden change in her tone. He felt a surge of compassion for her; it was clear that Viktor was abusing her. However, he didn't want to jump to conclusions, so he decided it was best to introduce himself first. "I'm officer Gabriel Wyndham of the Greenfield Police Department. You are in my home."

The emerald-eyed woman glared at him and tried to walk forward, but she managed to stumble. Gabriel stepped forward and caught her before she could collapse. In spite of her dire condition, she mustered the last of her energy in an attempt to distance him from her. This exertion pushed her further into a state of exhaustion, causing her to collapse into his arms.

Recognizing the seriousness of her condition, Gabriel gathered her into his arms with great care and secured the knife between his pants and his belt. As he gazed upon her grime-covered, passive face, he saw beyond the fierce exterior and glimpsed the softness that lay beneath the surface.

Dismissing the thought, he resumed his ascent up the stairway. Roughly halfway through the climb, he paused to check on the knife tucked into his waistband. The action proved a mistake, as the blade dug into his thigh and waist. Wincing through the pain, he resigned himself to enduring the discomfort until he could reach the third floor.

Upon reaching his attic room, he noticed a slight abrasion on his thigh. He was uncertain whether it was a result of a knife cut or not. In the center of his bed, he gently seated her. Placing a hand on her forehead, he sensed her elevated temperature.

Using his right hand, he thoroughly inspected his pants for any cuts while simultaneously using his left hand to remove the knife. Fortunately, there were none. From the bedside, Gabriel retrieved a pistol, and holster together, then attached it to his belt.

Descending back to the kitchen, he placed the knife in the rack, and slipped his phone into his pocket. He then collected a few hand towels, soaked them in cold water, and poured a glass of water. With these items in hand, he returned to the unconscious woman.

Upon entering the room, Gabriel's gaze fell upon her delicate form nestled in his bed. She appeared to be a helpless young woman, similar in age to Lesley. The sight of her triggered a sense of urgency as he noticed the traces of distress upon her countenance.

With tender care, Gabriel delicately grasped the moist cloth and proceeded to cleanse the dirt from her face. As he wiped away the gray grime, her features gradually transformed, unveiling a softened expression that radiated a captivating allure.

Her clothes looked more like something a martial artist would wear. Despite the gray soot and dirt, it was too nice for a common thief. The material is as soft as silk but shows little signs of wear or tear. Yet the subtle designs looked much more fashionable than functional.

In an effort to reduce her fever, Gabriel gently placed a clean, cool towel over her forehead. As he stood there, his hand resting on his chin, he contemplated his next move. Who was this woman? He wondered. He decided that before taking any official action, he needed to learn more about her. In the meantime, he would take care of her.

It didn't take long before the mysterious woman stirred from her slumber, blinking her eyes open. "Who are... Where am I?'" she said as she tried to sit up but fell back flat on her back.

"Take it easy. You passed out on me once already."

"Ah, yes, the guardsmen." Her soft facial expressions harden as she examines Gabriel and her surroundings. Then soften as she closes her eyes, pressing the cool cloth to her forehead. "Have you taken me to your bed chambers?"

"I thought that you might want to rest for a while."

"That's rather kind of you but aren't you concerned about what someone might think?" Once more, her facial expressions grew milder, and a sly grin emerged upon her lips.

It was clear to Gabriel that this mysterious woman was having fun with him. "I'm more concerned with who you are."

"Who I am? Do you bring strangers into your bedroom often? That's bold of you."

With a furrowed brow, Gabriel raised his hand to his mouth. He couldn't resist asking himself a similar question. It would have been more sensible, and required fewer flights of stairs, to have let her rest on the couch. Yet, he found himself walking her up three flights of stairs to lay her upon his bed. He brought her up to his room. Why on earth had he done that?

He cleared his throat deciding to ignore the question hoping that his thoughts didn't display on his face. "Have you taken any narcotics in the last twenty-four hours?"

The enigmatic woman maintained her mischievous smile, subtly infusing it with a tinge of bewilderment. "Narcotics?"

"Mind altering substances. Drugs." Gabriel paused for a few moments as she continued to stare at him. "Do you know who you are?"

"I am aware of my station, Guardsmen of Greenfield. It surprises me that you do not." She sat up in the bed letting the damp cloth slide off her forehead and drop into her hands. "I am fascinated by these Narcotics you speak of. However, I would argue that it is undesirable to alter one's mind to be forgetful. I would alter it for increased mental capacity, speed, and processing abilities."

"That's quite the hot take." Gabriel said sarcastically. He was taken aback by the Bizarre twist of meaning.

"What a fascinating turn of phrase." She said scrunching her brow. "I have not the slightest idea of what it means. Do the peasants around here say it?"

"Presents?" Gabriel was unable to determine if she was being sarcastic, but he was beginning to feel offended. Her tone was more like a formal question than an actual dig at his social class. "I'm sorry, your majesty," He said with a hint of sarcasm, "Us peasants have many strange phrases."

"Your majesty?" She echoed, tilted her head, and asked, "Are you aware of my identity?"

"What? No. I really don't." Skepticism had filled his face as he relaxed his arms, letting them fall to his sides. He had studied her face, trying to determine if she had been toying with him, or if this had been an illusion of grandeur or something more sinister.

A moment passed as her piercing green gaze bore into his own, sending a subtle wave of unease through him. Finally, a chuckle broke the tension as she settled back into the welcoming comfort of his bed. "That's. Interesting. Though Not unlikely." She shrugged. "You are unaware of my identity. This feeling is both peculiar and liberating."

Gabriel observed her behavior further. She had acted strangely, but did not appear to have been a criminal. He had been intrigued by her speech and her casual demeanor.

"I have no knowledge of my whereabouts or how I came to be here." With hands raised high, she let them fall, accompanied by a resounding clap. Her gaze wandered around the room, as if her mind was engrossed in a distant realm. "The last thing of which I have any recollection is a duel with my younger brother." she said to herself. "Then I find myself here with you in your bedchambers. Like a young maiden ready to give everything to my lord husband."

Gabriel tried to ignore the last part—she was definitely toying with him—and summarized what she had said. "A duel? You were fighting your brother? Then somehow ended up in my home?"

"To summarize the narrative, my brother gained enough influence and power to usurp my rightful claim to lead our empire."

"Empire?" he inquired with a dubious tone, a faint smile playing on his lips. The tale was far-fetched, but it wasn't the first he'd heard a crazy story from a perpetrator. Someone who was to lead an empire wouldn't be breaking into his home in the middle of the day. "I'm guessing that makes you a princess?"

She looked up at him with those emerald eyes now full of sparkling delight, "I am." She said with a grin. "I would properly introduce myself." she said, placing the cloth back on her forehead as she lowered back down into his bed, shutting her eyes once more. "But I am exhausted, Gabriel."

"I'm going to need your name princess." Gabriel was reluctant to admit that this was not the first time he had said this to someone.

"Oh yes." She said more than a little amused.

"Are you going to enlighten me?"

"It depends on what you can offer for it," she said, stretching and getting comfortable. The pillows and sheets became more disheveled. "Your bed is quite nice."

"I'm not playing a game with you. What is your name?"

"You will not take that tone with me, guardsmen." The strange woman laughs. "In my kingdom I'd have you in chains for such insolence."

Gabriel's scowl was a silent display of annoyance toward the princess as he positioned his hands on his hips. Her playfulness was beginning to irritate him.

"My name is Amelia Ascendant of the Empire of Silver Wolves."

"Ascendent as a family name or is that part of a title?"

Amelia stopped to think about it for a moment. "Well I guess it's a little bit of both. There is an interesting story to it."

"I'm sure there is." Gabriel rolled his eyes. "You seem like a nice lady, a little confused, but nice. If you could remember where you came from, I could take you home. I could speak to your brother about this." Gabriel was skeptical of her story. He knew she had been in a fight, and she looked exhausted, but he couldn't tell if she was covering up abuse or if she was telling the truth.

"You are going to talk to my brother on my behalf?" Amelia Scowls. "Such matters are above your station, and can not be interfered with. He is mine to deal with."

"I don't take kindly to matters of abuse. I can protect you from him if that is needed."

"And you're going to protect me from him?" A tinge of skepticism permeated her tone.

"Yes, I know I can."

"You are adorable. Like a little puppy." She looked out the window for a moment, then back at Gabriel. "He's powerful. Much stronger than I had anticipated." She paused, then continued, "You are correct, I can rectify this wrong and bring my brother down a peg or two. However, I need you to do something for me in return."

"What's that?"

"If you will swear your undying loyalty to my cause and to me, I will make you my first knight of this realm."

"First knight of the realm?" Gabriel did his best not to chuckle, but failed to cover his smirk. "Yeah. OK."

Amelia looked him dead in the eyes and narrowed her own. "If you intend to keep me safe then swear to me."

Gabriel found the theatrics to be unnecessary, but he played along to make her feel more comfortable. He was beginning to feel invested in the outcome, even though the situation was strange.

With an arched eyebrow, Amelia remarked, "Gabriel Wyndham, Do you swear to bear my arms in service to your cause Lady Amelia Ascendent."

"I swear."

"Under Sol's light Raise Sir Gabriel Wyndham, Knight of the Ascendent."

Gabriel's spine tingled, and goosebumps rose on his skin. A buzzing and ringing sound came from his pocket. He fished out his phone and saw that it was Lesley calling. He answered.

"It's not like you to call, what's wrong?" He raises an eyebrow at the lack of response. "Hello?"

"Gabreil? Come to the alleyway south of the school. It's the one. Wait, let go of me! Help!" The phone goes silent.

"Who was that?"

With eyes wide open, Gabriel stared at the phone, his disbelief palpable. "That sounded like my mother." Gabriel's hair stood on end. His skin crawled and his mind raced, but he knew what to do. "I've got to go."

"Sounds like trouble, guardsmen." The princess asks with a clear lack of worry.

"I'm a cop. Not a guard." As he glanced back at her, a startling realization hit him—he couldn't leave Amelia alone in his house. "I'm not going to leave you here. If you need help with your brother, come with me and stay out of sight."

"I will not stand by! You gave your support to me and I must return the favor. I'm your Lady now."

"Hey, easy now." Gabriel felt uncertain about the significance behind the words she uttered, yet he had a vague understanding of her intent. While Gabriel prided himself on being a man of his word, the notion of being honor-bound by an ancient oath unsettled him.

"You have made me, a stranger to you, a welcome guest in your own home. You have cared for my well-being and even aligned yourself to my cause. What kind of Queen would I be if I left you to venture into the dark all alone?"

Gabriel pondered for a moment, wondering if she was a member of a royal house or if that was a cover for some trauma she was dealing with.

Amelia rose from the bed, sliding into a standing position. Her every movement was deliberate and controlled. There was a strange, indefinable aura about her that he couldn't quite place. "I have been in worse condition than this and have walked far more difficult paths. I shall accompany you." Her emerald eyes sparkled with intense excitement for adventure.

With a shrug, very unsure of the sanity of this woman, or himself. Gabriel opens the top left drawer where he keeps his badge and handcuffs. Tucks them into his jeans pocket. "Let's go."

Amelia grabbed his arm as he started to turn away towards the door. "What about your blade?" She studied the blade with intense curiosity. "Interesting weapon."

Gabriel looked at her very confused, and followed her gaze to the sword. "My weapon is on my hip." He said while wrapping his right hand over the grip, "We don't use swords in the real world, princess."

Laughter emanated from her. "Real world?"

Gabriel searched his phone for Lesley's shared location, rummaging through it. She was still at school, but he had a terrible feeling. The location had been updated south of the school in an alley.

With a casual shrug, Amelia conveyed her feelings. "Lead the way, copsmen."

Chapter Two

Lesley

Lesley and her friend left school, both dressed in their school uniforms. The alleyway they passed through was ordinary, lined with garages, garbage containers, and the backs of houses and small yards.

"Looks like a clean getaway, Olivia," Lesley said as they turned the corner.

"Let's go down this alley." Olivia said, her long, curly blonde hair bouncing with excitement. She beamed with rebellious glee.

Lesley placed her hands on her friend's shoulders, her grin widening to match Olivia's. "Let's do it!"

Lesley felt a sudden chill run down her spine. The air was thick with a strange sense of foreboding. As they walked past an open garage door, they heard someone call out to them. The two turned around, expecting to see a member of the school staff catching them in the act. However, to their surprise and disgust, it was a couple of guys hanging out in their garage.

The first man was wearing blue jeans and a sleeveless shirt that showed off his muscular arms. His shaved head glistened in the midday sun. The second man was slimmer and shorter, with a long black ponytail. He was also wearing jeans, but his shirt was black.

"Hey, ladies!" The shorter of the two says to them as they approach them.

"Ladies?" Lesley sneered. "We are literally in school uniforms."

With a sideward tilt of her head and a narrowed gaze, Olivia extended her hand to rest protectively on Lesley's lower back. In response, Lesley assumed the role of a guardian, carefully guiding Olivia behind her and enveloping her in a protective embrace.

The smaller man moves around them. "You look old enough, baby. I can teach you something school can't, girl."

With a frown, Lesley examined the little man. He was shorter than her, with long hair slicked back into a ponytail. While he was correct in his assertion that she was of legal age, she still found his approach and demeanor distasteful. "I'm sure that's why you hang around in the alley in the middle of the day, huh? 'Oh, police! Police!'"

The smaller man flashed a brilliant smile, revealing his pearly white teeth. "Don't be like that, baby," he said, attempting to put his arm around Lesley. She raised her arm to create distance between them and backed away.

"I don't think she likes you much." The bald man laughed.

Lesley realized too late that the two men had blocked both ends of the alleyway, leaving her with no easy way out. "Oh, you can tell?" she asked, her voice dripping with sarcasm. She couldn't help but find the situation strange. These two men had seen her cut through this alleyway before.

"Oh look at that. Blondie locks are about to piss her pants." The bald man said with a laugh. "I enjoy your fear." Lesley could hear Olivia grunt behind her.

"God. You two are disgusting. What kind of fun do you think we are looking for?" Lesley cuts off the bald man as he begins to speak. "Ya know what? Don't waste your breath. I'm sure I'm not going to like what you have to say."

In that tense moment, Lesley pivoted, intercepting the bald man's attempt to reach Olivia. With a resounding slap she forced his arm away, asserting her dominance. Their gazes locked in a fierce and unyielding stare. "Looking is free, but touching is going to cost you."

"Oh you are a feisty one, ain't ya." He rubbed his smooth head with one hand. "I'm going to have to knock out all your teeth before I have fun with you."

"What?" Lesley's eyes go wide, unprepared to hear something so dark, and disgusting. Her stomach felt like a burning lead weight, unsettling and upsetting.

With a sudden grip, the bald man seized Lesley by the arm, jolting her back to reality. In a swift counter, Lesley's free arm shot forward, her open palm connecting firmly with the man's throat.

Clutching his throat, grimacing in pain, he stumbled backward and spat up blood. The bald man had recovered and glared at Lesley. "This one might be tougher than she looks."

"Damn! Don't get beat up by a girl now." With a little snicker, the smaller man said.

Amidst the chaos, Lesley's senses were flooded with a surge of endorphins. The world around her transformed, becoming crystal clear and vibrant in its every detail. In a protective instinct, she positioned Olivia behind her, shielding the young girl from harm. "I don't think you can afford to try touching us." With a mocking smile and a slight bounce in her heels, she bobbed on her feet and brought her hands to her face like a boxer in the ring.

"What are you two doing in the alley with these school girls?"

From behind the garage, a young woman stood before Lesley and Olivia. She was a few years older than them, with light brown hair curled in a bob and dressed in a shirt and skinny jeans.

The larger man pointed to Lesley. "This is the one we told you about. She needs to be taught a lesson."

"Oh please, teach me something!?" Lesley taunted her. "We are all having fun now!"

"I believe it is they who require 'a lesson'," Olivia stated with a frigid edge to her voice.

Lesley smiled with great intensity glad she had such a supportive friend even if it was an approval for a street fight.

"I ought to pull out all your hair, little girl."

With a narrowed gaze, Lesley focused her attention on her. "I'd like to see you try."

The woman took a deep breath. "Look. There is no need for violence. Why don't you come inside and we can discuss this?" The woman inquired in a polite and refined manner.

Lesley noticed that the woman's demeanor and body language had changed drastically. Lesley wondered if the woman was trying to trick her or if she was genuinely interested in talking. Lesley was willing to play along to see what the woman was up to, but she didn't want to put Olivia at risk. If Lesley fell for the woman's tricks, she knew that Olivia would be their next target. "After all this, you think we're going to go into your house and risk disappearing?"

"That's exactly what I'm saying. If you cooperate, you won't be harmed. You might even enjoy your new life." Lesley glanced down at the hand on her shoulder, where the woman had placed it. "Come on, darling. You'll be fine."

"What. In. The. Actual. Fuck. Is it wrong with you?" Lesley's fist shot out so fast that she hadn't time to register the motion. The impact of her knuckles against the woman's face caused a sickening crunch of bone and cartilage. Lesley's sapphire eyes turned a deep steely gray, like a storm brewing within her.

Lesley stayed in a side stance with the left side of her body leading and her hands up, ready for another attempt. "I thought you were going to teach me something?" She taunted again, so sure of her ability to fight.

The womans cool, seductive demeanor cracked worse than the bridge of her nose. She writhed on the ground blood flowing all over her face and chest.

Lesley was struck in the back of the head with a metal trash can lid, causing her to stagger and fall to the concrete ground. The smaller man tossed the lid away with a loud clunk, saying, "Today's lesson: always watch your back."

Lesley lifted her head, grimacing at the stab of pain. She let out a low, breathy moan as the memory of the attack came flooding back. She had been assaulted from behind. The bald man, still coughing, tried to help the strange woman with her broken nose, which was now crooked to one side.

As Lesley regained full clarity, she noticed Olivia being kicked while she was on the ground nearby. "You greasy ponytail shit." She muttered to herself.

Without a second thought, she threw herself between Olivia and the incoming kick, taking the full force of it. The force of the impact left her momentarily stunned and breathless. However, she regained her senses and turned the situation to her advantage. She gripped onto the attacker's foot, then slipped her legs up between his and began to roll. The attacker lost his balance and fell to the ground with a loud snap.

Lesley leaped to her feet, a little dazed, and rubbed the sore spot on the back of her head. The little man on the ground was moaning in pain. The bald man and the woman stared at the stormy-eyed girl in disbelief. "Weren't you going to teach me something?" Lesley breaks the man's ankle with her foot causing him to scream out for her to stop.

"Well, well. I like this one."

Ready to combat a new threat, Lesley whirled around but was both relieved and annoyed to find her brother approaching with a strange woman. She let out a weary sigh and lowered her guard and head. The adrenaline was wearing off, and the pain was beginning to take hold. Her head throbbed, and she could suddenly feel her heartbeat pulsing through the back of her ears.

Gabriel wrapped his arms around Lesley and said, "The police are on their way. It's going to be okay, baby girl."

"I don't need your help taking out the trash."

Gabriel rolled his eyes and gave chase as the other two fled. He ran past the woman and tackled the bald man around the waist, bringing him to the ground. Gabriel parried the blow from the bald man, who was lying on his back and attempting to strike him with his elbow. Gabriel seized the man's wrist and pulled it behind his back, handcuffing his arms together.

As the woman struggled to break free, Amelia firmly held both of her arms and stated, "Savages like you deserve death."

Two officers exited a squad car that had pulled up to the scene. One of them radioed in, "This is Officer Williams. We need medical attention on the south side of 76th and Conley, inside the alleyway south of the school. We have two or more injured."

"Looks like you got 'em, bubba," the other officer said.

Lesley turned to Olivia, who was on the ground, and helped her up. "Are you okay?"

Olivia shook her head. "No," she said, her voice a little shaky.

"It's the adrenaline coursing through your veins. You'll be okay." Lesley led Olivia to a nearby stoop and sat down. "Take a breather," she said, patting the concrete stairs.

"Why did this happen?"

"People are awful," Lesley shrugged.

"It can't be that simple."

"It usually is."

Gabriel, who was conversing with an officer near the end of the alley, abruptly turned around and jogged back to them. "Hey, are you okay, Baby girl?" he asked, kneeling down in front of her.

Lesley looked her brother in the eye and smiled. She knew that whenever he called her 'Baby girl,' he was deeply worried about her. He had his faults, and they didn't always see eye to eye, but she knew that he cared for her in his own way. "I'm going to be okay. I got a bump on the head, but it's not a big deal. I actually feel better than I have in a while. I'm not sure why."

With a warm and comforting embrace, Gabriel enveloped her in a big hug. He expressed his relief and joy, saying, "I'm so glad you are alright."

With tears welling in her eyes, Lesley nestled into her brother's embrace, expressing her heartfelt sentiment: "I love you too, old man."

Olivia clutched her cheek, her face contorted in pain. "He kicked me!" she cried, pointing at the small man being led away on a stretcher.

"You're such a cry baby. You might have gotten hit at most three times" She said with a sly grin. "Actually you did get hit more than me."

A pair of ambulances arrived and took away the little man on the ground, who was still moaning and complaining about his injured leg. Lesley found this amusing. "You deserved it."

"Are you sure you're okay?" Gabriel asked, his face a mask of concern, with furrowed eyebrows, a downturned mouth, and a tensed jaw.

"I'm fine." She said as a paramedic came running over. Lesley pulled her hand away from her matted, blood-stained hair with a dejected sneer. She waved him away without a word.

"You should let them take a look at you."

"No. I'm fine. I'm going to stay awake for some time and put some ice on my head." In a downward tilt, she supported her head with her arms, which were resting on her thighs.

With a half smile on her face, Amelia says, "She is resilient." As Lesley's head continued to throb, she found herself struggling to form an opinion about Amelia. The pain in her head made it difficult for her to concentrate and think deeply about the situation.

"No. Take a look at her." Gabriel pressed on, gesturing fervently for the paramedic's return. The latter, upon noticing, halted his movements and accessed the situation.

"I told you I'm fine. Do not lay a finger on me." With a narrowed gaze, the paramedic turned and walked away, leaving Lesley amused by his evident frustration. However, her laughter only intensified the throbbing pain in her head, causing her to wince involuntarily.

With a sullen expression, Gabriel crossed his arms over his chest and declared, "I am your legal guardian."

"Are you now?" From her seated position, Lesley lifted her gaze to meet Gabriel's eyes.

Gabriel frowned, then his eyes widened. "Oh, happy birthday!"

"You forgot, didn't you?" Lesley said with a roll of her eyes. "Thanks," she said, rubbing the back of her head again. The pain was already fading. "I'd say this is a good birthday so far. Nothing like a good fight."

Lesley struggled to her feet, her body protesting like that of an elderly woman. As she rose, she caught sight of a strange symbol painted on the ground in motor oil.

Lesley studied the circle, taking note of every minute detail. She found it increasingly intriguing. A triangle with a circle on each point, nestled inside a double circle with strange writing in between the lines. "These guys must have been really out of their minds."

"Things are getting stranger by the moment." Gabriel said. "Let's leave this for the police."

"It looks like a ritualistic circle." Olivia said. "Could be useful for something."

"Yes. They were planning to offer us as a sacrifice to their old gods." Lesley laughed, then frowned. "Wait, were they planning to sacrifice us to some ancient god?"

"Goddess." Olivia corrected. "Sounds pretty cool, right?" A radiant smile spread across her face.

Lesley was intrigued by the idea, and she cracked a small smile. "Depends on where you stand." Lesley whipped out her phone and snapped a photo of the circle before Gabriel could see. She did not want to hear him lecture her about taking pictures of crime scenes.

"Let's not tamper with the scene. If this becomes a murder investigation, I'd rather it not be us who contaminated the crime scene. We should leave." Lesley rolled her eyes and followed him out of the alley to his car.

Chapter Three

Gabriel

In the twilight's embrace, Gabriel drove home. Despite the sun's lingering presence in the sky, the radio's blare seemed a distant echo, drowned out by the collective indifference of its passengers. The news report of increasing random acts of violence droned on, but it fell on deaf ears. With a sigh, Gabriel reached for the dial and turned the radio off. The world's chaos and fear felt too close, especially after the recent events that had shaken his life.

Gabriel pulled into the driveway and, as they walked toward the house, he put his arm around Lesley and held her close. She gave him a confused look, but then smiled and leaned into him. He wanted to be furious with her, but he couldn't. He was grateful that she was safe.

"She is quite the warrior for a youngling." Amelia said, breaking the silence. "You must be proud to have a daughter like her, Gabriel."

"She is my sister." In a moment of contemplation, Gabriel allowed the memories of raising his sibling to flood his mind. Amidst a complex web of emotions, he found himself torn between feelings of pride and moments of reflection. Recognizing the intensity of her emotions, Gabriel acknowledged the profound impact that their parents' loss had on both of them. Even during times of turmoil and anger, he understood the root of her feelings. Despite the challenges they faced, Gabriel experienced a deep sense of accomplishment, believing that he had nurtured a compassionate and understanding individual. "I am very proud of her."

With a smile on her face, Lesley directed her full attention to Amelia, her brow furrowing in concentration as her features underwent a subtle transformation. "Who are you anyway?"

The princess smiled, glancing at Gabriel and then back to Lesley. "I'm Amelia Ascendant of the Empire of The Silver Wolves."

Lesley's eyes widened and her mouth hung open for a moment. She stared at her with raised eyebrows and a wrinkled forehead, then returned her gaze to the ground. "Right. I didn't expect you to be into roleplaying women, old man."

"It's a long, short story." As they ascended the steps to the porch, Gabriel released her. He then retrieved his keys, inserted one into the front door lock, and turned it. A sudden burst of energy blew the door off its hinges, showering the porch with wood and metal. A bolt of light then launched Gabriel backwards, and he landed in the front lawn.

A large man stood in the doorway, clad in form-fitting silver armor. His large plate shoulders were adorned with three distinct cascading ridges, and his gloves and boots were tipped with claws. A white cape draped down his back, and the top of his helmet came to several spikes angled at forty-five degrees. The knights, including himself, bore a crest depicting a wolf howling at the moon.

In his left hand, he carried a large tower shield with three wolf heads facing forward next to each other. The wolf in the center was larger than the others, and the shield had a hilt at the top. The details of the armor were etched with a soft shimmering white light.

The armor began to peel away, like water flowing over his skin, revealing the face of an older man. His jaw was as rigid as the armor he wore. He appeared unfazed by his surroundings and focused his attention on Amelia.

"Prince Viktor requests your presence, or your death, my lady," he said as he walked out the door into the yard. "I know we both prefer the former."

Gabriel rose to his feet, his sight obscured by a haze and a shrill ringing resonating within his ears. With deliberate movements, he reached for his holstered pistol, taking aim at the knights while issuing a stern command, "Surrender and drop your shields!" As he grappled to make sense of the surreal scene before him, his words emerged at a measured pace. It suddenly dawned on him that Amelia's claims were not delusions or fabrications.

"I was hoping to find a way back to Viktor before he found a way to me, Lord Commander Cecil. I guess I was being too optimistic." Amelia crosses her arms over her chest, resting her weight on one leg, giving her a tilted stance.

Cecil inclined his head. "We are not sure what happened, but we have discovered how you've fled."

"I did not flee." Amelia scoffed.

"Put your hands up!" Gabriel interrupted.

Cecil stopped and turned his head towards Gabriel. "I assume that you possess some sort of powerful weapon that gives you a false sense of superiority. If this be the case, you may try your strength against me." He glanced at Amelia, who shrugged, then back at Gabriel. "I accept your challenge."

"Sir, what about them?" One of the knights asked his commander, keeping Lesley in his grasp.

"Take them alive. All three of them. We could learn much about this place."

"No!" Gabriel yelled as he fired his pistol. The liquid armor that had slid down over Cecil's face solidified before the bullet could penetrate. The impact of the bullet against the armor was loud, like metal clanging against metal. Cecil's head did not jerk back.

Cecil observed the scene, turning to leave. "Pathetic. Challenge revoked," he called over his shoulder. "Lance, Edward. Take them."

"Lance and Edward as well." Amelia said with a smirk. "You have both grown so much. I'm sure you were both very interested in exploring wherever it is we are."

"Father was torn to bring us along on this unknown journey." Edward admitted. "I find it quite fascinating."

Another knight evaded Lesley's attempt to strike him and, in one swift motion, wrapped an arm around her waist and hoisted her over his shoulder. "Hey, what the fuck." Lesley said attempting to smack the knight but made no effort. He dragged her into the house.

"Yes, yes." Lance dismissed. "I was hoping for more action."

Gabriel shot at Lance, the bullet ricocheting off his armor.

Lance paused, glancing at his shoulder before returning his gaze to Gabriel. "Is that even a weapon?"

"This one has it in for you brother."

"I hope he puts up more of a fight than that." With a determined step, Lance descended from the porch, preparing himself for the impending confrontation. His muscles tensed and warmed up as he approached Gabriel, readying himself for the physical challenge that awaited him.

"Be lenient with him, for he is not yet accustomed to our manner of living." With her hands firmly planted on her hips, Amelia's gaze was fixed intensely on the duo, her countenance revealing a mixture of worry and determination.

Lance exhaled. "Yes. My lady." His tone carried a weight of sarcasm but also sincerity.

Edward shook his head and sighed, then gave Amelia a very small bow and led her inside. "I apologize for the inconvenience to my lady." With a sigh, Amelia trailed after him.

Gabriel aimed his pistol and fired, but each shot bounced off Lance's armor. As Lance lunged forward, Gabriel blocked his punch with his right forearm. A surge of energy rushed through Gabriel, like a warm simmering flame.

Gabriel had never faced an opponent as quick as Lance. The man moved like lightning, striking Gabriel's defenses with thunderous blows. Each impact sent a shockwave of pain through Gabriel's body, leaving him tingling and numb. Gabriel felt like a helpless mouse being toyed with by a cat, as Lance's strength was unreal.

Like a saint, Gabriel awaited Lance's next move. He parried a hard punch across Lance's body and stepped around to his flank. He followed up with an elbow to the side of his head, which landed with a loud clunk of bone on metal. Pain exploded in his own elbow, but Lance was left with little to no wound.

Gabriel held his elbow, wincing at the torn and bloody skin. He regretted the attack, but with Lance distracted, he shook off the pain and ran inside to pull Amelia away from Edward.

"Gabriel," Amelia exhaled with a hint of exasperation.

Edward spun and punched Gabriel, but Gabriel parried the blow. Gabriel then used his entire body weight to push Edward's arm across his own chest. The metal armor seemed much lighter than expected as the both crashed to the floor. Gabriel punched Edward in the solar plexus over and over, but the damage done was to Gabriel himself, as his blood splashed on the smooth silver armor.

Edward inserted a knee between them and shoved Gabriel off him, sending him into Lance's waiting arms, which were like a bear trap. Lance's arms wrapped around Gabriel's chest as he dragged him backwards into the kitchen.

"Cease your actions." Amelia ordered. Lance halted his advance, but kept his grip on Gabriel. Amelia placed a hand on Gabriel's chest to stop him. Her emerald eyes were filled with controlled determination and a hint of fury. "This is not a battle we want to fight, concede your challenge." The princess turned and followed Edward down the spiral staircase to the basement.

Gabriel's eyes widened in surprise, unsure of how to interpret her reaction. He watched in disbelief as she vanished around the corner, giving him one last stern look. He relaxed, feeling the defeat and exhaustion wash over him. He could feel the knight remove his arms from around him, allowing him to breathe.

He didn't see it coming, but he felt the knight's boot land on his back, launching him forward and down the flight of stairs. The short staircase seemed endless as he felt himself hit every step on the way down.

Gabriel, his face bloodied and his vision blurred, managed to lift his head. He landed at Cecil's feet, who paid him no heed as he lay there bleeding. In front of the Cecil, a silver rift opened up, with the three women standing in it. Lesley, Amelia and a silhouette of his mother. Gabriel tried to wipe the blood out of his eyes.

Edward knelt down and placed his hand under Gabriel's chin to support his head. "I am confident that he will recover."

Lance kicked him in the face as he walked past, saying, "I hope not." As he started to pass out, the last thing he saw was Amelia protesting to Cecil, who nodded in agreement. To what he could not tell.

One by one, the knights and hostages vanished into the vortex, with Lance pulling Lesley by the arm. In an attempt to fight back, Lesley was dragged by her heel. She punched and kicked Lance, but her efforts were futile. Lance continued to pull her along, shaking his head.

Cecil's unwavering gaze, marked by a clenched jaw and narrowed eyes, descended upon Gabriel, carrying a potent blend of disapproval and hostility. Though on the verge of speaking, Cecil remained silent, struggling to find the appropriate words. With a subtle shake of his head, his attention returned to the expanding vortex behind him. The vortex's incessant flashing intensified until it engulfed him entirely, disappearing into its dark core.

The shimmering object expanded, its edges taking on the appearance of tentacle-like appendages waving in the space around it. It continued to grow towards Gabriel, enveloping him in its warmth. It felt like a down feather comforter swaddling him to sleep, and its silver glow began to fade. Gabriel savored the warm feeling in the darkness before slipping into unconsciousness.

Chapter Four

Gabriel

Gabriel sprang awake, struggling to catch his breath. Minutes had passed while he lay on the frosty concrete floor, his body saturated with adrenaline and his heart throbbed within his chest. His gaze swept the room, seeking any trace of movement. Blood from his hands marked his knuckles, with his left hand bearing the brunt of the injury.

Regaining consciousness, his breathing gradually returned to a normal pace. To his dismay, he found himself on the cold, unforgiving basement floor. Agonizing pain shot through his hands as he attempted to move, as if the weight of the world was crushing his back. Every attempt to push himself up was met with excruciating discomfort, leaving him helpless on the cold, dark floor.

With his head in his hands, he contemplated the futility of existence. The vortex, Amelia, the knights, and, most significantly, Lesley were all gone. Apathy washed over him, prompting thoughts of surrender.

The thought of it had been nothing short of torment. An overwhelming sense of failure had consumed him, leaving him unable to escape its grasp. Desires to ignore it, to find solace in other thoughts, and to unleash his anger upon the world had only served to add to his guilt and emotional and physical distress. The situation had torn him apart, demanding action.

The emotional guilt and pain had morphed into an excruciating physical torment. As he attempted to rise from the floor, his arms trembled uncontrollably. His body felt utterly depleted and strained. His left arm buckled, causing him to fall onto his side before rolling onto his back. His chest heaved as he gasped for breath, feeling as though an invisible weight crushed it. The intensity of it all became unbearable.

In an effort to resolve the issue logically, Gabriel attempted to distance his feelings from the situation. Though he recognized the importance of this separation, he found it an insurmountable task. The fate of his sister's life precariously hung in the balance.

As anxiety gnawed at his very core, a buzzing numbness washed over him, eliciting a nauseating sensation. The stark revelation that his sister's existence could abruptly be terminated rendered him entirely powerless, gripped by an overwhelming sense of helplessness.

His jaw clenched tightly, a solitary tear traced a path down his cheek, eventually mingling with the cold pavement. Despite his best efforts to resist, his imagination relentlessly conjured up images of her untimely demise. In a mere heartbeat, Gabriel became a helpless spectator to his sister's tragic fate. Forever seared into his memory were the vivid details of her final moments, captured as fleeting seconds slipped away.

Her face plastered with an overwhelming sensation of dread. A jeweled dagger plunged into her chest, piercing her heart. Her blood soaked hands covered the gash through her abdomen. Lesley falls to her knees as she fails to keep her intestines inside her small frame. A looming shadow smashing her head with a rock to put her out of her misery. Her fine black hair matted with thick blood and brain tissue. One dangling blue eyes somehow watching him. Judging him. Accusing him.

In the grip of despair, Gabriel's fists pounded the unfeeling earth, a reflection of the chaos within him. His mind, a prisoner to the relentless torment of nightmarish thoughts, mirrored that of a disturbed man forced to witness the death of a loved one. Rage coursed through his veins, an inferno with no outlet, leaving him consumed by guilt. In a desperate attempt to find solace, he struggled to focus on his breathing, seeking a path to tranquility. Yet, like an unwanted guest, his thoughts kept circling back to her, always front and center.

A torrent of emotion surged through him, gripping his throat and causing it to tighten. His body trembled with an uncontrollable force. His hands, forming tight fists, dug the nails deeply into his palms, turning his knuckles pale. The prospect of losing her proved unbearable, and a stream of tears escaped his eyes, running down his face.

Taking a deep breath, he forcefully expelled the air from his lungs. He had to remind himself to breathe, to remember that she was still alive and that this wasn't real. Inhaling deeply, he held his breath until his lungs felt like they were on fire. When he could no longer contain the air, he exhaled, feeling a slight improvement.

He reminded himself that there was still hope. He repeated the deep breathing exercise a few more times, slowing his breaths until his breathing pattern returned to normal. Each exhale helped to lessen the existential dread, until it passed. He still didn't feel okay, and he knew he wouldn't until he found her.

Before he could address the issue, he needed to come to terms with it and take action. With each inhale and exhale, he steadied his breathing. It was remarkable how releasing his fear brought a tangible sense of relief.

"Alright," he said to himself as he collected himself and regained his composure.

Gabriel looked up from where he was lying on the floor to the vortex. Taking one last deep breath, Gabriel prepared himself for the reality of the situation. "So get up and do something," he muttered to himself.

Gabriel braced himself for pain as he rolled back over to his belly. Pushing himself up into a kneeling position was too easy. There was no pain when he felt like there should be. He planted his feet and stood up as if he didn't have any injuries at all.

Astonished at the lack of pain he lifted up his shirt, expecting to see a bruise or some other kind of wound, but there were none. The dried blood on his shirt and the pool of blood on the ground were the evidence that he had been injured. The blood was dark and dry, as if he had been lying there unconscious for some time. He couldn't help but think that he was dead. But at least he felt alive.

It was then he realized that everything seemed darker than normal. Being dead could explain why everything was more of a grayscale but so could a simple lack of lights. The thought unnerved him as he forced himself to take a deep breath and exhale.

Aware of the human's limited color perception in darkness, he grappled with an unsettling uncertainty. Was the inability to see color a consequence of blunt head trauma or an indication of death? The haunting possibility lingered in his thoughts, causing the hairs on his arms to rise. Exhaling deeply, he attempted to dispel the enveloping anxiety.

Gabriel thought about his sister with less dread. He felt his way forward in the darkness, looking for the vanished vortex. He found a knocked-over barbell when he stubbed his shin on it. The pain sharpened his senses as a little adrenaline rushed through his bloodstream.

He spun on his other leg, clenched his teeth, and let out a low groan. The brief burst of intense pain pulsed at the point of impact, but at least it told him he was alive.

Gabriel hobbled to the bottom of the stairs, where the light switch was on the wall. He flicked it on, and to his surprise, the basement became darker. He flicked it again, and the lights came back on, but it was still darker than usual. A little more dread crept in, but he felt a little more prepared.

Gabriel climbed the stairs into the kitchen, expecting to find a mess. However, the room was clean and well-lived-in. He walked into the dining area, half-expecting it to be a mess as well, but it was clean and set for dinner for a large family, including a high chair for a young child. Food was on trays, ready to be passed around the table. Plates were in place, and a large herb-crusted rib roast was in the center. Gabriel was overcome with nostalgia. He couldn't help but smile. He hadn't seen the table set like this in years.

Though he felt this way, something nagged at the back of his mind. Not allowing himself to dwell on it, he continued into the living room. The first odd thing he noticed was that the front door was still there. The same door that had been blown off in an explosion of white light and shimmering particles. He opened the door and looked at the dark, starless night sky. Everything seemed somewhat normal. He let go of the door and turned his attention back to the dinner table.

Gabriel felt that nothing was out of place, yet everything was. He felt drawn to the table as if he was being guided by a helping hand. It was intriguing. Having a huge Sunday dinner with his family was a nostalgic experience for him. He used to sit next to his dad, who always sat at the head of the table. His mother would sit across from him, always with that warm smile on her face.

Gabriel missed his family, but in that moment, he felt their presence. He reached out his hand to where his fathers would have been, in a gesture of remembrance. Then, out of habit, he reached out his left hand to the high chair where his baby sister used to sit.

"Lesley," he said aloud, feeling as though he was coming out of a trance. Longing, guilt, and dread all overwhelmed him, ruining the moment. The food before him transformed from a fresh meal to a rotting mess. A sudden wail of the ice wind sent shivers down his spine, causing Gabriel to jump out of his chair. In the distance, he could hear the faint sound of a toddler crying.

A sudden sense of unease crept over him, urging him to find the source. He walked through the kitchen and up the spiral staircase to the second floor. The crying grew louder and more frantic, and the feeling of unease grew stronger. He started to feel tense, sweaty, and his throat tightened in a familiar way.

Gabriel wanted to continue down the hallway, but his path was blocked by the first door on the right. It was Lesley's room, and the door was locked. Gabriel tried to open it, but it wouldn't budge. He was both irritated and worried now. He kicked the door three times before the wood gave way and cracked, letting it swing open.

A massive flash of light and the sounds of two gunshots blind and daze him. He raises his one arm to protect himself. Peering through his finger he pulls out a pistol and aims in the direction of the sound. The light faded revealing the inside the room was another darkened hallway. Identical to the one he stood in yet from the perspective from the stairs. In the distance he sees a shadowed figure lower a pistol.

"Don't move!" Gabriel yelled.

The young man looked back and spun towards Gabriel, raising his pistol. Gabriel was faster and fired two shots into the young man's torso. Instead of falling the young man dissipates into smoke. Vanishing in front of Gabriel's eyes. He takes a few steps forward and sees the open door ahead of him is to the master bedroom. Once occupied by his parents and now abandoned.

Two people lie on the floor in the master bedroom. One still alive. The faint wet sounds of the man trying to breathe as blood filled his lungs. The warm crimson liquid pooled into the soft carpet fibers on the floor underneath him.

Gabriel dropped the pistol, his hand shaking. "No. This can't be happening." The sound of a child crying brought him back to the present. Terror burrowed into his mind and festered. He turned and ran back the way he came, into the shadowy hallway.

The hallway became a series of identical hallways. No matter what door he ran though, it landed him into another hallway. He ran until his legs were numb; His lungs burned. He could feel terror breathing on the back of his neck pushing him forward. Like someone, or something, was tormenting him. He burst through another random door and found himself back in the master bedroom. He stared in shock.

He could feel heavy footsteps behind him. He spun around and nothing was there. When he turned back around the shadowy figure raised a pistol at him. Gabriel put his hand up and pleaded for his life in front of the figure of a shadowy young man. Its eyes started to shimmer dull red that grew in intensity.

Gabriel shouted "No!" as the figure fired two shots. The sound of the gunfire reverberated in his head, like incomprehensible screeching or electricity pulsing through his flesh. After a moment, Gabriel realized he was still alive and thinking, so he opened his eyes. The shadowy figure was gone.

Everything was gray except for the warm glow of the streetlights. He sat there for a moment, lost in his thoughts and guilt, before forcing himself to stand. He couldn't help but think that he deserved this. This had once been his parents' room. Its contents had been left undisturbed for many years. One large king-size bed, a huge dresser, and a master bathroom. The sword was resting on the side of the bed, hidden from view but ready to be used.

Gabriel smiled for the first time upon seeing it, but he couldn't remember bringing it in. Then, like a bolt of lightning, he remembered the knights and everything that had happened. Gabriel tilted his head and focused on the two windows. He realized that the warm lights were not coming from the streetlights outside. The source of light hovered in the two street-facing windows like a pair of large eyes watching him, studying him.

A shadowy figure wrapped its arms around Gabriel's chest from behind. The lights in the window grew brighter, almost as if they were enjoying the scene. He could feel an invisible force pressing against his skull, trying to bore into his mind. It felt like metaphysical claws were burning through his flesh.

Gabriel managed to break free from the figure's iron grip by pulling one of its arms away from his neck. Under the intense orange light, Gabriel could see that it was not an arm but a large, black tentacle. The smooth, slick surface slipped out of Gabriel's grasp, and the tentacle flopped back onto his chest with such force that it made him wheeze.

More tentacles slithered out of the darkness and wrapped themselves around Gabriel's body was trapped in place, tightly squeezed by the constricting pressure, preventing any movement. He felt like he was drowning under the constant pressure. Every time he exhaled, the tentacles squeezed a little tighter, reducing his lung capacity. The area around the windows darkened until all structural features vanished, leaving him lost in the void.

Eyeless facial features appeared in place of the windows. A shadowy face, more eye-like than ever, sneered at him. The tentacles dragged Gabriel into the hallway. The red orbs vanished, extinguishing the only source of light.

Everything was beyond dark and threw Gabriels other senses in a muddle. Gabriel lost his sense of movement, direction, sights, hearing and even smell. A strong sense of dread overwhelmed him, letting in a numb paralyzing feeling. It held him tight, his breathing shortened. His heart beats inside his chest like a jackhammer. Veins enlarged to capacity. Sharp pains exploded throughout his body as blood vessels began to burst.

On the verge of going unconscious, he all but gave up hope of saving himself, let alone his sister. He took this moment to cry for her and hope she was still alive. If he was going to die he would die with that hope in his heart.

A flash of light burst forth, pushing back the mass of tentacles in all directions. Gabriel fell to the floor, gasping for air. When he had regained his composure, he looked up at a wolf-hilt sword floating before him. He reached out and grasped its hilt, feeling its warmth flow through and around him. It felt wonderful as it coursed through his body, giving him a sense of euphoria and relief. He could figuratively and literally breathe again. Yet somehow, underneath all of that, there was a twinge of sadness. Something incomprehensible that Gabriel couldn't quite put his finger on. But it gave way to the release of heat flowing through his body and venting through his skin, a warm white flame illuminating the darkness around him.

Gabriel's senses returned to normal, and he attached the sheathed sword to his belt. The colors in his surroundings returned, but they faded to grayscale at the edges of the light, even with the runic blade illuminating his environment. He couldn't see anything beyond a few feet in front of him.

Gabriel was certain he was in the stairway at the entrance to the hallway. He couldn't see the tentacles, but he could still hear them, feel them, squirming out of sight, folding over and around themselves.

He forced his way back down the stairs, feeling the mass of tendrils react to his movement. It retreated out of sight and crept up behind him at the edge of the light. He kept going past the kitchen and back into the basement where he had last seen his sister. He was ready to move on and leave this place that was not quite his home, but then he stopped suddenly.

Gabriel saw a pair of glowing red orbs in the darkness before him again. The void swallowed the light around him, and he could feel the bitter cold encroaching. The grayscale obscured all details around him, so Gabriel couldn't tell how far away they were.

Gabriel drew his blade, its glowing runes illuminating the darkness. He walked forward, and the two orbs seemed to follow his progress, growing larger until they vanished. Gabriel found himself back in the mist-shrouded basement of his gym, standing in a dried pool of his own blood. The vortex was gone.

He reached out for the vortex, hoping to find it, but was instead pulled forward by an unseen force. Gabriel raised his sword, feeling it slip from his grasp. He slashed down, hoping to slay whatever had grabbed him. The sword rang out as it clashed with an unexpected object, the downward force redirected and parried away.

The pair of red orbs appeared before Gabriel again. The light aura surrounding Gabriel showed the silhouette of a large shadowy man. It wielded a sword and shield of black metal that glinted in the light. It was like a shadow of a man with no face. Two red snakelike glowing orbs where his eye should be.

Gabriel raised his sword at his side with both hands. He felt the heat intensify within him, sharpening his senses and illuminating more of the space around him.

With a gaping maw, the creature revealed a row of sharply pointed teeth, each marked with intricate patterns. Gabriel couldn't decipher if the creature was smiling or merely mocking him. Suddenly, the orbs surrounding them multiplied rapidly, resembling a myriad of serpent-like eyes observing their every move. In an instant, both the shadowy figure and the orbs disappeared, leaving Gabriel alone in the enveloping darkness.

In an abrupt moment, he found himself falling, surrounded by a distorted reality. A familiar silvery glow, reminiscent of a vortex, enveloped him, emanating a comforting warmth.

Chapter Five

Lesley

The warm feeling of the vortex disappeared as a cool breeze blew over her. It was like a refreshing summer breeze waking her from a deep sleep. She stretched her arms and legs out long and wide. She felt a light pull on her arm that seemed to slide away. It was a strange feeling that did not register with her. She yawned and opened her eyes. Her vision came into focus, and she realized she was falling.

"Oh Shit!" She yelled adrenaline pumping through her veins. Her long raven hair whipped around her. Swearing over and over she comes to the realization that she isn't about to die as there was no ground in sight. It is like a giant endless well, with no bottom or top, filled with a cool colored atmosphere. It was like an infinite cylinder with walls that are more like a thick silvery mist.

The mist swirled around her, clockwise. As it thinned and separated, she saw millions of twinkling stars, a giant blue sun, and countless giant gas nebulas. The multi-colored lights of each object illuminated through the gaps. The mists opened and closed tiny windows around her, and she realized that she must be inside the vortex.

In the distance, through the silver mist, she could see a figure made up of stars. A constellation. But in the blink of an eye, it was gone. Her eyes showed her that she was in free fall, but it felt more like she was being pulled forward. The unnatural sensation made her feel nauseous. Suddenly, the sensation changed to a push in the opposite direction, making her skin feel damp and her stomach churn even worse.

As the soothing lullaby of sleep whispered its invitation, her focus began to ebb away. A soft, silvery haze engulfed her surroundings, painting the world in a dreamy, hazy glow. Gradually succumbing to the irresistible pull of slumber, she embraced the sensation, allowing her eyes to gently close.

Everything went black, and she found herself floating comfortably in a void. New images assaulted her behind the safety of her eyelids, forcing her to refocus. A gray splotch grew and swirled frantically. It randomly grew, shrank, and contorted until it stopped and multiplied into two. They contorted themselves around each other and stretched into a pair of motionless curved horizontal lines.

A swirl of dark greens, reds, and violets bled into the darkness, vibrant by contrast. Shades of gray, dark green, dark red, and blue blurred together to form an abstract painting of a woman. Her features emerged around two curved lines, her closed eyes.

The realization made her skin crawl and the hair on her arms stand on end. She floated in a sea of darkness in front of a vibrant image of a woman. Her body buzzed with anticipation. Her arms twitched as she clasped her hands together in a praying gesture. More than anything, she wanted the eyes to open. She prayed for them to open, desperate for them to.

"Open your eyes," she repeated over and over again, her voice trembling. "Look at me!" she yelled in a raspy voice, her throat feeling dry and tight. She floated in darkness, surrounded by a nebula and dark colors. Exhausted, weak, alone, and desperate, tears began to stream down her face. "Look at me," she said, her voice shaking.

Two curved lines split open, revealing a pair of warm-colored eyes that stared back at her. Two glowing orbs like the sun rising over the horizon. The dark colors swirled into an image of a young woman with long flowing dark green hair, dark skin tones, and a cool color palette. The eyes were bright in the darkness. Lesley was drawn to them like a moth to a flame. It was a euphoric feeling.

Lesley felt her arms rise to touch the image of a woman. The dark lady's arms formed out of the same dark swirling colors and mirrored each other's movements in perfect symmetry. They smiled at each other. A warm and inviting sensation filled her. The image of the woman swirled into a perfect singularity and vanished into the darkness. Lesley was alone again.

"Please don't go!" Lesley begged, her throat tightening and burning with anger. "Open your eyes!" Tears welled up in the corners of her eyes as desperation and dread filled her again. "Wake up!"

Lesley felt herself smile as her eyes snapped open. Much to her dismay, she was still falling through the silver swirling mist. However, she was no longer scared, nor was she affected by the strange sensation of motion. She couldn't help but notice that she wasn't alone either. Lance was still holding her arm, the same arm he had used to drag her into the vortex. He looked sick and sweaty. Weak. She knitted her brow and studied him for a moment, asking, "Is this real?"

She realized Lance was unconscious with her free hand and she pokes him in the face. He lay motionless in a deep sleep. His face was soft, almost pleasant, but Lesley did not allow herself to feel any sympathy for him. She was going to get rid of him, no matter what it took.

Lesley wrenched her arm free and slipped from his grasp. She looked down to see Edward carrying Olivia in his arms, and below them, Amelia and the two Knights who had escorted her through the vortex. She looked around for Gabriel, but he was nowhere to be seen. Neither was the giant Knight, Cecil. "Did they even make it through?"

The harrowing image of her brother, lying battered and bloodied on the basement floor, resurfaced in her mind, inflicting a fresh wave of pain. "Is he even alive?" She shook her head to dismiss the awful thought. "No, he's alive, I've got this."

She massaged her aching wrist as she surveyed her surroundings. The situation was unsettling, but she couldn't help but feel liberated. She waved her hand, parting the silver mist to reveal the dark void beyond. It brought a smile to her face. She withdrew her arm after experiencing a sudden, sharp pain. The pain lingered for a while before fading away. This made her smile, too.

Her smile transformed into a mischievous grin that spread from ear to ear. She gave Lance a gentle push, sending him floating over the edge of the swirling mist. He slowed down and stopped before going beyond the horizon. Lesley's face twisted into a disappointed frown. "Well, that's a shame."

She took a step forward, but then remembered that there was no solid ground to push off from. "So..." She tried swimming over, but she didn't make any progress towards her target. "I'm going to push you though."

She was furious and snorted in disgust. "If only I had something to throw at him," she said to herself. "Wait." She looked down at her shoes and smiled again. "I got you this time." She looked back at him, took off her shoe, cocked her arm to throw, and Lance opened his eyes.

His movements appeared sluggish, but they transformed into erratic patterns. Fear consumed his gaze as he darted his eyes around, the intensity of his emotions evident in the wide-opened stare. "What's happening?!" he cried in a panic.

Lesley looked around, unsure of how to react. She put her shoe down, wondering if it was worth throwing. "Maybe he'll pass out again like... I did?" she said to herself, unsure if she had ever woken up. She realized that this could all be a dream.

"Youngling, what did you say?"

With a furrowed brow, Lesley replaced her shoe on her foot, conveying her evident irritation. "Youngling?"

"Where are we?" Lance said, surveying the vortex.

"I figured you'd know." Uninterested in conversation, she concentrated on her descent. Through wiggling and maneuvering, she maneuvered herself into a headfirst position. Although she didn't fully comprehend the physics at play, she gathered enough momentum to land mere inches from Olivia.

Despite Lance's efforts to mirror her movements by pivoting in place, he found himself immobilized, unable to move from his current position "What are you doing?"

Lesley shot him a glare, silencing his commentary with a brusque, "Shut up and watch." She extended her arm as far she could manage, her fingers just barely grazing Olivia's clothing. The fabric of Olivia's uniform slipped through her fingers, eluding her grasp.

In a swift motion, Lesley seized Olivia's hair, twisting it into a makeshift handle around her hand. With a gentle tug and an apologetic tone, Lesley applied minimal force, pulling them both upwards. Lesley managed to grip Olivia's arm, and they ascended as a pair, with Olivia still cradled in Edward's arms. When they reached the top, they were on equal footing with Lesley.

"What are you doing?" In a strained voice, Lance asked a question, his tone reflecting either panic or the enticement of cozy sleep. Unable to distinguish between the two, she showed indifference.

Lesley spun around and told Lance to be quiet. With great care she pulled Olivia from Edward's arms and turned her away from the knight. Lesley felt like an avenging angel, saving the world one friend at a time. She smiled as she examined Olivia's soft face and groomed her hair to make sure it was still in place.

"Okay!" Lesley said, turning back to Edward, her long hair flowing around her. "So you wanted to know what I was doing you piece of shit?" Her smile widened as she looked up at Lance.

Lance's eyes widened in alarm. "Wake up!" he shouted as he tried to swim down to them, but he was held in place. "Wake up!" he yelled again.

Lesley never thought she could enjoy someone else's panic, but now she did. It was a strange feeling, a mix of guilt and pleasure that was more euphoric than anything else. "Oh, are you going to miss your partner if I manage to push him through the, uh, swirling mist?" She taunted and laughed. She raised her leg and placed her foot on Edwards' armored chest.

"No!" Lanced yelled out.

She laughed again. "No?" she asked, continuing to tap her foot on Edward's chest. "I'll tell you what," she said with a laugh. "I'll toss him up to you, but you have to catch him." She said playfully, stretching out the syllables.

Lance yelled, "Get your foot off my brother!"

The realization shattered her euphoric feeling and brought out a cold cruelty in her. "Brother?" she repeated aloud. Lesley clenched her teeth as she thought about the last time she saw her brother, "I had, I have, a brother."

She imagines Gabriel laying on the basement floor, bleeding and near death, after being beaten by the two. "Your brother?" she said to herself with a touch of disdain. "Oh, that's rich." She pushed Edward into the silver mist.

"No!" Lance yelled, his voice was filled with hopelessness and fear.

Edward's eyes snapped open as a wave of light washed over him. He began to breathe, gasping, and the light faded. He looked around, taking it all in. Lance was above him, with Lesley and an unconscious Olivia behind her. The princess and two other knights were below, all of whom appeared to be unconscious. "What is this? Is this what happens between the realms?"

"Fucking, why!?" Lesley let out a piercing shriek that reverberated through the air, her vocal cords straining to produce the high-pitched sound.

Lance shouted, "Brother, that girl tried to kill you by pushing you through the mist!"

With a cautious touch, Edward brushed his fingers against the edge of the vortex, causing its misty tendrils to swirl and dance around him, resembling delicate strands of silver smoke. In a calm and composed voice, he expressed his understanding of the situation, saying, "I can't hold any resentment towards her." Following this, he withdrew his hand and rubbed his fingers together as if contemplating the implications of his words.

In a swift and forceful motion, he lunged his arm forward, capturing Lesley's arm in his grasp. The force of his pull caused her to violently collide with his armored chest, resulting in a splatter of blood and the disturbing sound of cartilage or bone being crushed beneath the impact.

As if experiencing a sudden sharp pain in his arm, Edward let go of Lesley's wrist. Seizing the opportunity, Lesley retaliated by shoving him with all her might. Edward was pushed closer to the perilous edge of the vortex, while Lesley was propelled away, beyond his reach.

Lesley groaned as blood trickled from her nose. She bumped into Olivia and continued to do so until they came to a stop before touching the silver mist. Lesley wiped the blood from her nose and smeared it across her face as it rolled up her cheeks and into her hair. The bleeding stopped, or perhaps the strange physics they were encountering were preventing the blood from flowing down her nose.

Edward admitted, "That was a little more violent than I expected." Lesley flipped him off. Edward shook his hand, extended his fingers, and clenched his fist repeatedly. "Where is father?" he asked without taking his eyes off Lesley.

"Father?!" Lesley had no doubt that he was talking about the Lord-Commander. "You are a whole family of murderous dogs?"

Lance looked around, but his father was nowhere to be seen. "You killed him before I woke up?"

"Yes." She lied, she held a concealed desire. It was not material possessions or worldly gains that she yearned for; instead, her sole aspiration was to inflict upon them the very torment that consumed her being, an agony that clawed at her soul. "He was the first one I pushed out into space. I'm sure he died an extremely painful death."

"You'll die for this!"

"Father would be furious if they were dead."

"He would rather be avenged."

"Yeah, and how are you going to do that from all the way over there?" With her thumbs, Lesley examined her nose for any fractures. Sharp pain shot through the point of contact, accompanied by a persistent, dull ache. "Are you going to throw your boots at me?"

With narrowed eyes and a grin, Lance questioned. "Is that why you had your shoe in your hand when I woke up?"

"Absolutely not! That's absurd." With a crimson blush spreading across her cheeks, she comprehended the foolishness of her actions.

"You woke up first. Pushed my father to his death. Then you tried to do the same to us but we woke up? Am I understanding the situation?"

"That sums up the situation pretty well." Lesley laughed, "I hope that eats you up inside."

"I'll kill you!" Lance screamed.

"Not if I kill you first!" Lesley's focused gaze narrowed, burdened by a combination of mental and physical exhaustion. The edges of her vision began to cloud and darken, encroaching upon her sight. "I'll kill all of you."

Edward shook his head in disappointment. "We don't know where we are, how long we've been here, or how long we'll be here. We don't know if we'll be able to sleep, or if we'll be knocked out and die. I don't know. But I do know that it will be painful. I felt it with this very hand."

Edward raised his arm and showed Lesley his palm, his fingers spread wide. "I don't want to imagine that pain all over my body. So with all that, it's too dangerous for you to be here." Edward paused to consider his next move. "I wish I knew what was going to happen to you," he said. "But if you survive, find me. I would like to document your experiences."

"What?" Lesley's face was a study in confusion as she tried to make sense of what he was saying.

A small pulse of light shot out of Edward's hand, hitting Lesley in the chest and sending her flying backwards into the silver mist. Her eyes widened in shock as time seemed to slow down, and she felt a sense of helplessness wash over her. A flash of silver mist swirled around her, accompanied by a flash of light.

The next thing she felt was a hard landing on a stone. Pain exploded in her knee as it smacked the cold surface. Light poured through a giant crack in the ceiling, assaulting her eyes and causing her to squint. Through the haze, Olivia's smiling face came into focus.

Olivia reached out and gently touched Lesley's face, brushing the hair away. Her hand was warm and comforting. "Are you okay?"

The question went in one ear and out the other as she sat there, unmoving. "I'm OK." Her mouth was dry and bitter akin to waking up after a long slumber. "Did I die?"

"What are you talking about? We're not dead."

"Not you. Me."

Olivia shook her head. "No, you're not."

Lesley's eyes dilated in agony as a piercing shriek erupted from her lips. With trembling hands, she removed them from her face, expecting to see blood. To her surprise, there was none. The excruciating pain receded, but Lesley continued rubbing her face, searching for any sign of injury.

Olivia seized her hands and made her look her in the eye. "What are you doing?"

Uncertainty engulfed Lesley's mind. Doubt crept in, casting shadows on her memories. She questioned the reality of her existence, wondering if it was an illusion or a dream. The boundaries between truth and fiction blurred, leaving her in a state of confusion

Chapter Six

Lesley

Sunlight streamed through a gaping hole in the roof and walls of the small, dilapidated gray brick building. Lesley sat in the midst of ancient, dusty tomes on half-broken, dusty shelves. In the center of the room, a silvery vortex of tendrils hummed within a circle of stones. Each stone was etched with a glowing blue rune-like symbol, not unlike old Nordic runes. The placement of the circle was too perfect to be a coincidence.

In the wake of the vortex's disappearance and the fading luster of the runes, Lesley's gaze remained intently fixed on the stones. With a glimmer of hope, she stretched out her hand, fearing that the doorway back home had sealed shut behind her. To her dismay, her touch elicited no response. The portal had vanished completely. If there were a way to revive it, it remained a mystery to her. In a brief moment of mounting anxiety, she took a deep, steadying breath, followed by a gradual release.

As the sound of birds chirping enveloped the air, she deduced that they were nesting somewhere nearby, likely in the old and worn-down wooden roof. In the distance, the gentle murmur of a river could be heard. The sounds of nature created a peaceful ambiance, but the gradual crescendo of human voices interrupted the tranquility.

With a narrowing gaze, Lesley noticed the hushed whispers between Edward and Lance. Unable to decipher their words, a sense of suspicion washed over her. Her eyes grew narrower, a mixture of anger and disgust brewing within.

"Are you sure you're OK?" Olivia asked, breaking Lesley of her fixated glare. "This is all really crazy."

"That's an understatement." In the quiet atmosphere, Lesley's thoughts escaped in a murmur. She had not anticipated any response from Olivia, and true to her expectation, Olivia remained silent.

With hurried steps, Edward approached, knelt, and gazed into Lesley's eyes. Instinctively, she averted her gaze. Edward gently cupped her cheek, turning her head toward him, compelling her to meet his stare. They remained in silence for a while before he released her, turning away to walk back to Lance.

Now, sitting on the hard surface, she felt a mix of rage and helplessness, trembling violently. It was now her and Olivia against the world. But she had realized that she couldn't protect herself, let alone Olivia. They were vulnerable, exposed, and completely overpowered. As frustration crept in, her face began to flush red, and she trembled uncontrollably.

Suddenly the vortex erupted open, its shimmering silver tendrils unraveled, exposing its brilliant white core. Her eyes dilated, and her heart momentarily faltered. Anticipation dried her throat, distorting time and quickening her pulse. A question lingered in her mind: could Gabriel have trailed them?

From the vortex's core emerged a colossal figure. His silver armor boasted broad platemail shoulders adorned with three cascading ridges, a testament to his stature. As his feet struck the ground, the vortex abruptly sealed, echoing with a resounding thud. Lesley's exasperation manifested in a deep sigh.

"Father!" Lance exclaimed, sprinting toward him, Edward trailing closely behind.

"We seem to have arrived in a different location that we entered."

"They're a family?" Olivia asks.

"Of course they are," Lesley muttered to herself, but she already knew. She continued to question the validity of the previous hour or so. She had been subconsciously picking up on subtle cues, and it was possible that she had dreamed everything up to this point. Perhaps she was still dreaming, having never woken from her bed. She had never gone to school, and she had never been attacked in an alley. It was all a dream.

The memory of a shattered bone haunted her. She rubbed the bridge of her nose, trying to alleviate the pain that still felt very real. It was as if she could still feel the thousand needles piercing her skin, and a cold shiver ran down her spine. She was haunted by the feeling of simultaneously burning and freezing in the vacuum of space. It all felt real. With her eyes closed, she had hoped to wake up in her own bed. However, when she opened them, she was still in the dilapidated building with a group of unusually strong knights.

She had kept an eye on them as they regrouped and met out of hearing range. She had looked for any sign that they were being genuine. But every glance had seemed natural, and every gesture could have been explained away. If it had been real, wouldn't they have said something by then? She had narrowed her eyes and gritted her teeth.

Lesley took a deep breath and tried to push her doubts aside. She did not enjoy doubting what she saw and felt, so she acknowledged the reality of the pack of murderous dogs in front of her. Despite being unable to comprehend their conversation, a skeptical part of her mind couldn't refrain from considering their possible motives toward her. The intensity of her anger and rage had gradually shifted, evolving into a profound sense of frustration. She had attempted to remain calm, but her blood had boiled and her body had trembled as she battled the internal struggle. She had had to find a way to escape before they had killed her.

In a surprising moment of solace, Lesley's hand was enveloped in warmth as she glanced down to find Olivia firmly holding it. Looking up at her serene friend, Lesley couldn't help but notice the striking calmness that radiated from Olivia. Unlike others in their dire situation, she remained unfazed, exuding an aura of unwavering confidence. As Lesley closed her eyes and drew a deep breath, she pushed aside any lingering worries. Despite the hopelessness that surrounded them, she had to hold onto the belief that their safety was assured.

Fighting back tears, she knew she couldn't just sit there. Lesley scanned the area until she saw the small runic symbols in a circle where the vortex had opened. She leaned over to Olivia and whispered, "I have an idea."

"What is it?"

"The portal thing. Let's jump back through."

With a melancholic gaze, Olivia uttered. "That's not going to work."

In a flash, Lesley rose to her feet, her heart pounding with hope that the portal would reappear. But her hopes were dashed as it remained closed. With a swift glance, she assessed the three knights, their gazes fixated on her. As Lesley's antics were dismissed, Edward offered a disarming smile and a subtle head shake, indicating his disapproval while allowing the conversation to continue smoothly. "Do they know something we don't?"

"They were messing around with it for a while but nothing seemed to activate it."

"There is a door right there." Lesley pointed out. "Let's make a break for it. Maybe we can outrun them."

"What if they are also super fast?"

"I guess we die?" Lesley shrugged, knowing she had made a foolish attempt at humor. The very real possibility of being murdered weighed heavily on her mind.

The two of them rose to their feet and made their way to the large wooden door. Edward spared her a fleeting glance before returning to his conversation, unconcerned. Lesley came to a complete stop and glared at the three of them. "They aren't worried about us at all."

Upon reaching the wooden door, Lesley let go of Olivia's hand. They now understood why the wolves had not been worried about their escape. The door was made of thick, heavy wood and reinforced with iron. Lesley tried to open the door with one hand, but it would not budge. "It's stuck." She tried again with one hand, then with two, until she cried out in exhaustion. She crossed her arms over her chest and narrowed her eyes. "Did they try and fail at the door too?"

"Not that I have seen."

Lesley felt a slight tap on her shoulder that sent a shiver down her spine. She turned around, expecting to see Lance or Edward, but to her surprise, it was one of the two unknown knights who had not removed their helmets the entire time. He carried her from the front yard to the basement.

Cecil remarked, "I'm surprised to hear you're eager to return." Lesley didn't know the man, but she could tell from the venom in his tone that he didn't mean it as a compliment. The princess sneered in response.

"Yes. We were on our way." The knight had spoken, her voice muffled and unusually gruff, as though she had been intentionally altering it to sound deeper.

Lesley's eyes widened and she tilted her head. "Why would you offer to help me? Aren't I your prisoner?"

"You still are. Do not forget that. We need the door open as much as you do, youngling."

Lesley took an abrupt breath, her distaste for the term palpable. She tried to conceal her emotions, knowing she would be hearing it often before she could find a way to get home—or die trying.

With a light-hearted tone, Amelia remarks, "She possesses a great sense of pride."

Lesley could not comprehend the puzzling dynamic between herself and Amelia, who, despite sharing the same status as a prisoner, exhibited starkly contrasting behaviors. Lesley's behavior was characterized by paranoia, while Amelia's disposition remained remarkably composed and peaceful.

"Let's open it together." The female knight, still trying to make her voice sound deeper than normal, placed her hands on the doorknob.

Lesley, despite her initial hesitation, found herself the center of attention. With everyone's eyes on her, she mustered the courage to grasp the knight's silver gloves. Together, they tugged at the heavy door. As it slowly creaked open, Lesley couldn't help but notice that the knight was doing most of the work. A pang of envy struck her as she marveled at the knight's remarkable strength.

The rusty metal hinges creaked in protest until the one of them snapped. The edge of the door dropped to the floor and lodged itself in a crack in the stone floor. The door stuck halfway open. Lesley starts to slide through but the female knight grabs her shoulder.

With unwavering composure, Lesley reiterated her earlier statement, reinforcing that the object remained firmly stuck. In response, Olivia's eyes narrowed, yet her smile remained gentle. Acknowledging the discomfort, Lesley averted her gaze, feeling a tinge of embarrassment.

In a hushed tone, the knight spoke, her voice now carrying a more genuine quality. "I couldn't have done it without you." She gestured for her companion to join her, and together, they deftly slipped through the narrow doorway.

Lesley carefully considered the tone of her voice and the words she had spoken, pondering their familiarity. An elusive sense of déjà vu lingered in her mind, accompanied by a tinge of discomfort. She grappled with discerning whether the other person's words carried genuine sincerity or a layer of sarcasm, but regardless, both possibilities left her feeling uneasy.

Through the ajar door, Lesley entered a larger room. It was a place of worship, akin to the sanctuary of a church. An undisturbed altar stood before a large room with long wooden benches. The two knights stood on either side of the door as each person entered the sanctuary. Cecil, however, had to work harder than most to squeeze his large body through the door. He scraped the floor as he pushed it open wider.

A worn mural of three women huddled together was behind it. They all wore simple cloth garments and hoods, similar to those seen in Renaissance paintings. The three women formed a triangle, with the dark green-haired woman with fair skin and warm-colored eyes at the top. She wrapped her arms around the other two women: a white-haired, thin, and frail woman with features of bone under her young dark skin; and an amber-haired woman who appeared more formless under her hood. They sat together in a clearing under a bright sun surrounded by a starry night. An arched shooting star appeared on each side of the painting.

Mesmerized by the art, Lesley resisted the urge to become lost in it. She was drawn to the deeper story of runic witchcraft, and her body ached for power. However, she knew she needed to stay focused on finding an opportunity to escape with Olivia.

Lance expressed his profound disdain by uttering the expletive, "What a contemptible place this is!" He then proceeded to forcefully propel an aged book with his foot, causing it to glide across the surface of the floor.

"It's an old temple of the three." With unwavering confidence and a determined stance, her hands boldly placed on her hips, Amelia's gaze swept across the temple, examining every intricate detail.

"Who are the three?" As Lesley posed her question, a sudden shift occurred in the room as every gaze swiveled in her direction, magnifying her feelings of isolation. The collective attention made her uncomfortable, and she wished they would cease their scrutiny.

"They are an old myth said to be worshiped in ancient times." Cecil added. "The religion of heretics."

"It is said the three goddesses govern the aspects of creation. They are one and three separate goddesses. Mind, Body, and Soul." Amelia knitted her brow in deep contemplation as her fingers grazed her chin in a thoughtful gesture. "Or was it Life, Death and Soul?"

"Past, present and future." Edward injected. "Urd, Verdandi, and Skold."

"I don't think so, though you can see their prince of time shifting throughout the piece." Suspended from the ceiling, a mural depicted the dilapidated image of the tree Yggdrasil spreading out into the cosmos. Amelia gestured toward the faint, haphazard bridge cascading from the mural.

"There is one true lord." Cecil proclaimed. "Sol. God of light and governor of all aspects."

"Come now, Cecil. No one is disputing that."

Lesley frowned as a religious disagreement erupted, regretting her question. She tried to ignore their diatribes. Olivia listened attentively without comment, promising to share any useful insights later. Meanwhile, Lesley scanned the room for a discreet exit. If she could slip away unnoticed, she would, but she wouldn't leave her friend behind.

In the room, two escape routes were visible: the vortex room door and a pair of double doors situated at the heart of the central aisle. However, both of these sturdy wooden passageways were guarded by watchful wolves, making a stealthy escape nearly impossible.

Edward and Lance sat by the large double doors. Lesley surmised that they did not want to hear the discussion either. Though it was more likely that they were guarding the door to prevent her from fleeing. Taking a bit of pride in her possible notoriety, she smiled; maybe they did care after all.

Once Lesley had a moment to collect her thoughts, she recognized that the other people in the group were ordinary men and women who wanted to return home, something she could understand. However, she could not bring herself to care about them.

Despite Amelia's sincere demeanor, Lesley was skeptical of her trustworthiness. While Amelia became an unwilling captive, her true allegiance remained uncertain. Among the group, Cecil resembled a grumpy patriarch, Lance exhibited tendencies of a violent narcissist, and Edward possessed exceptional observational skills.

While Lesley roamed the room, Edward seemingly ignored her, but Lesley knew better. She keenly sensed their watchful eyes on her, yet she couldn't help but notice that the focus was primarily on Amelia, while Olivia was overlooked. Their surveillance was continuous, yet it was executed with exceptional subtlety.

It was clear to her that they did not see her as a threat, nor did they believe she would try to escape. They were mistaken. She would attempt to flee if given the chance. However, she would not leave without Olivia. As Cecil and Amelia's argument grew more intense, she carefully maneuvered around them.

As she passed by, Edward and Lance stiffened. She wondered if she had missed a telltale sign that confirmed her suspicions. Could they have been discussing her or the events that transpired inside the vortex? Or had they simply become wary of her? She kept her distance from them and overheard them resume their conversation as she walked away towards the altar.

Once again, anxiety consumed her, and she wished the last few hours had been just a dream. If what had transpired in the vortex was reality, this day could mark her end. Maybe that was why they hadn't uttered a word; they too were uncertain whether it had been real.

She took a deep breath and carried on, doing her utmost to avoid dwelling on what had happened. Her focus was on living in the present and trying to block out the conversations happening around her. This proved to be a significant challenge as both her inner thoughts and the external conversations were saturated with pain, fear, and irritation.

Amidst the distressing turmoil and unexpected uncertainty, her mind wandered aimlessly. Fragments of their conversation drifted in and out of her consciousness - spiritual presence, holy light, corrupted ancient spirits, and the power of Sol. It seemed like yet another meaningless dogma from a foreign realm, leaving her disheartened and disconnected from their beliefs.

Despite the unfolding events, Olivia looked more intrigued than apprehensive. Blessed with a knack for spotting the good in people and situations, she couldn't shake a mix of envy and annoyance. It might seem irrational to feel this way, but for the moment, they appeared safe. She shivered as the thought crossed her mind. The gravity of their situation appeared lost on Olivia, as well as the swiftness with which it could all unravel. Lesley hesitated, questioning if her own perception was flawed.

"The trio utilizes Sol's energy to weave the reality we know." With her booming voice, Amelia rendered Lesley unable to disregard her.

"Do you mean that the existence of the universe is evidence of his existence? If so, then yes. Our existence is a testament to his power."

"No one questions the existence of Sol, nor the power that he wields. The three are part of Sol's plan for us."

Lesley rolled her eyes and let out a small sigh. Gazing at the mural of the three goddesses, she began to understand what they were discussing. The three goddesses were weaving a large tree that sprawled outward in multicolored branches. In the realm of existence, a tree stood as a symbolic representation of life, brought into being by the goddesses. The tree encapsulated the intricate connection between life, death, and the soul, a bond unique to this specific plane of existence. Amidst the cosmic confluence, a delicate interplay of forces carves out a unique realm, nurturing the emergence of life. Here, the convergence of energy, space, and matter gives rise to existence in all its wondrous forms.

Did these three entities collaborate to create existence by intertwining these concepts? Lesley expressed disdain, indifferent to the outcome, hoping for the cessation and obliteration of everything. Returning to where she had stopped Lesley climbed one of the two three-step walkways onto the stage. She stopped in front of the podium in the center. She felt like a pastor of a religious group looking down at her flock of simple folk. She couldn't help but imagine herself as their captor. No, their shepherd. A small grin crept across her face. It was a foolish thought, but it was a small measure of enjoyment in the strange situation.

Her mind began to wander. She imagined crowds of people entering through the large double doors, walking down the center aisles, and finding seats. This was a large place of worship, she thought, and the people filled the room to capacity. She cleared her throat and the crowd fell silent.

The last few people hurried to their seats. All eyes were on her, eagerly awaiting for the divine to flow through her.

The thought of so many people looking up to her and relying on her message to get through the day overwhelmed her. Her anxiety grew as the anticipation mounted. Her throat felt dry as bone and her skin grew damp. The crowd was deathly silent, waiting with bated breath. Their eyes were cold, distant, yet fixed on her.

As the crowd's attention waned, a sense of panic settled over the speaker. Her mind, once filled with eloquence, was now a barren void. Desperation fueled her words, but they tumbled out in a jumbled mess, barely resembling coherent speech. In an instant, the vibrant gathering dissolved, replaced by the ghostly echoes of an ancient temple hall, where religious debates had once echoed through time.

Lesley's gaze darted around the room, silently praying that she had not been caught. No telltale signs of lingering stares met her anxious scrutiny. One final sweep of her surroundings confirmed her temporary reprieve. Olivia's warm smile, as radiant as the sun, greeted Lesley, her hazel eyes twinkling with a comforting glow. In that smile, Lesley found a measure of solace, a cherished respite from the unease within.

Fear gripped Lesley's heart as she ran her fingers along the back wall behind the altar. Beneath the mural of the three, directly under its center, the once solid wood mysteriously gave way and slid open. The opening revealed a pitch-black void that swallowed any stray light, making it impossible to discern what lay within. The darkness enveloped her, a tangible entity that sent icy tendrils down her spine, reminding her of spiders crawling unbidden on her skin.

With a cautious glance back at The Silver Wolves, Lesley furtively opened the small door when she was sure no one was watching. She stepped inside, leaving the door ajar. Shining her phone's flashlight, she revealed a dimly lit room. An old wooden desk and chair, along with a bookshelf filled with dusty books, filled the space. The disrepair of the room was consistent with the state of the rest of the building.

A sense of hope guided her to the pastor's office. Her flashlight danced over the bookshelves until she froze at the title of one: "Keeping Darkness in the Dark." She weighed the hefty book in her hand, its unexpected lightness intriguing. With anticipation, she flipped through its pages, hoping for a secret compartment, but there was none. Disappointment washed over her as she returned it to the shelf.

Reluctantly, she turned off the flashlight and sat in the chair. Fear gnawed at her. Returning was not an option, but she worried about Olivia's fate. Her wish to find solace in the office indefinitely seemed like a distant dream. She closed her eyes, trying to find that same fleeting solace in forgetfulness, even if it were just for a moment. But blinding flashes of light pierced through her closed eyelids, accompanied by a loud thump. Resigned, she let out a weary sigh and lifted her head, knowing she had been found.

To her surprise, she found herself no longer in the office. The room was illuminated by the warm glow of the burning sconces. She found herself sitting at a similar desk, but the contents of the desk were vastly different. Vials of liquids and gasses of different colors filled the desk. She squinted, unsure of what to make of this. She felt like there were too many unanswered questions. Was this madness?

She glanced around and saw shelves lined with countless books and ancient alchemist tools. Wooden tablets were entwined with string, and paper scrolls and tomes filled every nook and cranny of every shelf. Strange pseudo-scientific equipment with uses that were far beyond her comprehension was also present.

As she slid the chair back to stand up, she felt something under her foot. She looked down and saw a large leather satchel covered in moss and dirt next to the desk. She picked it up by the handle and shook it, causing the debris to fall off. The way the debris fell off so easily made her stop and think. The material of the satchel was old leather, well-kept but worn.

She inspected the inside of the bag by the light of a sconce. There were no signs of decay, moss, insects, or parasites hiding in the nooks. The inside of the bag looked impossibly dark looking far deeper than the bag should be. After declaring it clean enough to use, she slung it over her shoulders. After a quick adjustment of the strap, it felt no different from her school bag.

She saw a dim violet light pulsing on the far side of the room. She walked towards it cautiously, her heart pounding in her chest. The color deepened as she got closer, until all she could see was the light coming from a fist-sized black gemstone that glowed with an eerie light. Runes etched into the gem pulsed with life, and as she looked at them, the color deepened even more. It was both eerie and inviting, and she knew she had to have it. She swung her leather bag down, shattering the glass case that held the gem.

Lesley reached out and placed her hand on the gemstone. She felt a sense of calmness wash over her, like a wave of endorphins flowing through her body and washing away her hardships and pain. The light of the gemstone pulsed in time with her excited heartbeat, its glow flickering and fading in and out of existence.

She used too much force to pick up the fist-sized gem, causing her hand to fling upward. A shield of energy materialized around her arm, protecting her from harm as she smashed through the glass. The shield disappeared as suddenly as it had appeared, and glass shards flew everywhere, shattering on the floor.

"Who's there?" she demanded, but the answer was the sound of the low crackling fires. She heard faint voices, but when she turned around, there was no one there. She took a few steps, looking down the old library aisles, but she couldn't find anyone lurking around.

When she was comfortable enough to know that she was alone she returned her attention to the stone. It synchronized its pulse with her heart beat. Peering intently beneath its sleek surface, she struggled to discern the swirling mist within. Its mesmerizing allure was undeniable.

As the lights went out, she was swallowed by darkness. She felt like she was drowning, unable to breathe. The darkness crawled over her body and hair, squirming in the back of her eyes. She heard a faint whisper, but couldn't make it out. In an abrupt shift, a blinding flash of light assaulted her vision, causing her to instinctively raise her hands to shield her eyes.

"There you are." A man's voice, dripping with venom, rang out.

"Here I am." Lesley confessed, her face flushed with embarrassment.

"Come. We are departing."

Her eyes adjusted to the light, revealing Lance and the hidden office. She shifted her eyes back and forth, which was enough to trigger his wrath. Without a moment's hesitation, he slapped her, knocking her back into the bookshelf.

Her face twisted with pain as blood gushed from her nose. She clasped her hands over it, but the blood seeped through her fingers. She had half-expected the violet shield to protect her once more, but she began to doubt even the reality of that occurrence. Standing up, she glared at Lance with fierce intensity.

The abrupt weight of the bag slung over Lesley's shoulder jolted her out of her reverie. She glanced down at it, then back up at Lance, her mind grappling with the perplexing situation. Uncertainty clouded her thoughts as she struggled to discern whether the bag had always been there or if its existence was a mere figment of her imagination. With a pang of uncertainty, she questioned whether Lance had taken notice, or if he even held any concern.

Chapter Seven

Gabriel

An overwhelming sensation of distortion whirled around him. Pulling as if to tear the very fabric of his being apart. The world turned to darkness and contrasted into flashing bright lights. He winced in pain and covered his face with his hands and closed his eyes.

The whole experience was over quicker than it began. He felt like something else may have transpired and faded away. Like the memory of a dream after you wake. But he still remembered that nightmare and shadows and tendrils. Horrors that he wished were dreams. But he could feel the sword in his hand. It must have been real.

The exit to the room was an old, half ajar, wood-iron door. Grabriel struggled to pull the door open and realized it was broken off its hinges. He slid through into the sanctuary of a church where people once gathered.

As fascinating as it all was, the first forty eight hours were the most dire. Time was of the essence and Gabriel knew he didn't have time to linger here for long. He walked down the aisle through open double doors that led into a stone path overtaken by nature. The stone pathway transitioned from well placed stone to broken stones of various sizes. Until the path was swallowed by nature in the form of dirt and mud.

A great blessing as there were a half dozen fresh footprints heading into the distance. Gabriel was not the most seasoned tracker but these were easy enough to read. As he followed the trail one set of prints became semi elongated and stopped. There was a little splash of semi-dried blood that made his stomach drop. Gabriel chest tightened at the thought of Lesley still trying to fight her captors. He suspected that his little sister was getting dragged by on her heels before being assaulted. Perhaps carried the rest of the way.

Despite the blood loss not being severe enough to be fatal, he assumed that she was likely uninjured. He remained hopeful. He inhaled again and swallowed before exhaling again. He followed the footprints until they ended. They must have entered some sort of vehicle but there was nothing that resembled tire tracks. There was a large square shape as if someone dragged a large stone that flattened grass and stone. A little further up the path there was something that looked like bear tracks. No. Of course. Wolves. The thought unnerved him. Wild or domesticated wolves were a dangerous threat.

Further on the ground became a stoney path again. "They must have gone this way." In a desperate internal monologue, he recognized the urgent need for certainty and decisive action. Stagnation was an unbearable option.

Gabreil walked westward into the direction of the setting sun for what seemed like hours. The stoney path that became more accommodating the further he went. In the distance he could see something of a small village growing on the horizon.

Gabriel turned east through a pathway that merges into something that seems to be a more well kept modern black top road. If Gabriel didn't know any better this road was part of the interstate highway system. Four lanes divided by heavy slabs of stones. Unlit street lights were few and far between but Gabriel could see a few of them along the highway.

The other fork seemed to continue to the village. As much he had wanted to press forward along the highway he knew he had to eat and learn something about where he was. Gabriel walked until his feet ached but he couldn't give up.

When Gabriel arrived at the town the sky transformed into warm pastel colors. He always loved this time of day. The mesmerizing colors always made him smile. He stood before a collection of buildings surrounded by a large wooden fence. If there was an entrance here it would have been long built over and even longer forgotten. Gabriel continued his walk along the edge of the fence until he found an entryway paved with stone.

Upon entering, he gained a clear view of the village. It had one major road where shops stood. A few unpaved roads that breached off in what he could tell were residential homes. People walked up and down the roads like any other population center. Shopping, eating, working. In the early nineteenth century, commoners wore handmade clothing made from various qualities of linen and wool.

The main street had a large building that Gabriel assumed was some sort of town hall. Its stone stairs meet the road that leads east into the large wooden wall. Gabriel mused that's where he came out of the forest and ran into the wall for the first time. This side of it was more clear that the wall was built some time after the road blocking off the way to the temple.

There is a far building with what looks like a classic forge and anvil. A large man came to check on the fires burning in the forge. The houses are made from a similar gray stone of the temple that the vortex was in but were by far more modern. Not all that different from the brick houses in his own neighborhood. Some extended and added on over the years after the original construction.

All these houses had access to electricity, which provided them with the power they needed. Each building was illuminated by distinctive light fixtures, both inside and out. However, he couldn't figure out where the power was coming from because there were no power cables connected to anything.

Next to the houses, various vehicles resembling cars and vans caught Gabriel's attention. Engineered uniquely, some of these vehicles lacked wheels. His eyes widened in amazement as one of these vehicles defied gravity, hovering before his eyes before disappearing down the stone road. Gabriel couldn't have believed it if he hadn't witnessed it himself. This place was a fascinating blend of traditional customs and cutting-edge technology, creating a remarkable juxtaposition.

As he walked among the villagers, an older man approached Gabriel. "Oh pardon me young warrior." The man says apologetically. With a sweeping gaze, he assessed Gabriel from head to toe, his attention ultimately drawn to the sword adorning his waist. "That is a fine weapon. You honor your ancestors by wielding such a blade."

Gabriel's gaze shifted from the gleaming blade to the aged man before him. With a determined resolve, he reached out and placed his hand upon the hilt, his fingers grazing the cool metal of the blade. "This." Gabriel paused to consider it. "This has been handed down through my family for generations."

"It will serve you well when the time comes. I'm sure." In a posture of reverence, his hands clasped together before him, a soft, radiant light emanated from his body. "Have you traveled far? I assume you are wondering and getting to know the villages of the land." Silently, he examines Gabriel's garments.

"Yes, a great distance," he lamented, his downtrodden eyes reflecting his disorientation. "I am utterly lost."

"Oh, you're in Lightforge Town. Renowned for its blacksmiths and warriors, I am Aaron Lightforge." With a profound reverence, he presented himself. A radiant glow illuminated his eyes as he regained composure, and he bestowed upon me a gentle, sincere smile.

Gabriel paused briefly, finally realizing that the elderly man was expectantly waiting for a reply. It was apparent that this was a formal introduction. "My name is Gabriel Wyndham."

"Well met my Sir Gabriel."

"Well met." With a somewhat tentative nod, Gabriel reciprocated the greeting. "You can call me Gabriel."

"Nonsense." With a dismissive wave of his hand, Aaron discarded the idea. "A Knight such as yourself deserves your title."

"I'm looking for my sister. She may have been traveling with the other Knights of The Silver Wolves led by Lord-Commander Cecil."

With a wrinkled brow, the elderly gentleman was deeply immersed in contemplation. "Lord-Commander Cecil is the "Lord of Sarum City North-East of here. It's a few hours ride." The old man rubbed his chin. "Just beyond the town's limits, there stands a military barracks that serves as a place of training and relaxation for our troops."

Unenthused about the prospect of entering barracks occupied by Silver Wolves, Gabriel brushed his fingers against the wolf-hilted sword. "Thank you." He gave his hand to the old man to shake but he looked at it confused by the gesture.

"Seeking shelter for the night, weary traveler? Behold, an inn awaits you," Aaron proclaimed, echoing Gabriel's unspoken thoughts. Mindful of his recent experiences, Gabriel refrained from entertaining any thoughts that could potentially expose him.

With a fluid, deliberate movement, Aaron extended his arm in the direction of a two-story structure. "Here, they can offer food, shelter, a shower and a change of clothes. It would be a much better option than the barracks."

"That certainly sounds more appealing than basic rations and water," he replied, a grin of relief spreading across his face. The prospect of a proper meal was enticing, but the thought of a cleansing shower and a refreshing change of clothes held equal allure. In his haste to find Lesley, he had not considered any of these things.

"Tell them that Sir Aaron Lightforged sent you if they give you any trouble."

"Thank you." Despite not feeling fatigued, Gabriel wondered how much longer he could continue before collapsing from exhaustion. A pang of guilt struck him, yet he clung to the hope that such a place could prove useful. Darkness was descending, marking the end of a long and extraordinary day.

Gabriel entered the inn. Its lower level was more of a tavern and a reception area. Bartenders serving drinks to small groups of high spirited patrons. Merry men and women, some in their songs and others relaxing in their drinks.

Only now did it occur to him that he hadn't considered how he would make purchases. What form did their money take? Did they even have a currency? Initially, he saw little of value being offered in exchange for goods.

As Gabriel observed them more closely, he noticed that they used devices resembling credit cards or smart devices for payment. These devices came in various forms, such as bracelets, rings, and even weapons. Notably, they did not possess anything similar to a smartphone.

"Are you drinking, need a bed, or are you going to creep on my customers?"

Gabriels train of thought was interrupted by the question. He looked down to see a short woman whom he hadn't noticed approaching him. He thought about the question for a moment unsure if he should ask for anything.

Gabriel felt sheepish as he hesitated before speaking. "I was interested in a place to stay for the night." He glanced around the room before returning his gaze to the sword. He tilted the hilt towards the innkeeper, hoping the gesture would convey his meaning.

With a wary look, the innkeeper evaluated the man and produced a tablet-like device to examine the sword's hilt. "Another wolf?" she inquired, nodding her head. "How about I arrange a meal and a room for you? I can fetch some ale in the meantime."

Gabriel was astounded by the unexpected success of the plan. The mechanism and reasoning behind it were beyond his comprehension. If it functioned similarly to a credit card, he was clueless about whose money he was spending, assuming there were funds available. "Something simple would be good but how about you surprise me."

Pausing for a moment, she inspected the unrecognized crest with a discerning gaze, scratching her chin thoughtfully. "Which clan does this symbol represent?"

Gabriel uttered his words while trying to maintain a rigid posture, displaying a mix of boredom and nervousness akin to a small animal finding itself amidst a tavern filled with dangerous warriors. "Sir Lightforge sent me."

"I see. Come along." The innkeeper walked Gabriel to the bar and poured him an ale. "Enjoy your stay. You are in the hospitality of the Blackanvil Clan!" The tone of her voice shifted and sounded more like a service employee handling a customer. "Yer food will be up shortly. We have savory pies you'd like."

Gabriel didn't want to ask too many questions that might give himself away as an outsider and nodded. The pie did sound good at least. He looked down into the glass and gave it a little sniff. It was indeed ale.

The clan name sounded like they either were, or used to be, blacksmiths. That would explain the old smithing station he found outside, more or less, not being used. If they were still smithing it wasn't there.

It wasn't long before his meal was presented to him. It smelled wonderful. A hunger inside of him unleashing he didn't even know he had. He took the first bite and it was delicious. It was like many savory pies that he has had before. The flavor was mildly different but if he didn't know any better this was pork. Or something close to it. The more he thought about it the more he realized he didn't want to think about it. The ale was ale and the food was more or less familiar. Languages were more or less the same. He couldn't help but to wonder how or why that is.

"Whenever you are ready you can head upstairs. Your room is the last room down the hall on the next floor."

"Before I go. You mentioned that I was another wolf. Was there more of us here?"

"Aye." The woman said. "Men from the barracks come from time to time. There was also a small band that came through for a bit before heading to Sarum."

"Did the band head to Sarum have a girl dressed in red and black with them?"

"Not that I have seen. It was a couple of Knights who came in here for a few ales before their commander bragged in to scold them."

"Did they say or do anything unusual?"

"Aye, they did." She said, "They discussed how they entered a wormhole and ended up in a strange place but weren't quite sure what was real." She squinted her eyes. "It wasn't the strangest story I heard here but that one reminded me of the old tales."

"Old Tales?"

"Yeah, the ones of the dark one ripping through the fabric of realities to undo creation. Though never do you hear about people going in let alone coming out." The short woman shudders. "Cold chill."

Gabriel had a lot to think about, dark thoughts that made him question reality. He didn't want to admit that the nightmare in his home might have been real, but the thought of black tentacles and glowing snake-like orbs filled him with a strange dread that lingered for far too long.

"Are you OK?" The barkeep asked. "You look like you've seen a ghost." She laughed. "They are stories. Creepy, but pure fantasy stories."

"Yeah, of course." Gabriel clears his throat. "Fantasy."

Chapter Eight

Gabriel

Awakened by the insistent sound of the alarm, Gabriel stirred from his slumber. Peering out the window, he beheld the sun's descent below the horizon, marking the dawn of a new day. In the distance, a menacing fire raged, casting an ominous glow upon the town. Gabriel donned his fresh medieval style clothes with haste, and descended the stairs in a flurry of motion. Bursting through the front entrance of the inn, he was met with a scene of utter chaos. The town was engulfed in pandemonium, with terrified screams echoing through the air as people fled for their lives. The fire was spreading relentlessly, its flames licking at the edges of the town, threatening to consume everything in its path. Realizing the urgency of the situation, Gabriel resolved to take action and rushed toward the heart of the inferno, determined to help in any way he could.

The clashing of metal echoed in his ears, yet its origin remained elusive. A sinking sensation overcame him, he desperately attempted to regain his balance, but it was an exercise in futility. His body tumbled uncontrollably, gravity's relentless pull forcing him into a dizzying descent. With a jarring impact, he hit the ground, momentarily stunned. His vision blurred as he slid helplessly along the rough grass.

"Medic!" He heard someone yell, his vision blurred. "Where's your armor?" The voice said again. The sword in his hand still hummed with a soft glow that dissipated until it was gone. He was being dragged away by a knight.

His vision cleared, revealing the chaos of a fierce battle. The air resonated with the clash of metal and the blinding flashes of energy attacks. The ground trembled beneath the might of their blows, and the shockwaves scattered debris. Amidst the raging inferno, Gabriel comprehended that the fire was the least of their concerns.

Amidst the chaos, silver-clad Silver Wolves clashed fiercely with warriors donning copper-colored armor. Although both sides were formidable, The Silver Wolves possessed a distinct style of armor that set them apart. Gabriel, caught in the midst of the fray, could only watch as blood splattered across his face when the man dragging him was abruptly cut down. The identity of these enigmatic copper warriors remained a mystery to him.

In a clash of blades, Gabriel faced the onslaught of copper knights. Their swords shone menacingly, and one knight advanced, his blade poised for a deadly strike. But as the copper knight's sword descended, Gabriel's blade seemed to come alive, parrying the attack effortlessly. His body, as if guided by an unseen force, rolled backward, granting him a reprieve from the onslaught. As he regained his footing, Gabriel found himself surrounded by several other copper-armored knights, one of whom wielded a spear adorned with a broken sword, half of which had been severed.

Simultaneously, they all launched an assault, forcing Gabriel into a defensive stance and pushing him backward. Blocking their blows rendered his arms numb. With a brilliant flash, his sword emitted warmth that flowed through him. Each strike seemed to invigorate him, making him feel stronger and faster. It was an extraordinary occurrence, like being exposed to a potent source of energy and absorbing it completely.

Gabriel parried a blade and countered with a slash, breaking through the neck guard of one man's armor. Blood splashed his comrade's face, followed by Gabriel's sword piercing it, causing more carnage to flow over his body. Two more fell by Gabriel's hand in quick succession until the only man left standing was a bannerman.

The bannerman thrust his banner into Gabriel's shoulder hilt deep. Gabriel parried too late, its tip biting into his flesh. He cringed in pain but slashed the banner in two. Blood poured out of the wound. Gabriel buckled to one knee and the warriors were on him. In a furious slashing motion, he swung his blade, but before he could complete the deadly arc, his own flesh split cleanly in half, in a vertical plane that defied all logic. His two halves separated in a gruesome spectacle, sliding apart as if unmoored from reality.

Adorned in lustrous silver armor that radiates an ethereal gleam, a warrior emerges. Atop his shoulder rests a resplendent crest depicting a brilliant burst of light erupting from an imposing anvil. "On your feet. The Shattered Swords shall not have us this day."

Gabriel gasped for air, as rivulets of blood trickled down his arm, where the tattered banner had become embedded. It was apparent that the Shattered Swords posed a clear threat to The Silver Wolves. He grappled with mixed emotions regarding fighting on their behalf, yet he couldn't deny his gratitude for being alive and able to contemplate such matters.

"Sol would be pleased by your bravery but you should fight with armor." The silver knight yanked the banner out and placed his hand on the wound. White light flowed from his palm, healing the wound.

The pain lingered longer than the wound but wasn't too far behind and vanished as well. Gabriel was amazed by the gesture clenching his hand a few times. "What."- Gabrild stopped himself from asking the wrong question. "What is happening?"

In a swift motion, the silver armored man's helmet retracted, unveiling his refined features and jet-black hair. With effortless ease, he lifted Gabriel to his feet as if he were a mere sheet of paper. "Battle."

Gabriel's eyes widened as he recognized the warrior standing before him. "Aaron Lightforge?" he questioned, surprised to see a younger version of the warrior he had encountered earlier that evening.

"Eric. I'm often told I look like my grandfather." He said laughing. "Take your fallen brother's armor, it will be more suitable than the cloth you wear." He ordered slapping Gabriel on the shoulder.

Gabriel winced in pain but tried not to show it. If that was a friendly shoulder slap Gabriel didn't want to feel what it meant to be attacked by such a man. Judging by the slain man cleaved clean in two. He had some notion.

Eric's act of compassion was evident as he carefully kneeled down and skillfully removed the armor from the fallen knight. As if performing a mystical transformation, the armor condensed, resembling melting ice in reverse, until it took the form of a small, compact silver cube. Without hesitation, Eric tossed the cube to Gabriels, symbolizing the transfer of a significant artifact.

As Gabriel seized the armor cube, the armor captivated his attention as it melted and seamlessly melded around his hands. This phenomenon was eerily familiar, reminiscent of the time when Cecil and his companions had invaded his home, evoking the same sense of dread and terror.

Gabriel panicked and tried to shake the liquid metal off his hands, but it was no use. He felt like water was rolling over his skin, and then he was submerged in it. The metal expanded and surged up his arm, covering his entire body and blocking his vision.

Unable to see and unable to get a grip He panicked and swiped metal from his face. Suddenly, light broke through and he could see. Gabriel took his hands off his face and saw Eric staring at him with a half-amused expression, but Gabriel couldn't help but feel like he was being judged. Gabriel moved his arms expecting the metal to be heavy but it was as light as air, tight and form fitting like a second skin.

A young man runs up to Eric panting. He didn't look so much like a warrior but like a squire. He wore light leather armor, a sword and shield. "My lord Lightforge, Their commander has landed on the field."

"Good!" Lightforge said with a smile. "I will put an end to him once and for all." He said clenching his fist. It hummed with yellow white energy.

"Incoming!" Another yelled!

Eric turns heavensward, putting up a shield in time to block a giant hammer exploding in vibrant light. The resulting clash surges enough energy to push Gabriel backwards. Their battle was a spectacle of lights and violent blows clashing in great concussive waves.

In the midst of the Shattered Swords' relentless assault, Gabriel found himself compelled to defend himself. The knights employed their skilled swordplay to probe his defenses. As a blade narrowly missed him, Gabriel instinctively raised his left arm, prompting a shield of liquid metal to emerge from his armor, blocking the blow. The clash between his radiant white light and the Shattered Swords' azure luminescence was a breathtaking spectacle.

The knight pounded on Gabriel's shield, but Gabriel thrust his shield forward and followed up with his humming runic sword. The sword pierced the knight's heart, and Gabriel withdrew it, followed by a spurt of thick blood. The knight fell lifelessly to the ground, his blood pooling around him.

Gabriel watched the man take his last breath as a flicker of light faded off his body and flew upward. Gabriel was knocked out of his train of thought by a bolt of light. He flew back several feet. A giant hammer came crashing downward, lighting burning in its wake. Gabriel rolled out of the way in time to avoid being crushed or worse. The blow of the impact sent him flying backward into a stone building.

The pair were still fighting blow for blow. Eric held the upper hand swinging two handed with his bastard sword. The shattered sword champion on the defensive with nothing but his wits and energy. The hammer leapt up and towards its master. Nearly hitting Eric on its way back. They clashed in a glorious light show of powers.

Eric lifted his sword with fierce determination, unleashing a mighty downward swing that found its mark on the champion's chest, cleaving through the hilt of the two-handed hammer. Blood and the echoes of clashing steel reverberated along the blade, striking Eric's body, though he remained unwavering, the power coursing through him. The mace, now reduced to a single hand, swung wildly downward, only to be met by Eric's shield arm, blocking the blow with unwavering strength.

"You disappoint me." Eric said, pushing the blade further into the man's chest.

With his visor retracted, the champion revealed his bloody grin as he spat on Eric's face. His teeth gritted, the champion snarled, "Such dishonor."

Eric grabbed the champion by the throat and slammed his face into the ground. The champion thrashed about, but Eric held him firm. Their energy swirled, reformed and funneled into Eric. The wolf revealed in his might, his aura glowing more vibrant. With a thunderous bellow, he unleashed a feral roar, echoing his unwavering determination: "No Mercy!"

Eric wipes the blood and spit off his face before running headfirst into the Shattered Swords. He cuts down one enemy after another, his silver light pulsing with power. The enemies are no match for him, and they fall to his blade one by one. Eric is a force to be reckoned with, and he shows no mercy to his enemies. He is determined to defeat them all, and he will not stop until they are all dead.

Eric ripped through the shattered swords as the battle intensified. The longer it raged, the more intense it became. Warriors burned with energy and their lights clashed in brilliant flashes of light, heat, and blood.

Gabriel paused for a few moments, leaning on the building, uncertain if he could complete his mission of finding his sister and bringing her home. His adrenaline was wearing off, and his body ached. His breathing became labored for a moment, but then it passed. The battle raged on, moving further away. After the roars died down, a mass of flickering lights rose into the air. They were the lights of dying men.

Gabriel heard a voice call out to him. "You there!" A mail wearing warrior with a mace runs up to him. "Let me check your wounds."

"I'm fine, I need to catch my breath." It took a moment for Girl to realize that the warrior running up to him was a woman. The weight of her voice was deep and smoky. Her red hair hung out of her mail cowell.

"I am Lisa, the Battle Medic," she said. Her index finger glowed bright, and she flashed it into Gabriel's eyes.

"My name." He cleared his throat and squinted. His vision blurred, and he groaned and shook his head. "My name is Gabriel."

"You're going to be OK." She said with a smile. "But you have a concussion."

"I need to get moving." Gabriel attempted to rise, but a pained groan escaped his lips. He did not want to be detained by a knight for questioning. He wanted to find his sister and leave before anyone knew he was there.

"Don't move yet." Lisa placed her hand on Gabril's head and bathed him in a silky green light. The sensation was soothing, and his head fog lifted. The relief was even greater than when Eric had healed his shoulder. He felt a pleasant numbness, similar to the effect of general anesthesia. "Stay with me, you're going to be alright." she asked. Gabreil didn't respond, she repeated the phrase louder.

Based on her facial expressions, she appeared to be concerned about his well-being. Her brow was furrowed, and her eyes were narrowed in worry. She kept glancing over at him, as if to check on him. She also seemed to be biting her lip, which is a common sign of anxiety. Overall, her body language suggested that she was genuinely concerned for his health and safety.

"How are you feeling now?" She uses her index finger to recheck Gabriel's eyes.

In a state of profound awe, he realized that not only had the pain completely vanished, but an extraordinary sensation of well-being had enveloped him. A mighty surge of energy roared through his body, culminating in a swell of vitality that resonated from deep within his chest.

"You are a very fast healer." Rising gracefully, Lisa extended her hand to Gabriel in a warm and inviting gesture. "Exceptionally so. Can you stand?"

With great caution, Gabriel grasped her hand while she ensured his wounds remained undisturbed. Gently, she assisted him to his feet, her strength surpassing even his expectations.

An airship soared overhead in a manner similar to a jet, its sleek hull cutting through the air. The airship's propellers whirred, propelling it forward, and its tail fin provided stability. The airship's passengers enjoyed the view from the cabin, which was equipped with comfortable seats and large windows. The airship was a marvel of engineering, and it was a testament to the ingenuity of its creators.

Witnessing the jet soar above, Lisa's eyes widened in awe. Gabriel, catching her gaze, couldn't help but notice the profound admiration radiating from her eyes as he traced her line of sight. "Lord Viktor must be going back to the capital."

Gabriel's astonishment and surprise were evident as he never anticipated such a swift encounter with Viktor. The notion of meeting him so soon had not crossed his mind. "Prince Viktor was here?"

"Yes. That was his royal jet that flew overhead."

Drawing a long, deep breath, Gabriel attempted to dispel the gnawing anxiety that had taken hold of him. Amelia explained that her family was the strongest in the kingdom. "How would you compare him to Eric Lightforged?"

"There is no one else like him. I had the privilege of witnessing Lord Viktor in combat once, during the battle against the savage uprising. Viktor single-handedly slew King Erik Carlsen with a single stroke of his sword. He moved with grace, speed, and strength. I swear he was the embodiment of the All-Father." Lisa said, "I couldn't dream of moving like Lord Viktor."

Gabriel pondered his choices, knowing that expressing enthusiasm for being on Viktor's bad side would be dishonest. He had witnessed Eric Lightforge effortlessly dispatching six men in a blink, possessing superhuman strength and speed. The concept of someone surpassing that level of power was beyond Gabriel's comprehension. While he hoped the tale of Viktor's god-like abilities were exaggerated, the events he had witnessed made him hesitate to discount them entirely.

Gabriel's initial support for Amelia and Viktor stemmed from his limited understanding of their remarkable powers. However, as he uncovered the true extent of their abilities, which exceeded his wildest imaginations, his confidence in them began to waver. Doubts about his ability to stay loyal gnawed at him. To minimize attention, he resolved to find Lesley and return home, prioritizing discretion over involvement.

"Are you ok?" Lisa asked. "You're still pale."

A vehicle resembling a truck hovered to a stop a few yards away. Lisa had never seen anything like it before. It was sleek, silver, and emitted an ethereal glow. A man emerged, wearing battle-worn armor similar to Lisa's, and asked, "A survivor?"

Lisa responded, "This knight sustained minor injuries during the battle."

"I'm fine." Gabriel, plagued by self-doubt, pondered his worthiness of the esteemed title of knight. While his disposition inclined him against deception, prudence dictated that he maintain the facade rather than risk disillusionment. Prior incidents, such as killing shattered swords in self-defense, had provided convenient pretexts to garner trust. This wasn't the first time he had found himself resorting to deception for what he perceived as the greater good.

"Well met, I'm Captain Edwin." The soldier said with a slight bow.

"Gabriel." He remained seated and nodded.

"Yes, it seems the Shattered Swords are intent on starting a glorious war," Edwin said as he waved to the truck as an invitation. "The battle wages on and I intend to join them in Glory."

Gabriel eyed the man, considering what to say to maintain his cover. "I have another task I've been assigned."

"Really?" Lisa inquired, raising her hand to her face. The gesture caught Gabriel's attention, finding it strangely appealing.

"Yes," Gabriel, fearing for his safety and liberty, decided to conceal the truth from Edwin to avoid potential harm or confinement. He hoped that his deception would be accepted and his lie would be believed.

Edwin narrowed his eyes, and Gabriel assumed he was suspicious, but he hoped Edwin wouldn't say anything that would give away Gabriel's false status as a knight. "I haven't seen this particular crest before."

Gabriel trailed Edwin's curious gaze to the crest on his shoulder, identical to the one adorning his sword. Puzzled by its sudden appearance, Gabriel was uncertain about the extent to which his disguise would continue to be effective. "We are a small clan."

"A small clan with a very impressive crest," Edwin said with a hint of disdain. "It's not so different from the great houses."

Gabriel was perspiring and at a loss for words. He was hoping that Edwin would drop the matter, but it didn't appear that he was going to. "Where is your clan from?"

Gabriel paused to think. He couldn't fabricate a location, or Edwin would see through his deception. "A little town called Greenfield."

"Greenfield?" Edwin inquired. "I am not familiar with a town with such a name."

As panic set in, Gabriel struggled to find the right words. on the verge of making self-incriminating statements, he was interrupted by Edwin, who resumed speaking.

"I'm from a little town north east of here called Moonbright."

The sky darkened, and lightning flashed. "Praise be to Sol." Lisa said. "A little rain will help the people combat the lingering fire."

Relieved, Gabriel was glad the topic had shifted from his clan to the weather. If Edwin suspected foul play, he didn't mention it. "Yes, very well," he said after a long pause. "Come, Lisa. Glory awaits."

A beam of ominous light pierced the night sky, casting its illumination across the horizon. Eric Lightforge plummeted from the sky and crashed at their feet. Lisa sprang into action, healing Eric with a large green aura. Eric stirred but remained unconscious. "Who could have done this to Lord Lightforged?"

With a smile, Edwin expressed his admiration "A worthy opponent." His posture and every inch of his being radiated a profound sense of pride.

The Silver Wolves and Shattered Swords continued to rage in their bloody battle. At first glance, it appeared as though they were still fighting each other, but Gabriel noticed that they had fought alongside each other against a massive beast.

"What is that?" With wide eyes, Gabriel absorbed the horrifying scene before him. The beast stood six feet tall and tore through the knights with ease, its skin like shadow and a pair of warm colored eyes raging through Silverwolf and Shatter Sword alike. After meaning and killing countless soldiers. It leapt on top of them, sending a shockwave that knocked them off their feet. Lisa managed to keep healing Eric.

He had already thought he could not defeat someone like Eric, but now he faced a foe that had nearly slain the great warrior. The beast emanated an aura similar to the extreme dread he felt in his home. The light around the beast dimmed, and absorbed the solar from its surroundings. His stomach sank as he feared a multitude of horrors: his home, his desire to avoid helplessness, and his immediate concern, his relative strength.

"It can't be," Edwin said under his breath. He was the first to attack, landing a blow to the beast's flank. The beast roared in pain and lashed out, knocking Edwin into a building.

Lisa stopped healing Eric and summoned a glimmer of lights around the four of them. Gabriel hummed in his light once more, feeling the sudden surge of power flow into him. Dread and anxiety fled from his thoughts. From head to toe, he emitted a soft, warm, white light around his body.

"For glory!" Edwin leaped back to his feet, his sword drawn. He charged at the beast, slashing and stabbing with all his might. With a resounding roar of agony, the beast swung its menacing claws at Edwin. However, with remarkable agility, Edwin evaded each strike, demonstrating his exceptional reflexes and quick wit.

Gabriel and Lisa joined the battle, and the three of them fought the fearsome creature back-to-back. Their combined might could keep the beast from tearing through their defensives. Every time they poked at the beast's hide they were met with a quick slash of its vicious claws. The beast was too fierce for the three of them to overcome alone.

Lisa and Edwin were slammed away by the beast once more, leaving Edwin lying on the ground and Lisa struggling to stand. Only Gabriel and the beast remained. The beast tried to overpower Gabriel, but Gabriel kept backing away. He was amazed at his own ability to keep up with the beast and stay out of its reach.

Gabriel fought the beast until he could no longer. The beast leaped and pinned Gabriel to the ground, its shadow teeth inches from his face. Its warm colored eyes burned into his mind. Gabriel knew that death was imminent. Fueled by desperation he thrust his sword upward into the beast's abdomen. A bright holy fire erupted from the sword, consuming the beast and leaving behind darkened ash.

Gabriel remained motionless on the sodden ground for a considerable period, attempting to grasp the sequence of events that had transpired.

"Well struck." Edwin exclaimed, helping Gabriel back onto his feet. "You are a glorious Paladin of Sol." Inwardly, Gabriel wondered. Was this his new identity? A consecrated warrior for an unfamiliar solar deity? "We must head back to base. Report this to the king."

"I must return to my own mission."

"Very well. Before you go, take this blessing," Lisa prayed. When she finished her murmur, Gabriel was enveloped in a cool white light. "May Sol be with you, Paladin." With a warm, inviting smile, she gently nibbled her lower lip.

"Thank you," Gabriel said, smiling awkwardly in return, feeling invigorated. It was as if a veil had been lifted from his eyes, allowing him to see a deeper truth that he couldn't quite articulate. A power that he could use to save his sister, and liberate his home.

Before leaving Gabriel alone in the misty rain, Eric and Lisa loaded their truck with as many soldiers as possible.

Chapter Nine

Gabriel

The sounds of battle fade into the sobs of loss and roars of outrage. The beam of light burned in the sky, then faded away. Despite the clear visibility, no one appeared to acknowledge or be concerned about the beam of light, as everyone continued to work diligently to extinguish the remnants of the spreading fire. The smell of the smoldering wood triggers fond memories of a fire pit blazing gently into the night but Gabriel felt guilty for conjuring up such a memory in the aftermath of some skirmish.

Gabriel wanted to forget the night and sleep, but even after all the fighting, he was surprised to find that he wasn't exhausted. The lights around him dimmed and vanished, but he could still feel the power flowing all around him.

The creature he had managed to kill was very similar to the knight in his home in many ways, and it haunted him. He tried to keep his thoughts on his objectives, his Sister, but the swirling darkness all but consumed his focus. In his journey through the town, he paused to scrutinize his surroundings and discovered that he had unwittingly returned to the familiar confines of the inn. In the distance, smoke billowed into the sky, growing denser despite the rain that was intended to help the townspeople.

Amidst the falling ash, Gabriel made his way towards the towering column of smoke. When he reached the scene, he witnessed the relentless inferno engulfing a large section of the roof, radiating intense heat. A small crowd had gathered near the house, standing passively without offering any help. Although there were murmurs among the crowd, the conversations were too hushed for Gabriel to decipher the content.

Amidst the cacophony of the crowd, Gabriel's attention was drawn to a young girl's distant cries. He navigated through the dense throng until he reached the child, who sat alone and tearful. Surprisingly, despite the sizable gathering, no one seemed concerned about her well-being. People moved about their business, oblivious to the girl's plight. As the crowd swelled, an air of indifference prevailed, and no one extended a helping hand.

No one came forward to assist a young child in distress. Initially, Gabriel hesitated to intervene, fearing attention and potential consequences. Yet, the child's cries stirred his empathy, evoking memories of Lesley. Unable to ignore the child's plight, he found himself drawn toward her. With a deep breath and a determined expression, Gabriel pushed through the crowd, resolved to offer help.

Gabriel knelt before her, gently brushing away the soot and tears from her face with his thumbs. Despite the grime covering her face, the girl's blue eyes shone brightly, reminiscent of Lesley's eyes in her youth. "You're going to be okay," he said to her. "What's your name?"

The girl's eyes widened momentarily, before her gaze shifted to her own hands which were surprisingly clean. "Celise." She said through whimpers.

"Where are your parents?" Gabriel's heart sank in his chest when Celise gestured back to the old, burning barnhouse. The lower level had once been used to keep animals, while the upper level had been living quarters. It was the oldest and ugliest building in the village. The house was decorated with totems made of animal bones and feathers.

"Papa ran in after mother." She said through her tears.

"OK," Gabriel uttered, his mind racing with uncertainty. Contemplating his next move, he wondered if there was anything he could do to help. Shifting his gaze toward the inferno engulfing the house, he knew he had to act. The realization settled in that he was the only one who could find his parents. "What are your parents' names?"

"Papa is James. Mama is Jennifer."

"Stay here." Gabriel charged into the blazing house, smoke billowing out of the front doors. The entrance opened onto a staircase that led up to a spacious living room. No sooner had he reached the top of the stairs than the roof collapsed behind him igniting the floor behind him. Gabriel regretted his actions, but it was too late to turn back.

Gabriel could not see through the smoke, but he could hear a man repeatedly calling out the name Jennifer. Gabriel kept going, waving the smoke away from his face. He tried his best to stay low to minimize breathing in the thick smoke and to keep it away from his eyes. Despite his best efforts, his lungs burned and his eyes watered.

As the noise of a collapsing object and stifled groans reached Gabriel's ears from a distance, he continued his journey through the constricted hallway. He could hear the sound of someone coughing and choking. There was someone ahead of him, but between the smoke and his own blurred vision it was hard to see anything past a few feet.

"Is someone there?" Gabriel asked as he continued to move forward. He approaches an open door as the ceiling collapses again, stopping before being crushed by it. On the other side of the door was a giant of a man holding up the ceiling with sheer strength, preventing it from further collapsing and blocking the path into the bedroom. He groans and growls as sweat poured down his face, his veins and muscles bulged, and he mutters under his breath.

"Jennifer!" the large man bellowed, trapped beneath the weight of the ceiling. "You! I can't, I can't move," the big man said. He nodded his head in the direction of an unconscious woman lying in bed. "My wife. Go, get her out."

"What about you?"

"The spirits shall not have me this day."

As Gabriel squeezed through the narrow door frame, he navigated around the large man, pressing close to him. Just then, the ceiling above James caved in, causing the floor to collapse and the entire structure to become unstable. The floor shook violently as James fell through into the fiery depths of the chamber below. Gabriel peered down through the gaping hole in the floor, but the smoke and flames obscured his vision. He hoped that James had survived the fall, but doubt crept into his heart. Horrified by the sight, Gabriel felt helpless to save James. Still driven by his guilt, he resolved to save Jennifer, for Celise's sake, and to appease his own troubled conscience.

As smoke billowed through a large hole in the ceiling, oxygen rushed in, fanning the flames. A wooden beam fell in front of Gabriel, blocking his path to Jennifer. Flames erupted at his feet, separating him from her. The temperature rose rapidly, and Gabriel felt the sting of smoke and sweat in his eyes. He tried to wipe it away with his arm but only made matters worse. Raising his arms to protect his face, Gabriel charged through the flames, determined to reach the other side.

Meanwhile, the ceiling continued to collapse, the structure failing in a cascading catastrophe, dropping burning debris through the floor. The impact knocked Gabriel off his feet and onto his face. He lay gasping for breath at the foot of the bed, his body aching from the fall.

Returning to his feet he found Jennifer as pale as a ghost and covered in sweat unconscious in the bed. The floor buckled, knocking him and the bed over. Then the floor gave way beneath him, and he fell through the hole.

Gabriel hit the ground with a thud as the bed crashed down next to him, launching Jennifer into his arms. He wrapped his arms around her and looked up in time to see a flaming wooden beam falling towards them. Gabriel's eyes widened in fear as he rolled them both out of the way, narrowly avoiding the wood beam as it crashed to the ground where they had been lying moments before.

The fire spread to the dry hay that was scattered throughout the area. Most of the animals had escaped, but a few unlucky ones were crushed by the debris. Gabriel knew that they could be next if they didn't get out soon.

Gabriel released Jennifer and stood up. A ceramic cup fell from the living quarters and struck him on the head, causing him to stagger and fall to his knees. Blood streamed from his head as he spread himself over Jennifer to protect her from anything else that might fall.

He tried to pick her up, but his strength started to fail him as his exhaustion caught up with him. His lungs felt like they were on fire as he gasped for air. His vision became blurry from the smoke, sweat, and blood, but he couldn't let go. He couldn't give in, not yet. He wasn't going to let Celise lose her parents. Gabriel struggled to drag Jennifer toward the half-broken double doors. The fire around him roared. The flames out paced them burning the surrounding walls and the double door ahead of them.

Gabriel fell to his knees, lowering Jennifer to the ground as gently as he could. He was gasping for air and his body started to fail him; His exhaustion from the last day was taking hold. He couldn't bring himself to move anymore. He could hear a low growl and the wall exploded showering wood and flames around them. Gabriel thought the house collapsed on them but James emerged rampaging toward them with the fury of a thousand warriors. The big man scooped up his wife and ran towards the door. Gabriel was inspired and found the second wind needed to press forward in his wake.

Fresh air was sucked inside engulfing the flames as James burst through the burning barn doors, carrying his wife in his arms. He placed her in the grass, then collapsed to his knees, exhausted. Gabriel could see the heat radiating off of James' body, and the steam rising from his clothes. He knew that James must have been in incredible pain, but he was too focused on saving his wife to care. Gabriel watched in awe as James stood up, his muscles rippling beneath his skin.

Jennifer, on the other hand, looked peaceful, despite being covered in a mixture of dirt, hay, and ash. Her hair was matted and her clothes were torn. She lay on her back, her chest rising and falling in shallow short bursts. Her eyes were closed, and her face was expressionless.

James placed his hand on her mouth to feel her breath. He sighed and tears welled up in his eyes. His hands started shaking from the sudden cold, adrenaline, and fury. "She's not breathing."

As the heat from his body radiated outward, the air around him grew warm. As they sat there in the light of the bonfire that had been their home, his breathing slowed and became more regular. His eyes became moist and red.

Weeping, Celise knelt by her mother's side. "No, Mommy, you can't be dead," she said, collapsing onto her mother's body.

"Move back, Celise," James said, pushing her to the side. He took a deep breath to steady his nerves. The seconds felt like minutes as they watched their home crumble around them.

Gabriel kneeled down beside him. He was trained for stuff like this. "I can help.", He said, moving into position kneeling beside her, opposite of James. He places two hands in the center of her chest, shoulders directly over his hands; elbows locked. He compressions her chest thirty times.

He lifted her chin, tilting her head to ensure a clear airway. To prevent air from escaping, he pinched her nose. With a complete seal formed over her mouth with his, he gave measured breaths, aiming to restore her breathing to its natural rhythm. While administering CPR, Gabriel continuously monitored to see if her chest rose with each breath, indicating a successful restoration of breathing. Taking a second breath, he exhaled, ensuring that her chest moved accordingly. Despite the movement, she still did not begin breathing independently.

Gabriel repeated the chest compressions and rescue breathing twice more, but still, there was no response. "Come on! Don't do this to us." Gabriel's actions became increasingly frantic as he placed his hands on her chest again. The images of his own parents dead on the bedroom floor flashing through his mind. A lingering feeling of guilt and helplessness fueling his actions, his need to save others.

James intervened, placing his hand over Gabriel's to stop him and signal the futile efforts. "She is close to death." He said in a low growl.

"No, she can't die!" Celise cried.

As darkness enveloped Gabriel's vision, the mournful sound of Cecile's tears transported him back to his thoughts of Lesley. In his mind, he could vividly recall her tearful cries echoing from her crib. A crimson stream flowing down her cheek.

"But there is another way." James said, tapping Gabriel on the chest, to bring him back to reality.

"I can help." Gabriels insisted. "I can save her."

"You can't but Sol, and the spirits of the wild can." James closed his eyes and inhaled the air around them and exhaled long and slow. "Hold her. Keep her in your thoughts. Pray."

Gabriel attempted to resume CPR, but James restrained him. As he watched James and Celise, Gabriel was reminded of his own experience with Lesley, and he did not want them to suffer as he and Lesley had.

"No." James placed one of Gabriel's hands on Jennifers belly and one behind her back of her head. "Pray." James releases Gabriel's arms. "Girl, pray."

Without hesitation, Celise knelt next to James. She clasped her hands together, tilted her head downward, and closed her eyes in silent prayer.

Despite his reluctance, Gabriel complied with James' request, burdened by a sense of failure for his inability to save another life. Jennifer's clammy, deathly pale skin was unnaturally cold to the touch. Her passing affected him profoundly, beyond what would be expected for someone he scarcely knew.

Gabriel moved her gently so her upper body was propped up over his legs and placed his hands where James had directed him to. One hand behind Jennifer's head and the other hand over her navel.

Following instructions, he closed his eyes and began to pray. The embers of his inner fire danced beyond his reach. He drew in a deep breath and fed the flames, causing them to grow larger and brighter. He exhaled, stoking the fire until it burned hot and strong. Gabriel's body began to emit a gentle glow, and waves of fiery light erupted all over it.

James placed one hand over Jennifer's heart and another in the air. "Hear me, spirits of the wild," he called out. The wind began to pick up around him, and his aura shifted from earth brown to lush green and back again. Celise hummed a deep crimson.

"Wild gods?!" one of the onlookers yelled. "Heretic! I knew it!" another added.

Gabriel had forgotten about the crowd, who had been silent onlookers until now. He could feel their energy shift from disgust to hatred. But something was holding them back. Gabriel realized it was him—or, more precisely, the uniform. James was a large, intimidating man, and Gabriel couldn't rule out the possibility that the crowd feared crossing him.

James closed his eyes and his expression became serene. He bit his finger and drew blood, which he then used to trace a set of runes in Jennifer's forehead. Someone in the crowd gasped audibly. If he heard them, he ignored them. "Spirits of the earth, strengthen her body to retain her soul."

"Spirit of the flame, light a beacon for mommy to follow!" Celise began by extending her aura, a brilliant red and orange flame, into Jennifer's body. All of their auras flowed into Jennifer, causing her to glow with vibrant energy.

James placed one hand on his wife's chest and another in the air. "Spirits of the wind, stoke the flames. Guide my Jennifer back to me!" James compressed his wife's chest a few times with one massive hand.

A single wisp of light appeared and floated down, landing on James' forehead. He closed his eyes and leaned down, creating a seal over their mouths and blew the life energy into her. In response, she emitted a brilliant glow, to be followed by violent coughing and rapid breathing. James lifted her into his arms, which resulted in her breathing stabilizing.

Jennifer's eyes flew open, and she gasped and coughed. Her voice was hoarse and raspy, but she managed to force out a few words. "Where am I? I was with Sol, she was beautiful."

"Don't speak my love. You are safe now." James scoops up his wife in his massive arms and lifts her as he comes to a stand. He looks down towards Gabriel grunts. "I am James. This is my wife Jennifer. The little one is Celise."

Celise blushed and smiled. "Thank you for your help with channeling the spirits."

Gabriel introduced himself as he stretched his lower back after standing. Tonight, he witnessed incredible and unimaginable events. He couldn't help but express his amazement, saying, "That was quite impressive."

"Sol's flames burned brightly in you, Sir." Jennfer said, placing a hand on Gabriel's chest.

The crowd appeared to be an angry mob, but they did not do anything to provoke them. The townspeople parted to allow them to pass, none daring to speak against him, but Gabriel could sense the entire town's disapproval.

Gabriel couldn't help but think that James expected this behavior from the people around him. They weren't violent towards him, but they continued to circle him and murmur things that sounded like religious doctrine. They continuously called James both a heretic and a savage. Despite the miracle they witnessed, the people here did not carry a high opinion of the man.

After the group disbanded, a few individuals lingered behind. Intrigued by their actions, Gabriel pondered their intentions. Did they remain to ensure the house burned down, to prevent the fire from spreading, to conclude it was unsalvageable, or perhaps they simply found pleasure in the sight of the flames? Questions about their motives remained unanswered, including whether their hesitation to attack was due to James' size or the intimidating presence of the Silver Armor of the Local Law Enforcement worn by him.

"Girl, come." James said, Jennifer resting her head on his shoulder. They had both been exhausted, James had had a rough exterior though she had started to show signs of fatigue.

As they moved farther from their home, the houses were less charred by the fires. Gabriel believed that the fire did not originate from the conflict, but rather from James's house. He could not help but suspect that this may have been a targeted attack using the battle as a cover.

"Where are you going?" Gabriel asked, his concern for their family is growing.

"We must find shelter," James said. He walked over to a nearby carriage-like vehicle, which resembled a minivan. "We will rest in the carriage and leave at first light."

James opened the back of the carriage and laid Jennifer on the bed inside. The interior was a decked-out tiny home used for camping. Although the carriage did not have a kitchen or shower, it had the well-used equipment for both.

In a childlike and whiny tone, Celise expressed her fondness for the place, stating, "But I like it here."

"We can't stay, little one."

Gabriel smiled empathetically at the pet name, understanding their situation. He extended an offer, stating that he had a room available at the INN, conveniently located in the heart of town.

"I know of it."

"You are welcome to join me for the night."

"They would not have us," the big man grunted. "It was only a matter of time before this happened. Wolves don't respect the spirits of the wild life from which they derive from. Now that they know. If we don't leave we will soon be driven out."

Gabriel thought he understood the situation: a large man, a heretic, and a savage. However, he wanted more information, so he asked, "Does this have something to do with them calling you a heretic?"

With a cautious gaze, James halted and directed his attention toward Gabriel. He seemed to be searching his face for any indication of what Gabriel was planning. "What clan are you from?" James asked with an abruptness that suggested he was struggling to keep his emotions in check.

"What if I told you I was not a silverwolf?"

"Then I'd call you a liar."

"Why's that?"

"Only wolves can use their weapons and armor because the weapons and armor can read your DNA. If you don't have the correct DNA, the weapons and armor will not work for you."

The revelation left Gabriel stunned. Raising the sword, he scrutinized the wolf crest with its solitary eye. Was it possible? For countless generations, this blade had been carried by his family, passed down through the ages. But no, it was impossible. "I am a silverwolf?" he uttered, his voice laced with incredulity.

Under a misapprehension, James interpreted Gabriel's question as a declarative statement: "I can see that." With a furrowed brow, Gabriel raised an eyebrow in disbelief. It seemed like a cosmic coincidence, something beyond mere chance.

"If you can't stay here, where will you go?"

"We will travel north over the mountains to my hometown of Snowfall Village." Directing his gaze towards Celise, James commanded, "Enter the carriage." Despite her initial hesitation, Celise complied and took her place in the back of the carriage alongside her mother.

Gabriel's smile was tinged with desperation as he inquired, "Is there any possibility that you'll be passing by Sarum City?"

In a moment of reflection, James lowered his gaze to the ground, forming a frown upon his lips. "Yes," he said at last. "We will stop there for supplies on our journey."

"You are welcome to join us. It's the least we can do." Jennifer injected.

"Thank you." Gabriel bowed graciously.

With a sneer directed at James and a subsequent smile for Gabriel, she graciously uttered, "It would be our honor."

"Very well." James said. "If that is what you desire, then meet us here at first light. We will leave without you if you are not punctual."

Chapter Ten

Lesley

Lesley wiped the blood from her nose onto her school uniform sleeve. She, Olivia, and Amelia were sitting in a carriage made of steel-like metal. The design combined a curious blend of contemporary and vintage styles, embodying a fusion of the new and the old. It merged functionality with opulent luxury, catering to both practical needs and indulgence.

"I can't believe he hit you like that." Olivia leaned over to inspect Lesley's nose. Lesley pushed her away and looked out the carriage window, wanting to forget her nose and the pain.

Accompanying them were their captors, a small group of knights riding alongside on militarized motorcycles, each motorcycle adorned with glowing wheels of radiant light. Though impressed, Lesley was in a foul mood. As she brushed her hair from her face, she winced in pain from her fingernails grazing her tender nose.

She was not accustomed to feeling helpless. She had always known her limits and when to use strength and finesse. But now, neither of those options were available to her. She touched her nose again to make sure the injury was real, and the self-inflicted pain caused her to wince.

Lesley was deep in thought as the lush forest gave way to open fields. The sun was sinking below the tree line, and the sky was ablaze with color.

The deep reds and oranges of the sunset were reflected in the still waters of a nearby pond, creating a mesmerizing sight. Lesley lingered in that moment, simply taking it all in. She felt a sense of peace and tranquility wash over her.

"This is the southern edge of my kingdom."

The peaceful atmosphere was shattered by Amelia's phrase, which greatly irritated Lesley. "Your kingdom, huh?" Lesley asked, not even looking at the princess. "I'd say I'm impressed, but considering you're locked up here with us." She let her accusation hang in the air, unable to stop herself from being rude.

"Why do you presume I am locked in here?" Amelia reclined, unwinding her shoulders and crossing her legs. "It is my will to return to the capital and face my brother again."

Lesley furrowed her brow. "Perhaps now is the time you tell us your story." She watched the scenery and the knights for a few moments more before turning her attention to the princess.

"Of course," she said, steeling herself. "I am Princess Amelia Ascendant of the Kingdom of The Silver Wolves, first child of Marcus Ascendant, King of the Wolves." She spoke with great pride.

Lesley folded her arms across her chest. "Oh," She tilted her head and glanced at the Knights outside before returning her gaze to Amelia. "You're the princess of the Knights who captured us and took us through a magical portal?" Her skepticism was palpable, almost venomous.

Amelia nodded in agreement. "Exactly."

"You can't order them to let us go?" Before Amelia could answer Lesley continued. "Of course not. A princess who orders her own knights around? How preposterous." Lesley looks back out the window, arms crossed over her chest.

"You speak of what you know very little of."

Lesley found herself chuckling and shifting in her seat. With a self-reflective remark, "God, you sound like Gabriel."

Amelia continued, "My brother challenged me for the right to rule. Our fight had yet to conclude when I found myself in your home."

"In a weird way that makes sense." Olivia shrugged.

Lesley's expressive hand gestures emphasized her disbelief as she exclaimed, "How on earth does that make any sense?"

With a noticeable undertone of contempt, Olivia remarked, "Solarians hold honor, loyalty, and strength as their highest values. Above all, they revere their deity, Sol. It appears to be the foundation upon which their society is based."

"You can rule a nation by winning a duel?"

"There are certain caveats in place to protect the integrity of the crown but in our particular case. Yes." Amelia folds her arms across her chest.

"Yes?" Lesley's eyes go wide. "Yes!? That's absurd!"

With a slight shift in her seat that exuded discomfort, Amelia questioned, "Is it?"

"Yes." With a resounding slap, Lesley forcefully brought her open hands together, conveying a firm and resolute stance.

"I don't know what it's like where you come from but the strength of a ruler can actually change the way of the world. And my family is the strongest."

"Hold on. If you're so strong, and the rightful ruler of these knights, why didn't you fight the knights yourself?" Her chest felt constricted, and the words lodged in her throat as anger surged through her veins. "The strongest of your people." With a contemptuous mutter, she expressed her disdain.

"My struggle is not with my people, but with my brother. I do not wish them ill."

"You could have protected Gabriel right? You could have stopped them!"

"Gabriel challenged them. It would have been improper for me to interfere."

"Improper? He could be dead!" She spoke with a hint of sadness in her eyes, which had turned from their usual sapphire blue to a steely gray. "He could be dead!"

Olivia placed her hand on Lesley's shoulder. "We don't know that."

"He was quite gallant." Her eyes darted away, but then returned to Lesley's. "I have no doubt he lives."

The rage inside of her was building to a breaking point, and she felt like she was going to explode. She wanted to cry, to lash out, but she couldn't. Then, Olivia wrapped her arms around her in a warm embrace, and the tears that Lesley couldn't summon fell from Olivia's eyes. Lesley released a breath of contentment, her tension easing.

She could feel the static in the air, and her skin tingled with goosebumps. As she watched the sun sink below the horizon, her eyes filled with tears. Olivia always knew how to make her feel better, but this was different. This was something new, something she had never experienced before. It was almost too much to take in. The experience was like being sucked into a whirlpool and dragged down to the bottom.

The sun set, and the stars came out, shining brightly. The moon was so big and bright, it looked like a second sun. Olivia had cried herself to sleep and was still whimpering. She was like a helpless child at times. Lesley couldn't blame her, even though she was the one who had lost her only family.

In a moment of self-reflection, Lesley recognized that her past actions had strained her relationships, leading to the loss of people she deeply cared about, much like Olivia had experienced. However, Olivia had the advantage of a larger family to find solace and support, something Lesley lacked.

Certain that Gabriel would not want to remain in this world either, Lesley attempted to push those thoughts from her mind. There was nothing to be done about it at this time. She stroked Olivia's hair as the girl lay her head in her lap. The carriage slowed as it passed a number of makeshift tents and people who all appeared to have been displaced.

With a raised voice, Amelia inquired, "What is happening out there?"

Gathering her composure, Lesley inquired, "I take it this isn't normal."

"No. It is not."

The carriage came to a halt, finding itself amidst a refugee settlement beyond the colossal gates. Each of the four-story towers in the wall was connected to the others by fortified metal and stone, providing an impenetrable barrier.

"What has happened to my people?"

Startled by the rhythmic clanging of metal on metal, Olivia awoke from her nap. The slow parting of the massive metal gates created an opening in the wall, and the carriage resumed its forward motion. When the loud bang signifying the gates' closure echoed through the air, Lesley realized they had successfully passed through.

Even though it was night, the city streets were still bustling with activity. From the moment they passed through the gates, it felt like they were driving through an endless sea of city buildings. There was more city around every corner.

After passing through yet another smaller gate, they came to a halt. Silence enveloped them for a few moments, only interrupted by the sound of the door latch opening. This signaled the culmination of their arduous journey. Anxiety churned Lesley's stomach, as she sensed that their end was imminent.

With astonishment, the guards watched Amelia emerge first. Confirming her presence, he acknowledged, "It's true." Lesley was unable to discern whether Amelia's quizzical expression conveyed hurt or annoyance. Following Amelia's lead, Lesley and Olivia exited as well.

"Amelia." In a well-maintained semi-medieval stone and metal fortress, Cecil stood proudly alongside a stern, older man. This man wore armor adorned with a silver wolf emblem on his chest, and his hands were clasped firmly behind his back. Soft lights emanated from the armor, walls, and even smaller objects and lamps, casting a warm glow over the entire scene.

As the carriage sped toward what appeared to be a garage filled with similar carriages, Lesley's eyes widened in astonishment. The dimness engulfed them as the carriage smoothly descended toward the ground.

"Uncle Arcturus. It's good to see you."

While conversing with Amelia, Arcturus strode over to Lesley and gave her an appraising look. "The existence of the vortexes is quite extraordinary, as are the intriguing people on the other side of them." Exhibiting a cordial smile that belied his ulterior motives. "I'm sure we have much to learn from the youngling."

Lesley's countenance contorted in revulsion as the word reached her ears. She had already cultivated a deep-seated loathing for Arcturus. As shadows crept along the periphery of her sight, a storm of malevolent thoughts swirled within Lesley's mind. Sinister fantasies emerged, envisioning their demise through cataclysmic downpours of shadowy energy, accompanied by flashes of lightning that would sear their flesh from their mortal frames.

"Take them to the Holding Cells." Cecil ordered.

Lance acknowledged with a salute. "You two," he said to the pair of unnamed knights, "You are relieved of duty. I will take over from here." The pair saluted Lance, then lingered for a few moments, turned and walked away.

Lesley watched Amelia and her entourage ascend the steps to the keep's main entrance for as long as she could. A part of her wished Amelia would turn around, show some last shred of humanity, use her title and privilege. It was a foolish hope. A harsh shove brought Lesley back to reality.

"Let's go, we don't have all night." Lance attempted to push her again, but she stepped aside and allowed herself to be led forward. "That's a good youngling." Lesley was disgusted by the word. The more she heard it, the more she despised it.

With a sweeping motion, a pair of guards swung wide the imposing double doors, unveiling a descending staircase. At the staircase's base, another duo of guards maintained a vigilant watch. As they steadily made their way down the flight of stairs, the guards encountered numerous additional guards stationed at various intervals.

"How deep does this go?" Lesley asked.

"Not deep enough for you." Lance said, his voice trembling with anger.

As they descended, the holding cells became darker and more squalid. The cells that housed a variety of people became more uncivilized and destitute. Many men and women were sickly and listless.

"This is where we part ways." Lance said as he opened the black bars of a prison cell. He grabs Lesley by the arm and tosses her inside causing her to trip and fall onto her shoulder. A sharp pain erupts, and she grimaces.

"That's no way to treat a lady." Lesley protested as she ran past Lance to help Lesley back up to her feet.

"You are no lady." He slammed the sliding door into place with a loud bang and walked away without saying another word. "You like pushing others around." He added with malice.

"Why is he treating you like that?" Olivia asked.

"Maybe it's revenge." Upon comprehending the occurrence of events within the vortex, Lesley found amusement in Lance's futile desire to harm her. His inability to do so elicited laughter from her. Yet the fact that he also remembered happened only confirms that the events in the vortex had taken place.

"Revenge? For what? They attacked us. Invaded your home and kidnapped us."

"You're right." As Lesley nursed her shoulder, the pain diminished with each cautious movement. "These guys are monsters and we'll make them pay somehow."

"Good." Olivia said, her lips curling into a grin.

"Now that we are alone, check this out." With her arm fully submerged in the bag, Lesley searched diligently for the runic gemstone she had previously tossed inside, her eyes scanning the contents thoroughly.

"Did you obtain this bag from the temple?" she inquired. Gently grazing her fingers over the delicate leather and intricate designs, she marveled at its beauty.

"Yes." Fixated on Olivia, Lesley halted, her gaze firmly fixed. "I didn't always have this bag?"

"No."

Once more, Lesley glances around, her demeanor exuding palpable insecurity. "Do you think they noticed?"

"I don't think so."

Amidst the bag's solitary contents, Lesley delves diligently, seeking the elusive runic gemstone. Surprisingly, its retrieval proves to be an arduous task, despite being the sole item within.

"Do you have something?"

With a nod, Lesley carefully wrapped her hand around the stone. In an instant, a quiet whisper emerged from behind her, causing her to furrow her brows and turn around.

A man of dubious character, dressed in black boiled leather armor and a black cloak, sat with a black wide-brimmed hat balanced on his knee. He was covered in old dirt and sweat and smelled like he hadn't bathed in years. It was clear that he had been there for some time.

Flashing a sly smile, his eyes swept over their school attire as he asked, "What are you wearing?" His voice was soft, but it seemed to echo in the darkness.

Olivia was startled by the sound of his voice and asked, "How long have you been there?"

"You already know the answer to that," he said, his words laden with hidden meaning. "I'm Raven," he said with a bow, not bothering to stand.

Olivia introduced herself and her best friend Lesley, and then she grabbed the side of her skirt and curtsied, saying, "And this is a school uniform." Surprisingly, she exuded a positive disposition.

"Olivia, don't waste your time with him. The guy is clearly unhinged," Lesley stated, her eyes rolling in exasperation. Leaning against the cold steel bar of the holding cell, Lesley idly swung one arm around.

"How long have you been here?" With a questioning look, Lesley rolled her eyes at Olivia. Lesley glanced around the room before fixing her stare on Olivia, wondering why she had repeated the same question.

"I've been here for about ten days," he snickered.

Lesley sighed and turned her attention back to the small hallway they were led down, and the guard at the very end of it.

"You're staring at that guard like you could kill him with your eyes." Raven chuckled. "Relax, sit back, and enjoy your time while you can."

"Because we are stuck together doesn't mean we have to talk."

"I could leave anytime I wish to."

"You must be biding your time." Lesley turned her gaze back down the hallway placing her arm between the bar.

"Indeed." The rogue lay down and covered himself with his blanket. "I have lived a long life, and my desires have all but been torn to shreds and scattered to the wind." he said with a mischievous grin.

Lesley expressed her disdain with a dismissive, "How poetic."

With a sense of defeat and helplessness weighing upon her, Lesley kept her gaze fixed on the guard. Suddenly, another guard emerged, noticeably shorter and thinner than the first. After a brief exchange of words, the smaller guard turned his attention toward Lesley, his stare unwavering.

Olivia walked over to stand next to Lesley and asked, "Do you hear what they're saying?"

"Does it even matter?" Without sparing the two girls a single look, Raven curled up into a tight ball beneath the protective cover of his cloak.

Lesley sighed, her admission tinged with defeat. "No. I guess it doesn't."

"Maybe you should challenge him?"

"Challenge him?" Lesley sneered at the thought. It was ridiculous. Absurd. "Sounds like a good way to die."

"Hmm. Maybe you're right." Raven scratched his chin. "He's a vicious one. You might be better off sitting down and eating your meals."

Inside the cramped confines of her cell, laughter echoed relentlessly, haunting her senses endlessly. Lesley's eyes strained against the encroaching darkness that warped and twisted her face. "Shut up" she snapped furiously. "I know I can take him. I fought bigger men and won."

"With full justification, issue him the challenge." A smile tugged at his lips as his gaze hardened.

"Lesley no!" Olivia yells. "How many times do you need them to show you they aren't normal."

"Provoke him into a fight," Raven chuckled again. "If you emerge victorious, I wager he'll set you free."

With a sharp gaze, Lesley scrutinized Raven, recognizing him as a naive and misguided individual in a similar predicament. She dismissed his words as lacking any significance or value. "You're hilarious."

"Silence yourselves." The small guard said with a foreboding chill in his voice.

"This is your chance at freedom." With astonishing swiftness, Raven inclined his head forward, raising both eyebrows in unison. A playful smile gradually spread across his face, hinting at mischievous intentions.

"Will you stop instigating a fight?"

"She is stronger than you think."

With a menacing glare, the guard locks eyes with Lesley, his steely blue eyes unwavering. In a chilling tone, "You will keep those eyes off of me or I will cut them out."

In a swift surge of emotion, Lesley's anger manifested visibly through the tightening of her facial features into a concentrated expression. Her eyes swept over the guard in a comprehensive assessment, taking in every detail from head to toe. "I'd like to see you try."

"You dare challenge me?" The guard's excitement was palpable as he eagerly awaited an engaging contest.

"No!" Olivia squeals.

"Do it." Raven murmurs softly, catching Olivia's attention. She turns to face him, her gaze sharp and disapproving. Unfazed, Raven holds her gaze, his eyes fixated on her hazel depths. In a bold gesture, he winks, leaving Olivia momentarily taken aback.

Lesley glanced about the cell, then back at the guard. Even she was surprised by what came out of her mouth next. "I challenge you to a duel."

As Olivia's eyes widened with tears, her voice quivered as she uttered, "Why are you doing this?" Raven watched Olivia's reaction with a face palm and a chuckle.

The guard looked perplexed, dumbfounded even. "Very well." The guard puts his hand on the metal bars and slides the door open. "We all love a good fight." The guardsman snarled, drawing his sword from his waist.

Lesley's eyes widened in fear. "Hold on, hold on," she said. "I didn't mean it. I don't have a weapon!"

With a steely gaze, the guard uttered a warning, "You ought to have reconsidered your decision to challenge me," before thrusting his blade forward.

Lesley raised her arms to protect herself and shut her eyes. The dark gem emitted a violet energy blast that deflected the sword's thrust. Lesley's eyes widened in astonishment. "What's going on?"

The gem pulsed with energy once more, blasting the sword out of his hands and sending it spinning away from him to clatter on the floor. "You're real?" she said to the gemstone.

"Mother of Sol," The guard said, raising his shield and pushing through the pulsating energy shield. The gem fell to the floor. He pushed her backwards and into the cell wall, his strength overwhelming her, much like the other knights. He lifted her off her feet and dragged her upward along the wall.

Lesley strained with all her might as a spark of electricity coursed down her arms and into the metal shield. The guard was thrown back a few feet and fell to his knees. Lesley collapsed onto the hard floor, gasping for air. She wasn't sure what had happened, but she was free. She jumped back to her feet, feeling energized. Her heart was racing with adrenaline.

The guard lunged, delivering an uppercut to Lesley's chin. Her head snapped back and hit the cell wall. He didn't stop there, continuing his assault with a series of punches that knocked the wind out of her.

"Perhaps this was a poor idea." Raven admitted looking away. Olivia exhaled sharply, wrapping her arms over her chest.

Lesley, dazed, tries her best to block the attacks, but many of them get through. Her entire body was in agony, and she collapsed against the wall, the only thing keeping her upright. A large violet aura of light emerged behind the guard. The gem shot through the guard's shoulder and into Lesley's hand. Her fingers clenched the gem, and dark runes emitted violet light that expanded outward.

The guard roared in agony, fueled by adrenaline, and kept coming. Lesley used the gem's shield-like properties to push aside his fist, following up with an elbow to the side of his head that knocked his helmet clean off with a loud crack like thunder.

Spotting an opening, she went on the offensive with a flying punch. Electricity crackled down her arm, causing a flash of light as she slammed her fist into his face. She watched in amazement as the energy flowed through her hand and between her fingertips.

Olivia leaped into the air with delight. "It looks like you've acquired some superpowers!"

"Powers?" Lesley asked, glancing from her fist to the guard, electricity buzzing up and down her arm and between her fingers.

"Yeah, like the Knights. But with electricity," Olivia shrugged. "Like Thor, yeah."

"The legend has come true! By the will of the gods, I am alive!" Lesley cheered out, lighting crackling in an aura around her. "Another!"

"Alright, it's time to make our exit," Raven declared as he stood up. "We won this challenge."

With a downturned mouth and narrowed eyes, Lesley placed her hands on her hips, "We?"

"Aren't we an adventuring group now?"

"You aren't going anywhere." With labored breaths, the guard leaped back to his feet, clutching his sword. Before Lesley could muster a response, he seized her and slammed her face into the metal bars of her prison cell, pinning her there. seething with rage, he spun her around. "No one will be able to recognize that pretty face when I'm done with you." With a glint of wicked delight in his eyes, the guard tightened his grip on her, holding her firmly in place. In a gruesome display, blood violently erupts from her lips and nose, drenching both the guard and herself in a crimson spray as he bludgeoned her face with the pommel of his sword.

"She won the challenge!" Olivia protested. "Let her go!"

"It's a good thing no one was here to bear witness to my folly." He smashes her in the face one more time. "It will be your turn as the next."

In a swift and courageous act, Olivia fearlessly threw herself in front of the guardsmen to protect Lesley. With unwavering determination, she forcefully pushed him back and freed Lesley from his grip.

The guard, taken aback by Olivia's audacity, could only let out a mocking laugh as he released Lesley, who crumbled to the floor. With a sinister grin, he uttered, "Are you challenging me?"

The guard grabs Olivia's shoulder and pulls her towards him, plunging his sword into her chest, up to the hilt, and then twists it, eviscerating her. Blood spurts from her mouth and drips down her chin. In a swift motion, the guard slid the blade horizontally, effortlessly slicing through flesh and causing blood to splatter across Lesley's face. Tears brimmed Lesley's widening eyes, mirroring her escalating emotions—first sheer terror, then profound loss.

Olivia's knees buckled beneath her as excruciating agony enveloped her. With each labored breath, wheezing and gurgling sounds escaped her lips, while her teeth remained tightly clenched in an effort to quell the overwhelming pain. Blood, the essence of her life force, flowed relentlessly from her side, draining her of color with every passing second. In a final gesture, she reached out to Lesley before succumbing to her injuries and collapsing to the ground.

With her voice grown hoarse, Lesley let out a mournful cry, calling out, "Olivia." The familiar world surrounding her appeared to melt away, gradually losing its distinctness and clarity. In a state of disbelief, she muttered, "This can't be true. This isn't real," her eyes reflecting the bewilderment in her soul.

Witnessing the fading light in Olivia's eyes, Lesley was gripped by a sense of paralyzing horror. Helplessness, numbness, and nausea overwhelmed her. Her limbs tingled with the buzzing of anxiety, while an unexplainable heat scorched the back of her throat. As the room darkened, the air swirled and shifted around her. A resounding cry of "No!" erupted from her voice, carrying the weight of her anguish and despair.

As the winds gusted with a fierce intensity, an eerie howling filled the air. The formidable force of the wind caused the stone walls to crumble into dust, unable to withstand its might. Electricity crackled and surged around her, emitting a vibrant violet glow. Her gaze remained fixed on the guard, tears streaking down her face. The steely gray of her eyes gradually transformed into deep, mesmerizing violet orbs.

As the wind around him gained intensity, the guard levitated, carried aloft by the powerful gusts. The ceiling above could not withstand the dark winds and was destroyed, propelling him upward through the roof. Suspended beneath the night sky, he found himself floating amidst a sphere of whipping wind, ominous clouds, and crackling bolts of lightning.

"No one will recognize you when I'm through with you," she taunted, echoing the guards' cruel words as the black wind howled around them. The violet gemstone in her hand throbbed with energy, emitting a powerful aura that radiated outward.

A piercing cry of anguish erupted from the guard's lips as his limbs contorted and twisted in an unnatural dance. The sickening snap of bones echoed through the air, lost amidst the howling wind. A crimson haze enveloped his form, veiling the gruesome transformation he underwent.

In the midst of the raging storm, Lesley found herself in an eerie serenity, transcending her initial fury into a brooding calm. The tempestuous tears shed in her unbridled rage were now whisked away by the swirling winds. A sudden burst of electric energy erupted from her palm, as a mysterious dark gem hovered in the center of her left hand. Shadows danced and flickered around her, mirroring the tumultuous thunder that reverberated all around.

With the gradual subsiding of her anger, a profound sense of loss washed over her, leaving her overwhelmed. Sinking to her knees, she crawled closer to Olivia's lifeless form, gathering her tenderly in her arms.

Chapter Eleven

Gabriel

Gabriel captivated James, Jennifer, and Celise with the tale of the knights' odyssey through the silver vortex. Yet, he strategically left out certain details he was hesitant to disclose, such as the dream-like battle in the darkness and the enigmatic knight with sharp, star-like teeth. Jennifer's curiosity heightened when she discovered that Amelia was a pivotal figure in the narrative. A distant look clouded her eyes, as if she were reliving a past memory she chose not to share. Regaining her composure, she turned her attention to Gabriel, studying him with intense focus.

"So you really aren't one of them." Jennifer gasped. "But you channel the power of Sol, I feel it in you."

Gabriel responded with a shrug, expressing his uncertainty with a mumbled, "I suppose I should say thank you?" The enigmatic nature of Sol and the beliefs surrounding the Solarian faith left him grappling with conflicting thoughts and emotions. Captivated by the enchanting realm, its mystical wonders stirred memories of his encounter with the villagers, igniting his thoughts. "Can you tell me why they call you guys heretics?"

Jennifer explained that the reason behind people viewing them as heretics stemmed from their worship of nature spirits and their audacity to challenge the forces of nature itself. Centuries ago, The Silver Wolves, a dominant clan in the land, had deemed all forms of magic associated with the realms of nature and the wild goddess, known as the Three, to be overly dangerous, and thus outlawed them.

Furthermore, she elaborated that The Silver Wolves were ardent worshipers of Sol, the God of Light, and their followers, the Paladins, were conduits of his power. They vehemently denounced any alternative forms of worship, particularly the worship of the void, labeling them as acts of heresy.

Gabriel yearned to believe in the legitimacy of magic, hoping that the formulation of a law surrounding its usage held some kernel of truth. Yet, from his observations, wielding magic appeared nothing less than a miraculous feat. He struggled to comprehend a rationale for outlawing such an extraordinary power.

Sol was the only explanation for the sudden emergence of white flames-like aura that covered his body on occasion. He clenched his fist in an attempt to summon it again, but to no avail. He felt its power within and without, but it was beyond his grasp. Gabriel pondered the void creatures in his home, still hoping that it was a dream, but seeing the beast in the town of Lightforge he knew that was not the case. He could not help but think that they would be a major problem for him in the future, and he was going to need Sol to do it.

"We are here." James growled from the driver's seat.

As the carriage rolled over the hill, Gabriel was astounded by the sight of Sarum Keep, a walled city situated in the center of an expansive plain. Even from a distance, it was apparent that the walls were colossal, though their true scale remained immeasurable. The skyline of the city exhibited a distinctive Romanesque style, with castle-like structures towering above the walls themselves. Underneath the azure glow of the second moon, the resplendent moonlight shimmered brilliantly off the silvery walls, enhancing their luminance.

Jennifer told him a tale about the second moon and the sacrifice of an old void knight who became a paladin of Sol. Cecil, the redeemed, gave his life to protect the world from The Void King and now watches over them from the night sky, emanating his light in the darkness as The twin of Mani, the silver moon in the sky.

"Cecil? Like Lord-Commander Cecil?"

"It's widely believed that he's from the redeemed lineage. However, I hold the opinion that he was simply named after him. The esteemed Lord-Commander Cecil hails from the Walled City of Sarum, one of the four prominent Great Cities of The Silver Wolves. These cities were meticulously established by the revered Wolves of Hati. Each of the four clans established a city, to the north Bremen, the Frozen City by the Wolves of Gerki. To the west The Coastal City by the Wolves of Freki. In the center of the Kingdom is Lyndell, the Capital City, established by the Wolves of Sköll."

"You seem to know a lot, it's rather impressive."

"I must confess I was not born of the druidic tribe with James, but as a child of Sol. My Father was a Knight in service of Sarum, and my mother was a cleric of Sol."

"They must have been furious when you left."

"They were, but I believe they came to comprehend in time. Sol is present in everything, including the realms of Nature. I would even go so far as to say that it exists among the void touched."

"Light exists even in the darkest of places." With a nod of approval, Gabriel released a breath through his nostrils.

"Nature and light are more intertwined than people think. Society is increasingly rejecting the gifts of nature, giving credit to the parts of nature that come from the Sol. This is a union that is more important than people realize."

Jennifer pointed to the towering Brisack Mountains, now visible in the distance, their peaks piercing the clouds. She said they would cross the mountains to reach Snowfall Village, James' hometown. She explained that the town was always covered in snow and that James' family raised rabbits and sold their meat and fur with the Frozen Monastery and with Druids along the river near Yggdrasil.

"Yggdrasil?" Gabriel said, recognizing the name of the Norse world tree. "In my world, there is a myth of a great tree of Yggdrasil. It is an ash tree that encompasses all nine realms, which are part of the ancient Norse view of the cosmos."

"Interesting. Here it is said that Yggdrasil's roots are the gateways to all other realms but such travel has been thought to be myth. According to legend, the Bifrost serves as a magnificent rainbow bridge, a path traversed by ancestors as they journey across the nine realms. Perhaps our worlds are more tied together, or have been in the past, than previously thought." Jennifer becomes lost in thought. "Given the chance I'd love to see your world."

Gabriel agreed, his voice tinged with sorrow. "The path leading to my arrival was devoid of color, without a hint of vividness. It was far from resembling a vibrant rainbow."

A large crowd of people living in tents was gathered at the gates. There were makeshift cooking stations and medical care facilities. The crowds grew thicker as he walked closer to the city walls. The southern gate was buried beneath the masses of people who were trying to enter. Many of them looked like they had been neglected for some time.

There was a clamor of people, as he made his way to the southern gate, Growing unruly as a fight broke out outside of their vehicle. One man hurled another into the side of the carriage, the sound reverberating loudly inside and causing Celise to cower in Jennifer's arms. "What is going on out there?"

"Trouble."

"I take it this isn't normal?" Amidst the throngs of people, Gabriel inquired, his gaze sweeping over the multitude.

James shook his head. "No, look at the giant's gates." He pointed with his chin and a small wave of his hand. "They've never been closed before."

Gabriel clenched his teeth, unsure of how to react to the situation. James drove the carriage down the streets. The sides of the road were filling up with men, women, and children living in makeshift tents or vehicles. The conditions looked uninhabitable. The further they went, it seemed like many of them had been there for some time.

Before Gabriel stood two men clad in basic armor. Their attire consisted of gray cloth and chain mail armor, featuring a sleeveless top, puffy pants tucked into matching gray boots. The distinguishing feature, however, was the metallic form-fitting armor worn beneath. Their shoulders bore the identical crest of Hati howling at the moon, a symbol shared by Cecil and his warriors.

James brought the carriage to a halt and beckoned the guard over. "What is going on here?"

"It has been commanded by the Crown that all towns and villages are to be evacuated. We are accepting people as quickly as we can. Please park your carriage wherever you can find space, as it will be sorted out later." The guard pats the door and resumes his patrol.

Celise, held in Jennifer's arms, lay on the mattress. "What does that mean, daddy?" she asked. The hulking man let out a low, menacing growl.

Unsure of what to think, Gabriel leaned back in the passenger seat. He couldn't help but think that the hulking beasts in Lightforged had something to do with this. Edwin and Lisa must have reported to the king, and this was the outcome of that report.

As the city walls grew nearer, Gabriel couldn't help but think of them as a massive gate that kept people out rather than a safe haven within. Despite the guards' actions, the police officer sympathized with them, having been in a similar situation himself. He believed they would not have done it without a good reason.

Two colossal slabs of metal, reaching up toward the sky, loomed ahead as Gabriel approached the city gates. He couldn't imagine anything big enough to require such a large door. But then he noticed that the larger door had a more reasonably sized one built into it, which could easily accommodate large vehicles. And even smaller than that was a door for individuals. A door within a door, within a door.

As the sky gradually transitioned into a dusky hue, James found himself pulling over to the side of the road. He gestured towards the sky, remarking that the sun would be setting soon. "We'll secure supplies outside the city if we need to," James continued. "We'll camp here for the night and leave in the morning."

"Are you sure you'll be okay?" Gabriel asked, placing a hand on James' shoulder.

Upon hearing the question, James's head subtly bobbed up and down in agreement. His verbal response consisted of a solitary, affirmative word: "Yes."

"You are welcome to journey with us when you complete your quest." Jennifer offered.

"We will be gone by first light." James grunted.

"I appreciate the offer, but if everything goes well, I'll be back home with my sister." For some reason unknown to Gabriel, this made him sigh. "Thank you for bringing me here."

"It was an honor to repay you."

Celise jumps up and gives Gabriel a huge hug from behind. "Thank you."

"Sure thing, kiddo." Gabriel returned the embrace with one arm, then opened the carriage door and slid down to the pavement of the street.

Nodding, James expresses his well wishes, "I hope you're able to locate your kin."

Gabriel nodded in response and closed the door. He could still hear Celise and Jennifer thanking him and wishing him luck. It filled him with warmth to know that he had been able to help save her.

Approaching the towering gate, Gabriel observed four guards arranged in pairs before each colossal door. The sigil of a wolf howling at the moon adorned their weapons and armor. Behind them, an intricately carved smaller door was embedded into the metallic wall. While it remained stationary, Gabriel surmised that its practicality made it the more frequently used entrance compared to the grander ones.

"We will have beds and food for everyone. There is a caregiver who provides medical care and food." The guard volunteered the information.

"I'm here for my sister. I have reason to believe she is inside already."

"Sister?" The first guard glanced at his partner before looking back at Gabriel. "I'm sorry, sir, but you'll have to wait with the other refugees. We'll let everyone in when we're ready to open the gate."

"You don't understand. I didn't come with these refugees."

"I regret to inform you that the city is under a temporary lockdown. This is an order from the highest authority. No one is allowed to enter or leave the city for the time being. We will resume admitting people into the city as soon as we can."

Gabriel's half-truth, "I have important business with the Lord-Commander," was a desperate attempt to convince them to allow his passage.

"We are bound by the direct orders of the Lord-Commander, and we will not deviate from them." The guard's eyes narrowed, his hands moving to rest on the hilts of his weapons. "No expectations."

With a gesture of surrender, Gabriel lifted his hands and retreated a few steps. Despite his efforts, entry was denied, yet he was resolute in finding a way in. Following the perimeter of the wall, he stumbled upon the food shelter. An extensive line of people extended far back along the wall and disappeared from view. It became evident to him that the number of people exceeded the availability of food.

Behind the makeshift tent's flaps, Gabriel discovered a small, inconspicuous opening that seemed to lead inside the wall—an unconventional yet potentially valuable entrance.

Gabriel moved behind the tent and slipped through the flaps, emerging in a cozy cooking area. The tantalizing aromas immediately enveloped him, causing his mouth to water uncontrollably. Following the delectable scent, he found himself standing before an enormous pot of stew, brimming with an assortment of vegetables and meats, each possessing its unique flavor.

Just as he was about to indulge in a spoonful of the savory stew, a loud, metallic clang abruptly interrupted his culinary reverie. The young woman tapped the soup ladle on the metal tabletop and asked, "What are you doing? You have to stand in line like everyone else."

Gabriel placed the ladle back in the pot and said, "I have urgent business to attend to inside."

'Inside?' she responded, her darting eyes betraying the intense mental activity happening behind them. She crossed her arms over her chest impatiently, the ladle still held firmly in her hand, as she declared, 'There's no way to get inside the city from here.'

With a swift turn, Gabriel's eyes caught an unexpected sight. The door had vanished, replaced by an impeccably smooth and seamless wall, leaving him in astonishment. Bewilderment creased his brow; doubt clouded his certainty. He was resolute, however; he trusted his memory. An entryway had, undeniably, been there.

"This is a kitchen. To go through the wall, you must go to the gate. No leave." She said, with an air of frustration.

Determined to uncover more, he meticulously ran his hand along the wall, searching for any indication of a concealed door. As he traversed the tent, the puzzle's pieces gradually aligned. In a sudden flash of insight, he glimpsed a hidden passage. Regret filled him for not having entertained this possibility earlier.

With a curious tone, the girl asked firmly, "What are you doing? I told you to leave."

With a dismissive gesture, Gabriel ran his fingers over the sleek metal surface. Its texture bore a striking resemblance to the knight's armor. The sensation beneath his touch was akin to running water or the caress of his own flesh.

As he heard footsteps approaching him, the door suddenly dissolved before his eyes. The liquid metal melted away, revealing a narrow passage. Within the dimly lit corridor stood a surprised man, his long beard and scraggly mustache framing his dirt-smudged face.

He looked at Gabriel with wide eyes and asked in a hoarse voice, "Who are you?" Gabriel was as surprised as the man and didn't know what to say.

In a commanding tone, the woman urged, "Let's take this inside, before someone catches sight of us." With a deliberate shift, her voice took on a venomous quality, adding weight to her words. Sensing a faint, pressing sensation of a weapon at his back, Gabriel hesitated, not daring to turn around and face the girl.

In a swift and lethal motion, the grizzled man brandished a dagger and charged at Gabriel, leaving no time for him to respond. "You heard the boss," the man growled, his voice grating. With a ruthless grip, he grabbed Gabriel's tabard and dragged him forward, the sharp blade of the dagger grazing his throat. As the liquid metal door sealed shut behind them, the corridor plunged into a state of darkness.

"Who are you?" The girl demanded, pressing her weapon across Gabriel's armor.

"I'm a man trying to get in through the wall." In an attempt to maintain his composure, he silently chided himself for being caught by surprise. Had his hunger not been so intense, he might have detected the peculiar demeanor of the girl.

In tense silence, Gabriel and the grizzled man stood motionless for several moments. The man's labored breathing fanned Gabriel's face, making him uncomfortably aware of the sweat beading on his forehead and the thunderous pounding of his heart. Gabriel knew that the man was waiting for him to make a move, ready to pounce in an instant.

Taking a deep breath, Gabriel attempted to steady his nerves. He understood that his survival depended on clear thinking. As he met the man's gaze, he recognized the chilling, calculating eyes of a killer.

In the confined space of the corridor, Gabriel fought off his assailant, evading the impending danger. As the grizzled man lunged forward, Gabriel twisted his arm. The knife left a thin crimson line across his armor, slicing through it with finesse. Simultaneously, Gabriel's sword rose; its hilt struck the man's jaw with resounding force. Using the newly created distance, he unleashed a powerful straight kick, sending the assailant crashing into the metal wall behind him. Regaining his balance, Gabriel spun around, fully prepared to meet any further attacks that may come his way.

As the armor sealed the wound on his chest, he winced from the lingering sting. Bewilderment washed over him, for the blade had sliced through his armor with effortless ease, while his pistol had failed to make a dent in his previous fight with Cecil and Lance.

"Nice move." The girl, donning a laid-back smile, turned her gaze back towards the man sprawled on the ground, her brows furrowing in consternation still holding the soup ladle. "This was supposed to be a diversion, giving him the chance to regain his feet and end you. Unfortunately, it appears he's lost consciousness."

Sensing a potential second trap, Gabriel struggled to resist the urge to turn around. However, he hesitated, torn between the need to ensure the man was incapacitated and the uncertainty of not wanting to look. With a swift motion, he twisted his body to catch a glimpse of the man on the floor. But as he turned back, he was met with an unexpected attack. The girl hurled the ladle at him and lunged forward, brandishing her own knife in a menacing manner.

Despite her rapid and forceful thrusts with her dagger, none of her strikes were successful in finding their intended target. Unable attempted to unsheathe his sword but accidentally slammed his elbow into the wall. He skillfully blocked the knife with the hilt of his sword and retaliated by slamming the hilt into the base of her wrist, sending the dagger upwards.

The blade effortlessly pierced through the metal ceiling, holding it in place as if it were flesh.

"Let me pass and I'll forget this ever happened." He glanced back at the downed man and turned back again. He half expected her to try again but she was still rubbing her wrists. It was then he realized that she was wearing some sort of bracers with a slight glimmer metal on them. "Whatever you're doing with your bracer, stop and listen to reason."

The young girl smiled. "You're good. Very perceptive." She raps her fingers on her wrists rapidly. She launches the dagger at Gabriel and to his own astonishment and catches it mid air inches before his face. "Holy shit." He says loudly, amazed at his own speed and dexterity.

The girl vanished from sight. Gabriel was perplexed and turned around, to be struck by a powerful sidekick. The force of the blow sent Gabriel reeling backward into the solid metal door. Gabriel fell to the ground, stunned. She stood over him, her eyes narrowed. "You should have stayed out of my business," she said, smashing her heel into Gabriels chest.

Fully aware of her correctness, Gabriel acknowledged his error and its subsequent consequences. In an attempt to defend himself, he raised his arms after she struck his chest with her foot twice. During the fourth stomp, he seized her foot and forcefully kicked her supporting leg. However, she skillfully shifted her weight onto her arms, demonstrating her resilience. Gabriel exerted outward pressure to prevent her from falling and managed to free her foot from his grasp. To his bewilderment, she disappeared, leaving him vulnerable and disoriented.

As he frantically searched for her, his eyes swept the area, but to no avail. The girl had vanished without a trace. He was baffled by her swift disappearance, yet he was determined to locate her before she could strike again. In the confined space of the narrow corridor, there was no place to seek refuge.

Suddenly, she descended from the ceiling, a dagger clutched in her hand. In a split-second reaction, Gabriel conjured the shield of his armor, deflecting the blow. A burst of white light erupted, propelling the girl backward. She stood defiantly between him and the other end of the passage.

"We don't have to keep fighting." Gabriel pleaded with her. "Let. Me. Pass."

The grizzled man groaned awake. "Akisu, you OK?"

"I'm fine, old man." Akisu took a deep breath and composed herself. She remained standing, observing Gabriel intently until an odd expression crossed his face. Gabriel couldn't decipher Akisu's thoughts, but something about him had clearly captured her attention. "I will let you pass but you have to tell me who you are."

Gabriel recognized the unfamiliar word—Akisu—which, to his surprise, meant thief in Japanese. It was peculiar enough that everyone appeared to communicate in a common language, but encountering fragments of an additional dialect from Earth further added to his astonishment. Gabriel pondered whether "Akisu" could be a nickname rather than the girl's actual name.

The shield melded back into the armor. "My name is Gabriel." He said, picking up his sword off the ground. "I need to get into the city to find my little sister and her friend. They have been taken by The Silver Wolves."

Akisu looked down and to the left for a second while exhaling. "OK." She said, snapping her gaze back onto him. "Come inside, have a drink. We can talk in more detail." Akisu placed her hand on the metal wall behind her and it slid open. "Come."

Barrels of beer stacked on top of each other. Boxes of miscellaneous alcohol types scattered all around in an organized fashion. Akisu led him through the storage until and up the stairs. Looking back he could see the grizzled man getting to his feet and disappearing behind the solidifying metal wall. The hidden passage becomes hidden once again.

The stairs led to a small room with a little door. On the other side was a typical slow ceiling fan spinning bar. A man stood behind the bar cleaning some glasses. The wall behind him lined up with multiple different brands of alcohol. The bartender glances at him and goes back to cleaning his glasses without even a word.

"Looking rough there boss, you ok?" The man asked Aksiu.

"Everything is fine." She said dismissively. "Give me a shot of whiskey."

At the bar, Gabriel made his order, requesting an ale and a burger. To his surprise, the menu listed a cheeseburger. Yet, when it was served, he discovered an unexpected presentation—the meat and cheese rested atop a bed of vegetables. Unable to identify the type of meat, which was not beef, Gabriel's hunger compelled him to devour the meal regardless. Commencing with a leisurely pace, he then devoured his meal. A single, sustained gulp sufficed to drain his ale, finishing his meal.

"You were really hungry." Akisu laughed. "So tell me your story."

Once more, he recounted the tale of his arrival in the world of Terra. He proceeded to narrate each event that had transpired in his life up until that moment, sharing everything with Akisu. Compelled by an enigmatic sense of trust, the story flowed effortlessly from his lips.

"That's a wild story." Swiveling away from him, she sips her drink and says, "I've heard crazier."

Gabriel's gaze lingered on her, his eyes darting back and forth as though the reality of the situation sank in. It was dawning on him that he had just unburdened himself, sharing his personal story with someone he had recently been at odds with. He realized this was something he wouldn't have normally done. Casting a suspicious gaze upon Akisu, he peered into the depths of the ale.

If Akisu noticed she didn't let on. Not skipping a beat she continued, "Lord Commander Cecil has been reported to come into the city with a caravan and entourage." She took a moment to sip her drink before continuing, "I had no idea that the princess was part of its cargo. I thought she was dead."

"Do you know where they went?"

"They went to the keep in the center of the city." With tender care, Akisu takes Gabriel's hand and traces a detailed map onto his palm. "Follow it and you can't miss it. It's the only giant castle in the city. Well the only castle with its own gate and courtyard." With a subtle flick of her eyebrow and a charming smile, Akisu exuded an alluring presence.

Gabriel slid from his stool and stood up, expressing his gratitude with a simple, "Thank you." However, the tenderness he felt from her was having an unexpected impact on him. There was a subtle force on the outskirts of his perception, seemingly trying to sway him. Despite this, Gabriel's intuition urged him to resist this influence, compelling him to rise and depart.

"No need to thank me, but consider yourself in my debt. The fight paid for your entrance, but the information I provided has a price tag. The drink, well that's on the house," Akisu said with a charming laugh.

Gabriel shrugged and tilted his head. "I thought my story paid for the information."

"No, that paid for the food."

Gabriel nodded, acknowledging the implications of the situation. While he yearned to depart without encountering the young girl once more, he couldn't shake the feeling that she held potential—a double-edged sword that could manifest as either trouble or an invaluable source of information. As he pivoted on his heel, preparing to exit, he caught sight of Akisu's watchful gaze fixed upon him.

With a wink and a tilt of her glass, she uttered a playful warning: "Don't die now."

Gabriel's attention was captivated by her grin, an intriguing blend of mischief and allure. He could sense her playful intention to tease him, yet beneath the surface, he detected a hint of darkness. The hunger lurking within the hidden depths of her soul was palpable. "I don't plan on it." Exiting with a subtle shake of his head, he ventured forth into the bustling heart of the city.

The towering skyscrapers loomed overhead, their structures resembling a winding river flowing through a monumental canyon. Not unlike any other sprawling metropolis, the city bustled with an array of people from all walks of life. The cacophony of horns echoed through the streets as cars, buses, and taxis maneuvered through traffic. Crowds of people hurried along the sidewalks, diligently moving to and from work or indulging in retail therapy.

The only thing missing was the smell of exhaust fumes that polluted the air. Even inside the city the air remained fresh and clear. It made the multitude of smells of food, people and their by products a lot more noticeable. But even in the midst of all this chaos, there was a sense of excitement and energy. This was a city that never slept, a city where anything was possible.

Gabriel navigated the map to the castle through the dense city. The streets were narrow and crowded, and the air was thick with the smell of sweat and sewage. The buildings were tall and close together, casting long shadows across the streets. Gabriel pushed his way through the crowd, his eyes scanning the map.

He turned a corner and saw the castle ahead of him. It was a massive, imposing structure, with high walls and towers. It was unique in that it was the only castle with both a gate and a courtyard. While other structures had one or the other, this one had both. Gabriel took a deep breath and started towards it.

People looked up and pointed as the dark cloud emerged and grew over the castle. It was a massive, ominous cloud that seemed to be sucking all the light out of the sky. The people below were terrified, and many of them began to run and scream. Gabriel looked up in the narrow corridors, and he saw a large castle-like structure with a dark and ominous storm cloud looming next to it.

The imposing castle stood tall with its sturdy gray stone and gleaming silver metal exterior. Its menacing gate bore the crest of a wolf howling at the moon. The surrounding storm cloud swirled and churned like a living entity, its darkness so profound it seemed to be made of pure void. Gabriel's gaze fell upon the castle and the ominous cloud, a sense of trepidation washing over him. He had an eerie premonition that something sinister was about to transpire.

Chapter Twelve

Gabriel

Guards and knights were in the process of evacuating the grounds as the dark storms brewed. Gabriel empathized as they struggled to keep control of the situation. One of the side buildings was covered in some sort of force field, blocking the entrance. The knights, in a valiant yet futile attempt, hurled themselves at the impenetrable barrier, only to be repelled with force. The ornate gate was flanked by two guards. A small implosion was followed by a huge explosion, showering stone and metal across the dusky sky.

The guard turned around and watched the chaos in front of them. But they did not leave their post. Gabriel was too far away to hear what they were saying, but he could tell that one of the guards was trying to convince the other not to intervene.

With a sinking feeling in his heart, Gabriel cautiously inspected the perimeter of the gate, searching for an opening. To his growing dread, he discovered a gaping hole where the gate had been reduced to rubble by relentless debris. Encircling the debris was a sinister, blood-like substance, intermingled with bone fragments and hair. A cold realization washed over Gabriel as he recognized the gruesome remains of a human being. His face turned pale, and a wave of nausea swept over him. Every few minutes, the storm surged with energy and then burst outward.

In the midst of a brewing storm that enveloped the knights and guards, Gabriel made his way through the courtyard, once again overwhelmed by nausea. As he battled his ailment, two knights approached him with a compassionate demeanor, offering first aid and a blessing. Recognizing the evident shock etched upon Gabriel's countenance, they extended their assistance. The knight gracefully waved runes in the air, infused with radiant light energy. With a flash, the runes cleansed Gabriel's aura, washing away the lingering traces of shock. The blessing bestowed upon him resonated with the one previously bestowed by Riza, yet this time, a profound sense of ease and comfort washed over his body, enveloping him in a calming embrace.

Gabriel, taken aback by the warm reception, smiled and uttered, "I'm well, tend to those who've fallen." Among them, he found an unexpected sense of comfort and ease, making it natural for him to move in their midst. The tremendous explosion flung him against the stone wall of the garage, leaving him disoriented. The two knights were nowhere in sight, sent hurtling in another direction, he assumed. Gabriel hoped they had survived but managed to pull himself to his feet despite the pain.

A huge wedge of stone from the castle wall was violently thrust outward, crashing into the building opposite. The structure shook intensely but managed to stay standing, although a gaping hole exposed the devastated interiors of residential dwellings.

As a loud noise reverberated through the air, a combination of cracking lighting and stone, Gabriel's gaze shot upwards. In that moment, he witnessed a colossal chunk of the building descending from the roof above. Pushing himself off the wall, he narrowly avoided the fallen stone. Propelled by the shockwave, he was thrown forward through the castle's double doors. In the immediate aftermath, he sought refuge from the falling rocks, only to find the interior conditions equally dire. The relentless shaking of the walls caused concealed dust to cascade in showers, further exacerbating his discomfort.

As he pressed forward he passed several guards grabbing one by the arm, forcing him to face him. "Lord-Commander Cecil ordered me to escort Princess Amelia-"

In a low, urgent voice, the knight interrupted, informing him of Amelia's location. He pointed to a spiral staircase nestled against the northernmost wall, indicating that she was housed in the highest tower's guest quarters. "If she is still alive," he added somberly, before turning on his heel and swiftly exiting the building.

His amusement at the princess's plight in the lofty tower gradually turned to worry as he realized the brewing storm posed a grave threat to the entire castle, including her and Lesley. Summoning his courage, he ran forward and began the arduous ascent up the winding staircase to the tower's top. The wind howled around him, and sweat trickled down his back as he focused on controlling his breathing.

With cautious steps, he ascended the stairs one at a time, treading carefully to avoid slipping on the loose gravel. As he climbed, the view became increasingly breathtaking. His vision expanded to encompass miles in all directions. He had reached an elevation above the storm, which appeared oddly unsettling. The low-hanging clouds above the bunker did not resemble a thunderstorm but rather resembled a dense fog. They moved in an unusual manner, and dark violet lightning unexpectedly flashed through them, leaving behind dark scars in their wake.

Upon reaching his destination, Gabriel encountered a solitary guard standing guard at the door. Summoning his courage, Gabriel approached the guard and assertively requested an audience with the princess. Despite the obvious brewing tempest, the guards exhibited a remarkable sense of composure. It appeared that the guards were either oblivious to the storm or had chosen to remain unperturbed by it.

"What is going on down there?" The guard inquired.

"You are relieved of your duty, Lord-Commander Cecil asked me-"

"That is no seal of Hati on your shoulder. Who are you?"

In his desperate pursuit to reunite with his family, to escape the castle, Gabriel, who was running short on time. He struck the guard in the temple, causing him to collapse to the ground. Instead of engaging in a lengthy struggle as anticipated the guard's fall left Gabriel in a state of astonishment.

Right behind the door he could hear Amelia talking to someone. Gabriel entered the room carrying the unconscious guard over his shoulder. He closed the door behind him and dropped onto the bed, propping the guard up next to him like a lifeless doll. "Your Highness," Gabriel said, looking around the room for Lesley. Gabriel's jaw clenched tightly, his blood surging with a tempestuous rage and profound disappointment, all trapped within him with no outlet for release.

"Copsmen. I see you still live."

With a hint of annoyance and frustration, Gabriel inquired, "Where is she?" Amelia wordlessly crossed her arms over her chest and raised an eyebrow. He took a deep breath and exhaled. "I'm glad you're okay, but where is Lesley?"

"She was taken to the holding cells," walking over to the window and pointing out the small structure beneath the storm clouds. The sphere of energy had already grown, pushing the knights further back.

"They're inside there?!" His boundless imagination was a relentless force that propelled his thoughts into a realm of infinite possibilities. He vividly envisioned Lesley trapped in the clutches of the raging storm, her body mercilessly buffeted by the tempest.

"It goes further underground than it looks. It is highly probable that they remain unscathed or have been safely relocated."

Gabriel's grip tightened around his sword's hilt, but his emotions were a maelstrom of numbness, helplessness, and burgeoning fear. The solace he had once found in the familiar touch of the blade now seemed distant and inadequate, leaving him feeling utterly vulnerable.

As the resplendent sun sank below the horizon, the vivid colors of twilight surrendered to the mesmerizing ascent of Cecil's celestial blue moon. Its radiant illumination embraced the cityscape, bestowing an ethereal glow that rivaled the luminosity of a second sun. In its full, majestic splendor, it shone brightly against the gathering storm, a beacon of brilliance amidst the darkening sky.

As the creaky door opened, Edward and Lance stepped into the room, their presence immediately captivating the attention of Gabriel and Amelia. The atmosphere in the room underwent a subtle transformation as all gazes converged upon the newcomers. With a faint, sinister smile playing across his lips, Lance's countenance transformed into a wicked grin as he uttered the words, "Behold, the one who dared to challenge the grasp of death itself."

"Today has been fraught with unforeseen problems." Edward grips the hilt of his sword. "Although I was aware that he would survive."

With a defensive stance, Amelia speaks with a cold yet formal tone. "Edward. Lance."

Gabriel's fiery passion became the antithesis of Amelia's cold, icy demeanor. With his hand firmly gripping the sword's wolf-shaped hilt, he issued a resolute command, "Take me to my sister."

"That is not feasible at this time. There is an emergency situation in the holding cells."

"She is bound to be dead by now." Laughter erupting from his lips, Lance's face transformed as a grin spread across its expanse.

"The probability of that is high."

Gabriel's heart bore a pang far more potent than any physical wound he had experienced, a searing ache that emanated from the depths of his soul. The overwhelming intensity of his emotions caused his grip on his sword's hilt to tighten with such force that his knuckles turned a stark, ashen hue.

With a hint of amusement, Lance inquired, "Are we repeating this? Your previous attempt didn't yield favorable results."

As Gabriel drew forth the wolf blade inscribed with runes, the tension that had consumed him started to fade. A gentle and luminescent white light emanated from him, exuding a harmonious aura.

"He bears our armor, wields our swords, and even channels the power of Sol?" Edward noted. "Interesting."

"This is my sword." A mix of astonishment and revulsion played across Gabriel's face, contorting his features into a striking expression. His eyes widened, his jaw dropped, and his eyebrows arched upward in unison, conveying his surprise. At the same time, his nose wrinkled, and his lips curled downward into a disgusted frown, expressing his clear displeasure. The conflicting emotions left him bewildered, uncertain of how to process what he was feeling.

"Upon beholding an uncommon crest, I am intrigued by the runic symbols engraved into its surface. I ponder their meaning, wondering if they are a symbol of power or protection, or perhaps a warning to those who would dare to cross the owner of the crest. I would be most interested in learning more about their history and significance."

"Let's see if you've improved this time," Lance taunted, his grin widening as he drew his sword in a swift motion. Lance charged forward, unleashing a rapid onslaught of attacks that forced Gabriel to retreat towards the far wall.

As their swords clashed, Gabriel was unnerved by the surprising power in his opponent's arms. It was as if he was not fighting a regular human, but rather a being composed entirely of muscle and sinew. Gabriel found it increasingly challenging to maintain his balance as his adversary's relentless strikes rained down upon him with incredible speed and force.

"It is inadvisable to engage in combat in this location. We must immediately evacuate the premises."

"Silence, Edward," Lance's armor underwent a transformation, as he drew his sword and charged at Gabriel. The protective covering extended from his forearm, forming an impenetrable shield that defended him during the charge.

With astonishing agility, Gabriel swerved to his left, causing his blade to graze against Lance's shield. In a fluid motion, Gabriel spun around, bringing the flat side of his sword crashing down upon the back of Lance's head.

Stunned and disoriented, Lance struggled to regain his footing as blood trickled down his neck. Despite the brutal blow, Gabriel couldn't help but marvel at Lance's indomitable spirit, as he managed to stay standing against all odds.

"You? How is this possible?" Gabriel glanced over to see the Lord-Commander Cecil staring at him, his eyes wide with disbelief. Cecil unsheathed his sword from his back and raised his shield in a defensive stance.

"Sir Gabriel is a knight in the service of Sol. Surely you do not intend to wage war against the house of your future Queen, thus courting the risk of civil war within our realms?"

Cecil's lips curled into a sneer, a contemptuous expression that radiated disdain and mockery. His eyes narrowed, glinting with icy contempt as he regarded Gabriel was beneath his notice and unworthy of his respect. Turning to Amelia, he eyed her intently. "So you still claim the throne? And this stranger is one of your knights?"

With unwavering conviction, Amelia gave a firm nod.

"This stranger?" Cecil let out an incredulous snort. "Absurd."

Gabriel's initial surprise soon yielded to the memory of his solemn vow to aid her. He hadn't realized such a vow could have been considered a legally binding verbal contract. Given the chance, his immediate desire would be to find his sister and return home, steering clear of the entanglements of this world's political affairs.

With hands planted firmly on her hips, she makes an exaggeratedly grand gesture towards the armor worn by Gabriel. "Observe the sword he bears and the armor on his back. The man is clearly connected to us by genetics."

Observing the intricate wolf pommel and family crest etched upon its surface, Cecil thoroughly scrutinized the sword. "He could have gotten that anywhere."

"This sword has been in my family for generations," Gabriel admitted.

"I wouldn't trust this wild dog. That's a stolen blade that he ruined with heretic writing."

"It is true, Cecil," Amelia affirmed. "I have seen it in his home."

Gabriel's brow furrowed as the conversation veered into uncharted territory. Despite the unexpected turn, he resolved to exploit the ensuing confusion, if indeed that was what it truly was. pondering James's words, the notion that only wolves could wield their arms began to seem plausible. If so, then it would imply that Gabriel shared a genetic connection to them. "Our two worlds may be connected in some way," he said to himself, but the words seemed to resonate with the others in the room.

"Those who bear our armor must have the appropriate genetic markers to wield it. You are surely aware of what this means." Amelia said.

"We shall observe how your honor fares." Cecil spat, glaring at Gabriel.

With a mix of frustration and silent determination, Lance's gaze burned into Gabriel. As he retracted his shield back into his armor and sheathed his sword, his body language conveyed a sense of pent-up emotions, yet he maintained a resolute quiet.

Amelia shifted her right hand from her hip to her waist. "Observing your combat was exhausting," she declared while gently placing her hand on Gabriel's shoulder. She then slid back and leaned against the wall, urging him, "Gabriel, we must make haste."

Gabriel gazed downward at the intensifying storm that was wreaking havoc on the residents of Sarum. "Those are the holding cells?" he questioned, his disbelief evident in his tone.

Amelia sighed, directed her gaze towards the window, then turned to Gabriel, whose expression was etched with pain, and spoke candidly. "They had the chance to escape," she insisted. unconvinced, Gabriel met her gaze and she reached out to caress his cheek. "I've weathered greater storms before."

Although he didn't have the heart to believe her, he couldn't deny the possibility of her statement being true. Additionally, he found the way she phrased it unpleasant.

Leaning in and resting her head on his shoulder, she expressed, "Sol is the embodiment of hope." Pausing, she pulls him away from the window to establish eye contact. "And I see him in you Sir Gabriel."

In his current state, hope was the vital elixir he craved. If Sol could bestow that upon him, then let it be so. Sol represented the essence of life, an omnipresent force that coursed through every living being, including himself. Taking a contemplative pause, he allowed his thoughts to wander to the timeless tale of Cecil's redemption. Its simplicity resonated deeply within him, as if he could see his own reflection woven into the narrative. Perhaps this is why the story had endured the trials of time.

In an attempt to compose himself, Gabriel took slow, calculated breaths. The likelihood of someone surviving within a tornado was minimal at best. While bracing himself for the worst, he clung steadfastly to his hope. She had to be alive. He had to descend and discover the truth.

Outside, a resounding explosion reverberated, heralding the arrival of a tempest that unleashed its fury upon the fortress. Through the window, a sinister wind entered, howling ominously. The violent tremors of the ground threw everyone off balance as the tempest expanded at an alarming rate. Its swirling winds relentlessly tore apart the surrounding area.

"The dark storm coming from the dungeons could destroy this building, or even the city. We need to hurry and finish this discussion later."

"Yes. You are correct my son. We can settle this matter after we determine the nature of this attack, and eliminate it." With a caring gesture, Cecil reached out and placed his hand on Edward's shoulder.

With a bitter smile and a shrug, Lance conveyed his resignation. Gabriel recognized the similarities between his family and Lance's. Both families desired happiness, safety, and love. While they faced challenges, they possessed strengths and, most importantly, each other. In spite of their differences, Lesley remained the last family Gabriel had left.

Despite the agreement, palpable tension lingered in the air. Cecil fixed his stern gaze upon Gabriel, his eyes lingering meaningfully on the sword. Though Cecil's thoughts remained concealed, Gabriel sensed a flicker of recognition, as if the sword held personal significance.

An abrupt explosion shattered a large portion of the building, leaving a gaping hole in the wall. The shockwave rocked the entire structure. Lance attempted to shield himself from the flying debris, but he was no match for the powerful gust of wind that swept him out through the broken wall. Edward cried out in pain and shock, while Cecil clung to him tightly as the floor beneath them cracked and crumbled.

"He'll survive. We must depart!" Commanded Cecil as he effortlessly scooped up Edward and sprinted out of the room, carrying him. "Move, Move!" The building shook and rattled, now unstable, and the floors started to shift beneath them. "Princess, follow closely or you will face our wrath." Amelia's emerald eyes blazed with fury as she sneered at him yet followed close on his tail.

As the building shuddered, the group hurried down the staircase. Small stones and loose dust cascaded down as the tremors intensified. Suddenly, a violent jolt sent Amelia tumbling, but Gabriel's swift reflexes caught her before she hit the ground. In that instant, their gazes locked as the building trembled once more.

Descending the stairs, they encountered numerous floors obstructed by debris. Gabriel, keen-eyed, detected a hallway free from obstacles, offering an opportunity to evade their wolf escorts. He seized Amelia's arm, urging her towards the alternative path. However, she resisted, conveying her disapproval with a resolute shake of her head. "We have to ditch them and find Lesley."

In a stern voice, she firmly declared, "Absolutely not! I will not have my honor questioned again. Should I leave at this moment, the chance to rectify my mistakes will be forever lost. I cannot simply disappear once again. We wolves are a family, and as such, we will find your sister and protect her. In return, I ask that you aid me in dethroning my brother. Please have faith in my abilities."

In this captivating moment, her mesmerizing emerald eyes held him spellbound, prompting an involuntary nod of agreement. The attraction between them was effortless, as if guided by an unseen force. Yet, deep within him, a persistent compulsion lingered—a stark contrast to the emotions he experienced while conversing with Akisu.

Exhaling a deep breath, Amelia released the tension in her body, allowing herself to fully relax. "I wish my brother were more like you, Gabriel. Your care and compassion for her is remarkable but if you go your own way now I cannot follow."

"Amelia!" Amid the air, Cecil's urgent yell broke through, prompting Amelia to whirl around while tightening her grasp on Gabriel. Gabriel, caught unprepared by her swift action and lacking the time to stop his advancing momentum, crashed into her. Contrary to his expectations, Amelia remained steadfast, as if he had run into an immovable wall.

A thunderous crack resonated throughout the halls, causing a rift in reality to split open between Cecil and Edward. This rift separated them from Gabriel and Amelia. The tear pulsed with swirling blue and green energy, expanding in size with every passing moment.

"What is this?" Edward leaned in.

"Stay back son."

"It is as if a black hole is distorting reality around itself. A sudden and unexpected split or break in reality."

"This must be why I was spirited away from my duel with Viktor."

With a hint of skepticism, Cecil responded, "Perhaps."

A sense of unease washed over Gabriel as he contemplated the eerie darkness. The vortex bore a striking resemblance to the one that had transported him here, yet it was devoid of any light, casting a sinister atmosphere. "Besides the color, there's something different about this one."

Gabriel peered into the rift and saw a star-filled sky, with millions and billions of warm-colored stars. His eyes widened as he recognized the contents of the rift: an infinite swarm of warm-colored orbs circling and darting about like a million bees ready to swarm out of their nest. "Let's go," Gabriel said, pulling Amelia by the arm and leading her away from the rift. "Go!" he said again, more forcefully.

The tear expanded quickly and grew larger. The forces of the expansion propelled all four of them backwards. Dark void creatures with warm-colored eyes poured out. Their bodies formed around their orbs, filling out from the dark swirling mists. They became small, bulging, tentacled monstrosities.

"Darklings!" Amidst the chaos, a single knight's desperate cry echoed before he succumbed to a gruesome fate, torn asunder by dark creatures.

"For Sol!" With a swift and lighting-fast movement, Cecil released a powerful ray of light that illuminated the room. The intense brightness momentarily blinded everyone present. Acting swiftly, Amelia shielded the body of Gabriel from the blinding light and tightly shut her eyes. "We are not prepared for this. Go!"

Blinded by the sudden light, the Darklings lost sight of Gabriel and Amelia as they darted back into the hallway. The pair located another flight of stairs and escaped into the courtyard. They slammed the door shut, using their body weight to keep it closed. Outside, the Darklings' screeching and banging on the door only intensified as they erupted into the courtyard.

The Silver Wolves' forces engaged the Darklings. A line of knights, ablaze with radiance, collided with the void creatures. As the dark cloud intensified, lightning flashed and the sun was obscured. The Darklings became difficult to see, their warm-hued eyes visible in The Silver Wolves' armor and Sol's Light. Guards formed a line and marched through the open gates. "We will tend to any injuries once we are a safe distance away," one guard informed the group of people. Arcturus stood in the open, offering aid to his people. His hand glowed with light as he healed the injured.

A lightning bolt struck Arcturus's office tower, destroying it and sending debris flying into the crowd. Several people were crushed or impaled by the falling rocks and glass. Panic spread as people began to trample each other in an attempt to reach the gates. Cracks opened in the sky, and creatures fell from them into the fields.

The urgent exclamation, "We are being overrun," resounded from one of the guards' mouths, conveying a sense of alarm and urgency.

"Fight on to your dying breath!" A piercing arrow abruptly ended Arcturus's speech, impaling his body and emerging from the other side. As he collapsed to the ground, a bewildered guardsman caught him. Miraculously, the arrow dissipated into thin air, dissolving like smoke and carried away by the gentle breeze.

"Lord Arcturus!" the guard yelled. With urgency, he lifted Lord Arcturus and carried him away alongside the evacuation group. However, the sight was grim as blood began to gather and form pools around them on the ground, he stopped amidst the chaos and yelled out, "Medic!"

Panic ensued as the void-like creatures tore through the Wolves. Men and women lay scattered on the ground, the storm-torn area transformed into a battlefield. The air was thick with the smell of blood and smoke, and the screams of the dying filled the air. The Wolves let out war cries as they charged into the mass of void creatures, yet they were no match for the void creatures, and they were overwhelmed.

Gabriel seized Amelia by the hand, but she pulled away. "We have to fight through this," she insisted. She enveloped herself in light that burned out, causing her to collapse to the ground.

Gabriel grabbed her hand again and said, "I see you are eager to die, but I don't think you can help anyone." He pulled her close and led her through the open battlefield. The darkness grew thicker, shrouding his vision and blocking out the light of the twin moons. Gabriel, unable to see more than a few feet in front of him, drew his sword and engulfed it in a white flame to allow himself to see her clearly.

Darklings attacked him, and he fought them off, killing many. When they died, the warm light of their eyes extinguished and their bodies faded into the darkness as if their physical form was reabsorbed by a larger formless entity.

Gabriel led her to the front gate, where a throng of people were trying to squeeze through. The most experienced warriors were left behind, holding back an endless horde of creatures that were flooding out of the castle.

The cold night grew warmer as the mob's body heat increased. They were civilians, who lacked the wolves' great strength. Gabriel helped them push through the gate, breaking it down. The people fled the keep, with Gabriel urging them to keep going. Upon the evacuation of civilians, The Silver Wolves and Darklings stood their ground. A profound clash of luminous and dark energy filled the air.

"I have to get into the holding cells, but you need to escape. You're in no shape to fight."

"I need to help them fight," she insisted. "Our goals are the same. We'll have to fight our way to the holding chambers if she's still there." She looked at him with pleading eyes. "Give me some of your strength."

With an impassive expression, he returned her gaze. "How?"

"Reach out to me with your spirit."

Gabriel sensed a subtle depletion within himself as a portion of his energy left his body and surrounded Amelia. A gentle, pale green aura enveloped her as she leaned in and pressed her lips against his. Caught off guard by this unexpected gesture, Gabriel's eyes widened in astonishment. "That didn't hurt, did it?"

"Far from it," he said, a blush tingling his cheeks. "It's more like you've become an extension of me." In reality, a fleeting sensation of exhaustion washed over him.

With amusement dancing in her eyes, Amelia flashed a wide grin. "You're quite the softie, aren't you? However, it has become imperative that we reconvene with Cecil." She playfully struck his shoulder before dashing around the newly formed line of soldiers. Gabriel followed suit.

The light of the full moons pierced the darkness and served as the sole luminous beacons. The Silver Wolves rallied together forming a line surrounding the castle. Lord Commander Cecil, a fervent conduit of energy and prayer, radiated that sacred luminance upon his loyal men. The wolves, turning the tide of battle, valiantly vanquished the Darklings and forced their retreat into the rifts. In harmonious union, paladins and clerics wielded their radiant light to mend the rifts, bringing forth a healing touch to any wounded they could reach.

With a dry tone, Cecil addressed Amelia, "You didn't run away."

Fury gleamed in Amelia's narrowed gaze as she vehemently denied the accusations. Her anger and frustration coursed through Gabriel, as if they were tangible entities. This sensation intrigued him, like discovering a part of his body he'd never known existed. It felt both intrinsic to him and yet oddly detached, like an objective observer watching his own emotions unfold.

"I apologize for questioning your honor. There are much larger problems to be addressed now." said with a heavy sigh.

"Apology accepted." Amelia said with a graceful smile. Gabriel continued to feel the shift in her emotions as the anger lifted replaced with a cooler sensation under his skin.

Cecil assessed the battlefield as his troops valiantly fought to repel the encroaching darkness, their relentless advance pushing back the shadows that hungered for their destruction. "Sol's light mends the rifts the Darklings spill from but it takes a tremendous vigor." With a prayer on his lips, he bestowed blessings upon Gabriel and Amelia. A radiant light, shaped like a crescent moon, emanated from them, enveloping them in its glow. "Now we take the fight to the darkness."

"And your son?"

With a heavy sigh, Cecil exhales deeply. "We'll have to fight our way back in, seal the rifts, and destroy the Darklings. If the light is with us, he'll live."

"They do not seem to be as vicious as I had anticipated." With a single sweeping motion, Edwards unleashed a brilliant wave of light, annihilating numerous small Darklings in its path.

With a determined gaze, Cecil conducted another evaluation of the intense battle unfolding before him. His forces were relentless in their assault against the darkling, overpowering them with a ratio of approximately one hundred to one. "I am skeptical that these small creatures are the same as those of old. They fall easily enough, but they seem to be limitless in number."

"I will eliminate as many Darklings as necessary to extract my sister." Gabriel declared, his resolve igniting a fierce desire to annihilate them. He paused, his gaze falling upon Amelia, who observed him with an enigmatic smile. Uncertain whether her expression mirrored his true feelings or hers, Gabriel's emotions surged within him.

Cecil's gaze narrowed, and Gabriel sensed both his annoyance and probing stare. Cecil then issued a series of commands to Edward, instructing him to lead the men in an advance toward the keep, with the high priests positioned at the rear. Additionally, Cecil ordered Edward to eliminate any Darklings they encountered and to utilize Sol's Light to heal any wounds sustained. Following the issuance of these commands, the Lord-Commander redirected his attention to Gabriel and Amelia. "You both accompany me into the Holding Cells."

"You still don't trust my honor?" Amelia asks, folding her arms over her chest.

With a stern expression, Cecil nods in the direction of Gabriel. "His honor is still questionable."

In response to the question about his honor, Gabriel let out a hearty laugh. With a mixture of disbelief and indignation, he retorted, "You broke into my home and dare to question my honor? You dragged my family here against their will, and yet you have the audacity to doubt my integrity?" The two locked eyes, their gazes intense, as the tension in the air crackled between them. Normally, Gabriel would have overlooked it, especially since he was about to get what he desired. However, there was something about Cecil that particularly irritated him.

"These things are not necessarily dishonorable actions." Pivoting away from Gabriel, Cecil allowed his helmet to settle back into place, a sneer forming on his lips. "This weapon you carry is not for anyone. Only the most skilled warriors in the clans are worthy of wielding them. It is curious that you can use them, outsider, but whether you are truly worthy of them remains to be seen."

In the midst of the Darklings' throng, Cecil led the way, holding his three wolf head tower shield high. The trio formed a triangular formation, ensuring they covered each other's blind spots. To their right, a knight suddenly took a fatal blow while protecting Amelia's flank. Amelia retaliated by unleashing a blast of green energy, incinerating the beast from the inside out.

Kneeling, Amelia reached for the knight's hand, intending to help him back to his feet. When she paused and her facial expression softened, Gabriel realized that the knight had already succumbed to his wounds and she relinquished her attempt. From the armor, smooth silver metal transformed and enveloped her arm, creating protective armor over her sturdy martial gear. A crest was emblazoned on the armor, depicting a wolf in unrelenting pursuit of the radiant sun, reflecting her unwavering determination. "I hope we are reunited in Valhalla." She said, as she took the knight's longsword, and placed it on her hip.

"Keep moving!" Cecil yelled, spraying white energy in front of him burning a wave of Darklings in front of them. Together, They exhibited exceptional teamwork as they advanced, the trio fearlessly fought off any darkling that dared come near. Their combined energies created a dazzling display of vibrant colors, intermingling and illuminating the air around them.

As they approached the holding cells, they encountered a purple barrier that blocked their way to the prison. Gabriel extended his hand toward the forcefield, feeling the energy tingle across his fingertips. Through this energy, he could sense a surge of emotions—sadness, loss, and grief—that permeated the atmosphere.

"Step aside, Gabriel!" Amelia landed a blow that stirred the shield, her green tinted light clashed with the violet shield, releasing muddy gray colored sparks, but the shield remained unyielding. Her relentless attempts were proved ineffective as the shield showed no signs of damage.

Cecil positioned Amelia and Gabriel behind him. Cecil invoked a fervent prayer, channeling pulsating waves of blue, silver, and white energy into his sword. Raising it high, he brought it down upon the force field, shattering it into countless fragments that shimmered briefly in the light before dissolving into the vastness of space. "Come, we have no time for your nonsense." Cecil said, signaling the two to follow him inside.

Delving deeper into the holding cell, the heroes faced a surprise attack from a horde of diminutive and nimble Darklings. Their sharp claws and teeth were put to use as they swarmed over Cecil and Gabriel, relentlessly slashing and biting. Despite their valiant efforts, the heroes battled against overwhelming odds, struggling to fend off the sheer number and ferocity of their assailants.

In a mesmerizing display of agility, Amelia brandished a longsword, launching a relentless assault upon the nimble darkling. With cat-like grace, she soared through the air, skillfully evading his counterattacks with surgical precision. One by one, the Darklings fell before her, as she danced through the fight with deadly finesse.

For every darkling they slew, two more appeared, then three. It was as if the Darklings were multiplying in the very presence of the warriors. The warriors fought valiantly, but it seemed like an impossible battle. The Darklings were relentless, and they seemed to be getting stronger with each passing moment.

Amidst the blood-soaked air and the lingering scent of ash, the trio engaged in a fierce battle as they navigated through the holding cells. Their determined advance led them to a vast chamber, where they were confronted by a spectacle that sent shivers down their spines. Before them lay a rift, a swirling vortex of darkness that exuded a palpable aura of malevolence, as if it were a conduit for some ancient force.

"Hold them while I channel more strength!" With his sword held close to his face, Cecil enveloped himself in the gentle, pale blue light of the redeemer. He then solemnly recited a prayer dedicated to the deity of Sol.

Amelia and Gabriel stood between Cecil and the growing horde of Darklings. They fought back-to-back, their swords flashing through the air as they cut down the endless wave of creatures. The Darklings poured through them like a river of darkness, but the two warriors fought on, their strength and skill unmatched. However, it was clear that they were outnumbered and outmatched.

Amelia and Gabriel were aware that they could not continue to fight for much longer. They were both exhausted, and their weapons were starting to show signs of wear. However, they refused to give up. They knew that if they did, the Darklings would overrun the city and destroy everything they held dear. Sol is the embodiment of hope and Ganriel summoned channeled his strength through him. He flashed brightly with a white flame aura bringing more light to the darkness.

Amelia took cover behind Gabriel, frantically throwing daggers over his shoulder. She aimed for any Darkling that managed to get past him, her jade daggers finding their mark with deadly accuracy. Gabriel raised his shield in a defensive stance, fending off all who approached him and slaying those who dared to test his fiery sword. When it seemed like they were about to be overwhelmed, Cecil managed to summon a powerful blast of energy that decimated the Darklings and sealed the rift.

Having vanquished the creatures, they ventured deeper into the lair of the holding cells. Death encompassed them; only the corpses of prisoners and guards remained. Before them loomed a gaping chasm, a treacherous passage to the depths below. As they gazed upward, the turbulent clouds and raging storms intensified. Dark violet lightning crackled and danced against the stone and metal of the imposing keep.

"This is where Lance must have fallen." Cecil said.

"That is a huge drop. I don't think he could have survived falling from that height." Gabriel couldn't help but entertain the notion that perhaps death would have been a more favorable outcome for the person involved.

"I fear you are correct." With a deep breath, Cecil let his eyes flutter shut and released a quiet sigh. "By Sols light I will find him alive or dead." With a brilliant flash, Cecil's aura burst forth, casting an enchanting glow upon the path.

They went deeper into the darkness, their hearts pounding in their chests. The sound was the dripping of water and the occasional rustle of leaves. Then they heard it: a faint crying sound. It was coming from somewhere up ahead. They crept forward, their eyes straining to see in the darkness. They came to a small clearing. In the middle of the clearing was a small child, huddled on the ground and crying. The child looked up at them, its eyes wide with fear. "Help me," it said. "Please help me."

"Lesley." Before his very eyes, the child undergoes a remarkable transformation, emerging as a young woman. Lesley, her face stained with a mix of blood and tears, found herself seated on the floor.

Lesley turned around, her eyes wide with fear. "Stay back!" she howled. Lightning crackled around her, and her aura pulsed out like a dark flame burning in the shadows.

"Whoa, whoa, whoa, baby girl." Sheathing his sword, Gabriel raised his hands. "It's me, Gabriel."

"Her aura is dark." Amelia's wrinkled nose and furrowed brow conveyed a sense of skepticism. "Is she the catalyst of the storm?"

Gabriel was entirely unaware of the significance behind those words. All that registered in his mind was the image of his baby sister, isolated and terrified. Compelled by an overwhelming urge, Gabriel drew nearer. "Lesley, listen, it's going to be okay."

Lesley's lighting, a menacing whip of energy, crackled in the air and struck the ground near Gabriel's feet, a warning for him to stay back, a warning he chose to ignore. In an instant, a bolt of lightning descended from the sky, piercing Gabriel's chest and sending him hurtling into the far wall. Through gritted teeth, Lesley vowed, "I won't let you harm us."

Amidst a symphony of coughing and wheezing, Gabriel's vision wavered, distorting reality with flashes of light. Determined to regain clarity, he resolutely shook his head, commanding his gaze to sharpen and bring the world back into focus.. Gabriel attempted to rise to his feet, only to discover himself amidst a pool of crimson pulp.

As he brought his hand to his face, a realization washed over him—the substance coating his skin was a macabre mixture of blood, bone, sinew, metal fragments, and stone. The question that echoed in his mind was whether this amalgamation originated from a single individual or multiple unfortunate souls.

"What am I going to do?" Lesley said with tears streaming down her face, Lesley whirled around abruptly as Cecil approached her.

With a startle, Lesley's gaze shifted from the vibrant, violet bubble back to Lance, who was floating levitating within it. In a voice that sounded unnaturally strained, Lesley uttered, "Lance. Yes. He was cruel. He broke my nose! He brought us to this fucking dungeon."

"Lesley. Did you kill the guards?" Struggling to his feet, Gabriel stumbled, his armor smeared with the remnants of a protein substance of human remains.

"The accusations! It's... It's not my fault." From her hands, she unleashed a shadowy bolt of lightning, which dissipated and faded into the surrounding air. "They made me. Forced me."

"She is too far gone." With a resolute expression, Cecil unsheathed his sword, channeling the radiant energy of Sol to imbue his weapons with its celestial power. "We must finish her before it is too late."

With a sudden lunge, Amelia propelled herself towards Lesley. However, a mysterious and formidable dark forcefield acted as an impenetrable barrier, repelling her attack. The impact caused Amelia to crash hard onto the unforgiving stone surface, rendering her unconscious.

"The mighty princess." With a deranged cackle, Lesley unleashed her maniacal laughter.

Gabriel unsheathed his sword, his heart wavering over its intended target. Darkness ominously swirled around Lesley, yet he had come here for her protection. Consumed by the radiance of Sol, Cecil gradually moved nearer, his sole mission being to obliterate her. "No. Stand down. Both of you."

In the dark corridors, Cecil brandished his raised sword as he charged at Lesley. However, his blade met resistance when it clashed against Gabriel's sword, which emitted a fiery white glow. Undeterred, Cecil pressed on, launching a series of attacks as the two engaged in a fierce duel. The echoing sound of their swords clashing resonated through the empty space, and the sparks that flew from their blades briefly illuminated the darkness.

In their relentless advance, a thunderous cacophony of clashing metal erupts, illuminating the scene with sporadic flashes from their intersecting swords. Among them, Cecil, the indomitable warrior, unleashes his formidable might, dominating Gabriel. The air is saturated with the pungent aroma of perspiration and the metallic tang of blood.

Gabriel battled to control his itching sword from inching closer to his armor, his muscles flexed and quivered. In a sudden burst of power, the blade effortlessly sliced through his armor and plunged deep into his flesh.

Fueled by the unrelenting pain, Gabriel's fury intensified, kindling a fierce determination within him. A shadowy light engulfed him, casting an ethereal glow as if emanating from his very essence. He deflected Cecil's blade and unleashed a relentless assault, forcing Cecil to adopt a defensive stance. Gabriel's precise slashes, parries, and disarming maneuvers left Cecil vulnerable.

In a decisive strike, Gabriel channeled the energy of the starlit void into his sword hilt and unleashed a formidable blow upon Cecil. The impact caused Cecil to plummet to the ground, helpless before Gabriel's dominant stance. With his sword poised menacingly at Cecil's throat, Gabriel asserted his commanding advantage.

"You are him, dressed as a wolf. Maybe you always were one. Maybe.' Pausing for a moment, she darted her gaze around the room, her deep-set eyes growing wide. With newfound determination, she directed her gaze toward Gabriel and made her proposition. With a venomous tone devoid of empathy, her spiteful words resonated through the atmosphere as she uttered them. "You should kill him Gabriel."

"Please Lesley. Stand down." With a determined grip, Gabriel raised his sword, directing its sharp edge towards Lesley.

Lesley gave a contemptuous snort. "These wolves perceive your benevolence as a sign of weakness. The honor I've witnessed is discarded without hesitation when it becomes inconvenient." With a commanding gesture, she conjured a powerful gale in her hand, causing Lance behind her, to writhe and scream as the fierce winds relentlessly squeezed the air from his lungs within the confines of the ominous violet sphere.

"Lesley, please. Release him and we can move on, I promise you that."

"There is no moving on Gabriel. They are all monsters here."

"For Sol!" From Cecil's hands, a radiant spear emerged, piercing through Lesley's protective shield with relentless force. The impact shattered the defense as if it were mere glass. In the wake of fading light, both Lesley and Lance vanished without a trace. The only remnants of their presence were the charred marks and smoldering ash, a testament to the immense power unleashed.

"What have you done?" Gabriel's eyes went wide, tears streamed down his face.

"What you couldn't, Coward. That darkspawn was corrupted and had to be put down at any cost."

"No, not dead." With narrowed eyes, Lesley stood there, half-shrouded in darkness and thunder. Lance floated within the sphere. Inside, the wind shifted, and Lance writhed in pain. He held his breath, trying to breathe, and then the sphere vanished, dropping his limp body to the floor. "You see how he is willing to sacrifice his own son to get to me? Disgusting."

Every shallow breath sent a burning constriction through Gabriel's chest. Uncomfortable tingling sensations prickled across his skin while an electric buzz surged through his limbs. The tranquil stillness that had surrounded him shattered, replaced by an eruption of rage. His knuckles whitened as they tightened around his sword's hilt. Darkness encroached upon the edges of his vision, threatening to consume it entirely.

In the shadowy confines of the holding cells, Gabriel and Cecil's swords clashed once more. The ringing sound of clashing steel and flashes of light illuminated the darkness. With a resounding thud, Gabriel struck Cecil's face with the flat of his blade, rendering him unconscious as he collapsed to the cold floor.

"You should kill him." Lesley's icy words were in stark contrast to the warm colored fury that burned in her eyes.

With his gaze fixed on Cecil, Gabriel's eyes narrowed. A part of him craved the man's demise. As his thoughts raced, he became convinced that Cecil posed a future threat to Lesley and himself. Almost instinctively, he found his sword at Cecil's throat. However, he managed to regain control, retracting the blade and turning his attention to Lesley. With a sigh of relief, he allowed the light to once again fill his heart. His facial features relaxed, revealing a gentler expression. "Let him go, and we can go home."

"No, this is all their fault Gabriel. Kill him!" In response to her unbridled fury, the atmosphere crackled with flashes of lightning, as if nature itself mirrored the intensity of her emotions.

"We are OK. We can still go home." In the depths of darkness, he found himself frozen, deprived of breath and thought. His home, engulfed in shadow, concealed beneath slithering tendrils that eluded sight.

Amidst the surrounding darkness, flashes of lightning crackled, triggering a tempestuous response as they lashed out with unrestrained force. Lesley sighed in resignation, acknowledging, "Maybe you're right." Abruptly, a concentrated burst of darkened lighting crashed into Cecil, his body contorted and motionless. Gabriel's eyes widened in shock. In a chilling tone, her voice devoid of emotion, she countered, "Maybe you're wrong."

Gabriel sighs, "Yeah." He knew it was the right move, but guilt started to creep into him like poison running through him. "They don't have to know about this, let's call it a day." He held out his hand. With a chuckle, Lesley shook her head. However, the runic gemstone started to glow brightly the moment his fingers made contact with hers.

A radiant pulse from the gem expanded outwards, distorting the fabric of space around them. A portal abruptly materialized in the air, exerting an irresistible force that drew loose debris towards its vortex. Lesley's eyes widened in terror as she was pulled into the void. Gabriel desperately shouted in a futile attempt to stop her, but his efforts were rendered useless. In an instant, she had vanished without a trace.

As the wind's fury abated, Gabriel found himself tumbling to the ground. Struggling to catch his breath, he rolled over and stared out into the expansive emptiness that stretched before him. Bewilderment swept over him, as he grappled with the reality of the situation. In an instant, Lesley had vanished once more, leaving him without any means to pursue her.

With a heavy sigh, Gabriel covered his face with his hands. He was struggling to decide on a course of action and whether he should take it. The absence of Lesley and his repeated failures weighed heavily on him, fueling his anxiety and inner rage. He made a conscious effort to relax his muscles, allowing his body to go limp. Tears rolled down his cheeks from the corners of his eyes, illuminated by the vibrant light of the twin moons shining through a hole in the ceiling above. Ironically, he felt exposed, as if he were under a spotlight. Yet, amidst the turmoil, a sense of unexpected calmness washed over him.

He lay there, his gaze fixed on the twin moons until their brilliance seared his retinas. With a sigh, he closed his eyes and turned his head away, the image of the dazzling blue and silver moons still etched behind his eyelids. When he opened them once more, his gaze fell upon Amelia, lying motionless on the ground. A tender expression softened his features as he watched her chest rise and fall gently with each steady breath. This small victory brought a smile to his face, a glimmer of hope in the midst of the chaos.

Gabriel struggled to accept the possibility that everybody around him had become monsters, including himself. They were individuals raised with somewhat distinct moral principles compared to his own, or perhaps they were fundamentally the same and unapologetically so. They didn't conceal their authentic selves. His thoughts drifted toward his parents, but he promptly dismissed the notion.

He looked back up at the bright moon again and smiled. He wanted to believe this was all happening for a reason. Gabriel rolls over, and pushes himself up to his feet. He sheathed his sword and walked over to Amelia slumped on the wall. Gabriel picks Amelia up and walks out of the holding cells. The long climb up was difficult and tiring but somehow it felt like a burden was lifted from him. He felt weak and wanted to give up, but he forced himself to keep going.

As Gabriel traversed the holding cells, an unexpected blinding flash of light compelled him to squint. Fortunately, he encountered a group of knights who granted him passage. Continuing onward through the battleground, Gabriel was met once more with a humbling sight—numerous lifeless bodies. Despite his own survival, a pang of guilt weighed upon him, as he struggled to dismiss the haunting thought that this tragic outcome was partly his doing.

Continuing his journey amidst the battlefield, Gabriel found himself overwhelmed once again by a profound sense of humility. While countless casualties surrounded him, he had somehow managed to survive. Yet, a part of him could not shake the lingering guilt, haunted by the inescapable notion that this devastating outcome bore his partial responsibility.

Bands of weary soldiers and the remains of hard-fought battles occupied the battlefield, leaving no Darklings in sight. Overhead, dark clouds passed, revealing a night sky that twinkled with stars next to Cecil's moon.

Edward was in the distance giving orders to his men when he noticed Gabriel emerge. "Where is my father? Lance?"

Gabriel didn't know what to tell him, but decided to tell him what he had to. "Cecil fought bravely." With a hint of a tear glistening at the edge of his eyes, he uttered those words, his gaze devoid of life. "But they were killed in the storm. Amelia and I made it out."

"Thank you." Edward said looking downward then back to Gabriel. "There is honor in falling in battle. I am certain that he did everything in his power." Edward waved over a few Soldiers, "Come, we must retrieve our honored fallen." and they disappeared into the holding cells and out of sight.

"I offer my sincere apologies for the events which have transpired. It was impossible to foresee any of this." Edward patted Gabriel on the shoulder then followed his knights into the holding cells.

When he realized no one was watching he walked out into the streets, where he found a motorcycle with a sidecar. He placed Amelia inside and hopped on the motorcycle. He fumbled with the controls until he found the ignition switch, which lit up with a familiar white glow. The motorcycle lifted off the ground, and Gabriel drove away from the keep.

Gabriel looked over at Amelia's soft face and whispered an apology. Tears welled up in his eyes, making it difficult to see the road. He drove until he reached the open city gates. They must have opened the gates to evacuate the city. He drove through the checkpoint, not caring if he hurt anyone, leaving a trail of light in his wake.

Chapter Thirteen

Gabriel

Gabriel entered the dense forest, his car climbed a modest hill before descending into a narrow path. The engine's steady hum was reminiscent of a jet ski gliding over open water, gently rocking from side to side as if navigating a series of invisible waves.

In a trance-like state, guided solely by instincts, Gabriel found himself propelling forward on autopilot. With no clear destination in mind, he continued to drive along the empty roads, bathed in the golden glow of the morning sun rising on the horizon. Suddenly, he noticed a military caravan approaching in the distance. Without hesitation, he swerved sharply, veering the motorcycle off the road and into the dense forest. Determined to remain unseen, Gabriel pressed on, navigating through the thick foliage, ensuring his presence remained concealed from the approaching caravan.

Amidst the forest, Gabriel stumbled upon a diminutive clearing, where a cavern, crafted by nature itself, awaited his discovery. The green grass contrasted with the dark gray stone of the cave, which was located on the side of a hill and surrounded by trees and grass. The darkness inside the cave seemed even more ominous, but there was something alluring about it. He slowed down and entered, as if being drawn in.

Gabriel's eyes adjusted to the darkness inside the cave. The stone walls were the same as those outside, with teal lines running through them. The lines seemed to glow, and Gabriel could feel a strange energy emanating from them.

In a small clearing, he came to a halt and dismounted from his bike. He stretched his back as he paced around the walls. The walls were adorned with old paintings, while the floor was cluttered with tiny trinkets. A growing sense of isolation began to creep over him.

Overwhelmed by nausea and anxiety, his breaths became shallow and irregular. He was filled with regret, unable to shake the feeling that he could have done things differently. His head rested against the wall, his chest tightening as he closed his eyes, his mind flooded with images of Lesley's darkened face.

His heart ached with shock and pain, and doubt crept into his thoughts. If Lesley were still alive, would she be spared by the merciless Darklings? Questions swirled in his mind, making it impossible to ignore the changes he felt inside.

His home, once a place of comfort and familiarity, now held no solace. A peculiar freedom had taken hold of him, despite feeling lost. Amelia's presence by his side offered companionship, but he questioned the nature of their bond. Was it love, or something else entirely? Did it matter in the grand scheme of things?

In the tranquility of the cave, Amelia's gentle moan shattered Gabriel's inner turmoil. Gabriel stirred, casting a tender glance at her serene slumber. Her peaceful features captivated him, yet doubts lingered in the recesses of his mind. He admonished himself, shaking his head in frustration at his reckless actions that led to Amelia's flight with him. As she stirred from sleep, a premonition of the impending conversation washed over him.

Gabriel inhaled deeply through his nose, attempting to quell the tingling sensation on his skin. With each steady breath, he endeavored to regain his composure. Moving on was imperative, even though returning home no longer held any allure. This world, though unfamiliar, beckoned to him, and he could envision settling down here. The power he felt in this realm was intoxicating.

"Regrettably," she said with a small yawn then emitting a weary sigh, "it appears that the conditions within the holding cells were less than satisfactory." Glancing at her surroundings, she let out a soft murmur.

In the hopes of her not having witnessed anything significant or incriminating against him or Lesley, he cautiously asked, "What do you recall?" Although a part of him wanted to conceal the truth from her, he also worried that their lingering connection could expose him. Moreover, he was reluctant to reveal the information he had acquired about The Silver Wolves caravan on the road, fearing that if she learned of them, her impulsive nature would lead her to join them.

"I vaguely recall Abyssal Thunder. Could you please elaborate on the events that transpired subsequent to the incident in which I was subjected to a forceful expulsion of lighting?"

Gabriel gulped nervously as he sensed the profound connection between them, feeling the raw emotions that surged through each other's minds. He could sense her growing concern for him but chose to deceive her. With a trembling voice, he managed to utter, "Cecil attempted to murder Lesley but ended up taking his and Lance's lives in a catastrophic explosion."

Amelia's inner anguish swelled, burst, and vanished as if she were processing her grief at an accelerated pace. His lie caused a wave of pain to surge through her. "I'm unsure of Lesley's fate; she could be dead." With a glimmer of moisture in his eyes, he uttered a statement that contained only a partial truth. As far as he knew, her unfortunate fall into the swirling vortex might have sealed her destiny.

"I see." In a gesture of frustration, she rested her hands on her hips, letting out a deep breath. "Then you brought me here?"

"Yes, that's the gist of it."

"They'll think I ran away." She said, narrowing her eyes.

Gabriel realized grief was not the emotion he felt within her, but rather frustration. With a slight turn, Gabriel spoke, trying to hide his vulnerability. "I'm sorry." Blinking rapidly, he fought against the welling tears, determined not to let them spill. Squinting his eyes, he used both hands to rub his forehead, effectively wiping away the evidence of his emotional struggle. In an attempt to regain composure, he inhaled deeply and exhaled slowly, seeking solace and strength within himself. "I had more pressing matters on my mind."

"Notwithstanding its potential to cause annoyance, the current situation remains salvageable." Emerging from the compact passenger car, Amelia stretched and extended her limbs. "Yet, Lesley's existence may endure." Amelia's furrowed brow reflected her deep contemplation, her thoughts wandering in a realm of uncertainty.

Gabriel could discern an unspoken truth, a secret she was hesitant to unveil—a revelation that held the potential to unnerve him. With a hopeful glint in his eyes, he uttered, "If she still draws breath, there's a chance for salvation." His words captured her attention, and a gentle smile blossomed on her lips.

"Your unwavering devotion to her is charming," she expressed with a warm wide smile and gleam in her eyes.

Gabriel was momentarily stunned, causing a flush to spread across his cheek. Amidst their connection, he perceived her genuine intentions, finding solace in the temporary protective nature of her words. The sincerity in her voice confirmed her true concern for his feelings.

"Come with me, I think this will cheer you up." Amelia said, biting her lower lip and leading Gabriel deeper into the cave.

Gabriel felt a surge of energy enveloping him, as if he had crossed an invisible energy barrier. The warmth and allure of the sensation washed over him. The teal stone embedded in the rocks bore a striking resemblance to ore, arranged in layers much like sedimentary rock formations. The varying hues of teal stood out against the backdrop of gray stone, creating a captivating visual symphony. "What is this place?"

"This cave is a natural healing place."

As he roamed through the room, he stumbled upon a captivating series of primitive cave paintings. The rudimentary drawings depicted a group of people frantically seeking refuge in caves to escape colossal, threatening beasts. Surprisingly, these immense creatures appeared incapable or hesitant to enter the caves. Their appearance differed significantly from the small, mischievous creatures he encountered in Sarum, resembling more closely the creature he confronted in Lightforge, only magnified tenfold.

Gabriel felt the warm teal stone beneath his fingertips, and a wave of tingling sensation traveled up his arm. When he let go, the feeling faded but he could still sense its presence reaching out to him, comforting him. He curled his fingers rhythmically, touching each one to his thumb in succession. The presence seemed to be gone, but the feeling lingered for a few moments.

"These caves once served as a sanctuary for my ancestors as they embarked on their sacred journey," she explained, gesturing toward the captivating images that depicted their nomadic quest for safe havens and the creation of temporary encampments. "Legends speak of ancient times when our people sought refuge in caves similar to these, perpetually hunted by sinister and evil beings of darkness. Prior to undertaking the pilgrimage, such caves served as essential shelters for my ancestors."

"They look so much larger than the ones we fought in Sarum or even the one in Lightforge."

"One can only hope that the size is artistic license and not the true scale." Amelia gestured for Gabriel to follow her into a small open path inside the far wall. The path descended at a sharp forty-five-degree angle. With each step, the teal stone became more and more prominent. They started to look more like veins in an arm leading them to a central point.

"What does it mean to go on a pilgrimage?"

"The pilgrimages were once a rite of passage into adulthood, but they later became more of a spiritual journey to hone their survival skills and help others in the clans. There were many times in history when kingdoms were at war and pilgrimages were very dangerous." As she walked down a spiraling corridor, she traced her hand along the wall. "Come along," she said. "There is something wonderful ahead. I feel it."

"Something wonderful, huh? What is it?"

"Just wait and see," she said, her tone infused with a playful undercurrent.

Gabriel followed Amelia, doing his best to mimic her movements, over the moss-covered rocks. The stones beneath him merged with a stream of water, making the path very slippery. It looked like no one had walked this path in a long time. All the better, he hoped, as no one would think to follow them into this forgotten cave.

Gabriel crouched lower as the opening became narrower. He dragged his fingers along the stone to steady himself, sometimes leaning against the wall to make sure he had a good grip on the rocks beneath his feet. As they got closer to their destination, he noticed that the water was getting warmer, and the teal veins in the stone were thicker and warmer as well.

Amelia turned to him and smiled. "A friend of mine, a cleric, shared a fascinating story. In ancient times, the pilgrimage was a powerful weapon against the dark forces that threatened the world. It involved the use of unconventional heretic magic in conjunction with Sol's light. However, discussing such matters is considered sacrilege."

His thoughts shifted to James and Jennifer. Their uncommon partnership intrigued him. He entertained the notion that they embodied an extraordinary convergence of enchantment, Cecile being embodiment of their union of magic and love. An idea that provided a glimpse into the rationale behind the animosity they faced from the people of Lightforge.

Gabriel's attention was captivated by the cave paintings adorning the walls. A recurring theme emerged as he examined each depiction, as most, if not all, of the paintings featured various beasts. Gabriel's eyes narrowed in displeasure. "Those are the Darklings we fought."

Amelia gave a half-hearted shrug. "The very same, I'm sure. Creatures that haven't been seen since Cecil the Redeemed."

"I've heard the story."

With a furrowed brow, a smile emerged from Amelia's lips as she gazed upon him. "Have you?"

"From the family that drove me to Sarum." Gabriel frowned as he thought about waking up in his basement and the nightmare that had taken place there. The shadowy figure, if it was real, could be connected to the creature in this religion. Given the events, Gabriel hoped that it had been a nightmare. "I've encountered one in my home."

Amelia turns around and faces Gabriel. "In your home in Greenfield?"

"It was like the shadow of a man with no face. Two red snakelike glowing orbs where his eye should be. Its teeth were sharp with steller patterns."

"That's terrifying. I've never heard of one like that. Unless." With a thoughtful expression, she scrunched her face as he bit her thumb.

"It was a void knight like Cecil the redeemed." With a displeased scowl, Gabriel concluded her sentence.

Amelia nodded thoughtfully. "Precisely. But the knights had long since been killed, it's terrifying that they might have existed in another realm."

"After you were taken through the portal, I had a nightmare when I woke up. It was like fighting the Darklings, with thick dark tendrils and other nightmare fuel. When I got back to the vortex, I was attacked by the void knight and then fell through the vortex into an old temple."

In a sudden halt, Amelia stood frozen before Gabriel, her wide eyes betraying the intense terror consuming her. Gathering her composure, she resumed her journey along the designated route. "I do not know how to say this but, if true, it appears that your world is being corrupted by the void."

Gabriel could no longer see her face, yet the chilling gaze she directed toward him lingered in his memory. A wave of anguish washed over Gabriel, as if a part of his soul had withered away. Now more than ever, he yearned for Sol, the embodiment of hope, as a desperate internal plea to help him navigate through the darkness.

A broad cavern with enormous bubbling pools of heated water and stone greeted the narrow corridor as it opened. Some of the stone had been carved into seats in the structure, giving the area the appearance of having once been home to a long-forgotten civilization. The cave walls had become more structured, with broken passageways resembling crude halls. Looking back the way they came, Gabriel could see the long eroded stone stairs that led into the cavern.

They kept walking through the old structures carved out of the cave walls until they came across a natural spring. The hot water steamed in the cool and damp eroded building. "Are we going to take a bath?" Gabriel asked with a smile curled on his lips.

Amelia shrugged half-heartedly, then bent down and unlaced her boots and placed them on one of the stone-carved benches. She ripped off her top and pants and then on top of her boots. "It would be wise of you to undress before entering the pool."

With a graceful motion, she slipped into the water. It came up to her neck as she sat down. She relaxed her shoulders and rested her head on the rock behind her. A glowing light emanated from her, changing from a noticeable grayish hue to a brilliant jade, illuminating the cavern walls.

The light grew brighter and brighter, until it was blinding. Gabriel raised his hand to shield his eyes. The light faded into a soft glow around her. She looked up at Gabriel, who was rubbing his eyes. "May I assume that some advance notification would have been appreciated?" She inquired, her lips curling into a broad grin.

His awe-struck words, "You're glowing," encapsulated the radiant beauty that emanated from her, leaving him astounded and utterly captivated.

"It's my spirit resonating out of my body. The waters here heal the spirit as well as the body." She tilts her head back and closes her eyes. Her whole body relaxes, melting over the rocks like wax, molding on and resting in whatever nook it fills in. "We have been blessed by Sol, emitting his light."

With her words, it all came together for him. The sensation of touching the cave walls, even his sword. The feeling of an untapped potential within him, something that had always been there but was now growing exponentially. This too was the power of Sol, and the surge of energy he had been feeling seemed even closer to his grasp.

"Get in the water." Amelia's smile vanished from her sharp angular features as she closed her eyes again.

Gabriel removed his clothes and placed them next to Amelia's. He dipped his toes in the water and tested its temperature by wading around. It was warm but not hot. A pleasant warmth rushed up his leg, and he closed his eyes, unable to describe the feeling that had touched a part of him that he had never known existed. Glancing at Amelia, Gabriel saw one of her eyes open, staring at him. As he pulled his foot from the water, his faint glow lingered, warming his skin like a lit fire.

Bringing her hands down, she said with a laugh, "By Sol, you burn hot." Her smile widened and she bit her lower lip.

Gabriel sank into the water across from Amelia, and the feeling consumed him. The dim light around him grew brighter. His mind drifted back to his youth or even a few years before he joined the police force.

Gabriel smiled back, "When I used to compete in martial arts events, my father made me meditate before and after every match and training session. I always felt so warm, even hot inside, but it never manifested like this before I came to your world." he said, looking down at the white fiery aura around his body.

"You are not ignorant of the ways of the spirit, but it has never appeared to you before. This is indeed strange."

He closed his eyes and focused on the feeling in his hand. The flame grew, dancing in his palm. "Ever since you came into my life, everything I thought I knew has been shattered."

Amelia's tone was notably more serious, yet she maintained a friendly and welcoming demeanor during the conversation. "Sol's spirit is present in the air you breathe, the water you drink, and the rocks upon which you now sit." Amelia moved closer to Gabriel and placed her hand on his chest.

"But it also comes from inside you. Your spiritual energy burns hot and playfully."

Gabriel was struck by the raw conviction in her words—her genuine desire to awaken his senses and tease his primal instincts. Her words and actions danced on the precipice of his conscience, while their spiritual connection, consciously or not, toyed with his physical desires.

"Places like this are considered to be places of power," she continued. "The reason we were able to heal so quickly is due to the energy stored in the earth around us." She spread her arms wide and closed her eyes. "Do you still not feel it? The planet's song, humming its tune into your being?" She drew in a breath, allowing the energy to course through her, and she began to glow a green hue that matched the gemstones and stone around them.

The spectacle brought warm feelings and a sense of jubilation. He closed his eyes to restrict his vision. To devote all his senses in exploring the feeling. It waves around him, floating around him causing his skin to tingle. When he opened his eyes Amelia stared at him, the light around him flared green but just for a moment. "The color is different now." Gabriel pointed out, childlike.

Amelia raised an eyebrow and smiled. "I found that the color of the energy to be irrelevant."

"How so?" He asked, cocking his head as he studied her features, the curve of her cheekbones, the dimple on her cheek. He soaked in her radiant aura like a man watching a goddess float ever closer from the heavens. Intoxicated by a vision of a goddess.

"I can feel this energy as revitalization energy and it could be why the power is green but I have also seen the power of the same color destroy and erode. Some people are more gifted at healing than at fighting. Energy is power."

"And power is everything."

"It is apparent that you do know how to start a fire." She said, biting her lower lip again. Amelia leaned forward and crawled toward Gabriel, sitting down next to him. She placed her hand in his, allowing their auras to intertwine. "Power can manifest itself in many ways."

Amelia's light and free energy mixed with Gabriel's denser and hotter energy. He felt a playful back-and-forth of their spiritual energies merging. Every time it started to feel overwhelming, he could feel her pull back her energy. It was a strange, intimate, and pleasurable sensation. Opening his eyes, he looked at her amused face. He was swept away by the gale winds of her emerald eyes leaned in and kissed her.

Chapter Fourteen

Lesley

"Please, wait," Lesley begged, but it was too late. Olivia was already gone. Lesley could feel the cold, hard floor beneath her and the damp air on her skin. She could hear the sound of her own breathing, ragged and panicked. She could see Olivia's body, lying still and lifeless on the floor. Lesley reached out and touched Olivia's face, her skin cold and clammy. She felt Olivia's hair, soft and silky beneath her fingers. "Wake up." She said, tears flowing down her face. The fresh wound of losing Olivia cut even deeper. "Open your eyes."

Lesley was floating in an empty space, her senses completely gone. There was no light, no sound, no smell, no taste, and no physical sensation. Only the void, numbness, and the screaming ghost of an echo in her mind. She was all alone.

A beam of light suddenly appeared before her, screeching as it cut through the air. The radiant energy left in its wake stung her eyes, causing her to flinch.

Lesley hated the beam of light because it represented hope. She didn't want to be hopeful. She wanted to wallow in her misery. She wanted to believe that there was no way out of her situation. The beam of light was a reminder that she was wrong, and that made her angry.

Lesley had been through a lot in her life. She had lost her home, her family, and now Olivia. She felt like she had hit rock bottom, and she didn't see any way out.

The beam of light was a reminder of everything that Lesley had lost. It was a reminder of the life that she used to have, and the life that she would never have again. It was a reminder of all the pain and suffering that she had endured.

Lesley didn't want to be reminded of all of that. She wanted to wallow in her misery and feel sorry for herself. The beam of light was a reminder that she couldn't do that. It was a reminder that she had to keep going, even though she didn't want to.

The beam of light was a symbol of hope, but Lesley didn't want hope. She wanted to give up. She wanted to die. The beam of light was a reminder that she couldn't do that either. It was a reminder that she had to keep fighting, even though she didn't want to.

Lesley hated the beam of light, but she knew that she needed it. She needed it to remind her that there was still hope, even though she didn't believe it. She needed it to remind her that she had to keep going, even though she didn't want to.

The beam of light was a symbol of hope, but it was also a symbol of pain. It was a reminder of everything that Lesley had lost, and everything that she would never have again. But it was also a reminder that she had to keep going, even though it was hard.

Seeking solace in the back of her eyelids she shut her eyes. Lesley floated in the ocean, her long black hair spread out around her. The radiant light warmed her skin, and the waves rocked her gently. All she knows is the comfort in the darkness behind her eyelids is keeping the pain away.

She rocks up and down as pain buzzes in, and fades away, swaying up and down, back and forth. A sensation of sudden pain wrecks her body, causing her to curl into a ball then eases away into the dark depths. She stirs, imagining that she is turning over, face down, on the surface of a body of water, hearing a voice calling out to her.

"Lesley," the voice said.

She opened her eyes and saw the waves moving all around her. They were beautiful, like rays of light and sound working in a symphony. The water pushed and pulled her back and forth, like a hand rocking a cradle. The water stirs; Pushing and pulling her back and forth like a hand rocking a cradle.

"Lesley," the voice said again, and the water stirred more violently. A smile grew on her face as she swam downward into the depths, wanting to surround herself with the waves.

In the chaos she recognized the sweet voice. It was Olivia. She did her best to swim upward but the force of the current was too strong. The more she tried to fight the currents tried to match. It was an uphill battle Lesley had to chance of winning. She was drowning.

"Lesley?" the voice asked, and the ocean raged out of control. Lesley turned upward, fighting the rough waters as best she could. She made it to the surface in time to see the clouds forming, blocking out the sun and darkening the sky. Waves ripped back and forth, twisting and tossing Lesley like a ragdoll. She started to swim downward into the depths, but it didn't seem to make any difference. She was at the mercy of the storm.

"Lesley!" the voice cried, pushing her even further down into the depths. Lesley could not fight it anymore. She could not swim in the rough currents. She soon realized that she was not swimming downward, but being pulled into the depths. She reached up to where she thought the surface was, but everything had gone black. She screamed, but bubbles rushed out of her mouth as she spiraled downward into the dark depths.

A calm stillness came over her, and her face turned placid. She felt embraced, warm, and comforted in the darkness. The embrace felt like being enveloped in a warm, comforting hug, but instead of arms, it was tendrils flowing over her skin.

Lesley fell to her knees coughing up sea water. She catches her breath and realizes she is covered in blood. Shadows swirled like a darkmist in the corner of her eye, and solidified and formed into matter when looked at.

She is the holding cells, but everything was obscured in darkness. But it was different, the obsidian walls, dark colored braziers, casting eerie, flickering shadows on the walls.

Lesley sat there catching her breath when she noticed the weight in her arms. Olivia, cold and pale. Lesley was filled with a lifetime of regrets as she brushed her hair away from her face. Her sweet cheeks frozen in time, still and beautiful.

Lesley, careful not to drop Olivia, groaned in pain as she stood up. She was exhausted, her breathing was labored. She took one step after another into the swirling darkness, which formed into a hall. As she walked, wall braziers lit up in pairs. The only sound was the soft echo of her breathing and the gentle shuffle of her feet on the stone floor.

The hallway stretched on endlessly, with no apparent end in sight. The walls were bare and featureless. The shadows seemed to dance and shift in the darkness, and it was hard to tell where one hallway ended and another began. The air was cold and still, and there was a sense of unease that hung over the place. It was as if the hallway was trying to swallow me whole.

Lesley wondered where they were as she watched the image of the Gem appear before her. It was intangible, like a ghost, but it still pulsed with violet light.

Tears spilled from Lesley's eyes, gliding down her cheeks like a gentle stream, and landing softly on Olivia's delicate features. Caring for Olivia weighed heavily on Lesley, both physically and emotionally, as if the burden was more than she could bear. Lesley's strength waned, making it increasingly difficult to move forward. The seemingly endless dark hallways appeared to swallow her whole, and her shuffling feet were more like a sliding motion now. Suddenly, the world around her spiraled into a swirling vortex of darkness, causing her to lose her balance and fall. Lesley's hair whipped wildly as she descended, once again trapped within the swirling, shadowy mist, with Olivia still cradled in her arms.

Lesley chuckled, recalling the sensation of this place. The gravity feels random while also appearing in free fall. Shades of gray, dark green, dark red, and blue blurred together to create an abstract painting of a woman who appeared before her once more. Lesley knew her but couldn't figure out how. Her presence was calming.

Lesley's eyes widened as a sudden force propelled her through the mist. The biting cold instantly froze her skin, while the sun's rays simultaneously began to boil her flesh. The pain was like being stabbed by frozen needles that were then heated until they were blazing hot, destroying her pain receptors. Her nervous system gave up, and she lost her sense of touch, her pain disappeared.

The constellations appear to be moving in unison. Lesley began to black out, her vision fading in and out. The stars warped around her, much closer than they had previously appeared, like little fireflies gathering around her. They formed a large hand that lifted her out of the void of space. It was a constellation of a woman smiling back at her. "Olivia?" Lesley attempted to say waving her own hand out as if to tough the face of a goddess.

Lesley landed on the hardened floor, her knees exploding with pain upon impact. She felt the skin on her knees scrape against the rough surface, and she bit back a cry of pain. She took a deep breath and tried to calm down. She found herself in a small, circular room with a black stone altar covered in strange runic symbols. The words were familiar to her, and they produced an aura of deep green, red, and blue colors. Lesley gently placed Olivia's body on the altar.

She had no idea where she was or how she got there. Tears streamed down her face as reality hit her. Olivia was dead, and Gabriel may be dead to her. She was all alone. Pain surged through Lesley again, but this time it manifested as tears. A small storm ran down her face.

She pressed her forehead against Olivia's, praying that she would open her eyes. She was desperate for Olivia to wake up. She felt a buzzing of frustration and anxiety fill her, and her hair stood on end as electricity crackled between the strands. Trembling violently, she muttered through her tears. "Please, please, please open your eyes."

Lesley was startled by the sound of a woman humming. It was Olivia, she was sure of it. The woman was humming a lullaby that Lesley remembered from her childhood. It was a warm and comforting memory. Lesley closed her eyes and listened to the lullaby, letting it wash over her. She felt herself relax, her breathing slowing down. She felt the warmth of Olivia's hand on her hair, stroking her gently. She felt safe and loved.

Lesley found herself back in her cell, the world swirling around her. She looked up at the stars and the blue second moon, and took a deep breath floating in Harmony with the first silver moon. The runic gemstone hovering above her, pulsing light in the darkened room.

She had her head in Olivia's lap. Olivia stroked her hair and hummed a lullaby. She was as Lesley remembered her, with curly blonde hair and hazel colored eyes full in her rosy cheeks. Her eyes are warm and full of life, compassion and empathy.

With eyes stretched wide, Lesley reacted in astonishment. "You're dead aren't you?"

"I know, Isn't this strange? Magic and Madness?" She said with a dark laugh, resonating with an ominous presence.

"Am I going mad?"

"I don't think so." In a gentle gesture of affection, Olivia playfully prodded Lesley's nose.

"I never got to tell you."

Olivia put a finger on Lesley's lips to hush her. "I know.".

With a sorrowful expression, Lesley's eyes remained steadfastly focused forward, reflecting the depth of her grief. "I'm sorry."

"It's OK." Olivia leaned down and rested her forehead on Lesley's. "I'll always be with you," she whispered. "In your head, your heart, and your soul."

Gazing into Olivia's hazel eyes, Lesley lifted her head, realizing she was back at the altar. Olivia's pale, cold body lay before Lesley. Her wounds had healed, but she was very much dead. Lesley let out a cry of anguish and collapsed to her knees beside Olivia. She cradled Olivia's head in her arms and sobbed.

With a constricted throat and dry eyes, Lesley was unable to cry, even if she wanted to. She struggled to her feet and stood there, dry-sniffing, staring at Olivia's corpse. Lesley was unaware of the passage of time as she stood over Olivia. Her face was red and puffy, her eyes swollen, and her nose sore, giving the impression that she had been crying for hours and long since ran out of tears.

Amidst the somber darkness of the altar, a fitting tribute to Olivia's memory, Lesley stood resolute. She knew Olivia would have found solace in this final resting place, a dark throne for the living goddess she held dear. As much as Lesley yearned to linger by her side, she understood the gravity of her mission. Vowing to avenge Olivia's death was the only path forward, for without retribution, Lesley could never find peace within herself. The road ahead was clear, and there was no turning back from this unwavering resolve.

In addition to her other concerns, she had to think about Gabriel. He had a strong sense of duty, and she was sure that the wolves, and Amelia in particular, were leading him astray. She knew that she would eventually have to confront him, as he would be a hindrance to her.

She clasped her hands together and offered one more prayer. The dark hallways turned to gas, and she reappeared in her cell. It was the time to move forward. The twin moons in the night sky were still visible through the massive hole in the ceiling. She felt the surge of electricity course through her. She was astonished that her school uniform was repaired, and her wounds were all healed.

She walked out of her cell, her pace quickening with each step. She was eager to begin her purge, but she knew that taking them head on would be foolish. She needed to find out the limits of her newfound strength before she could face them.

She ascended the stairs to the open courtyard, and was shocked by the devastation that the storm had caused. Bodies, buildings, and vehicles were all in ruins. The devastation was immense, and she felt responsible for it all.

Chapter Fifteen

Lesley

Gazing upward from the ground, Lesley encountered a familiar face atop a towering structure. The man, her former cellmate, offered her a smile. After a brief moment of recognition, she uttered a dismissive, "Oh. It's you."

Touching down beside Lesley, he spoke softly, "Come, my dear. Surely, you're a formidable opponent?" Lesley wore a blank expression, causing him to squint his eyes in response. He cleared his throat and said, "I am Raven. Do you recall me?"

Lesley released a deep breath as she replied, "Certainly, Mr. Instigator," before turning away to begin walking away. After putting a sizable distance between them, she glanced over her shoulder to find Raven still grinning as he followed her. His expression was beginning to irritate her. "Don't follow me."

"You were more than willing to fight that guard. It seems you are still looking for a fight."

Not having compelled her to confront the guard, everything that transpired was of her own doing. Lesley whirled around to face him. Electricity gathered between her palms, coalescing into a massive ball of lightning.

Her chest tightened with anxiety, making it hard to breathe. Her vision blurred, and she squinted her eyes. "I'm still looking for a fight."

"I am pleased to deliver good news, even if you only require a slight push in the right direction. You, I, and the guild can be allies."

Lesley paused, unsure of whether to trust Raven, but intrigued nonetheless. "Why shouldn't I fry you into a crisp?"

"I have noticed that you and I have a shared disdain for The Silver Wolves. As a member of a certain underground guild, I believe that we could be of great help to each other in our fight against them. I would like to propose that we form an alliance for this purpose."

Lesley let the crackling ball of electricity in her hand dissipate and relaxed her stance. "Continue."

"It would be foolhardy to attempt to fight them all on your own. You are not an army, and they are many. I have connections within the guild that can help us acquire the resources we need to achieve our goals. Together, we can get revenge for your friend."

"You want to help me get revenge?"

"You are not the only one who wants to see the empire burn."

"Who is the guild?"

"They are a group of ruthless thieves and unscrupulous mercenaries who operate globally."

Lesley found the idea of living underground appealing, as it would mean having little to no one to lord over her life. "As long as our goals are aligned, I'm interested."

"Phenomenal."

"This is unbelievable." With a snap of her fingers, lightning crackled between them. "Is this really my life?" Lesley uttered, a soft chuckle escaping her lips. In her mind's eye, she conjured a majestic storm, encompassing the entire world. Majestic thunder roared, causing buildings to crumble and fall.

"Yes, it's real and together we can kill more wolves than you can dream of." A malicious smile crept on Raven's thin lips. "Follow me."

Lesley and Raven hid themselves as they made their way through the bustling city streets. Lesley was shocked at how quickly their lives had returned to normal, with damage being repaired and reinforced.

The city was a bustling hive of activity, with new construction projects underway everywhere. The most impressive of these were the gigantic teal natural crystal towers being built on the great wall surrounding the city. These towers were said to be a new type of defense system that would protect the city from attack. Smaller crystal towers were also being built throughout the city. Objectively the city was a splendor, and she had reservations on its destruction.

Lesley overheard many conversations about Darklings laying siege to the city, coming from the very heart of Sarum City. She was able to gather information about what they were and where they came from from various conversations. The hastily built towers were meant to keep rifts from opening in the city. If a new age of darkness was to come about, the cities would be a great safe haven. Refugees from all over the city were being consolidated for their own safety.

The city was a place of hope and fear, of progress and danger. It was a place where people were working together to build a better future, but also a place where they were looking over their shoulders, afraid of what might come next.

The Darklings were intriguing to Lesley, creatures of pure darkness sounded outlandish even by the standards the people of this world had set for her. But the reality of their supposed nature tugged at her primal fears. She remembered bits of the conversation she tried to ignore back in the temple. Gods of light and Shadows, Time and space. There was more to it in life, more than dreams and hallucinations.

"Do we need to be worried about the Darklings?"

"Darklings will be the least of our problems for the time being. However, their arrival was quite unexpected."

"Did I do that too?"

"I don't think so. You shouldn't be concerned about them."

Dawn was approaching as they made their way down the dimly lit street, a single source of light coming from the occasional streetlamp. The air was thick with the smell of stale beer and cigarettes. Stepping into the confines of the diminutive bar, they couldn't help but notice the faint murmur of chatter emanating from its occupants. The bar was dark and dingy, with a few pool tables in the back and a jukebox playing in the corner.

Raven greeted the young woman sitting at the end of the bar with a friendly "Hello, old friend." The gruff bartender glanced up at him before returning his attention to the other customers.

Akisu's emerald eyes widen with astonishment while Raven gently nudges her with his elbow, urging her to take notice. "It's a pleasure to see you again Raven. I'm glad to see you well."

"No, it has managed to spare my life for the moment." He said with a laugh. "It was pretty crazy out there. Darklings in the city? Can you imagine?"

"Yeah, I can." Akisu takes a shot of whiskey. "Bloody terrifying to bear witness too. They kill indiscriminately."

"Has everything returned to normal now that the issue has been resolved?" Lesley found herself struggling to make sense of the cryptic conversation, which came across more like a coded exchange rather than a meaningful dialogue. Despite her unease, an odd sense of trust towards Akisu was gradually infiltrating her thoughts, creeping in and taking hold.

"Everything is about to change." Akisu gestured for them to follow her. As they ascended the staircase to the second floor, they found themselves engulfed in the darkness of a long, narrow hallway. The creaking of the floorboards beneath their feet echoed through the silence, serving as the sole accompaniment to their cautious steps.

"Oh, sorry." Akisu flicks the light switch, and the hallway is bathed in light. As they made their way down the hallway, they noticed the closed doors lining both sides. Akisu reached for the doorknob, opening it, and they entered the room. Inside, the office was surprisingly small yet opulently furnished.

There is a desk in the center of the room, with a chair behind it and two chairs in front of it. There was also a filing cabinet against one wall and a bookcase against the other, both filled with all sorts of exotic trinkets. Behind the desk was a lard square window looking over the streets. Akisu lounged at her desk, her feet up and her chair tilted back. "So what do you need?" She asked, tilting her head toward Lesley.

"I want you to help us kill as many wolves as possible."

"I see." Akisu's gaze lingered on the young girl for an extended duration, scrutinizing her every nuance. "You're Gabriel's little sister aren't you?"

"You know my brother?" With uncertainty clouding her thoughts, Lesley narrowed her eyes, questioning whether her initial feelings for Akisu had changed.

"Indeed, we have met. Your resemblance is uncanny. He was very thorough in regards to your origin story into our world."

"Another world?" Raven asked, "Is that why you're so strange?"

"I'm not so sure. I don't always feel like I fit in anywhere I go."

Raven placed a gentle hand on Lesley's shoulder and with a swift motion, Lesley brushed his hand away. She was still wary of his intentions, sensing his subtle advances. Resisting the urge to give him an electric shock, she maintained her composure. As Raven kept his gaze fixed on Lesley, he continued his conversation with Akisu. "Lesley possessed the potential to become an invaluable and formidable ally."

"Oh, I see." Akisu said. She threw a dagger that landed harmlessly on Lesley personal force field. "Oh, that's interesting."

With a contemptuous sneer, Lesley directed her attention toward Akisu and demanded, "What on earth was that?" As she spoke, crackling sounds erupted around her, creating an electrifying aura of lightning.

"I was testing your reflexes. I was not expecting that kind of display from you. Lighting too. I'm already very impressed with your work out there." Akisu waves her hand to the window where repairs are underway. "That was you wasn't it?"

"Yes." Lesley said, narrowing her eyes.

"Of course, Raven loves powerful women."

With a mischievous grin, he uttered the word, "Guilty."

"How are the Darklings tied to you?"

"I don't think that was me." She said, "Surely that was a coincidence."

"Coincidence?" Akisu shrugged. "I am highly skeptical of that claim. However, it is impossible to know for certain." She said with a shrug. "So you wish to get in bed with the guild. OK."

"So let's go out there and kill some wolves." Lesley declared, her fists colliding with a resounding thud. Bolts of lightning erupted from her hands.

"Not so fast." With a thoughtful gesture, Akisu scratched her chin, then proceeded to place her feet up on the desk in an unladylike manner.

"She is not going to help. Maybe it was foolish for us to even come here." Lesley slumped in her chain folding her arms over her chest.

"I will honor my word youngling."

Upon hearing the word, Lesley's spine tingled with a sudden chill. Her jaw clenched and her eyes narrowed into a focused glare. "Don't call me that."

With a narrowed gaze, Akisu shifted her attention from Lesley to Raven before returning it to Lesley. "As you wish." With gentle care, Akisu lifted her hands and delicately rested them upon the desk. "Instead of a hammer I'd rather use you as a scalpel."

With a sneer, Lesley uttered her words. "I'd rather go in a blaze of glory and be done with it."

"Let's think of a more sustainable solution to our problems. We want to eliminate the entire empire, not a couple of wolves."

"I thought we wanted the same thing. Dead wolves. I'll get that with or without your help."

"There will be plenty of time to rage Lesley. Hear us out."

Lesley stormed away from the conversation and she was growing frustrated, her head pounding. She still felt powerless to make any change. She inhaled deeply and focused on the shelf before her. She found a map of the region on a shelf in the bookcase. She studied the map of the country and the locations of the four major cities. The three major cities were arranged in a triangular formation with the great city of Lyndell at the center.

"Located in the lower left is the city where we are. Gabriel and Amelia are headed to the city northeast of here, the Grand city of Lyndell."

"Gabriel and Amelia." Lesley said with a laugh. "What do you want with them?"

"Your brother? Nothing. The princess? I want you to kill her the first chance you get."

"A royal assassination." Raven said excitedly. "We can kill all of them in one fell swoop. You and I can take the princess, then the king. The entire family."

"Easy, we have other people to kill Prince Viktor, and King Marcus. I just want you two to focus on Princess Amelia."

"How is killing the royal family going to help eliminate the wolves? Wouldn't they replace them with a successor?"

"All in due time. You'll get your fight and we will topple an empire." Akisu stated, a confident smile playing on her lips. Her gaze shifted from Raven to Lesley, and back again.

With a disdainful sneer, Lesley glared at Akisu, expressing her displeasure at being left in the dark, unaware of the complete narrative. "I'm not here to be your errand girl."

"I'd hardly call assassination of royal members an errand girl. This partnership will be more rewarding than you can ever imagine."

With a mischievous smile playing on his lips, Raven spoke. "Lesley, I assure you we want the same thing."

"Partner?" Lesley felt a surge of validation and respect as the concept resonated with her. While some details remained elusive, she chose to temporarily set them aside and focus on the bigger picture. "Gabriel won't stand by and let me kill her."

"I'm not asking you to do anything you aren't willing to do. Find a way to separate them if necessary and kill her." Lesley realized Akisu didn't care if Gabriel Lived or died.

If Gabriel chose them over her, she would have no choice but to let him go. She frowned, not wanting to see him harmed but she wouldn't allow him to stand in the way of her revenge. Amelia was at fault as much as any of them.

"You really should leave the city before they lock down everything."

With his head tilted to the side, Raven inquired, "They're locking the city down?"

"They are letting people in, not out."

With a furrowed brow, Raven contemplated the situation for a moment. Then, with a decisive nod, he rose from his seat. "Let us proceed with haste."

Exiting the bar, Raven and Lesley stroll down the hallway and out onto the street. As soon as they step outside, Lesley brings Raven to a halt. "I don't think I can do this if Gabriel gets involved."

As Raven rested a finger on Lesley's lips, Lesley promptly slapped it away. The unexpected jolt of electricity from the contact startled Raven, causing him to jump back in surprise. "You'll be fine, Gabriel will be fine."

Lesley's initial surge of anger gradually subsided, transforming into an audible sigh of relief. The realization washed over her that Raven had been correct all along—everything would turn out well. Perhaps it was due to her exhaustion or simply her desire to avoid thinking about it right then, but something about Raven's presence instilled a growing sense of comfort within Lesley. Together, they retraced their steps, exiting the building and finding themselves on the bustling streets once more. Raven confidently strode towards an SUV parked nearby.

"So we are stealing a car?" With a raised eyebrow, Lesley conveyed a sense of skepticism or surprise.

"Not just any car. Akisu's SUV."

"So you are going to steal from your friend?"

"She'll understand." With a small crystal in hand, Raven acquires entry into the SUV. However, Lesley's unimpressed glare greets him. "There is an artform to it."

"That's what all thieves say."

"You see this?" With a grand flourish, Raven displayed the gemstone using hand gestures. However, Lesley remained unimpressed. "This is an Aura Catalyst. With this you can store your own spiritual aura and use it like a key. Drawing quickly can cause discomfort but if you do it gradually enough, or when someone is distracted they will not even notice." He said with an air of confidence. "It's a technique I alone developed."

"Like a spiritual pickpocket." With a laugh, Lesley expressed her amusement, but to her surprise, Raven continued to gaze at her with unwavering attention, unfazed by her words.

"You really aren't from around here." Despite his frown, Lesley's laughter persisted. "Yeah. So now we have the keys to Akisu's SUV."

"Get in," Gracefully, Raven spoke as he extended his hand, inviting Lesley to enter the passenger door. Despite his charismatic efforts, Lesley sensed his growing irritation beneath the surface.

With a hint of amusement, she playfully remarked, "How romantic."

With a furrowed brow, he held the door open, allowing her to enter. Once she was inside, he closed the door and walked to the driver's side. Settling into the seat, he turned the key in the ignition, preparing to drive.

Lost in thought, she gazed out the window. A myriad of emotions overwhelmed her, and the idea of Gabriel transforming into a pseudo-silver wolf troubled her deeply. It was a real possibility, and she dreaded the thought of fighting with him, yet it seemed inevitable.

Glancing up, she noticed Akisu standing in front of her office window, watching them steal her SUV. Akisu's expression was unreadable, neither pleased nor disapproving. The enigmatic grin on her face might have been her default.

Chapter Sixteen

Lesley

Lesley abruptly sat up, throwing her arms into the air and screaming at the top of her lungs. She slammed her hands against the metal, recoiling in pain as she pulled them back to her chest. She felt something pinning her down, and her breathing became heavy as she gasped for air, tears rolling down her soft cheeks.

Lesley looked around, her face full of uncertainty. She was sitting in Akisu's SUV with Raven in the driver's seat. Looking up, she realized that she had slammed her hand into the roof. The skin on her hand was ripped, and there were traces of blood on her knuckles. She continued to pant, still taking everything in, tears welling up in her eyes.

"Are you OK?" Raven removed his arm from around her body and placed his hand on her shoulder. Lesley pulled away and tried her best to crawl out of his reach. "You started to cry out and trash in your sleep."

They sat silently for a few moments, allowing her time to regain her composure. Breaking the silence, she posed a question: "Where am I?"

Although Raven's smile was intended to convey reassurance and comfort, she struggled to accept it as a genuine reflection of the situation. The weight of her doubts made it difficult for her to fully believe that everything would be okay. "You're in Akisu's sweet SUV," his sly grin returned. "Do you remember falling asleep after we left Sarum?"

In a dismissive manner, she uttered her words while simultaneously yawning. "Does anyone remember exactly when they fall asleep?"

"Don't worry," he said, placing a hand on her shoulder. "I'm here for you."

"Thanks." It was a small gesture but it was nice to know she wasn't all alone. She sat up straight in her chair and thought about Olivia, and the pain of her loss stabbed her again. She looked away from Raven and put her head in her hands. She was devastated and felt like she was all alone in the world. She wanted to scream and shout, but all she could do was cry. "I'm sorry, I had a bad dream."

"What was it about?"

"I don't even remember. Something painful. Yeah, a million mealworms burrowing into my flesh and eating the metaphysical contents of my brain." Lesley laughs, "It sounds funny when I say it aloud."

Raven grimaced. "That's not funny."

A small village was visible in the distance, nestled in the rolling countryside among farms and livestock. The village was surrounded by a stone wall, and the roofs of the houses were made of thatch. There was a small church in the center of the village, and a few shops and taverns. The villagers were busy going about their daily lives, and the air was filled with the sound of chickens clucking and cows mooing. The village was a peaceful and idyllic place, and it seemed like a world away from the hustle and bustle of the city.

"What are you doing?" Asked surprised that they were headed toward such a small town. "You know where we are supposed to be going right?"

"We might be able to get a good meal and a night's sleep here, my dear." Raven glances at her, his face full of concern. "You clearly need it." Lesley's eyes were heavy but she fought the urge to sleep, not wanting to be burdened by the nightmares that were to follow.

As they approached, they noticed an elderly man standing by the open entrance gate, patiently waiting for their arrival. Beside him was a young woman with striking black hair. Lesley imagined what her mother might have looked like if she had been around. She furrowed her brow and shook the intrusive thought away.

Exiting the SUV, Raven approached the man who greeted him with a low bow. "Greetings, I am Raven, a traveler from the Land of the Rising Sun. My companion and I have journeyed far on our pilgrimage and are in need of shelter and supplies. The lady is exhausted and in need of much-needed rest. We would be most grateful for your assistance," With a flamboyant bow, he gestured toward Lesley, who was sitting in the passenger seat.

"I am Gregor, the representative of the village of Moonbright. It is a pleasure to welcome you to our humble village, my friend. We do not often receive warriors on their pilgrimage, but we are always happy to offer hospitality to those who come in peace."

Lesley got out of the car and looked at Raven with a mixture of confusion and suspicion. He winked at her, and she knew he was trying to manipulate them into giving him food and shelter. She was clueless as to the purpose of a pilgrimage, but they seemed to become more communicative when he brought it up.

"Welcome, pilgrims, to Moonbright!," said the raven-haired woman as she approached them.

"Allow me to introduce my daughter Lillyanna, who will be delighted to show you to your room for the night and prepare you a well-deserved meal."

Without hesitation, Lesley seized Lillyanna's outstretched hand and promptly yanked her arm back. Although her primal instinct encouraged her to trust the woman, a nagging voice of caution whispered within her, urging her to maintain vigilance. Bewildered by her impulsive actions, Lesley attributed them to her lingering drowsiness.

"It's okay, my dear," Lillyanna extends her arm in a protective gesture around Lesley. "I don't mean to harm you. Please, come inside and have something to eat."

Lesley hesitated for a moment before asking, "Why are you willing to help us?"

"Honor of course." A radiant grin stretched across Lillyanna's face, her eyes widening in sheer delight. In response, Lesley's face scrunched up, and she narrowed her eyes, as Lillyanna described. "It is a great honor to assist those on their pilgrimage."

With a monotonous voice, she uttered the words, "Honor, huh?" It wasn't long ago that she had held Olivia's hand in the same way. The thought brought on a sudden pang of sadness that she could not hide. A teardrop slid down her smooth cheek as the sky burst open with a sudden downpour. Lesley couldn't tell if the storm was natural or caused by her own emotions.

"Oh dear." Gregor gestured for the group to follow him inside. "Let's hurry along."

The group shuffled into the small house. The air was filled with the smell of stewed herbs and vegetables. The entryway opened into a large living area that flowed seamlessly into the kitchen and great room, the two rooms separated by a kitchen island with a bar countertop. A small staircase led to a catwalk with several doors that opened onto the second floor.

Lesley remained focused on the island. It was overall different but it reminded her of home. Eating berries with Gabriel before she skipped school with Olivia. It made her smile. It already felt like it was a million years ago but in reality it had been a couple of days. Life was funny like that. Everything can change in the blink of an eye.

Lillyanna ushered Lesley to the dining table and invited her to sit. "Please, have a seat," she said before walking into the kitchen.

Lesley sat down and observed Lillyanna as she moved around the kitchen. She was a graceful woman with long dark hair and olive skin. She moved with purpose. Lillyanna filled a kettle with water and set it on the empty counter. She then placed several cups and herbs on a serving tray. Lesley could smell the sweet, earthy aroma of the herbs as Lillyanna carried the tray to the table.

"I hope you like chamomile tea," Lillyanna said. "It's my favorite."

Lesley smiled, surprised by her own genuineness. "I love chamomile tea," As her thoughts drifted towards sleep, she found herself ensnared by the haunting grip of recurring nightmares. Inhaling deeply through her nose, she tried to push the thoughts away as she exhaled through her mouth. Despite her drowsiness, sleep eluded her. "But won't that put me to sleep?"

"To sleep? I don't think so but I can make you something else if you'd like."

"No, no, this is fine." Lesley said with a smile. This was turning into the most normal encounter she's had since she was brought to this world. "I guess that's something people say where I'm from."

"Is that so?" Lillyanna said with a warm smile. Lesley was reminded of a kind and nonjudgmental mother by her tone. She served four cups of tea, distributing one to each person at the table. Then she went straight back to the kitchen and began stirring a large pot of stew.

Raven scanned the room before returning his attention to the elderly man. "Is there anything we can help you with while we're here?"

Gregor took a long drag from his pipe before answering. "Actually, there might be something," he said. "I'm not sure if you've noticed, since you're from the Emerald Empire, but Prince Viktor has declared that small villages, like ours, are to abandon our homes and take refuge in the fortress cities."

"I have witnessed the Walled City of Sarum and the abundance of refugees outside the walls." Raven responded. "They slowly filter people into slums and homelessness."

"That is worse news than I expected."

"Why would they want us to leave our home for that?" Lillyana asked. "We live in the fringe parts of the kingdom."

Lesley Found the news of the wolves distasteful; she was starting to hate everything about them. "Maybe they are cruel animals."

With a sip of tea, Raven inquired, "Is he attempting to seize control of all small-scale endeavors, like farming?"

"Perhaps. He may intend to take our fertile lands but as king he already has rights to our crops." The elderly man said with a sigh, "It is not clear what he wants. I doubt it's because of the skirmishes between The Silver Wolves and the Shattered Swords."

Gregor scratches his chin. "The shocking news of Prince Viktor usurping Princess Amelia's rightful claim to rule reached our ears, leaving us in astonishment. Regrettably, she appeared to possess admirable qualities. I have no doubt that Viktor's reign as king will be marked by great strength and influence." The man looked conflicted between the two rulers, but he was not concerned about who ruled, only how it would affect his town. "However, what is important to us here in Moonbright is that we will not leave our homes."

"So you are asking us to defend you from your own kingdom? That sounds like it could be." He paused and Lesley could feel his lingering gaze upon her. "Fun." Raven said with a smile.

"Fun? Well, yes, you seem like a spry young man. But the lesson is "Power respects power." Gregor said with a stern look. "They will leave us alone if we win a fair duel."

Lesley's enjoyment of the situation was shattered by the outdated and cringe-worthy concept. She shook her head and looked into the bottom of her teacup. When pushed the wolves had no such honor.

As someone who likes fighting, Lesley understood that fighting can be respected when it is done for a cause, such as defending one's country, protecting the innocent, getting revenge. She could not prevent herself from snickering at the last thought. No one appeared to notice.

Though, she came to understand that the violence here was not for a righteous cause, but for power and control. It was violence cloaked in a thin veil of honor and glory. Violence is what they want and violence is what Lesley was prepared to give them.

Forever changed by The Silver Wolves, Lesley had lost everything. She could find honor in the bloodshed by fighting for the people of Moonbright. The dark thought escalated within her becoming more violent, brutal even. And yet she smiles at the many ways she could bring harm to the wolves. Darkness began to consume the edges of her vision.

Lillyanna startled Lesley by placing a bowl of stew and a cup of tea in front of her. Lesley had been lost in thought and hadn't noticed Lillyanna approach. The kindness in Lillyanna's eyes disarmed her forcing her to smile.

"You're looking quite pale, my dear," Lillyanna said, placing her hand on Lesley's forehead. "If you're ready to lie down, I have an empty bed for you."

Lesley nodded, grateful for Lillyanna's kindness. "Thank you, but I really don't want to sleep right now."

Raven looked concerned and said, "You should eat something. You'll need your strength."

Lesley nodded in agreement. She was drained, but not hungry. She stood up from her chair. "I'll be fine, I need, I don't know, some time alone."

"I need your strength." Raven insisted, tilting her head forward and raising both of his eyebrows.

Aware of the subject he was alluding to, Lesley recognized the validity of his words. Should the unfortunate circumstance of Amelia's demise come to pass, Lesley would require all her strength. Therefore, rest was essential, regardless of the potential for nightmares. "I'm fine."

"Come with me." Lillyanna takes Lesley's hand and leads her up a case of small wooden stairs that lead to a small catwalk. The catwalk served as the second floor hallway leading with three doors along it. Lillyanna led her to the middle door that opened up into a bedroom. She looked back down and could see Raven, who was still watching her, and Gregor sitting at the table slurping down his stew.

In the room there are two twin sized beds, a large bookcase filled with both books and toys. Next to that a pair of heavily used wooden swords. A single window lit the room with natural light. Above it a large plaque with a pair of steel swords crossed over each other. One reading "Edwin" and the other "Alphonse." Lillyanna waved her hand from one bed to the other. "You can take either one." she said with a warm smile.

"I really don't want to sleep."

"You don't have to, but no one will bother you in here. You can stay here until you're ready to sleep."

Lesley perched on the edge of the wooden-framed bed, surprised by the softness of the mattress. "This bed is lovely," she remarked. She lay down, feeling vulnerable and small. Despite her resistance to sleep, her body succumbed to exhaustion without a struggle, slipping into a deep slumber.

Lillyanna smoothed the covers over Lesley and tucked her in, then sat on the stool between the beds and brushed Lesley's hair with her hand. "I used to do this with my boys when I put them to sleep," she said, beginning to hum a slow melody.

The song was soothing and brought back long-forgotten emotions. Lesley shook off the feeling as a tear rolled down her cheek.

The song reminded Lesley of a time in her life when she was happy and carefree. The emotions that the song brought up were both happy and sad. She was happy to remember the good times, but she was also sad because she knew that those times were gone.

Lesley tried to shake off the feeling, but it was too strong. She let the tear fall and closed her eyes, remembering the past.

"Are you ok?" Lillyanna wiped the tear away from Lesley's cheek.

"I'm fine," she said. But lesley was not fine. She thought about the mother she never knew, who had been taken from her far too soon. She wondered what their relationship could have been like.

Lillyanna turned to leave, but then she paused and turned back to Lesley. "Oh," she said. "I almost forgot. I have something for you." She reached into her pocket and pulled out a small, wrapped package. She handed it to Lesley.

"What is it?"

"It's a little something to help you relax," Lillyanna said. "I feel you've been through a lot lately."

Lesley unwrapped the package and found a beautiful, hand-carved wooden box. She opened the box and found a small, smooth teal chalcedony stone inside on the end of a string.

"It's a worry stone necklace," Lillyanna said. "Hold it in your hand and focus on your worries. The stone will help you to let them go."

Lesley took the stone from the box and held it in her hand. She closed her eyes and took a deep breath. She could feel the warmth of the stone in her hand, and she felt her worries start to melt away.

"Thank you," she said to Lillyanna. "This is perfect."

Lillyanna smiled. "I'm glad you like it," she said. "I know I shouldn't treat you like a youngling now that you are on your pilgrimage but you are still so young despite your strength." A warm smile spread across her face, elegantly curving her cheek upward and enhancing the corners of her mouth.

Lesley heard hearsay youngling but somehow it didn't seem to bother her. "My strength?" Lesley mocked with a slight laugh. "I don't feel very strong."

Lillyanna placed a hand on Lesley's forehead. "I can definitely feel your strength brewing and churning inside of you."

"I'm sorry." Lesley added, shaking her head. "How long has it been?" she asked, looking around the room in an attempt to change the subject.

"Since I have seen my boys?" She asked, quite perky and happy. "My sons have long left on their pilgrimage. But I haven't heard anything of them in quite some time. A long time. It's almost been ten years. They must have found their destinies in distant lands or within the great cities."

"I've seen how hard this world can be." Lesley started to say thinking of Olivia and the crazy road that she has been on over the course of the last few days. She was thinking that Lillyanna's sons, like Olivia, have been killed in cold blood by some soldier or knight but couldn't bring herself to say it. It was clear to Lesley that she wasn't the other person here struck with sadness. "And they haven't contacted you in all this time?" Her voice was shaken in concern for them and for Lillyanna.

"If their true calling is to return home, they will do so when the time is right," she said with a warm smile. She giggled. "Those two were always so independent."

As Lesley contemplated her actions, her thoughts drifted toward her parents.

She couldn't shake the feeling of guilt, wondering if they would be worried

about her whereabouts. While they patiently waited for her return home, Lesley

couldn't help but smile, knowing full well that Gabriel disapproved of her

staying out late with friends or skipping school with Olivia.

Although he was not her biological father, he did his best to be a good father to her. She could not blame him for that. Their parents had been taken away from them when she was too young to remember them, so she had no recollection of what they looked like. All she knew was that people often told her that she looked like her father and Gabriel looked like their mother. Thinking about it, she could not help but smile.

It had been a long time since she had given much thought to her parents. Gabriel never spoke of them after he became her guardian. He refused to tell her what had happened to them. Sometimes she wondered if something had happened to them because of her. She knew that was unlikely, but she couldn't help but dwell on the thought. She pushed the worry stone in her hand, trying to smooth out the ridges.

Lesley's thoughts drifted to Olivia, and the way she had failed her. The thought made her stomach drop and her skin crawl. Guilt crept in, flying around her like a swarm of birds flapping their wings violently, blowing winds around her. She suddenly snapped back to reality.

As Lesley looked up into Lilyana's deep blue eyes, her anxiety melted away. They were like a soothing sea to her raging ocean. She found her touch both warm and comforting, so she welcomed it as she brushed her hair to the side. She felt that she would do anything to help protect her if there was anything she could do.

Lillyanna was a mother without children, and Lesley was a child without parents. Together, they made a sorrowful pair. Lesley considered staying with Lillyanna, but she knew that The Silver Wolves would eventually come and disrupt their home. Lesley had her own plans to execute, but for now she could at least pretend.

Chapter Seventeen

Gabriel

Gabriel squinted and shielded his face as his eyes adjusted to bright sunlight. He heard the spear before he saw it and instinctively moved to the left, pushing Amelia out of the way and shielding her body behind him. The spear whizzed past them and lodged itself in the cave wall.

Gabriel felt a sharp pain in his ear and warm blood running down his neck. A group of warriors emerged from the forest, looking more like barbarians than the knights Gabriel had been expecting. Gabriel recognized some of the totems. They were very similar to the ones that James wore around his neck. But worn with the intention form others to see where as James wore his under his clothing or his them in more discreet locations around his house. "Heretics?"

"Savages." Amelia responded coldly, narrowing her eyes on the biggest man. Gabriel could still sense her emotions, though it was very faint, he could sense her disgust for the savages, and that she was ready to kill them all. Adorned in a unique blend of leather, fur, and remnants of old chainmail, this group of men exemplified the quintessential barbarian ensemble.

The air was thick with tension, and something else. It was an oddly familiar sensation that made Gabriel uneasy. He narrowed his eyes and looked around the forest feeling as though they were being watched. "There may be more. We should get on the bike and leave."

"We don't need to fear these savages." Amelia whispered to him, her voice filled with disdain. She moved from behind Gabriel to stand at his side.

"Allow us to show you how savage we are," said the large barbarian. He raised his hand and the spear shook and suddenly flew past Gabriel hitting him in the shoulder again, forcing him to stay focused on the warrior. "You will have to stay focused." He flips his spear in his hand and points its blade at Gabriel. The warrior lung, spear in hand, closing the gap between them, and in an instant, he lunged at Gabriel.

It was fast, almost too fast, for Gabriel to react. He shifted his weight to his left leg and managed to pin the spear between his body and his arm. Gabriel tried to push him back with brute force but the warrior was too strong to move.

The warrior seized Gabriel by the back of his head and slammed their foreheads together. Gabriel was momentarily stunned, but before he could react, the warrior slammed their heads together again and again, stunning him further. The warrior then drew back his spear and slashed Gabriel a second time, this cut deeper than the first, and blood splattered across his chest. Freeing himself from Gabriel's grasp, the warrior, still holding him by the back of his head, tossed Gabriel aside, his body limp.

"Oh Gabriel." Amelia sighed and crossed her arms over her chest.

"I was expecting more." The warrior said, spitting on the ground. The rest of the war party pounded their spears on the ground in unison.

Gabriel's body felt heavy, but his resolve was unyielding as he struggled to his feet. The metallic taste of blood filled his mouth, and he realized with a jolt of surprise that the crimson staining his shirt was his own. It was a superficial wound, just a scratch, yet the pain was sharp and insistent.

"Perhaps I can show you what I'm made of." With a determined expression, Amelia intertwines her fingers and cracks her knuckles, producing a satisfying popping sound.

"That's not necessary," Into view strode a seasoned warrior, surpassing the last in distinction. "Yet," his eyes narrowed in a menacing manner. His long, messy hair was tinged with shades of gray. His face was withered from living through the hardships of many long years in the wild. "We are aware of your strength, Princess Amelia."

"That is comforting, I suppose, but hardly as entertaining as a good fight."

"Oh, so now we are willing to talk?" Gabriel said, wiping the blood from his chest with his hand.

"We wanted to test you of course. You are a gifted youngling. To survive Berenger's spear is no small feat.'

"Youngling?" Gabriel echoed, his aura flaring, the small wound on his ear and chest healing and the blood burning away. His shirt, ruined by the faint slash across his chest. "Maybe Berenger and I can go for a second round."

"Oh, you are indeed a gifted youngling," The seasoned warrior let out a low, sinister chuckle, with a menacing expression etched across his aged countenance. "Healing in such a manner is quite a rare gift." The seasoned warriors countenance transforms from a state of astonishment to one of intensity and fierceness. "Why is the princess of the wolves in our lands? Our ancient grounds?"

"We wanted to get away from the capital for a while. Perhaps a parley?"

Gabriel felt a faint sense of deception coming from Amelia. He could tell the spirit link between them was fading from the previous day. Emotional insights become less and less clear with each passing moment.

"Parley? Ha! You of all people should know the wolves are not welcome here anymore." The older savage frowned. "And why."

Gabriel arched an eyebrow at the comment and said nothing. Everything in this world has been more than a little disconcerting. "We are not all that different as you think."

"The wolves have abandoned their ways for giant constructs that do nothing but stand in the way of ascension."

"Ascension?" Gabriel whispered to Amelia.

Amelia kept her focus on the older warrior and responded, "For Sol." In the midst of formulating a retort, Amelia halted and adjusted her approach. "As you may know my brother and I no longer see eye to eye on many issues."

With a venomous hiss, the warrior spat upon the earth, his voice dripping with disdain. "All we hear is that the supposedly proud Amelia Ascendant, Princess of Wolves, is nothing more than a gutless deserter."

With a narrowed gaze, Amelia issued a stern warning: "Call me a coward one more time and I'll gut you before your next breath."

"I see the rumors aren't so true." The seasoned warrior sneers, lifting his weapon defensively. "So why do you come?"

Gabriel started to speak but Amelia raised a hand to silence him. "I wish to speak with your village elder." Gabriel was taken aback, but he felt like he should trust her in navigating this exchange.

"Tell me, Why shouldn't we kill you?"

"Perhaps we could be allies in the coming years and find a place for the old ways in my new world." Amelia responded, opening her arms wide.

"Your new world is a contradiction to the old ways. Clans must fight. Clans must have war. Clans must feed and become stronger."

"To strengthen the greater whole." Amelia interrupts the seasoned warrior. "That much, I do agree with."

"So you would have us ally with you to fight the rest of the wolves? You seek to march us to our defeat or do you truly wish the wolves to fall?"

"I seek to strengthen both of our clans and take my rightful place at the head of the wolves."

"I see. Your position was taken from you."

"A temporary discourse."

"How fragile this new world of peace is." The seasoned warrior stopped and turned away to the princess. "Your peace is a lie. In all your life, have you ever felt at peace? To live is to be in conflict of passions clashing against each other. Weaklings exist to feed the strong and make them powerful. Only then can they attain true victory over their enemies."

Gabriel sensed Amelia's anger despite her calm physical demeanor. Amelia felt disrespected but controlled her emotions to remain composed and rational. Then the feeling faded and he felt nothing at all from her. The spirit link between them expired and in its place he felt a longing to reconnect to her. For the briefest of moments he thought she shook her head and smiled.

"In this united world we can lessen the deaths of our young while maintaining the strength at our peoples core."

"But you aren't strong enough."

"You could always test me." Amelia said with a grimace that revealed a hint of glee.

"You wish to be tested? Very well. I hope it is as entertaining as you expected." The seasoned warrior turns to Berenger who nods in acceptance. "She shall be a good meal for you. It is pointless to say more until we know your strength."

"The arrogance. I accept this challenge." Amelia snickers to herself and clenches her fists. "Hand to hand. I wouldn't want to kill you just yet savage. Not for this."

"Very well." Berenger lunges at Amelia with a speedy flurry of attacks. Amelia blocks all his attacks at first, but she starts to lose her footing as Berenger's attacks become more and more powerful. Berenger's attacks are so fast that Gabriel can barely see them.

Amelia gathered her strength and launched a counterattack, but Berenger proved to be the quicker still. He dodged her attacks and continued to pummel her with his own. She fainted with her left hand, and then struck with her right. Berenger is caught off guard, and Amelia's attack connected with his chin. Berenger staggered back, and Amelia took the opportunity to attack again. Striking Berenger with a series of powerful blows, he fell to the ground defeated.

Amelia composes her breathing. "Have I passed your test?"

"You don't want to kill him?" With a fierce scowl, the seasoned warrior spits upon the earth.

"In my world, death to a man like this weakens us all." Trembling, Amelia extends her hand toward the fallen warrior. "He can still grow."

"Your words are humbling yet strike true." Berenger says, his voice trembling with exhaustion. He accepts Amelia's hand and lets her help him to his feet. "You would be a worthy ally in a fight with the wolves."

"I must admit I underestimate you." With a malevolent smile gracing her features, Amelia proclaimed, "I won't make that mistake again."

To Gabriel's astonishment, he hears the resounding chants of "War" repeatedly echoing from the savage individuals surrounding them, as they vigorously pound their chests.

In a single, fluid gesture, the seasoned warrior brought the warriors to silence, ending their rhythmic chants. "Berenger." The seasoned warrior's voice rang out, breaking the hushed stillness. "I'll give you the final word."

"The wolf princess has proven herself to clan Stonewrath and we shall honor the old ways with the bloodshed of our enemies." He turns to the rest of his people. "Let us be off and tell the rest of our people to prepare for war!"

"War?" From the depths of the woods, a chilling voice emerged.

"Who's there?!" With the sudden surge in the power of Berenger and his warriors' light auras, a multitude of colors and intensities were now present. The seasoned warrior aura burns a deep deep hunter green, similar to the green now flickering off Berenger form.

"Do you think these savages can best the empire?"

"Your blood will flow." Amidst the silent trees, Berenger's voice reverberates through the forest as he lets out a resounding shout, its echoes dancing in the darkness.

From the treetops, a silver beam erupts, and Amelia redirects it upward and away with a deft motion of her right hand. Gabriel stands in awe, captivated by the explosive impact as the energies clash and dissipate, leaving a dazzling trail in their wake. A second blast of light connects with the seasoned warrior, when the flash of light dissipates he is simply gone.

Berenger's face was a mask of anguish. His eyes, wide and filled with tears, stared at the lifeless charred remains. His lips parted in a silent cry, and a single word escaped his trembling lips: "Brother!" The green aura hung in the air before surrounding Berenger and absorbing into him.

A silver clad knight hung off the side of the tree with three points of contact leaving his right hand free. His limbs imbued with a cold blue energy acting as adhesive keeping him firm and in place.

With a flick of his arm, Berenger hurls his spear towards the silver warrior, leaving a trail of vibrant green energy in its wake. However, his aim proves to be off, and the spear narrowly misses its intended target.

The knight unsheathed a bastard sword, and ignited its edge with a deep silver energy. He suddenly leapt down at Berenger, his energy sword raised for a swift kill. Gabriel tried to leap in to intervene but the knight spun mid fall and fired a blast of energy out of his free hand forcing him into a defensive stance. He continued the spin as he landed, slashing out, mid crouch, at Berenger again.

Berenger stood tall, his spear halting the knight's blade. The knight was momentarily stunned, but it was a moment too long. Berenger's heavy foot slammed into the knight's armored face, pushing him backward but not down.

"That was a good move, assassin," Berenger said, raising his spear and engulfing it in green energy. He was about to finish the knight when suddenly fired a beam of silver energy from his open palm. The beam was aimed at Berenger's heart, but Gabriel was there in time to catch it in the white flame surrounding his hand. The silver energy did not spark or flash, but faded harmlessly between Gabriel's fingers like ash in the wind.

Berenger didn't hesitate for a moment as he let the spear fly through the short distance into the face of his attacker. The green energy clashed with silver for a mere moment. But to their surprise the Spear was caught in the knight's hand. "He was one of your wolves." Berenger announced. "There must be more nearby. We must slay him and head to Stonewrath's defense at once."

"It is far too late to save your people, Savage."

Amelia's eyes shoot open as a surge of terror engulfs her. Her face contorts in a blend of fear and determination, signaling an inward battle against the overwhelming emotions.

The knight lifted his bastard sword and charged into the throng of savages. His blade was a blur as he cut down one enemy after another. The savages were no match for his skill and ferocity. They fell before him like wheat before a scythe.

Time seemed to slow as Gabriel witnessed the carnage, for many moments, measured in rapid heart beats, the only sounds that could be heard were the ringing of steel against steel and the anguished cries of the fallen. Standing amidst the carnage, the lone knight reveled in his triumphant victory.

In a venomous and malicious tone, the knight icily declares. "We will have a lovely reunion."

"Gabriel, no matter what happens do not interfere." Amelia insisted through gritted teeth.

From the depths of his pocket, Gabriel retrieved the cube. Its power surged through him, forming a protective liquid armor around his body. With renewed confidence, he drew his sword, its gleaming blade catching the radiant light and reflecting it in a mesmerizing display.

With a hint of astonishment, tilt of his head, the knight inquired, "You are a paladin of Sol? Who might you be?"

Gabriel dashed at the knight forcing him into the defensive. The two men fought fiercely, their swords clashing against each other. Gabriel was no match for the knight's strength, but he was determined to win. He dodged the knight's blows and struck back whenever he could. The battle raged for several minutes, neither man able to gain an advantage. Finally, Gabriel saw an opening and thrust his sword into the knight's chest but his sword was easily parried away.

The lingering spirits of the fallen savages lingered in the air. Their ethereal energies shimmered and danced, swirling around Berenger like a tornado. As they converged on him, they surged into his body, further empowering him. Berenger's form transformed. His muscles bulged with supernatural strength. He raised his hand forward, and the spear twitched and struggled, trying in vain to free itself from the knight's grasp.

Amelia, clad in her own ornate armor, thrust her armored fist through Berenger's chest. His eyes widened in shock as his blood spurted from his mouth and his aura flickered and transferred into her. When life faded from his eyes, she slid him off her arm and he slumped to the ground. She then stood poised for battle, sword and shield in hand.

Gabriel yelled in disgust and horror, "What are you doing?!"

"These savages were never going to be useful." Amelia's gaze remained fixed upon the knight as her icy words landed with precision. Her narrowed eyes bore into the knight, exuding an air of unyielding resolve. "Viktor."

"Their power won't help you sister."

Viktor rescinds his helmet off his face. He is a pale man with black hair and even darker eyes. Now that he was still, Gabriel could see that his armor was far more ornate than he had realized.

"Did you think I wouldn't hear of your reemergence?"

With an outburst of rage, "I did not flee!". Her powerful voice resonated, accompanied by a teal aura radiating fervently around her. "I will finish the duel."

Viktor furrows his brow and his mouth hangs open, as if he witnessed something foul to his senses. "Finish? Is that a joke? Our duel has long been concluded. You have lost. Let go of that delusion."

Amelia cried out, "Never!" and lunged at with a swift thrust. He parried her attack with his bastard sword. She pushed out with her shield, knocking him backward, and sliced downward. But her blade was blocked by 's sword once more.

Viktor pivoted and struck Berenger's spear against Amelia's shield, the force of the blow sending a shockwave through the air. Amelia staggered back, but managed to keep her balance. Viktor pressed his attack, swinging the spear again and again. Amelia blocked each blow with her shield, until the spear began to glow with silver energy. With a final blow, the spear shattered upon impact.

"You are far too slow." Viktor plunged his sword into the earth and slipped inside Amelia's defenses. He grasped her sword wrist and twisted, disarming her. The sword fell to the ground. With his other hand, he struck her across the face with the back of his hand, knocking her to the ground before she could react.

Gabriel lunged forward, his sword raised high but Viktor seized him by the throat and lifted him off the ground with one hand. "You will reveal yourself to me, Who are you?!"

"Gabriel you fool." Amelia resends the armor over her head. "You can't interfere with establishing duels."

"This was not a duel sister. I will not entertain the notion!" Fury laced Viktor's voice as he expressed his feelings, his aura exploding outwards with every syllable.

Gabriel swung his sword downward with great force, but Viktor deftly caught the blade with his armored glove. The impact reverberated down the length of the sword, causing Gabriel's arm to shake. A sense of dread washed over Gabriel as he realized his efforts were futile. Viktor's defense, though effortless, proved impenetrable, and his offense, though restrained, remained deadly. It was clear that if Viktor had wished them dead, they would have been.

Viktors eyes narrowed on the hilt of the sword then to the crest on Gabriel's shoulder. "So this is the one; You are the one from the other realm."

With labored breaths and a heaving chest, Gabriel managed to utter a single word, "Yes." He confirmed what Viktor already knew.

Viktor's grip, akin to an iron vice, tightened around Gabriel, making it difficult for him to escape. As Gabriel's vision began to blur, he realized the gravity of his situation.

"You will need your lungs to speak properly." Viktor uttered as he let go of Gabriel. The impact of Gabriel's body striking the ground was forceful, leaving him gasping for air. He fought to inhale, his gasps accompanied by a bloody cough.

"That is a very interesting crest you have there." Viktor sneered and spat on the ground. "Fenrir the devourer. The wolf of Ragnarok. Five thousand years ago the master of your fallen clan turned their backs on Sol, and ushered in an age of darkness. Tell me Gabriel, Did you usher in the way for this new wave of Darklings?" Viktor asked as he pulled his sword from the ground.

"I don't think so." He said at last. He unfocused his eyes, lost in thought. "I've seen them before I arrived, or something like it. I don't think he followed me."

"You don't think he followed you?" With narrowed eyes, Viktor gazed intensely at him. "Explain yourself."

With a stammer and a fit of coughs, Gabriel attempted to formulate a response, but hesitation gripped him. He remained motionless, his mind grappling with the implications of his situation. Memories of plummeting through the portal flooded his thoughts, darkness enveloping him. A void knight materialized before him, adorned with sharp, star-like teeth and mesmerizing, glowing eyes. The sheer multitude of eyes was overwhelming.

Was he the reason they came into this realm? The strange void warriors in his house. Did they follow him through when he fell through the vortex? Gabriel narrowed his eyes. Did he push him through?

Gabriel looks at Amelia who seemed equally interested in what Gabriel had to say next. Continuing his explanation, he recounted the events that transpired after Cecil guided Amelia and Lesley through the portal. He vividly described the Void knight's eyes, which gleamed with warm colors even in the enveloping darkness, and the brilliant light that radiated from his sword. He also recounted his encounter with the Void knight before being transported away through the silver vortex.

With eyes widening, Viktor sneered and let out a hearty laugh in Gabriel's direction. "Your realm is doomed. Tainted by your fallen house. And now you spread its darkness back to ours? Fool." Viktor concluded with a sneer twisting his lips.

Turning his attention from Viktor, Gabriel's eyes settled on the family crest displayed proudly on Viktor's shoulder—a design depicting a wolf in pursuit of the sun.

He then glanced down to the crest etched on his sword—a raven-circled, one-eyed wolf. "Fallen house? My family have been warriors, diplomates, artists and everything else under the sun." Despite his attempt to hide his true feelings, Gabriel's face revealed his inner turmoil. His gaze shifted away as he sought refuge in his thoughts, his voice wavering with disbelief as he spoke. "That cannot be a representation of who we are."

In the depths of his soul, Gabriel wrestled with the encroaching darkness. Flickering across his mind like a haunting film, the memories of his deceased parents tugged at him. Yet, he refused to yield to their grasp, pushing those thoughts aside with unwavering determination.

The image of Lesley, engulfed in shadows as she held the lifeless body of a woman, mirrored Gabriel's internal struggle. Like her, he grappled with hidden burdens, refusing to succumb to the darkness that threatened to consume him.

"This union makes me question your loyalty to our people," Viktor said to Amelia.

"My loyalty is not up for debate." Amelia said, crossing her arms over her chest.

"Then fall in line. You failed in your conquest. I will be king. If you cannot accept that, I will cull your life right now along with your void knight."

Amelia clenched her teeth looking down to the ground, then to Gabriel. "I submit."

"He has his claws in you, sister." Viktor said with a laugh, turning his attention back to Gabriel, "As for you, Gabriel. You will live for now despite the folly for your clan."

"What did they do exactly?"

"Oh, you don't know? Your kin turned their backs on their people. Turned their back to Sol and allied themselves with the dark one, Oblivion, becoming the first Void Knights." Viktor kneeled down to look Gabriel in the eyes. "The shadowed warrior you described is undoubtedly a man steeped in abyssal magic. Your clansmen."

With a profound sense of connection, I perceive the divine presence of Sol deeply embedded within my existence. As a prayer is offered to Sol, a radiant and soothing light encompasses me.

"Lookup." Viktor points up to the radiant blue moon. "Lo and behold, another member of your clan has come to the realization of their misguided actions. This is the final fate of Cecil, the redeemed: a self-sacrificing act to mend a significant rift in reality."

"Cecil the redeemed." Gabriel's emotions were torn between fascination and terror as he contemplated the idea. However, on some level, it resonated with him. He yearned to believe Viktor's words, yet at the same time, he prayed for them to be untrue. Lowering his head, he averted his gaze from Viktor.

"All that remains is that second moon watching over our realm." Viktor studied him for another moment before coming to a stand. "There is honor in that."

Viktor turned his attention back to Amelia, "Did you know of his connection to the clan?"

"I did not." Amelia directed her unwavering gaze upon Gabriel, meticulously studying his every feature. "I have a hard time reconciling that."

In the throes of a disease, Gabriel experienced a profound sense of alienation, akin to that of a lab rat, a wild specimen corrupted by an insidious force. Despite this, Gabriel's introspection surpassed that of Viktor, as he grappled with his inner turmoil and the complexities of his situation.

"The fact that you utilized the light of Sol is one of two reasons you still live."

"What's the other reason?"

"I would like to learn more about your world, as I am considering claiming it for Sol."

Gabriel clenched his jaw. Gabriel wasn't sure if the nations of the world could withstand the might of the Empire of Silver Wolves. They seem impervious to small arms, absurdly fast and strong. Gabriel feared any march on Earth would be disastrous. But if the void knights are what he saw in his home, then maybe it would be best if The Silver Wolves stopped them before they could wreak havoc upon earth.

Gabriel's steely gaze bore into Viktor as he proclaimed, "Sol possesses the power to purge corruption." Should corruption truly defile his homeland, Gabriel will seek the aid of The Silver Wolves to cleanse and eliminate it from existence.

Viktor's gaze shifted from Gabriel's sword back to Gabriel's face. He tilted his head slightly backward and furrowed his brow in a frown. Even with the sneer on his face, Gabriel could sense that Viktor had a certain fondness for him. "Anything is possible through Sol."

There was something behind his dark eyes, a thought, but Gabriel couldn't tell his intentions. Amelia looked defeated, having been bested by her brother once again. This time, she had no excuses for her loss. She looked at Gabriel, her eyes soft, yet narrowed. He was starting to think he may be losing favor with her. Gabriel retreated within himself, wrestling with both realizations.

He couldn't hold any resentment towards her, for he shared her defeat. It was almost unfathomable to consider the possibility that he might be related to a fallen house of silver wolves transformed into void knights. Gabriel was both fascinated and repulsed by what Viktor had told him about his family. He wondered if his father had known, or if it was even true. Either way, he was shaken to the core.

Could it be his fault that the Darklings manifested in this realm? Could they have sent him here to usher in their darkness? Or was it Lesley? He swallowed hard and searched within himself. Lesley's lighting and dark storms were more like the natural magic that James used, but there was a lingering darkness within her.

The more he thought about it the more he wished it was all a dream. He wished he didn't wake up that morning to find Amelia weakened in his basement. He inhaled deeply and exhaled the dread away. It was futile to engage in such unproductive thoughts. He could only focus on the tasks immediately before him and deal with them accordingly.

"My Lord." Another knight, bedecked in armor even more ornate than some of the lights he'd encountered thus far, "The savage village that has been conquered is ready for you."

"Thank you Sir Kain." Viktor's piercing gaze shifted in Amelia's direction. He was keenly aware of the incredulity radiating from her unwavering stare. Viktor seized the moment to address her, "Does it astonish you that I utilize The Kingsguard?" In response, Amelia remained silent, humbly bowing her head as a sign of respect.

At Kain's command, The Kingsguard encircled them in a tight formation and advanced, following Viktor through the forest. As more kingsguard members arrived and closed in on them, one made a daring attempt to seize Gabriel's weapons, but he adamantly refused to hand them over. When another tried to take his sword, a powerful and sinister energy erupted, propelling the assailant backward. Gabriel was taken aback by the profound darkness that emanated from his sword, as if it held a void-like quality.

"Now that is interesting." Viktor narrowed his eyes on Gabriel then turned his gaze to Kain and the other Kingguard. "They are of no threat to me. Leave them armed."

Realizing their defeat, The Kingsguard reluctantly complied. Gabriel returned his sword to its sheath and assisted Amelia to her feet. The Kingsguard then guided them through the woods and down a rocky trail that led into the Village of Stonewrath.

Chapter Eighteen

Lesley

In the murky depths of darkness, Lesley had found herself ensnared by a million shadowy hands that had pulled her under, drowning her in an abyss of despair. She had fought valiantly, thrashing against the relentless hold of her captors, but her efforts had proven futile. Slowly, she had succumbed to the enveloping darkness, her body sinking deeper into the watery abyss. Yet, just when hope had seemed lost, a glimmer of light had pierced through the gloom. With a sudden burst of strength, Lesley had broken free from her shadowy confinement, gasping for breath as she had emerged from the depths. In a sudden moment of clarity, she recognized the terrors that enveloped her as she sat upright, fully awake in her twin-sized bed.

"Are you OK little bird?" Raven was sitting on the edge of the bed, looking at Lesley with concern, holding a warmed bowl of stew.

Lesley rubbed the sleep out of her eyes. For a brief second, Raven appeared to be completely inverted, with his long black hair, black eyes, and fair skin transformed into long white hair, white eyes, and grayscale skin. Her eyes widened, but after a blink, he looked completely normal. "Did you call me a little bird?" she asked.

Raven smiled. "Yes."

With a mirthful giggle, Lesley's joy was infectious. "Raven and his little bird?"

"Well, yeah." Raven gets up from the bed. "And this little bird was having another bad dream." He said, poking his finger on her nose.

With a blush, Lesley swiped his hand dismissively. "How did you know that I was having a bad dream?"

Raven walked over to the window and looked out at the old town below. "You chirp in your sleep."

Lesley laughed again. It was so silly that she couldn't help but to allow herself to laugh. "I do not!" She said.

With a swift turn, Raven's gaze settled upon her. "Yes, you do. It's quite cute."

With a rosy flush on her cheeks, Leslie used her hands to conceal her face from view. "I'm not cute."

"You are to me."

A broad smile involuntarily spread across Lesley's face. "Thank you?"

Raven returned the smile with a gracious, "You're most welcome." Curiosity piqued, he inquired, "May I ask what your dream entailed? Was it, perchance, another delightful encounter with mealworms?"

With a furrowed brow, Lesley immersed herself deep in contemplation. "I don't want to talk about it."

"Okay, but if you ever want to talk about it, I'm here for you."

With a radiant grin, Lesley expressed her joy. "Thank you. I'm glad you're here."

"Me too," Raven said, placing his hand on her head. "Since you're awake, you really should eat now." Raven handed her a bowl of leftover stew.

Lesley smiled as she realized the food was for her, but expressed little enthusiasm. She confessed that she didn't have an appetite.

"Well, you need to eat something," Raven said. "You haven't eaten anything since, I actually haven't seen you eat anything in the last two days."

"I know." In an instant, a pang of hunger jolted her senses. It was as if her stomach,

in response to her thoughts, rumbled loudly, demanding nourishment. Despite the lack of appetite, her body instinctively yearned for sustenance, an undeniable protest that couldn't be ignored.

She reluctantly grabbed the bowl of stew and ate a spoonful of its contents. It tasted as if it was reheated some time ago and then allowed to cool gradually. Lesley realized that Raven must have been in the room for some time, waiting for her to wake up. The bed across from hers had been slept in, which meant he must have slept there, woken up, and then gone to get her the stew. It was actually a thoughtful gesture on his part.

It was salty, savory, and aromatic, like the smell that had filled the house when they arrived. "It's actually good." With a silent shake of his head, Raven let out a small smile.

In the distance, Lesley's ears picked up the faint sound of someone weeping. She abruptly sat up in her bed and leaned against the wall. The source of the crying seemed to be coming from the other side. Lesley instinctively assumed it was Lillyanna, grieving over her lost sons. She could not shake the chilling thought that they were irrevocably lost and had met their demise.

"In this crazy world where strength is valued above all else you couldn't bring yourself to cry in front of others." She whispered to herself. She did her best to make sense of it but that was the only thing she could think of. Looking around the room now it seems obvious why this room has been left exactly the same since they left. It wasn't because she thought they were going to come home but the opposite.

"She misses her family." In Raven's words, if Lesley had been less informed, she might have interpreted his feelings as empathetic.

With eyes cast low, Said uttered. "I know the feeling too well."

Raven echoed the sentiment, addressing the little bird. With a darkening expression, he tilted his head before turning toward the door and announcing the arrival of The Silver Wolves. Raven exited the room, gazing down from the balcony, where he leaned against the wall near the bedroom door.

Lesley follows and leans over the railing with her arms crossed. Over looking at the small dining area and entryway she sees Lillyanna and Gregor at the door. "How did she get down there so fast?" Lesley asked. She squinted her eyes and looked back towards the last room. The door was shut.

Raven meekly shrugged. "I was really hoping to be gone before they arrived."

"I thought you said this would be fun." With a mischievous glint in her eyes, Lesley playfully prodded Raven's ribs, unable to resist the temptation to tease him.

Lillyanna moves back and into the dining area with a visitor in her wake. There was no mistaking his seamless silver armor and wolf cloth tabard. He was a knight of The Silver Wolves. A large man with pale skin and dark hair and eyes. The sight of him makes Lesley's skin crawl. A spark of electricity flows down her arm. A few moments ago she felt like she didn't understand these people, but now, in the presence of this wolf, she couldn't think of anything else.

"Is that Lance?" Lesley asked, but then realized it was someone else entirely. She looked back at the Raven. "How did you know?" \

Raven shrugged again. "I heard them. I mean there is a feeling of uneasiness in the air." He said, wiggling his fingers in the air.

"Yeah, OK." Lesley nodded, feeling uneasy. She couldn't tell if it was her dislike for them or her own nerves that was making her feel this way. "I want to help her." Lesley says.

"I'm always willing to fight." Raven said, narrowing his eyes at the wolf. "If that is your will, I advise you to wait and listen for now."

"Listen for what?"

"To make sure we actually have allies on the battlefield."

Lesley thought about it and was reluctant to agree. They had met these people less than a day ago. No matter how nice they seemed to be, they could turn on them at any moment. Lesley silently agreed to wait and listen to the conversation.

Lillyanna showed the knight to a seat and went into the kitchen. Gregor sat down across from the knight. They sat in silence for a few moments until Lillyanna returned with a steaming kettle and a tea set. She poured tea for both men, and they continued to sit in silence.

"I, Sir Alphonse, have been charged with the safe extraction and transportation of the people of Moonbright," the knight said, breaking the silence. "By order of King Marcus Ascendant, all residents of Moonbright are ordered to withdraw to safety behind the walls of the capital city of Lyndell. From here, we will head north and meet up with a larger caravan heading into the city."

"Now that is interesting." Raven whispered loud enough for Lesley to hear.

Lesley looked back at Raven and said with a sigh, "Is it?" She then turned her attention back to the conversation. "That's something we already figured out."

"You're slow sometimes."

With a piercing gaze, Lesley fixed her eyes on him, expressing her intense disapproval.

"You'll see."

Gregor slowly sipped his tea and then proceeded to rub his small gray beard. "I heard this was coming." He said with a heavy sigh. "Did they send you to make sure we comply?" The old man spits on the floor. "Dirty."

Alphonse slouched in his chair. "I have been commanded to bring as many people as possible to the capital that will safeguard our future."

"So are we to live outside or inside the walls?" Gregor asked.

"Inside, of course. I will make sure to get you inside as soon as I can. You will have a place to rest." Alphonse replied.

"We have that right here." Gregor said, gesturing to his small home.

"Look, I'm not trying to scare you, but there have been reports of Darklings inside the walls of Sarum. They showed up during the skirmish with the Shattered Swords, and in a bunch of other places too." Alphonse said.

"Darklings? That's absurd. That's a fairy tale. This must be how Viktor manipulates you." Gregor said, scoffing.

"Father, Darklings are not a fairy tale. You know this."

"The only thing I know is the church speaks of them. I've never seen one."

"Are you being intentionally obtuse?." Alphonse asked, his voice hardening. "I have seen them."

"I evoke my right of challenge." Gregor said, drawing his sword.

"Did you not hear me old man? Darklings have been manifesting. You are not safe." Alphonse said.

Lillyanna looked toward Gregor and back to Alphonse. "What if we don't want to leave?" she asked. "What will happen?"

"I am not going to leave you two here." Alphonse said, placing his hand on the hilt of his sword. "This place will not be safe if the Darklings invade and spill into our realm. We must consolidate as many people as we can where we are fortifying cities. I am authorized to remove you by force. I would prefer that it doesn't come to that."

Lillyanna looked hesitant for a moment. "Maybe we should go with him." she said to her father. "If what he says is true then the city might be the best place for us to go."

"No, I have made up my mind. We are going to stay here." Gregor said, his eyes narrowing.

"Father, you know Alphones wouldn't lie to us. We need to stop being stubborn, there is more to this migration than we originally thought."

"Why is he saying that?" Lesley whispered.

"He's being very defensive. He's not going to listen to anything the knight says." Raven whispered back. "Though I'm not convinced there will be blood."

"You are being a fool!" Alphonse retorted.

"Fool?!" Gregor's fierce anger turns to more curiosity mixed with concern. "We have survived the many wars of clans, wild tribes, and many more deadly attacks throughout the ages without hiding behind your walls." Gregor pointed out. "Now it will be the fairy tale your prince has spun up."

"Father, think of the people of Moonbright. We cannot let them suffer when they do not have to."

"I am ordering it on behalf of the crown. Anything other than compliance can be seen as treason." Alphonse said, his voice cold.

"We will not leave our home!" Gregor said, his voice rising in defiance.

With a heavy sigh, Lillyanna expressed her disapproval, addressing her father with a drawn-out, "Father..."

"I've had enough of this. You will come along with some belongings or you will be taken by force with nothing but the rags on your back old man."

"We chose to fight."

"Very well, with nothing but the clothes on your back it is." Alphonse abruptly came to a stand. He throws the table aside and in a quick movement grabs Gregor by the collar. Gregor, surprisingly nimble for his age, steps back and infuses his sword with light.

"I can't believe how quickly that escalated into violence." Lesley snickered. "Is he really going to kill him?"

With a downward turn of his mouth, Raven expressed his disagreement, "I don't think so."

"We have no choice but to help. We have to protect them from these monsters." With an exaggerated hand gesture, Lesley conveyed her message.

"There are always choices." Raven retorted. "They aren't going to kill them. Let's keep moving north to the city. We could even join the caravan. We are already going to the same place."

"This was your idea wasn't it?" Lesley clutches the worry stone that Lillyanna gave her. "I thought you said that this would be fun."

"Didn't I also say I don't like working for my meals?" Raven takes a deep breath. "I want to make sure that you know where you'll stand if this doesn't end in your favor." Raven said, pulling out his daggers in anticipation of a fight. "If we die here your brother may be lost to the wolves."

"That has nothing to do with this."

"Are you sure?" Raven interjected, "I'm on board, if this isn't about killing wolves."

"What happened to killing as many wolves as you can dream of?"

"I didn't mean to be as reckless as possible while doing so. We have a mission to consider as well."

"I'm killing this bastard and any other wolves in the area." Lesley moved to the top of the stairs. She could feel Raven's eyes on her. She glanced over at him, and he was still watching her.

"Let us proceed with the slaughter." He says. Raven leaps over the balcony and lands softly on the first floor. He feels slow, more like a glide dropping.

"Who are you?" Alphonse draws his sword and points it at Raven.

"I am Raven. Champion of Moonbright."

"You will disarm. Fall in line, stranger." Alphonse orders.

"He is our champion." Gregor confirmed. "One on one combat."

"There will be no combat trials on this day. I already told you this was a non-negotiable old man."

"Wait. I want to take him." Lesley says.

"OK." Raven smiles, placing his hand back down onto his hips.

Lesley held the runic gemstone in her left hand, halfway up the stairs. Her eyes were locked with Alphonse. Her aura grew in intensity, The wind and electricity buzzed around her.swirling around her. She took a deep breath and started to creep down the stairs.

"What is this?" Alphonse asked. "It can't be. You're dead!"

The dark colored gems light up infusing her with energy. She can feel it lifting her upward. She can feel a storm raging inside of her. It swells though and around her, manifesting as lightning cracking over her body.

Alphonse draws his sword, his wolf engraved shield in the other. "By the light." He whispered. With one quick movement the knight stepped forward, his shield held high beaming with a cool white light.

She could see the face of the wolf, glowing brightly, light flowing off of it like tethered cords. His sword flashed with light as it trusted forward. It sparked and clashed on the aura of dark colored infused lighting surrounding Lesley. He pressed firmly on the shield-like aura. It cracked in protest as he inched the sword toward her. The attack took more effort to block than she anticipated as she strained to hold him back.

With an exerted push, Lesley strained every muscle to keep him at bay.

Meanwhile, Raven moved to the knight's flank and delivered a stabbing blow to his abdomen with one of her daggers.

"NO!" Lillyanna cried out.

Alphonse swings his sword to his left, forcing Raven to step backwards to evade, at the same time trusts with his shield against Lesley's aura. "Hertics!"

"Honorable combat is one on one!" Gregor yelled.

Raven moves to Alphonse's backside and attacks again forcing the knight to spin around to defend himself. The knight spins back and swipes out with his shield hitting nothing but air. Raven stepped back into Lillyanna.

"Oh apologies." He said. But Lillyanna pushed him back into the wall. "I guess I can't persuade you to look the other way?"

"No, you can't." She responded by attacking Raven with a sudden flash of her sword made out of pure light.

"When did you get a sword?" As Raven scrutinized the dagger, he deftly evaded its swift thrust. The dagger possessed a unique property - light effortlessly flowed through it, converging into a radiant blade composed entirely of pure energy. "Oh, that's a neat trick."

In an astonishing display of speed and agility, Lillyanna surpassed Raven's expectations. The two warriors exchanged blows, but Lillyanna's exceptional reflexes allowed her to evade Raven's attacks and retaliate with remarkable precision. Despite facing Raven's dual daggers, Lillyanna held her ground with her solitary aura sword. However, the tide of the battle shifted as Raven gained momentum. The turning point came when Lillyanna unleashed a decisive strike with a second dagger, pinning Raven to the wall. The icy white light of her blade pierced his shoulder, anchoring him to the surface with unwavering resolve.

"You are full of surprises." Raven said, smiling through the pain.

Lesley reached deep within herself, to the raging storm inside. She summoned its power into her palm, where it hovered wildly and uncontrollably before lashing out.

Alphonse and Gregor were blasted backwards. The knight slammed hard into the far wall and landed with a loud clank of metal on stone. Electricity coursed through his body, causing him to convulse on the floor. Gregor broke through the wooden table, slashing lukewarm stew all over the floor.

Lesley raises one hand, summoning the great storm once again. It's raw energy rushing to her palm. Tears started to flow from her steely blue eyes. Its lightning sparks and clashes all around. Burning the wood, stone and finally snapping onto Gregor.

Lillyanna leaps into between her and Alphonse. "Lesley stop!" Raising her own arm in defense of the knight for the oncoming blast.

"Lily no!" Gregor yells out to his daughter hacking up his own blood. The lighting burned through his cloth garments revealing a smoking blast to his chest.

Lesley's eyes go shockingly wide for a second as the darkness swirled all around her. In that instant she remembered the warmth of Lily's touch. The unusual strength she has about her and the tears she secretly kept away from view. "Move away."

Images of her beloved friend Olivia racking her mind. "Kill them both." She could hear Olivia saying as if she stood right behind her.

"I will not." Lillyana mumbles something under her breath. It sounded like a prayer. Suddenly light hummed engulfed her and the knight. She was protecting him. "I know not of the turmoil you must be enduring but you are a good person! I see the storm brewing inside of you. You don't have to do this!"

"Move!" Lesley asks again. The storm grew rapidly, the lighting infused with the power of the illuminating gem. The clouds grow darker and winds pick up in speed, whipping her hair and loose clothing around.

"I. Will Not!" The light around her humming enlarges and covers Gregor.

"Why!?" Lesley demanded.

Olivia appears behind Lesley placing her arms around her shoulder. "Kill them all."

"No." Lesley shakes her head. "I can't."

"They are all wolves." Ovelia's disembodied whisper grazed Lesley's ears, brushing the edge of her consciousness.

Alphonse rolls over and weakly whispers. "Mother, I'm sorry."

"Mother?! You're one of them." Lesley whispered to herself, unsure if she had even said the words out loud. The worry stone around her neck hummed with a soft light, and she suddenly realized something that hit her like a thunderbolt: her son was not dead, but a Silverwolf. She was a Silverwolf too.

Lesley was in a sea of pain, torn and twisted, pulled back and forth. Lesley was unwilling to take anything from Lillyanna, as she only wanted to protect her. Lesley also wanted her dead for being a Silverwolf. It was a bitter betrayal, a train wreck of inevitabilities, a hard call to make.

Lesley wondered if this was how Gabriel felt. Part of her understood why he acted the way he did, but she was not Gabriel. She could make the tough decision. She had no love for The Silver Wolves and wanted nothing more than to kill them all for Olivia. The storm continued to grow in size and intensity, and Lesley closed her eyes as she released the storm within.

Lesley stood frozen in time, a dark shadow casting over everything and obscuring their faces with sketchy dark lines. She heard her name echoing, "Lesley." The voice said again tugging at Lesley's attention, forcing her to see her.

Spinning around, Lesley saw Olivia sitting at the top of the stairs. She was still wearing her school uniform, her dirty blond hair freshly made. Her hazel eyes were full of life. As Lesley ran up the stairs, her storm-steel eyes turned deep blue. She embraced her friend, and they tumbled backward through the floor. They landed gently in Lesley's bed in her home.

"They are all wolves." Lesley cried.

"You wanted to help her but her betrayal was clear." Olivia said, brushing Lesley's head with her hand. The darkness obscured the windows but the room was illuminated in a warm color. "Lesley. It's OK. You need to kill them. All of them."

Lesley sits up and watches her. "I, I know."

"They only want to fight. Kill. and devour. Before they do it to you, you must kill them first."

Lesley rolled over onto her back. The shadows between the popcorn ceiling grew larger and larger, until they looked like a starry night sky. The stars twinkled brightly. "Yeah." she said. "Okay." She closed her eyes and prayed into the darkness behind her eyelids. When she opened them, she was standing in front of the wolves again. Her dark storm surrounded everything.

"I'm slow sometimes." She said laughing to herself echoing Raven's words to her. "I didn't want to see it. It was so obvious. You are a wolf and you have to die."

Lillyanna Summons a beam of white light into the palm and forms a bow and brightly lit arrow. "I won't let you hurt my family."

Lesley frowned. "I'm sorry." Olivia stood behind her and whispered in her ear and together they spoke in union. "It's inevitable."

Lillyanna fired a blast that exploded on the violet shield. The energy dithered and vanished but the force of the blow pushed Lesley back. Lillyanna fired shot after shot slamming on the shield. Lillyanna's arrows rained down on Lesley like a storm of her own coming from all directions. Lesley tried to dodge them, but it was impossible. She was soon covered in wounds, and she could feel her strength ebbing away.

Lesley dodged Lillyanna's arrows and retaliated with her own magic spells. Dark infused lighting drifted and crackled. Lesley could feel the power inside of her swell but this time in a more controlled manner. Lesley retaliated with streams for lightning slamming into Lillyanna. Unlike lesley she was not shielded. But she remained on her feet. Lesley commanded the winds around her to lift Lillyanna off her feet.

Lesley could feel the power inside of her swell, but this time in a more controlled manner. She retaliated with streams of lightning, which slammed into Lillyanna. Unlike Lesley, Lillyanna was not shielded. But she remained on her feet. Lesley commanded the winds around her to lift Lillyanna off her feet. Lillyanna fought against the wind, but it was too powerful. She was lifted into the air, and Lesley blasted her with another stream of lightning. Lillyanna screamed in pain as the lightning arced through her body.

With each step forward, Lesley surged Lillyanna with unyielding energy. She came to a halt, standing directly before her. "It didn't have to be this way." Lesley cried. "You only had to move."

Alphonse stabs lesley in the abdomen. Lesley's eyes go wide. She slammed her attention to the young wolf. She pulls him closer by grabbing his head. She jolts him with all the fury she could muster. The ground infuses in her dark violet energy. Darkness caved in around the edges of her senses.

She grabbed the blade with her bare hand and shot electricity down the hilt of the blade. Alphonse convoluted in pain, his body writhing as the electricity coursed through him. The old man tried to step in and raise the weapon high and was instantly electrified. She held him in place, steaming more electricity from her free hand.

Lillyanna cried out in pain, "No!" as she watched her father and son suffer. The runic gemstone pulsed gradually stronger and outward until its dark pulse was the only remaining light. Pushing the energy out behind them and being absorbed into the orb.

The orb grew brighter and brighter, until it was too bright to look at. Then, with a flash of light, everyone was gone, and Lesley was left alone, standing in the dim violet light of the gemstone.

A sense of replenishment waved over her. It made her smile, frown and then her eyes went wide. "What happened?" She said aloud. Lesley scrambled her senses. She felt the phantom pain in her abdomen but there was no wound. Her uniform wasn't even cut or ripped.

Raven placed a hand on Lesley's shoulder causing her to leap in place. She didn't even hear him approach. "This is what you wanted. You killed the wolves and everyone who stands with them." Raven kneeled down and found Lillyanna's twin daggers, examined them and placed them into his belt.

Even if she knew what to say she didn't have the words for it. Earlier that day she went from vowing to protect a stranger to being completely numb to their pain. But deep down she knew he was right. This is what she wanted. They all had to die not for any other reason outside of her will. It wasn't a want anymore but a need. A hunger.

She stood amid the wreckage, her hair whipping around her face in the wind. She raised her hand and called forth a mighty wind, rain, and lightning. The storm raged around her, and she laughed, unable to describe the feeling of power coursing through her veins. She felt like a goddess, a force of nature, unstoppable. The storm was hers to command, and she reveled in it.

Her joyous expression twists into introspection and sorrow. "I don't even know who I am anymore." Lesley clutches the worry stone in her hands as if in prayer. It's dim and flickering light peeking between interlocked fingers. The runic gemstone hovers over her shoulder pulsing violet light among the rain and ruin. The village of Moonbright was a scene of devastation.

"Of course" Raven puts his hand on her shoulders. "You are exactly who you are meant to be."

"Vengeance."

Chapter Nineteen

Gabriel

There was a battle here but it was long over before they were dragged through the gates of Stonewrath. The village was constructed of wood and stone, lacking the more modern touches of anything he had seen before. Everything here was crudely hand-built and much more primitive. The buildings were small and simple, with thatched roofs and dirt floors.

The streets were unpaved and muddy, and light came from the second moon and the fires that burned in the villagers' homes. The people themselves were dressed in simple clothes made of rough-hewn cloth. He felt like he had stepped back in time, to a world that was long forgotten. Until the knights half destroyed it. No home was left untouched. The lucky few were partially destroyed.

Amidst the chaos, several brave locals refused to surrender and made a final, desperate stand, fiercely battling against the overwhelming force of the wolves. Their valiant efforts, though admirable, were ultimately futile as they succumbed to the superior strength of their adversaries. Gabriel realized that The Kingsguard were not killing anyone. The people of Stonewrath were being subdued and arrested. People lined the streets, dragged out of their homes, handcuffed kneeling on the ground.

The Kingsguard ripped the weak, the elderly and children from their homes. Anyone that resisted were brutally attacked but not killed. Any injured or unconscious were forced to be carried by another captive. Gathered them into a large group. They were all moving in the same direction.

With a clenched jaw, Gabriel grappled with the profound injustice of the situation. Throughout his career as a law enforcement officer, he had encountered numerous disheartening incidents, yet this particular case stood apart as singularly egregious. The sole factor offering him a momentary pause was the fact that the perpetrators had been apprehended alive.

"Why are they ripping these people from their homes?"

"They are The Kingsguard." Amelia explained. "They serve the Royal family without question."

"That doesn't answer my question."

"I fail to comprehend their motivations, and honestly, I find them utterly inconsequential."

Gabriel looks down and away, then back at the families shackled in chains. He had to remind himself that he was not in failed lands, even though this looked like the start of a massive war crime. He turned his gaze back to Amelia. "Are you not a member of the royal family?"

"Yes, but I fear I've been away too long." Amelia meets Gabriel's stare lifting an eyebrow. "I cannot blame them. To them, I have been missing for months. And now I reappear with a relative of the fallen house? I would be cautious too."

"Why would they doubt you?"

"Trust me, you don't know the stories. Even if they are half true I wouldn't take what I say as truth. The void, the darkness and the fury of the Ravenous one and the corruption he represents isn't something to take lightly."

As Gabriel breathed in deeply, his thoughts wandered to the intriguing crest and its symbolic representation. The image portrayed a majestic one-eyed wolf surrounded by a circle of ravens, evoking a sense of mystery and power. "Did you really not know about my crest when we met?"

"I was intrigued by the sight, but I did not realize it was the fallen house. In hindsight it was rather foolish of me to have not seen it."

"Before I die I'd like to know more about this Fenrir clan. Who were they, why did they embrace darkness, and how did they end up on earth? There are so many things our people have in common yet we have so many differences. Did we start here or on earth?"

"I had not considered that. Are my people from Earth or Terra? It's hard to say. I've always assumed Terra was Midgard of the Legends."

"Everything is aggravating," Gabriel said, his rising voice betraying his irritation. His heart began to pound, his palms became clammy, and his breathing became shallow. He felt like he was going to be ill. He attempted to concentrate on his breathing, but it was difficult. All he could think about was the anxiety and how it was going to ruin everything.

With immense effort, he slowly trudged forward, his feet feeling like heavy weights made of lead. Each step was a struggle, as his weary muscles protested with aching pain. The mere act of lifting his feet seemed insurmountable. He gritted his teeth and forced himself to keep going, one foot in front of the other.

On the verge of losing his composure he knew he had to face his fear and find a way to calm himself. He took several deep breaths and concentrated on the present. He felt the air entering and leaving his lungs, the beat of his heart, and the sensation of his feet on the ground. Gradually, he began to feel better. His anxiety began to dissipate. Although he was still anxious, it was manageable. He knew he could get through this.

Gabriel's head began to throb as if someone was pounding on it with a hammer. He fell to one knee, clutching his throbbing eye. The pain was so intense that he felt like he was going to be sick. He closed his eyes and tried to breathe through the pain, but it was no use. Everything went black.

Gabriel dredged his way through the darkness, his arms outstretched before him. He felt something coming after him and instinctively drew his sword to meet it. A sudden clang of steel on steel rang out in the darkness. He reeled back, blocking and parrying the attacks, but could see nothing.

His arms are shaking with fatigue and is on the defensive. His breathing is labored and he's covered in sweat and the chill wind is cutting him to the bone. He struggles to keep up with the onslaught of devastating blows barely stopping the massive two handed blade from ending his own existence. The sound of the steel clashes and reverberates into physical force pushing him backwards and landing in the dirt and mud.

The metallic tang of blood lingered in Gabriel's mouth. A dull ache and harsh rawness of his throat that caused him to cough blood. He was dragged, his body semi-limp, through the open wooden gates of a small village. He could hear the familiar sounds of armored combat and the sounds of energy concussion blasts.

Surveying the area, Gabriel murmured, "It feels as though he's physically present with us."

"Who are you referring to?"

"The void knight I fought back at my home."

"Keep moving." One of the knights demanded pushing Gabriel forward forcing him to move forward.

"Touch him again and I'll break your arms." With her usual formal demeanor gone, Amelia spoke coldly. Gabriel was not touched again by The Kingsguard, who repeated the order. Amelia turned back around and continued to walk with him.

"It looks like you have some authority."

"There exists a particular point at which strength is revered. At this juncture, without Viktor, they are aware that they would be incapable of preventing me from fulfilling that threat."

"How is he so much stronger than everyone? I've never seen someone move like him, even here in Terra."

"I have my suspensions but that is a sensitive subject. All I can say is that he was not this strong when we last engaged in combat."

"Is that why you killed Berenger?"

"I realized I needed his strength in order to face Viktor, so I absorbed it. He didn't have much use beyond that." she said in a matter-of-fact tone.

"I thought so," Gabriel said. "I have seen it happen on many occasions that one can absorb the spirit of another and gain power. But life has value. He could have aided us in other ways." He knew she was right; yet he couldn't help but to feel guilty for their deaths.

"Trust me Gabriel, there was no saving him from Viktor." She said grimly. "If it wasn't me then it was going to be him."

"How are you so certain of that?"

"You're aware of how he killed those savages. Your firsthand experience battling Viktor confirms it." Amelia momentarily halted, gazing upwards and to the right. "During my fight with Berenger, I feigned weakness to earn his trust. Viktor's arrival rendered him irrelevant to us."

Gabriel had a difficult time accepting the harsh reality, but he couldn't deny the underlying logic. In the heat of the moment, a tough decision had to be made. While part of him acknowledged its necessity, he couldn't help but wish it would have a more significant impact on the outcome.

Realizing Viktor wouldn't have spared their lives if he intended to kill them, Gabriel's mood darkened, and his thoughts shifted. He couldn't help but question the true extent of the Fenrir house's vulnerability, especially considering The Silver Wolves' utilitarian evaluation of individuals. However, he also recognized that he might be conflating two separate issues in his mind.

"I perceive that you are agitated. His energy gave us a better chance of victory; however, I did not realize how little it would have mattered."

"I have no right to pass judgment upon you. You merely acted in accordance with what you perceived as the righteous path." Gabriel's jaw clenched tightly as his mind delved into the deepest, darkest corners of his thoughts. Gabriel's mind lingered on thoughts of Lesley and his parents. Even after all this time, he still yearned for them deeply. The traumatic experience had shaped him into the man he had become. However, this transformation came with a heavy heart.

"I regret nothing." Amelia said, forcing Gabriels attention on her.

With grim determination, he responded, acknowledging their contrasting viewpoints, "I understand, that's one area where we differ."

Locking eyes with Gabriel, Amelia detached her hand from his. Her expression was unreadable, leaving Gabriel uncertain if she was assessing or scrutinizing him.

To divert her attention, Gabriel scanned the area and inquired, "Where is Viktor?"

"He went ahead into the village. Most likely fighting the strongest among them himself."

"It sounds simple, he fought the strongest and absorbed their strength. I've witnessed this a few times already."

"Be assured, it cannot account for the vast difference in strength in such a short period."

"If you collect every drop of water you can create an ocean." Gabriel reasoned.

"There may be a lot of people in this world, he would have been on a mass genocide to reach this level of strength."

The village was small, and they soon arrived at its center, where they were all herded around a large, burning pyre. In the light of its flames, families were reunited, desperately clutching one another for what little comfort they could find. Their faces were filled with terror and helplessness. The knights methodically arranged the locals in a circle around the pyre.

Viktor, transfixed by the great flame, stood mesmerized by its hypnotic waves. A great barbarian warrior knelt at his feet. Viktor, the clear victor, must have dragged the giant warrior to where he was kneeling, as there were signs of a duel between them.

"What are you doing with them?" Gabriel asked.

"I've recently discovered a hidden secret within our own civilization. I'm testing a hypothesis."

"I'm sure if you burn them they will die."

"Burn them?" Viktor laughed while taking a burning stick from the pyre. "Showing them the wrath of Sol?" He said waving the flames at the captives. "No." He placed the flaming stick into the soil extinguishing its fire. Viktor drags the stick carefully behind him as he walks in a circle around the pyre. "It would be a waste to burn them. A matter not worth my time."

"Then what are you doing? Why attack a small village?"

"As I told you, I am merely testing a hypothesis." He dragged the stick behind him as he walked in a line and then drew a little circle at the end of it.

"Using the lives of your people as test subjects?"

"My people, ah, yes. The strange man from a strange world." Viktor said with a smile. "I am familiar with your name from the Lord-Commander's report." He dragged the stick behind him as he walked in a line and then drew a little circle at the end of it. "His unfortunate fate is lamentable, but it is commendable that he perished nobly."

"Don't they live in your lands? Doesn't that make it your responsibility to protect and teach? Can't you show them the true value of life?"

"Do you really think these savages are my people?" He dragged the stick behind him as he walked in a line and then drew a little circle at the end of it. "These same people who reject all that our empire has built? Attack and raid our small towns and villages and feed on their spirits, are my people? No Strange man, these are not my people. These savages see my people as meals to devour and grow stronger. Worse than animals, parasites."

"As it was in the old ways!" An older warrior among them said. The man had a look in his eyes that told Gabriel that he had already forfeited his own life. "Lord Fenrir, devourer of souls, kings and gods lead us this path. A gift to all of the wolves."

"You see? They openly admit it." Viktor around the pyre for a second time. "Savages that reject the gifts of Sol. God of the energy that gives life to all." Viktor sighed and knelt in front of Gabriel. "We've taught all that can be taught to those who are willing to learn. The value of their lives is the sum of its potential energy."

"Wait, I've seen this image before." Gabriel had seen such circles before, like the one he saw in the alley when he found Lesley. There was a similar symbol on the floor of the garage, but this one was much larger, big enough to fit a whole village.

The Kingguard force the people in place, with force when necessary. "What is the purpose of this magic circle?"

"That is what we are here to test."

"At least let these people go, they are innocent."

"Innocent? How absurd. I am not doing anything to them that they wouldn't do to me or my people. If they were in my place they would be feasting on my spirit. As it was in the old ways." Viktor turns to the old man who turns his gaze away suddenly.

"You mean to kill all these people?" Gabriel's eyes go wide. "Is that how you become so powerful?"

"Not exactly."

Amelia's grim expression was a clear indication that she was concealing something. She may have been afraid of what would happen if she told the truth, or she may have been protecting someone or something. Whatever the reason, it was clear that she was not ready to share what she knew. However it was also clear by her reactions that she was invested in knowing the outcome of the experiment.

With a solemn gaze fixed upon Gabriel, the colossal warrior conceded, "Youngling, irrespective of your beliefs, our defeat is an unavoidable fate."

Gabriel studied the man's features and he bore a remarkable resemblance to Berenge. He is, or was, Lord of Stonewrath, his existence possibly shattered by the loss of his sons. He carried the same full expression as the old warrior who spoke before.

With their leader's words a palpable transformation had swept over the inhabitants of Stonewrath, rendering them complacent and subservient, meekly surrendering to their leader's words.

"Your spirit will endure within my beating heart. Together, we will defend our world from all who would do it harm. As in the old ways." However, despite the sincerity in his words, Gabriel couldn't help but notice the mischievous glint in his eyes, belying the gravity of his statement.

The giant warrior sighs and nods. "As in the old ways."

Gabriel surveyed the group of prisoners, recognizing the fragility and preciousness of life. He couldn't stand by and did nothing to protect them. There had to be a way to stop this, a way to keep them safe. Gabriel leaned closer to Amelia and whispered. "He is about to get even stronger. How can we stop this from happening?"

"I don't think we can." Amelia said defeated. "These simple people have already surrendered their right to live. You can not save them."

"I can not accept that." Gabriel stood up, but was knocked back to his knees. "You can't do this to them! They have value far beyond the sum of their spiritual powers."

"Gabriel, you cannot defeat him."

"I can't allow him to kill these helpless people."

"A public challenge?" Viktor waved his hand to order The Kingsguard away from Gabriel. "Very well. I'll accept this challenge if only to humble you. What are your terms?"

"If I put you into the dirt you let these people go."

"A deathless duel, then? That is wise of you. Should I emerge victorious, I shall proceed with the ritual as planned. Is it agreed?"

In the initial confrontation, Gabriel initiated the physical altercation by throwing the first punch. However, Viktor demonstrated remarkable agility and successfully evaded the incoming blow.

"Terms accepted." Viktor began to toy with Gabriel, dodging his punches and landing his own with devastating force. Gabriel was no match for 's superior skill, speed, and strength. Viktor counter attacked, landing a direct blow to Gabriels nose. Blood explodes on his face.

Blinded by free flowing blood from multiple wounds Gabriel swung repeatedly, but Viktor was too quick to be hit. Gabriel's aura glowed brighter and brighter, until it was almost blinding. With his speed and strength enhanced, Gabriel was able to match Viktor's speed, forcing Viktor to block Gabriel's attacks.

Viktor's dodging became less frequent as he continued, and he blocked more and more. Viktor faints and Gabriel falls for the opening and Viktor counters again but this time Gabriel stops the punch. Viktor feigns a faint, Gabriel takes the bait, and Viktor counters with a punch that Gabriel blocks by grabbing his fist.

With remarkable speed, Gabriel's facial wounds mend, giving him an advantage in the fight. His relentless assault forces Viktor to adopt a defensive stance, struggling to withstand the powerful blows.

With a burst of his radiant silver aura, Viktor's movements became a blur, leaving Gabriel struggling to keep up. Relentlessly, Viktor pounded Gabriel's face into a bloody pulp once more. Standing tall above his vanquished opponent, Viktor reveled in his triumph. Gabriel's luminous energy waned as he lay sprawled on the ground, fresh blood seeping from his wounds.

"You have great potential," Viktor said. "Someone like you could be more valuable than all of your spiritual powers combined, but not these savages and heretics who reject Sol."

A grimace of agony twisted Gabriel's features, as a crimson spray of blood erupted from his mouth. Viktor turned to one of his Kingguard and ordered, "Heal him. I don't want him dying yet."

With a gentle touch, The Kingsguard's hands bestowed a surge of vitality upon Gabriel, pulling him back from the brink of death. An inexplicable compulsion seized Gabriel, urging him to wrest the life force from The Kingsguard. The Kingsguard crumpled to the ground, but still breathing shallowly, in a state of shock but still alive. In a sudden, swift motion, Gabriel stood ablaze with a muted gray energy, his sword brandished with unpredictable ferocity.

"It seems that you possess the undying spirit of Fenrir, after all. Perhaps there is some of his blood coursing through your veins."

In Gabriel's mind, a persistent ringing resonated, assaulting his senses with an intense and clamorous noise. It felt as though an unspoken summons, an irresistible and undeniable call, was emanating from deep within him. "I can't let you do this to these people."

"I see why she likes you. However, I perceive the darkness that resides within you. It burdens you, distorts your perceptions, and obscures your inner light." Viktor tightened his clenched jaw, his gaze fixed firmly as he uttered, "We shall witness the outcome."

Under the twin moons, With dexterous precision, Viktor wielded his bastard sword, effortlessly deflecting and countering each attack. The swiftness of his movements formed a mesmerizing spectacle, a blur of steel and skill. His opponent's blade flashed menacingly in the darkness, each exchanging a testament to their evenly matched skills and experience. The air crackled with the resonant clash of steel, mingling with the scents of blood and smoke.

As the battle raged on, neither combatant could gain an advantage. It was a grueling test of endurance and skill. Gabriel's arms ached, and his lungs burned. He realized he couldn't maintain the relentless pace much longer.

In a moment of desperation, Gabriel launched a wild attack. He instantly regretted his mistake, for Viktor seized the opportunity. With a cunning feint, Viktor lured Gabriel's blade to one side, unleashing a devastating cut to the other. Gabriel's sword was deflected, and Viktor's blade sliced through the air, burying itself deep within his opponent's chest.

As Gabriel plummeted to the ground, astonishment flickered across his widening eyes. With great effort, he drew shallow breaths as a crimson cascade spilled from his lips. Deprived of the strength to rise, he resigned himself to the adversaries before him. A steady flow of blood from his wounds merged with the encroaching darkness that veiled his sight, an ominous harbinger of his impending demise.

"Pity." Amidst the chaos, Viktor's voice reached Gabriel's ears, but his sight was obstructed. His vision drifted heavenward, and the twin moons caught his attention. They resembled a pair of indifferent eyes observing the unfolding events, one glowing a vibrant blue and the other a steely gray. Gabriel, a faint smile playing on his lips, lifted a hand toward the celestial bodies.

In a state of panic, Amelia grasped Gabriel's hand and firmly returned it to the ground, urging him to cease his restless movements. However, her words fell on deaf ears as Gabriel succumbed to an overwhelming lethargy.

Gabriel's voice quivered as he feebly extended his hand towards the descending light. "What is that?" he inquired, his confusion evident. On the edges of his sight, a deep, taunting sound reverberated through the obscurity. He abruptly felt immersed in waves of darkness, while simultaneously, a substantial beacon of light drew him forward. It was as though two potent forces were ripping him apart.

"What are you referring to?" Amelia responded, her tone laced with concern.

Immersed in profound darkness, Gabriel's vision was shrouded, rendering the world around him into an abyss of shadows. However, in a startling instant, his sight was miraculously restored, as if a blinding white light had pierced through the veil of obscurity, allowing him to perceive the world in its natural clarity once again. A lingering familiarity of a delightful dream was all that lingered in his thoughts, intermingled with the echoes of a sweet voice resonating within his consciousness.

Although the bleeding had ceased, Gabriel's strength had waned, leaving him pale and weakened. His blurred vision and surreal detachment from reality made everything appear as if he were experiencing a waking dream.

Under the glow of the full moons, Viktor commenced the ritual. With hands clasped together in prayer, he raised them towards the sky, then lowered them to the center of his chest. A radiant silver aura emanated from Viktor, spreading outward until it enveloped the entire circle.

"Sol is with us." A knight said. "Praise be." Another said. The Silver Wolves look upon their prince with the reverence of a god as they praise Sol as if they were one and the same.

Amidst the darkness, the magnificent pyre erupted in a mesmerizing dance of flames. Their vibrant hues transformed from reddish orange to ethereal silver and white, remnants of their original colors still lingering. An intense heat radiated from the pyre, accompanied by a thick, smoky atmosphere. The deafening symphony of crackling flames and burning wood filled the air, while the overwhelming scent of smoke permeated everything, making it difficult to draw breath. The brilliance of the flames was almost blinding, creating a spectacle that left onlookers in awe.

Within the circle, agonizing cries echoed as people's auras and energies poured forth, drawn irresistibly toward Viktor. Hovering above the ground, he reveled in the sensation of absorption, his face a mask of pleasure and power.

Amidst the hushed cries of anguish, a dazzling light burst forth, quelling the mournful sounds. Descending gracefully, Viktor unleashed his ethereal silver light, igniting a captivating flame with enchanting hues. The flames, imbued with a profound silver radiance, danced around him, illuminating the darkness with a vibrant glow.

In the wake of his power, the people within the circles lay reduced to mere ash and bone, their souls claimed by Viktor. Now more formidable than ever, he hungered to unleash his newfound strength and seize his ambitions.

With a malevolent grin adorning his face, Viktor proclaimed, "Sol has blessed us this day."

With disbelief, Gabriel observed the devastation that unfolded before his eyes as he lay there, his wounds miraculously healing. A surge of raw grief swept over him as the villagers crumbled into dust, disappearing in the wind. Despite the pain, a sense of numbness enveloped him, accompanied by a somber gratitude for being spared from the fate of those who perished. Sol was with them, Gabriel agreed.

Chapter Twenty

Lesley

Lesley digs through the back of the SUV where Raven kept all of the weapons and armor they found in Moonbright village. They took Alphones sword, shield and Armor. and condensed it down into a small fist sized cube. A Giant two handed sword that seemed impossible to weld lays across the back and into the rear seats of the suv. Lesley was glad she didn't encounter the person who swung this thing around. The weapon was so massive and heavy only a real monster could weld such a weapon. Daggers and every type of weapon and tool in between.

"When did you grab this stuff?" Lesley asked, breaking the silence.

"If I told you I'd have to kill you." Raven said with a laugh as he drove the SUV though rocky terrain. Lesley bounces sharply, the blades and armor cubes fall over. One of the blades cut Lesley's clothing. She pulls her arm in, fusing over it but the clothing stitches itself back together. Lesley blinked her eyes in surprise, and she studied the fabric. And trace of the cut was gone, she even questioned whether it actually happened. Raven half heartedly apologized but Lesley was too immersed in her sleeve to notice. Shaking the thought away she turned her attention back to the assortment of weapons.

"OK then, why did you take this stuff?"

"I'm clearly going to sell it once we get to Lyndell."

Lesley conveyed her sarcasm as she replied in an obvious tone, "Yeah, clearly. I mean, that's obvious I guess."

As Lesley grasped Lillyanas' daggers, a pang of betrayal pierced her heart. In contrast, her face softened, yearning for the tenderness of Lillyanas' voice and touch. In an alternate reality, they could have been family. Yet, this remained a mere fantasy. Ultimately, Lillyanas belonged to The Silver Wolves.

Despite coming to this realization, Lesley's spirit bore the enduring weight of the daggers' presence. She felt an inseparable connection to them, as if they were woven into her very essence. A sense of despair and longing lingered, refusing to be dismissed. "I'm going to keep Lillyana daggers."

"No. They don't work."

"All the more reason for you to give them to me. I doubt someone would buy broken daggers." With a mischievous giggle, she stole a quick glance at Raven, gauging her reaction before tossing the letters into the depths of her bag. Raven's opinions held no sway over her; she was determined to keep the letters close, a secret treasure she refused to part with.

Her mind drifted to the wolf sword displayed in Gabriel's room, a symbol now repugnant to her. While the thought of claiming the bastard sword held a certain appeal, the practicality of wielding such a formidable blade began to sink in.

"You really don't need to use any of those. You are curiously powerful."

"Yeah." Despite her increasing strength, Lesley couldn't quite grasp the extent of her growing power. Each passing moment felt like a gradual ascent in strength. Determined, she reached for the colossal sword and strained to lift it, only to find it immovable. A chuckle escaped her. After all, the sword's size was daunting.

The SUV hits another giant bump knocking the stack of armor cubes over, like tossing a fistful of oversized dice. She instinctively reacted to try to stop them from falling and the sleeve of her uniform suddenly morphed into small arms that reached for the cubes as well. Lesley screamed in fright and pulled her arm back, causing the sleeve to return to normal.

"What are you doing back there?" Raven looks back in the rear view mirror.

"My uniform did something weird."

"Weird like how?"

"It turned into little wiggly arms with little hands."

Ravens face scrunches as he looks back at her in the rear view mirror. "Are you sure?"

"No. I'm not." She reaches out her arm and paws at the fabric. Nothing notable happened. "Am I going insane?"

Raven looked back at her again but he remained silent for a long moment. "Would you like to?"

"Just tell me no."

"No, you're not going crazy."

Lesley continued to rub her sleeves, but there was nothing strange about them.

"You still didn't find anything? I grabbed a lot of things."

"How do these armors work?" Lesley asked, picking up a cube. Relieved that she didn't see the little hands again.

"They are some sort of Biological material and crystals that form a super lightweight armor. It's all science fiction to me. They fetch a good price on the black market. But they are basically useless as is. At least I don't understand how they work."

The armor starts to mold down Lesley's arm. Forming a clawed gauntlet. "Holyshit!" Lesley says her eyes are wide.

The SUV comes to a sudden halt, Raven turning around and watching in disbelief.

"How are you doing that?"

"I don't know." The liquid armor slides over her forming a unique set of armor. Her family crest appears on the clawed gauntlet. Her school uniform starts to meld with the armor, making the illustrious silver armor more of a darksteel. It was all over faster than it bargained. Lesley lay in the back of the SUV panting unsure how to react.

"Well you definitely look different." As Raven spoke, Lesley's attention was drawn to the family crest, where she observed his stare linger for a moment. "What is that crest? I haven't seen it before."

With a tilt of her head, Lesley's intuition stirred, sensing a deceit in Raven's words. "It's my family crest. It dates back countless generations." She lifts her arm up and examines the intricate details. "How could it possibly know this crest?"

Lesley sat up, revealing that she was wearing armor. Her family crest was displayed on her shoulder and gauntlets. Her uniform was still on, but it was also changed. The top was more like something she had seen Amelia wear, with part of it being a hooded knight's tabard that was black and red, while she still wore a long skirt over the metal leggings.

Raven borrowed his eyes from her. "How did you do that with the armor? Your uniform changed too."

"That's not normal?"

"No, not even a little bit."

Exiting the SUV, Raven circled around to the rear of the vehicle. He opened the hatch, allowing her to exit the vehicle. "That's incredible. I mean you also look stunning."

"Oh, thanks, you flatter me sir."

"Only wolves and their clans can use the armor. It's something in it that reads DNA markers to identify clans. In essence you are a wolf."

Lesley's eyes go wide for a moment, then her face twists in rage. "No, don't say that. That's not even funny." She said, shoving a finger in Raven's chest.

"It's true, only wolves can use-"

"Don't say that!" Electricity buzzing around Lesley. "I am not a wolf. I will never be a wolf. Do you understand!?" In a surge of pent-up emotion, Lesley clenched her teeth, embodying the spirit of a wild animal. Her fierce growl and bared teeth resembled those of a wolf. This transformation intensified her anger, fueling it further.

With a deep inhalation, Lesley calmed herself. "Yeah. I'm sorry. It doesn't make sense but in a strange way I can see it. I don't want it to be true."

"It's ok. It doesn't have to be true. The people you are descendants of don't have to define you or your future."

Lesley sighed and turned her gaze away, brushing her hair behind her ear. "You're absolutely right." Suddenly, her exclamation of surprise cut through the air, "Oh my god, what is that?!"

In the distance, Lesley's gaze fell upon the towering silhouette of a gigantic tree. This colossus illuminated the heart of a sprawling metropolis, an urban landscape of impressive scale. Its majestic height caused its summit to vanish amongst the clouds, while its expansive branches stretched out, seemingly enveloping the entire city. The luminescence emanating from the tree possessed such intensity that Lesley averted her eyes, unable to withstand its direct brilliance. The sheer magnitude and exquisite beauty of this natural wonder left her in awe.

With a grand flourish, Raven's hand sliced through the air, gesturing towards the majestic city of Lyndell in the distance. "I truly desired for you to witness the city from this vantage point."

"It's beautiful." Lesley said with a genuine smile. "What's with the tree?"

"It's a sapling of Yggdrasil planted at the fall of the Void King 5000 years ago by Cecil and Blessed by Sol himself."

"That's so cool. I wish Olivia was here to see it." Inhaling deeply through her nose, a smile involuntarily formed on her lips. While the ache of her loss still lingered, its intensity was notably diminished. Though physically apart, the presence of her familiar scent, carried by the wind, brought a smile to her face. "It's a shame that I aim to destroy it."

"I'm glad to hear that." A broad smile stretched across Raven's face, revealing a dazzling array of fang-like teeth. "We are so close to correcting an old mistake."

It becomes apparent to Lesley that she was previously unaware of the reason behind Raven's animosity toward the empire. "Why do you hate the empire so much?"

"They stole something from me."

"Like what?" She asked, placing her hand on Raven's back.

Raven looks down over the edge of the cliff and waves Lesley to come to his side. "There they are. It's as Alphonese has said." A large caravan of vehicles and people on foot traveling in large clusters stretch for miles. Silver Wolves flank each side as well as traveling between the clusters. "Once we reach the city we can infiltrate and find our target."

"Why does Akisu want us to kill Amelia knowing that Gabriel might still be with her?"

"That connection might allow you to get close to her without being suspected of being a threat."

"That's, uh, logical, but it's still a risk. They know I destroyed part of that city. And killed some people who deserved to die."

"Maybe we can rephrase the narrative. Moment of grief you accidentally destroyed part of the city. The people who died were collateral damage and not intentional. I'm sure Gabriel will understand."

"Gabriel has a history of assuming the worst before anything."

"But he does want to protect you. We can turn that to our advantage in a pinch."

"Maybe. But I'd rather avoid his involvement if possible. His initial reaction will be to save Amelia."

"Perhaps you are right. We will need to catch her alone then we can use Gabriel as a shield to protect you."

With a determined expression, Lesley delves into the depths of her bag, reaching

for Lillyanna's daggers. However, an unexpected sensation meets her as the bag

appears to possess an unusual depth. "I can never find anything in this thing." As Lesley opened the bag, she was met with an unexpected surprise—it had no bottom. In an instant, the daggers materialized before her eyes. "Oh there is it." Lesley pulls out one to the daggers, thinking nothing of it.

"Hey, I said you can't have those."

"And I told you I was going to take them anyway." Lesley uses it to summon a lighting blade. "This is perfect. So I guess they work."

"Wolf girl."

"Ya know, I'm sorry I took the daggers, but please don't call me that!" Lesley yelled, sending a spark of electricity down her arms.

With a rosy flush gracing his features, Raven raised his hands as a clear sign he was yielding. "I apologize, I shouldn't have called you that. Daggers are kind of my thing but don't need them. They look as though they suit you."

Feeling mischievous, Lesley smiled, swinging the dagger around her. "How about a lesson in melee combat?"

"Oh, I assumed you already knew how to fight."

"I've been winging it this entire time." Lesley puts one finger on her nose and points her other hand at Raven. "You see what I did there?"

He smiles, getting to position, pulling out his daggers. "Yeah, yeah, OK."

In the training grounds, Raven and Lesley diligently honed their dagger skills. With deliberate movements, Raven instructed Lesley on the correct stances and combat maneuvers, ensuring a solid foundation for her eager apprentice. Lesley's swift learning ability shone through as she grasped the fundamentals, impressing Raven with her potential.

A playful smile tugged at Raven's lips as he gently pushed Lesley away. "Are you toying with me, dear Lesley? Your prowess in melee combat is truly remarkable."

With a roll of her eyes and a smile, she spoke. "OK I have received some training from Gabriel, along with attending various classes here and there."

"Oh, I'd love to hear more."

"Gabriel got me into it because he wanted to keep me safe even when he wasn't around. I took a Krav Maga class with Gabriel. I kept up with it because I liked fighting. I really liked Taekwondo too, I got, like, really good at that style."

"I'm intrigued by Krav Maga Class and Taekwondotoo."

"Krav Maga, Taekwondo."

"In my defense, you stated it quite oddly." Raven laughed as Lesley playfully pushed him back, both of them filled with amusement. "Oh, sorry, how about we make a game out of it. You show me your two styles if you disarm you. But if you can hit me with your dagger at all, I'll do whatever you like."

"Sounds like a deal." Lesley grinned playfully.

"The dagger, not the lighting that comes from it." Raven leans forward, extending an index finger. "I mean it."

Lesley perceived him as a teacher-like figure, assuming the role of a disciplinarian if necessary, which amused her. "Ok, OK."

Raven and Lesley sparred with daggers. Lesley was overwhelmed by Raven's experience and speed, but she felt like he was going easy on her. She knew that if he wanted to win, he could have easily done so. However, he was teaching her the intricate ways of grappling and keeping safe in close quarters combat with a dagger. He was making sure that she knew what to do in any situation. Raven almost disarmed her multiple times, but she managed to stay armed all while Lesley could not land any kind of blow against him. It was like trying to hit a shadow.

The two continued to spar through the night, their movements a dance of shadows and moonlight. Suddenly, Lesley's foot caught on a hidden root, and she began to fall. Instinctively, Raven reached out to stop her, but she grabbed his arm and dragged him down with her. The two tumbled back onto the grass, gasping for breath.

"Are you ok?" Raven asked, brushing her hair out of her face.

"Yeah, but are you, loser?" Lesley grins.

Raven's eyes widened in astonishment, and her grin stretched even wider in an exaggerated manner as she exclaimed, "What!?" Lesley taps Raven's abdomen with the hilt of her dagger. "Clever girl, what style was that?

"Some might call that feminine charms?" She said with a blushing smile.

"It worked." Raven leaned in and kissed her.

The two lovers lay in the grass, kissing and gazing out over the city of Lyndell. The caravan of refugees was a long way off, but they could still see the dust rising from their feet. The twin moons were full and bright, and they cast a blue silvery light over the landscape. The urd tree stood tall and proud in the distance, its branches reaching up to the sky illuminating the horizon. It was a beautiful night, and the two lovers were lost in each other's arms.

Chapter Twenty-One

Gabriel

Gabriel and Amelia stood side by side in front of a large picture window, their eyes drinking in the breathtaking panorama of the countryside. Verdant fields, like a patchwork quilt, stretched as far as the eye could see. In the distance, the faint outline of a city could be discerned, a mere speck on the horizon. The sun hung low in the sky, casting a golden glow on the rolling hills and distant forests.

The panorama was breathtaking, a tapestry of vibrant hues and intricate landscapes. Majestic mountains kissed the heavens, their snow-capped peaks gleaming under the setting sun's gentle caress. Verdant valleys cascaded down the slopes, adorned with lush forests and sparkling rivers. It was a scene of breathtaking beauty, a testament to the wonder and grandeur of nature.

But for Gabriel, the moment was tinged with a profound sorrow. His heart ached with the weight of the past, the memories of countless lives he had failed to save. The entire village of Stonewrath lay in ruins, another grim reminder of his inability to protect those he held dear. The specter of his failures haunted him, whispering doubts and eroding his resolve.

His gaze shifted to Amelia, who stood beside him, her eyes reflecting both concern and unwavering support. In her presence, he found a glimmer of hope, a lifeline amidst the storm of despair. He knew that he could not afford to fail her as well. The love and trust she had placed in him fueled his determination, igniting a spark of resilience within his weary soul.

With a heavy sigh, Gabriel turned away from the breathtaking vista, his heart still burdened but his spirit renewed. He knew that the path ahead would be fraught with challenges and heartache, but he was resolved to fight on, to protect Amelia and to honor the memory of those he had lost.

Amelia pulled Gabriel close to her, interlocking their arms by the elbow. "This is a good moment, to reflect, and see the Kingdom from above."

Gabriel weakly smiled, feeling the warmth of his body, comforted his weary mind and body. "That looks like one of the great cities, which one is it?"

"That is the city of Bremen. It's the northern coastal city."

Given all that had happened, he felt foolish for attempting small talk. He felt even more powerless to make a difference as they stood there leaning on each other for support. He said to himself, "What a pair we make."

"Yes, it's very lovely. Very cold." Amelia averted her eyes as she spoke. Gabriel couldn't tell if she had even heard him.

As the airship soared gracefully through the skies, Gabriel could not help but be awestruck by the sight of the approaching city. Its walls, towering and imposing, seemed to stretch on endlessly, forming an almost impenetrable barrier. However, as they drew closer, they noticed something unusual. A large caravan had set up camp just outside the city walls.

Tent checkpoints and armed guards were scattered strategically in front of the gates, reminiscent of the situation they had encountered in Sarum. But there was one significant difference this time: the gates were wide open, and people were being admitted at a much faster pace than had been the case in Sarum. This observation piqued the travelers' curiosity, and they exchanged puzzled glances among themselves.

"This again?" Gabriel said. "Why are they bringing people to the cities and keeping them on the outside of the walls?"

"The unforeseen act of introducing a large number of people at once has left us ill-equipped. In addition to thoroughly checking for any signs of corruption that people may have." Viktor said as he approached. "Their safety is paramount. When Darklings invade our realm, they must find shelter. I shall stand guard over them."

"You do care about some people." Gabriel said, surprised to hear any trace of humanity from him.

"Yes. My people."

"And for good reason." Amelia's snarky remark elicited a silent, piercing glare from Viktor. It was evident that there was an unspoken secret between them, excluding Gabriel from their shared connection. Amelia looked toward the skyline and continued. "Has there been more incidents outside of Serum?"

Gabriel distanced himself from the conversation to closely observe the siblings.

He discovered a greater similarity between them than Amelia had initially revealed. Moreover, he grew increasingly skeptical of Viktor's intentions behind gathering people into the large cities, suspecting that his motives weren't as altruistic as they seemed.

"Unfortunately there has, we are expediting the processes of letting people in the cities. With the new defensive measures in place these camps outside of the walls will no longer be necessary."

"Where do the Darklings come from? What are they exactly?"

"They originate from the void. They infect everything they encounter. And they seek to destroy us. However Their return is inevitable." Viktor said sternly.

Gabriel noticed Amelia avert her eyes again this time adding a sigh. He gave her a reassuring touch on the shoulder and asked, "Are you OK?" With an angry glare, she shook her head at him in disapproval.

"Yes, and no. This is not exactly the way I wanted to return." Amelia crosses her arms over her chest and looks downward out of the windows. "I was whisked away merely days ago, and I come back with a looming threat of Darklings on the horizon? How am I to be queen in these circumstances?" The sudden change in Amelia's speech to an extraordinarily formal tone caused a slight unease in Gabriel.

"Our arrival is imminent," Kain informed Viktor before giving Gabriel a frosty sneer.

Recognizing The Kingsguard as the one he had drained strength from, Gabriel felt a mix of relief for sparing his life and a lack of remorse for the act.

"Thank you Kain." Viktor turned away, "Kindly direct The Kingsguard to escort us forthwith to the throne room upon landing."

The ship turned sharply allowing the group to see the full view of the City of Lyndell. Gabriel's eyes went wide as he stood in awe. The marvel of engineering was a sight to behold. Gleaming silver buildings rose up from the ground, their sleek surfaces reflecting the sunlight. The buildings were designed to integrate nature into their designs, with large windows that let in natural light and green spaces that provided a sense of peace and tranquility. The overall effect was one of beauty, efficiency, and sustainability.

The city was even more marvelous than the great walled city. The buildings were tall and slender, with intricate designs that seemed to defy gravity. As far as the eye could see, it was a massive city, similar in scope to New York City combined with all five boroughs.

Beneath the colossal tree canopy, a soft glow persisted, even during the night, casting its radiance upon the immaculate and meticulously paved streets. A subtle smile graced Gabriel's lips as he envisioned the impending chaos that autumn would inevitably bring upon the city. His imagination painted vivid scenes of leaves transforming their hues, the air assuming a crisp quality, and the inhabitants bustling about with an air of exhilaration. Gabriel recognized that autumn symbolized a period of transition, and he eagerly anticipated the opportunity to experience its essence – if he were granted the privilege of longevity.

As he reflected on Lesley, thoughts of autumn suddenly weighed heavily on his mind. It was her cherished time of year, and he recalled her delight in watching the falling leaves. Memories of her as a toddler, enthusiastically building piles of leaves and jumping in them, flooded his thoughts. It was her favorite season. With a deep breath, he shook his head and forced himself to focus on something else. He wasn't prepared to confront his overwhelming grief yet.

In a sudden movement, Amelia leaned against him. Gabriel lowered his gaze to meet her eyes, filled with a blend of grief and sorrow, yet still blessed by the radiant light of Sol. He gently wrapped his arm around her, and together, they began to emit a soft glow, emanating from within. A smile involuntarily spread across Gabriel's face as he embraced her.

"What are these fresh constructions?" Amelia abruptly inquired as her eyes fell upon the colossal teal statues and mounted guns adorning the expansive walls.

"They are a part of a new defensive strategy to keep the darkling out of the city." Viktor replied.

"Like the caves where people once took shelter." Gabriel reasoned.

"Indeed, our esteemed scientists have uncovered a remarkable breakthrough, granting us the ability to not only construct defensive structures but also transform them into formidable weapons." Viktor reaches into his pocket and delicately extracts a small, teal gemstone. "As we delve into the abundant life stones, the defensive strategies of our ancestors from the past have evolved into the potent weapons of the future for all of Terra."

With a genuine sense of pride and no malicious intent, Gabriel observed the prince as they approached the city walls. It was clear that the prince desired a bright future not only for his own clan, the Ascendant clan, but for the entire world. However, the skeptic within Gabriel harbored doubts about the prince's chosen path to achieve this vision.

"Demonstrate your worth and survive the impending moments," Viktor sneered. "We shall soon discover if you are a true reflection of your clan."

As Gabriel narrowed his gaze upon Viktor, his hands instinctively found their place on his sword. "What is the implication behind those words?" he inquired, his voice tense.

Amused, Viktor extended one hand, palm outward. "There is no necessity for violence," he replied with a grin. "Yet."

Panic surged through Gabriel's body, bringing with it an intense wave of nausea. Fortunately, the sensation soon subsided, but in its wake, he was left with a profound sense of vertigo and weakness. He could no longer stand and collapsed onto one knee, drained of all strength.

"You made it through the force field alive at least. Perhaps there is still hope for your redemption."

"I'm sorry to disappoint you."

"Warrior, I hold no grudge against you. In fact, I applaud the potential that you possess. Indeed, you are quite fortunate." Viktor said coldly. "It is possible that your sister may not be as fortunate as you. It seems that she, like the rest of your clan, has succumbed to corruption."

Gabriel managed a half-hearted smile as he uttered the words, "She's a survivor."

"Your sister is much more than a survivor. She is a destroyer. In a sudden and tragic event, the entire village of Moonbright was obliterated in the blink of an eye, resulting in the loss of every single life within its borders, including the innocent children who resided there."

Although a sense of relief washed over Gabriel upon learning Lesley had survived Sarum, the realization that she had succumbed to corruption gnawed at his mind, stirring foreboding and unsettling emotions. Gabriel was haunted by the chilling possibility that Lesley may have committed acts of genocide.

When he had last seen her, she had appeared utterly broken, and a deep-seated fear gripped him that their next encounter might reveal her beyond redemption. The weight of his heavy heart and gloomy outlook was compounded by the faint echoes of laughter that seemed to emanate from the surrounding darkness.

Interrupting him, Amelia retorted, "Enough torment, Viktor."

Viktor sneered, "Troublesome sisters. It seems we have something in common."

The sprawling streets, adorned with their ample width, teemed with well-attired individuals who emanated an aura of gentle warriorship. As Gabriel beheld the cityscape, he couldn't help but notice the presence of religious figures stemming from varied backgrounds. Among them were monks drawing inspiration from Tibetan, Shinto, and Christian traditions. While they shared certain similarities, they also possessed distinct characteristics that set them apart from the religions Gabriel had encountered on Earth.

They appear to be monks, priests, and clerics from different faiths coexist harmoniously, mingling throughout the city's bustling thoroughfares. However Gabriel has learned not to trust in his implicit biases and asks, "Does everyone worship Sol or are there different religions?"

"We all kneel to Sol, some in different ways than others." Amelia said. "Many of the religious temples are of the Druids and Shaman of Yggdrasil, Warriors and Priests of the Emerald Empire, Sand Empire and our own Paladins and Clerics of The Silver Wolves."

"It's incredible." In the heart of the city, a colossal, luminescent tree stood tall, serving as the centerpiece of this thriving community. Atop its expansive branches, a magnificent palace proudly rested. Gabriel marveled at the vast canopy that reached high into the sky, casting a majestic shadow over the city.

Despite the thin mist that hung in the air, the sun's rays illuminated everything with crystal clarity. Peace and prosperity permeated every corner of this remarkable city, filling Gabriel with an overwhelming sense of happiness and contentment. As he soared through the city, taking in its unique spectacles, he couldn't help but notice an electrifying energy that infused the very air.

Feeling invigorated and rejuvenated, Gabriel spread his arms wide, flexing and relaxing his muscles. He stood there, basking in the positive energy that enveloped him, filling him with optimistic hope for the future.

"What are you doing, you weirdo?" Amelia laughed, giving him a little nudge.

"There is something special here. It feels wonderful."

"It's the spirit of Sol you feel?"

With a prayerful gesture, Gabriel clasped his hands together and gently closed his eyes, his mind clouded with uncertainty. A pure white flame, an embodiment of his aura, enveloped him, dancing playfully around his body. The jubilant dance of the fire mirrored the profound joy and benediction that Gabriel experienced, evoking a tearful response. As the lingering echoes of laughter gradually dissipated into nothingness, a sense of tranquility and peace descended upon him, bringing a calming influence to his thoughts. "I feel his presence."

Gliding to a sudden halt, the ship lands smoothly yet abruptly. Exiting the vessel, they make their way to the palace. With a sudden jolt, Amelia loses her footing, only to be steadied by Gabriel.

The grand entrance boasts massive, ornate doors that creak open slowly, revealing an awe-inspiring sight. The passengers step inside, their eyes immediately drawn to the vast, domed ceiling. Intricate murals adorn the dome, depicting the rich history of the kingdom. The opulent interior features a plush carpet covering the floor, while exquisite tapestries adorn the walls. The air is thick with the heady fragrance of incense.

Under the watchful eyes of Kain and The Kingsguard, the passengers are guided through the palace in two parallel lines along the hallways. Meanwhile, Viktor, Amelia, and Gabriel make their way down the center. Gabriel experiences conflicting emotions of security and confinement simultaneously. They traverse a succession of magnificent halls, each surpassing the grandeur of the previous one. At long last, the throne room majestically stands before them.

"This is the palace, where I grew up." Amelia said. "Perhaps I can show you my chambers this time around." Amelia whispered in Gabriels ear.

"You might want to talk to Father before planning any romantic evenings." Viktor interrupted, pushing her forward and away from Gabriel, then walking past her.

"We should take Gabriel to the temple for further healing before meeting father."

"I feel fine." Gabriel touched his armor cover chest where Viktor had cut him.

"The rate that you heal is quite remarkable but not all wounds are physical. Sol, be praised."

"Unfortunately, neither of you has the freedom to move around independently. I understand that this is an unfamiliar sensation for you, sister, but it is something you will need to adjust to."

As they journey through the lavish silver palace, their footsteps resonating against the lustrous marble floors, the group is enveloped in an atmosphere of grandeur. The walls showcase an array of intricate tapestries that narrate the kingdom's storied history, while the expansive ceiling is supported by elegant marble pillars. The air carries a heady fragrance of incense, and the only discernible sound is the hushed murmuring of guards vigilantly stationed at the entrance to the throne room.

The large double-wide gates opened to a giant throne room. The room was massive, with high ceilings and walls made of smooth, polished stone. Light flooded through three large arch cathedral windows, which let in a soft glow from the sun and the great tree outside. In the center of the room was a raised platform, upon which sat a large, ornate throne.

King Marcus Ascendant of Sol sat on his throne, his silver hair flowing upward like a fiery halo, illuminating his stern expression. He does not move as the group enters the room, and his silence is deafening. He was notably older, relaxed and in control, but he radiated with power. He was dressed in a long, flowing robe, and his hands were clasped in his lap.

"So it is true. My daughter has come home." Marcus said his voice boomed in the throne room.

In a graceful motion, Amelia gently bends her body downward, expressing a gesture of respect and reverence. "Yes father, the last couple of days have been strange."

Marcus rubs his chin, his tone cold and dismissive. "And this is him, the knight from the Fenrir clan?"

Gabriel walks forward. Looking at the king reminded him of his own father. Their likeness is uncanny given that they must have been separated by countless generations. "I am Gabriel Wyndham."

"Wyndham? You don't carry the old name? The original name of your fallen clan has faded into the shadows, and its betrayal of Sol and the other four clans shall remain undisclosed, concealed in the depths of time. This is not the moment to dredge up bitter memories and remind them of their treachery during these desperate hours."

Amelia's budding protest is cut short by her father's interjection. "I know your intentions are honorable and true, despite your unconventional actions. You may not have the strength to rule, but you are still my daughter. There is value in that."

Without uttering a word, Viktor shot Amelia a contemptuous glare. His voice dripped with disdain as he declared, "Ultimately, you shall face the consequences of your actions. Your dishonorable behavior will be your undoing."

"Dishonorable conduct," Amelia echoed her brother's words which caused Viktor to jab her ribs.

"I should have killed you for being so weak." His laughter expressed through a sly, self-satisfied smirk.

"Put an end to your bickering, children," Marcus commanded, sensing the tension between his siblings escalating in their father's presence. Despite their occasional quarrels, at their core, they were merely children who held no genuine animosity towards each other.

"I'm sure you know of the Darklings reemergence across the country. We have gathered intelligence from all the kingdoms in the realm to know this is not a matter of our kingdom alone. Against great odds the monks, druids and clerics have ushered peace between the three great nations. The Shattered Swords of the Sand Empire and Emerald Empires both have agreed to sign peace treaties, and aid each other in combating the threat. The citizens of Yggdrasil continue to show us that serenity and peace are merits to strive for."

"Father, I know it's a long shot, but all I wish for is once more a chance to right my folly."

"You were given the chance to defend yourself months ago. You failed to do so. We need to be uniformed once and for all."

"That wasn't my fault I couldn't have known I'd be transported to another realm!"

"Outstanding circumstances and excuses are not withstanding. In order to secure the integrity of the rights of dueling there must not be exceptions."

"But father!"

"Enough!" the king bellowed. "Your desperation is unbecoming. We are not dogs fighting over scraps of meat. Only one of you can lead this nation after I am gone, and the time to decide has long since passed. Viktor will be king and will ascend when my time is over."

Marcus sighed. "So many things have changed in your absence. War with the Shatter Swords, an uneasy alliance with the Emerald Empire. The difference in your strengths is obvious."

"Father there is more to leading than strength."

"Do you take me for a fool?" Marcus asked. "Do you think we'd let anyone waltz in here and duel for the crown if they are stronger? Maybe from your perspective that's what it looks like. Let me explain further. We left the chaos of clans and bound the five most powerful clans together with law and order."

"Viktor had drawn power from the tithe to achieve his newfound strength. To use that as justification to deny me rectification is abysmal." Viktor's gaze narrowed in response, his eyes fixed on her with intensity.

In response, Marcus raised his hand to quiet Amelia and fixed his gaze upon her for a prolonged moment. "It was long after your duel and at my request."

"Tithe?" Gabriel notices the floor has a map of the kingdom engraved in it. Dinard, Great coastal city to the West, Sarum, Great Walled city to the South, Bremen The Great Frozen City to the North and in the center Lyndell where the Throne sits. At the heart of the Kingdom, a peculiar circle appeared. It bore a striking resemblance to the one Viktor had drawn as well as the circle he found in the garage where he discovered Lesley. This circle, in fact, was none other than the map of the Empire of Wolves.

"At your request? Then allow me the same treatment."

"No." Marcus growled angrily.

"What do you know? What has Sol shown you?"

"Sol exclusively presents me with pertinent information. Consequently, this matter is now concluded."

In the presence of King Marcus, a man clad in shimmering silver armor, donning a concealed black leather armor underneath, approaches with an air of nonchalance. He leans in to whisper something private in the king's ear, and then remains standing attentively until King Marcus dismisses him with a simple gesture. This enigmatic individual exudes a distinct aura of coldness.

Gabriel poses a hypothetical scenario: "What if I were to issue a challenge for a duel against you, with the crown as the prize?"

"While your ancestors may have had a legitimate claim to the throne once, you do not. You have no legal right to the throne, and you are not an eligible claimant as an outsider."

"I have some experience upholding the law where I am from."

"Then you understand my position as well. Take Gabriel Wyndham to the Holding Cells."

"Gabriel is an official knight, he has taken an oath to me, and I will not permit him to the holding cells."

"That is interesting. You aligned yourself to the Fallen house?"

"He has formally associated himself with House Ascendant and Sol. At the time, neither I nor he were cognizant of his lineage. If he is indeed an ancestor to the House of Fenrir, he has shown great fortitude in channeling the essence of Sol. I hereby entreat the throne to bestow upon him the title of Redeemed."

"I shall deliberate on your proposal." Marcus said. "In the interim, he shall be placed in the holding cells, but he may retain his armor. He will be honored, but monitored in the holding cells."

Chapter Twenty-Two

Lesley

Without arousing any suspicion, Lesley and Raven successfully joined the caravan. They proceeded at a sluggish pace, inching forward. The caravan, a motley collection of groups and civilians, stretched across the entire highway and continued to swell as more troops and civilians joined their ranks. It was evident that the people joining the caravan were entire towns and villages being escorted to Lyndell. The shortage of vehicles meant some people had to walk the road. Lesley couldn't help but think that this was the reason for their slow progress.

Impatience was beginning to fray Lesley's nerves. Though eager to maintain her momentum, she recognized that proceeding cautiously might be her best opportunity to enter the city without being discovered. Of course, that depended on whether anyone was searching for her.

"Does this thing have a radio? I really don't enjoy deafening silence." Lesley asked then suddenly looking out the window. "Did you hear that?"

"I didn't hear anything." In a desperate search for music, Raven switched on the radio, only to be met with unsettling broadcasts. Most stations were airing an urgent emergency alert, instructing all citizens to head toward the major cities. Surprisingly, a plea was extended to non-citizens, offering them an opportunity to enter the cities and submit to the crown's authority. This unexpected directive was portrayed as the ultimate solution for surviving the imminent threat posed by the emergence of the Darklings.

Raven flipped through the channels until they finally found a music station. They listened to half a song before it was interrupted by an emergency broadcast. "Civilians, please keep your radios on. Keep your personal devices close by. This is how we will communicate with you and provide instructions to make this transition as smooth as possible."

Engrossed in adjusting the controls, Lesley's ears perked up at the sound of a low, rumbling growl emanating from an unexpectedly close location. Casting her gaze outside once more, she was met with the same sight—a sea of unfamiliar faces.

While readjusting the radio, she inadvertently came across a concealed channel. To her astonishment, it was not a broadcasted message but an ongoing conversation between a group of knights. They were assigning duties and synchronizing their actions. "Whoa, ho, ho. I have a feeling this is no ordinary radio,"

Raven gave the console a wry smile, her expression carrying a hint of amusement. "Akisu sure has some fascinating gadgets. What is a BFG?"

While listening to the broadcast, Lesley and Raven learned of the princess's recapture alongside a mysterious knight rumored to be from another realm. They engaged in a conversation until they were instructed to stay tuned to the channel. Subsequently, Lesley intercepted information about several prisoners being held captive in a sizable truck.

"That has to be Gabriel right?" Lesley asked.

"The only other realm hopper I know is sitting right next to me."

"We need to get further up and find him. If he's locked up maybe he'll see reason."

Rising from her seat, Lesley resolutely headed towards the rear of the SUV. With a determined glint in her eyes, she meticulously combed through the stolen items that once belonged to Raven, intent on unearthing any concealed clues that could shed light on the mystery.

"What are you up to?" Raven inquired, his voice filled with curiosity and a hint of apprehension.

Placing all of the random weapons and items Raven had picked up into her bag, it began to swallow them up one by one, disappearing into its mysterious void. "Wow, this thing is amazing!" she exclaimed. Once she had cleared the mess, she tossed the bag aside and concentrated on her breathing, wanting to test the limits of her newfound extraordinary possession.

At the sudden intrusion of a piercing screech, Lesley sprang to her feet. The high-pitched sound reverberated within her ears, echoing in her mind. "OK, you had to have heard that right?"

"That, I heard." In a swift maneuver, Raven abruptly veered into the midst of a cluster of Darklings, causing their ebon colored blood to splatter across the windshield, resembling a trail of motor oil. With deliberate action, Raven gradually applies pressure on the brake pedal, decelerating the SUV until it comes to a complete standstill. "I'm sorry, are you OK?"

Amidst an array of weapons and armor, Lesley's form succumbed to gravity, tumbling over the stacked cubes. "I'm fine. But thanks."

In a sudden assault, Darklings, ominous creatures of the void, launched an attack on the unsuspecting caravan. The paladins, valiant warriors, valiantly fought against the shadowy assailants. The explosion that erupted from the creatures' midst was a devastating surprise, hurling travelers from their vehicles and leaving them sprawled on the ground.

The Darklings swarmed upon the caravan like a relentless storm, their sharp talons and teeth a formidable threat. Despite their brave efforts, the paladins were overwhelmed by the sheer number and ferocity of their opponents. Many succumbed to the onslaught, while the survivors strategized a desperate regrouping.

Amidst the chaos, Lesley navigated the treacherous terrain, her keen eyes scanning the surroundings for any sign of the prison vehicle. With determination burning in her gaze, she identified the heavily guarded truck and assessed the situation. She knew that liberating the captives was paramount, but her primary objective was to locate Gabriel, whose safety weighed heavily on her mind.

With the element of surprise on her side, Lesley engaged in stealthy combat, silently eliminating the guards and clearing a path toward the truck. Darklings and knights alike fell under her swift and precise strikes as she expertly weaved through the shadows. The clashing of swords and the occasional flash of lighting painted a vivid tapestry of her relentless pursuit.

Finally, she reached the truck, its doors secured with heavy locks. Lesley's nimble fingers made quick work of the mechanisms, and with a satisfying click, the doors swung open. Inside, she found a multitude of prisoners, their faces etched with both relief and despair. However, her heart sank as her eyes swept across the huddled figures.

"Gabriel! Are you in there!"

Through the open door, men, women, and children raced past Lesley,

their uncivilized leathers and furs flying. Unconcerned with their presence, Lesley's focus remained solely on locating Gabriel, whose absence was keenly felt.

A large man approached, causing Lesley to retreat. Meanwhile, James skillfully jumped from the prison vehicle, landing on his feet with a resounding thud.

"You look like him. The same crest of a one-eyed wolf surrounded by Ravens."

Lesley's eyes were filled with disdain as she glared at the large man before her. The idea that he would speak to her about some ridiculous family crest was offensive. She instinctively attempted to hide them with her hands. "You know Gabriel?"

"Gabriel is not among us. He did not find you in Sarum?"

Lesley's face scrunched in a mixture of curiosity and astonishment as she voiced her question, "Who are you?" The fact that everyone appeared to be familiar with Gabriel had left her rather surprised.

"Friends." James uttered, his tone devoid of ambiguity.

Lesley continued to stare at the giant and shook her head. "Are you simple?"

With a plea, Jennifer exclaimed, "Please forgive my husband." We were compelled to join the caravan, so thank you for your help. As she reclaimed her weapons from the vehicle's side storage, Jennifer briefly introduced herself.

"You brother saved my life, and now so have you." Jennifer smiled warmly.

"I wouldn't exactly say that." A surge of lightning crackled down Lesley's wrist, infusing her response with a touch of coldness. The thought of annihilating the group with a swift, electrifying strike crossed her mind. However, the presence of a small child among them halted her intentions. Her gaze softened, and the impending lightning dissipated into nothingness.

"You have our thanks regardless." Jennifer reassured her.

"We must take advantage and retrieve our things and head over the mountains." With a scowl etched across his face, James gazed into the distance. His nostrils flared as he inhaled deeply, as if attempting to discern the direction through scent alone.

Placing a comforting hand on James' shoulder, Jennifer uttered a gentle reminder. "Our chances of success are slim if the Darklings remain persistent in their pursuit," she cautioned softly.

In response to Lesley's suggestion, James emitted a grunt, which she interpreted as his tacit agreement. Meanwhile, Celise exited the vehicle, positioning herself behind James. With a fierce declaration of their impending retribution against the wolves, she unleashed fiery projectiles from her hands. With a gentle pat on Celise's head, Jennifer firmly told her to cease her actions.

With a raised eyebrow, Lesley dismissed the child's actions. "Are you implying that you aren't wolves?"

"On the contrary, we most certainly are not." James growls.

Despite her reservations, Lesley made a concerted effort to lower her guard as much as possible. She cautiously inquired, "Do you have any idea of his whereabouts?"

"Though we are acquainted with him, his current location remains unknown to us. Our last encounter with him occurred in Sarum before he entered the city," Jennifer replied.

Taking a deep breath, James exhaled with a sigh. "As a means of repaying our debt, we will join you," he declared.

Lesley scowled, her voice laced with disdain, "Your options are severely limited." The approaching horde of Darklings emitted a bone-chilling screech.

Amidst the swarm of Darklings that surrounded Jennifer and her family, James roared in defiance and charged at them. With each step, his strength increased, and his form became more ursine, his sharp claws tearing and ripping. However, he was overwhelmed. Seeing this, Jennifer and Celise rushed to his aid. Jennifer cast a light spell to enhance their strength. As they fought, James shouted, "Where are we going?"

"Follow me," Lesley said, gesturing for them to accompany her back to her SUV.

James hacked and slashed his way through the Darklings, while Celise ran behind him, shooting fire in every direction to keep his flanks covered. Her childlike maniacal laughter was unnerving, to say the least. Jennifer covered their rear with a Mace and shield infused with pure silver light. The three of them worked well together, and Lesley envied their teamwork. Even on her best days, she had never experienced that level of cooperation with anyone.

Lesley took the lead and tried to push the Darklings back by enacting the giant violet shield, but the darkling passed right through without being hindered at all.

"How can they pass right through my shield?"

Lesley called down a powerful lightning storm that struck down many creatures at once. The lightning rained down in terrible devastation. Darklings swarmed her, forcing her to draw her new dagger and summon the sword of lightning. She held the dagger in one hand and the runic crystal in the other. Lesley changed Electrons in the Gemstone and let it crash out lighting. In all directions. She drew the other dagger with her left hand. Doing her best to keep the creatures at bay.

The group fought their way through the Darklings until they reached a crack in reality. Darklings poured out of the crack, but Jennifer sealed it with Sol's light. However, the Darklings continued to swarm the group. "Keep moving!" Lesley yelled.

The SUV found the group before they found it. "Get in!" Raven yelled. "The wolves are pushing out to slay the Darklings, we need to make it to the city gates before they use the big guns!"

The group continued to fight as they got into the SUV. Jennifer and Celise got in first, followed by Lesley in the passenger seat.

"This better be what I think it is," Raven said as she found a weapon control and a cannon formed on the top of the SUV.

"I guess we know what the black market uses all that old armor for?" Lesley says.

James, cheered on by his companions, climbed on top of the SUV and used the guns to blast the Darklings. The weapons fired powerful energy blasts, incinerating the Darklings. Everyone who could shoot an energy projectile joined in the fight as the SUV sped towards the city.

Lesley pulled out an armor cube from her bag.

"What are you doing with that?"

"Hey Jennifer!"

Amidst her fierce battle against the Darklings, she uttered a resolute, "Yes?"

"You're not a Silverwolf right?"

"I already told you I am not."

As Lesley hurls the armor towards Jennifer, it miraculously molds itself around her, transforming into an epic chain mail over her pristine white gown. Jennifer's eyes widen in astonishment as the Darklings from the wing launch a relentless assault, their claws scraping against the metallic armor. Unfazed, Jennifer unleashes a series of chain blasts, taking down several of them. With a stern expression, she demands, "Give me a warning next time!"

Raven exclaimed, "Hey, that's mine!" in a commanding tone.

Celise couldn't contain her excitement as she jumped up and shouted, "Do me, do me!"

Simultaneously, Jennifer and James uttered in unison, "Don't give that to her!"

Lesley turned to Raven and, with a hint of exasperation, asked, "What's the worst that could happen?" She then handed Celise another armor cube, perfectly molded around her form, enhancing her fire blasts. With a grin, Lesley encouraged, "Burn, baby, burn!"

"Is she okay?" James inquired with concern.

Lesley responded enthusiastically, "She's incredible! And so adorable!"

The intensity of the fighting escalates significantly before subsiding. An opening appears, and numerous caravans head toward the city gates. The party valiantly protects the remaining vulnerable vehicles. Subsequently, a fleet of military vehicles and airships sweep through the area, clearing the path and sealing the rifts.

"Descend, big man!" Raven called out with amusement. "I'll neutralize the heavy artillery before The Silver Wolves catch on."

After the cannon's remnants dissipated, the seat underwent a remarkable transformation, morphing into a ladder. This ingenious mechanism facilitated James's descent to the SUV, providing a safe and convenient means of egress.

"They considered every detail," Raven remarked.

With the Darklings annihilated, a chilling realization emerged. The battlefield was a haunting sight, littered with the fallen bodies of both civilians and soldiers, victims of the merciless slaughter. In that somber moment, they recognized the sheer fortune that had spared them from the deadly clutches of the Darklings.

As the city gates swung open, the remaining people outside were ushered to safety within the walls. In a dramatic arrival, the caravan raced into the city, its elite guards and warriors from The Silver Wolves valiantly suppressing the spontaneous siege.

The final Darklings met their demise as they futilely hurled themselves against the city's impenetrable forcefield. Cannons unleashed their thunderous fury upon the endless hordes of creatures swarming the city, while the massive gates swung shut with a resounding thud.

A city-wide announcement played on everyone's personal devices, delivered by Jennifer. The message aimed to reassure the public, declaring that the darkling threat had been neutralized. It urged any injured individuals to seek medical attention and emphasized that the city remained secure. The cannons were efficiently destroying any potential rifts, ensuring the city's safety. The announcement concluded by urging citizens to remain vigilant and stay safe, as the situation was now under control.

Chapter Twenty-Three

Lesley

As Raven navigated the congested entryways, the sight before him was disheartening. The roads were littered with the wounded and dying, as medics rushed to provide aid to those they could amidst the chaos.

With her arms crossed over her chest, Lesley contemplated their next move as she sat in the SUV. "How are we going to gain entry into the palace?"

"I know of a way in." Jennifer says.

With a voice that carried a shade of doubt, James queried, expressing his uncertainty. "Are you positive that returning to the palace is your heart's desire?" Jennifer's response was a resolute shake of her head, her gaze narrowing in determination. In response, Lesley turned her attention to Jennifer, narrowing her eyes in a scrutinizing manner.

Jennifer places a hand on James' giant arm. "I was once of Priestss of Sol in Sarum. Most holy people are trained here in Lyndell inside the temple that is the base of the palace. There is a hidden elevator in the tree we can utilize to get to the top where the royalty is."

Raven drove through the crowded city while Jennifer attempted to recall the route. Pedestrians, cars, trucks, and people filled the streets. The city center was a walled-off kingdom, guarded by a pair of soldiers, separate from the rest of the city. Raven pulled over and peered out the window. "What's the best way in?" Raven asked, surveying the area.

"I am a cleric of Sol. They will let us enter if we wish to visit the Temple of Light."

"They might let you in but that's not to say they will let us all in." Raven countered. "It would be in our best interests to avoid possible conflict."

With a sly smirk, Lesley yearned for an explosive rampage through the temple, obliterating any Silverwolf who dared oppose her.

"Why wouldn't they let you in?"

"It's a feeling." Raven responded. "I see a potential spot to get over the wall, if you distract the guards we can get over."

"We don't have to do that, everyone is welcomed to the Temple of Sol."

"Yeah, let's take the front entrance." Lesley said crackling lighting and she clashed her fist into her palm.

"Subtlety will be our ticket in, and once we're inside, nothing will be able to stop us." Raven whispered with a smile. Raven always had something up his sleeve, Lesley noted with a furrowed brow.

As they came near the guards, Lesley grew uneasy, but to her surprise, they passed through the gates without a second glance. James, however, naturally drew attention to himself, but fortunately, it was nothing more than a mix of dirty and curious looks. They walked right through the front door of the giant cathedral.

The main temple of Sol is adorned with a mural of a being of light infused with blue and silver light, breaking the horizon over an uncultivated garden. The mural also depicts men and women hiding in dark caves, with teal stone carvings intertwined from the lands and into the being of light. The head priest of the temple, an older man of many years, greets them.

"Father Alexander Lancaster, it is so great to see you." Within a warm and comforting hug, Jennifer tenderly embraces the priest rocking back and forth.

"Oh my, sweet Sister Jennifer. You have grown so much. I'm glad to see you are well in such troublesome times."

Lesley released a breath through her nostrils and tapped her foot, her trust

Jennifer deteriorates with each passing moment. She looked around, shadowing shifting in the corner of her eyes. She interpreted it as a signal to remain vigilant, perceiving it as a message from Olivia.

"This was my mentor many years ago." Jennifer explained, smiling warmly at Lesley.

"What draws you back to Lyndell again?" His lips curled into a gentle smile as he uttered these words, his expression filled with warmth and kindness.

"We were on our journey to Snowfall Village but we were brought to Lyndell by force."

"Ah, yes, they are bringing people to the major cities. It's the Darklings, they have returned. We don't know how or why, but the great war is upon our people again."

"We were outside of the city when our caravan was attacked." In a swift motion, Celise reached for Jennifer's hand, and without a moment's hesitation, Jennifer effortlessly lifted her up.

Aware of Celise's watchful gaze, Lesley struggled to quell her unease, knowing that her actions mustn't harm Jenifer while she held her. Celise's suspicions were indeed valid. Having lost her own parents, Lesley felt an intense connection with the child, unable to bear inflicting upon her the same pain she had endured.

However, despite Lesley's genuine affection for the child, she recognized that her prolonged, unwavering gaze had become increasingly apparent.

"So you have seen them first hand, the Darklings seem to be appearing in waves. There have been at least a dozen in the last day. Each one is larger and more fierce than the last."

"That explains why the military was so prepared for them." James growled low.

"Rifts have been randomly appearing all over the realm. More and More and more frequently. I fear it's only a matter of time before we are huddling in caves again."

"But that's why they fortified the cities with the life stone?"

"Yes, it's known, and now proven to be effective at preventing the dark ones from crossing into its protective field." At the remark, a light of recognition spread across Raven's face, which prompted Lesley to wonder whether he possessed secret knowledge that they were unaware of.

In the heart of the sprawling city, shrouded in an aura of reverence, stood the Temple of Light. Its majestic architecture, adorned with intricate carvings and shimmering golden accents, reflected the profound significance it held within the Solarian faith.

As the acolytes and believers approached the temple, their steps grew lighter, their hearts filled with anticipation and devotion. The air itself seemed charged with an ethereal energy, emanating from the temple's hallowed walls. The Temple of Light was a place of solace, where the faithful could find refuge and rejuvenation in the presence of their divine patron. It made Lesley want to puke.

Within its grand chambers, adorned with vibrant murals depicting scenes from Sol's celestial journey, devotees gathered to offer prayers and supplications. The gentle glow of countless candles illuminated the sacred space, casting a warm and comforting light upon the faces of those gathered in worship. The scent of incense wafted through the air, creating an atmosphere of serenity and devotion.

At the heart of the temple stood an awe-inspiring statue of Sol, sculpted from pure white marble. The deity's radiant countenance exuded compassion and wisdom, while his outstretched arms seemed to embrace all who sought his divine light. Devotees would approach the statue, placing their hands upon its surface and offering silent prayers, seeking guidance and blessings from their revered deity.

In this sacred sanctuary, the teachings of the Solarian faith were imparted to eager disciples. Clerics and Paladins, clad in flowing robes, would gather their students in the temple's chambers, sharing the wisdom of Sol's divine revelations. Through stories, parables, and meditative practices, the teachings of life, love, and spiritual growth were passed down from generation to generation.

The Temple of Light was not merely a place of worship but also a center for healing and transformation. Those afflicted with physical or emotional ailments would come seeking solace and restoration. Within the temple's inner sanctum, healers and wise practitioners would employ ancient techniques and rituals, guiding the wounded souls on their journey toward wholeness.

As the sun's rays bathed the temple in a golden hue, the faithful would emerge from its sacred embrace, their hearts and minds aglow with renewed faith and purpose. The Temple of Life remained a beacon of hope and inspiration, a sanctuary where the divine light of Sol touched the lives of all who sought its embrace.

In that overly bright room, Lesley and Raven's presence was strikingly distinct, resembling a sliver of darkness. A deep sense of revulsion washed over Lesley as she stood before the Temple, an involuntary wave of disgust emanating from the depths of her being.

"This place brings back so many memories," As Jennifer twirled around, she marveled at the splendid view of the magnificent temple, taking in all of its grandeur.

With an uncaring cough, Lesley attempted to redirect Jennifer's focus. Meanwhile, Raven couldn't help but silently chuckle.

With an arched eyebrow, Jennifer inched closer to Father Lancaster. "I must utilize the secret passage leading into the palace," she murmured. James let out a grunt in response.

"Oh? Why?"

Despite Jennifer's growing agitation, Lesley maintained her composure and addressed the others. "We need to discreetly enter the palace. We are on a mission for the crown."

"We must not delay, the matter is urgent." With an air of gravity and urgency, Raven conveyed the significance of their entrance.

"A secret mission to the crown? I thought you were forced to come here because of the Darklings." With a furrowed brow and a thoughtful scratch to his chin, Father Lancaster focused his gaze on them.

"My friends here need to see Amelia." Jennifer insisted.

"Yes, of course, I understand." Father Lancaster, nodded.

"You do?" With a furrowed brow and whispered words, Lesley's thoughts swirled around Jennifer's connection to Amelia. The lingering question of whether Jennifer knew Amelia hung heavy in the air, sparking Lesley's suspicion. The fear of a potential trap gnawed at her, causing uneasiness to ripple through her being. In a hushed tone, she leaned in close to Raven and whispered her concerns. "Maybe we should find our own way."

"No, this is the way." Raven whispered back to her. "Trust me."

Lesley felt uncertain as Raven exhibited a declining sense of patience and precision, contrasting his usual demeanor. Taking a moment to closely scrutinize him, she turned to him with a perplexed expression. "Fine but if this goes sideways I'm going to kill that wolf loving woman."

"Wolf loving, He's a druid isn't he?" He uttered those words in a flat, expressionless tone while inclining his head slightly downward in her direction.

"Not him." With a contemptuous expression, Lesley sneered. "Besides, he's a bear."

Across Raven's lips, a sly smile emerged, spreading its mischievous charm. "How do you think Jennifer knows Amelia?"

Lesley offered a casual shrug, "I don't know."

"Come this way. This passageway is usually reserved for Royalty and the church." Father Lancaster announced, turning and walking through the cathedral. Within the temple, they discovered a concealed passage carved into the tree that led to the palace. Inside, a moderately sized room with a platform was illuminated by the tree's own light, creating a bright and vibrant atmosphere. Remarkably, a mechanized elevator was built within the tree, enhancing its functionality.

"Get on, this will take you to the temple inside the palace." Father Lancaster said.

At the platform, Raven and Lesley bid farewell to the rest of the group who chose to remain behind.

"Aren't you joining us?" Lesley asked, puzzled.

James replied, "We have our own journey to continue."

"Wait, you're already leaving for Snowfall? But isn't the city under lockdown?" With a questioning gaze, Raven gestured emphatically, one hand resting on his hip, the other extended into the air before him.

"Oh, right," James acknowledged.

With a scornful expression, Lesley assessed the man, convinced that his simple-minded nature was evident and impossible to conceal. She then surveyed the entire group with a cold, contemptuous gaze. seething with anger, Lesley's voice resonated with hostility as she confronted them, demanding an explanation for their actions. "What exactly are you all up to?" she inquired, her tone laced with accusation and impatience.

"It doesn't matter." Raven sported a knowing wink, exuding an air of wisdom. In an uncharacteristically incautious manner, Raven asserted his dominance by taking the lead. "We will be fine."

"I don't know what you mean?" Jennifer looked at her with a kind, yet confused expression. "Maybe we will meet again."

"Byebye!" Celise crys.

"Maybe?" With narrowed eyes, Lesley addressed the group, her gaze focused intently upon them. "Sus." The platform rose into the towering tree, ascending higher and higher until the group below became mere specks, lost from sight.

The area around her darkened. And in that darkness, a gray mist blew in and around her, until she was completely surrounded in a thick fog. In the blink of an eye Lesley was floating in a void space, then landed on hard ground. "What the hell? Did we make it?"

Lesley grabbed the smooth worry stone she was rubbing between her thumb and forefinger. The smooth edges of the object calmed her anxiety. Her lingering feelings of doubt drifted away from her mind. She felt more relaxed and focused.

She removed the glowing gemstone from her bag allowing its energy to illuminate the area around her. "Raven, where are you?"

Darkness surrounded her like a vast open field of nothing but she felt compelled to move in a certain direction. As she pushed through the vastness felt like it was shirking. She couldn't see anything but she felt the walls closing in on her shoulders. The pathway is growing more and more narrow by the moment. a narrow opening, she was blinded by a sudden flash of light.

The light faded, revealing a small room with six pillars that formed a walkway to a gated door. "Where am I now? This doesn't look like a temple of Sol." The first two pillars had two dimly glowing braziers, which emitted blue flames that radiated intense heat. As she walked down the pillared walkway, the next set of braziers erupted into flames, followed by the next, until she reached the steel black barred gate, which was flanked by two braziers of its own.

The wind blew gently and rhythmically through the metal bars, stirring her clothing and hair wildly. The door opened with a loud squeak, and she saw that her hand was clasped around the ornate engravings on the metal door handle. The airflow stopped, followed by another flash of warm light. In the distance, she could hear the faint sounds of the wind picking up as a sudden gust blew around her. Lesley covered her face as the wind pushed her backward, but it suddenly stopped as she encased herself in an illuminated violet shield.

The wind howled mercilessly against the shield, but Lesley inched forward. The next thing she felt was landing on a hard stone. Her vision returned as her eyes adjusted to her surroundings. She was startled but unharmed. As she heard a murmur in the darkness before her, shadowed light radiated coming from the gemstone. Startled, Lesley jumped to her feet. "Who's there?" she called out, but her question was met with deafening silence. She then heard someone whisper. "Raven? Olivia? Is that you?" she asked. Lesley forces open the door and walk into a small root filled room.

Amid the chaos of the trembling earth covered in dust and debris, a single ray of light pierced through the cracks in the ceiling. The faint glimmer illuminated the decayed remains of a human, bound tightly to a chair and entangled in a network of invasive roots. The corpse, beyond recognition, carried an eerie aura that chilled Lesley to the bone. Waves of dark energy radiated from the body, fueling the roots that ensnared it. Despite the advanced state of decay, Lesley detected a faint sound of breathing, a sign that the creature was barely clinging to life.

Two warm eyes suddenly opened and fixed their gaze on her. The corpse tried to get up tugging at its restraints weakly, whispering menacingly, "Free me." Energy clashes on Lesley violet shield-like aura. The ground began to tremble. "Closer." The voice said again.

Lesley was irresistibly drawn to the creature, despite her better judgment. She reached out her hand, and the clothes she wore melted out of the links of her armor, forming a thousand tiny hands that reached out with her.

The cloth of her clothing and tabard melded outwards, desperately trying to connect with the corpse.

A woman's silhouette appeared in the darkness, towering over the corpse. She looked up at Lesley with warm-colored eyes with snake-like irises. "Olivia?" In the darkness of her form stellar patterns emerged. Her bright stare flooded the room with light, causing Lesley to shield her eyes.

The light vanished before the pain, and she opened her eyes to find herself standing next to Raven, who was walking ahead of her. She was standing on the platform in a nearly identical room from their departure point. She assumed they had been teleported to another hidden room carved into the tree.

"Looks like we made it." Raven turned around to regard her. "What is it?"

"Yeah." Lesley looked around shaken. "Did you have any strange dreams when we were transported?"

"Yeah. I had a dream that you and I joined both mentally and physically and made sweet love in the starlit night for all eternity." Raven winked slyly.

"Not like that. Nevermind." With a flushed cheeks, Lesley sighed through her nose, lingering in her state of dejection. The hours she had been away, she believed would have been noticeable, but to her dismay, her absence was not acknowledged. "I was teleported to a different place."

"You seemed unusually quiet during the ride."

"Wait." Lesley carefully looked around the room, before her eyes went wide and she pulled at the fabric of her Black and Red Tabard. "What was that? Something moved."

With a smile, Amelia approached Lesley and exclaimed, "Oh, my! Look who graced us with their presence! You appear to be in excellent health and spirits, not to mention looking absolutely stunning." She conducted a thorough, doctor-like examination of Lesley, from head to toe, in a swift and practiced manner.

Lesley was utterly surprised by the suddenness of Amelia's approach, leaving her momentarily off guard. However, as the situation unfolded, Lesley's immediate reaction was to forcefully push Amelia away, recognizing the urgency of the moment.

"You have grown quite considerably." Amelia smiles. "I'm glad you are safe."

Thrilling currents surged through Lesley's very existence. The utterance, a simple, yet powerful "You," punctuated the air.

As Raven retrieved his daggers, a purring sound emanated from his throat. "All alone, are we?"

"How did you know we were here?" As the bolts of lightning coursed through her body, Lesley let out a soft sigh. Crackling and sparking, the electricity surged within her.

Arching her brow, Amelia addressed Shrek with a quizzical tone, "I heard you shriek, was that you trying to be stealthy?"

"She's working on it." Raven said with a laugh Lesley shooting him with a deadly glare.

"Jennifer warned you, didn't she?"

"Jennifer? I knew Jennifer once." Amelia's lips curled into a smile. "Ah, the mention of that name evokes a rush of cherished memories. It's been quite some time since we last had any kind of communication."

Lesley's suspicions were confirmed as she realized she had fallen into a treacherous trap. Her mind whirled with thoughts of betrayal as she grappled with the realization that Jennifer and her family had deceived her. Fuelled by a burning desire for vengeance, Lesley vowed that their paths would cross again, and this time, they would face the ultimate consequence, joining the ranks of the deceased.

"Where is Gabriel? Why aren't you with him?"

"He is in the holding cells." Amelia said, placing her hands on her hips.

"Of course he is. You people and your prisons." With a narrowing of her eyes, Lesley conveyed a sense of skepticism and determination.

"I assure you he is safe."

"I remember having that kind of reinsurance when Olivia was killed."

A look of bewilderment caused Amelia's face to contort into a puzzled expression. "Who?"

With an intensified aura, Lesley summoned crackles of lightning around her. Her eyes narrowed as she drew Lillyanna's dagger, channeling electricity through the blade, causing it to elongate.

"Marvelous." Amelia said in awe. "Gabriel is under my protection of course."

"So your people have taken you back?" Raven asks, circling around the Amelia side.

"Fortunately so." Amelia looks back to Lesley. "Who is your friend?"

Lesley's gaze was locked onto Amelia as she uttered the words, "Gabriel, please take me to him." She attempted to control her rising anger by taking deep breaths. Deep-rooted within her was an unwavering resolve to safeguard her brother's welfare, a commitment that transcended her initial perception.

"Let's take care of her now. It's an opportune moment." Raven said coldly.

"Take care of me? You two mean to kill me? I'm not too sure if Gabriel would survive should I perish. And I don't think he could forgive me if I killed you." Amelia smiles, "But then again he thinks you're dead already. Oh, how could I ever look him in the eyes again knowing I've killed his little sister the next time we make sweet love."

Lesley's eyes widened in astonishment, her head cocking to one side as her gaze sharpened. "Yeah. What?" she inquired, her voice tinged with curiosity and disbelief.

Raven shot a quick glance at Lesley before replying quietly, "There's a lot to unpack there."

Lesley breathed out deeply as the harsh lights grew brighter. "And the holding cells, where might they be?"

"I would have told you before the threats. I don't want to fight you and I won't allow you to kill me. It's in our best interests to get along. If I die, so does Gabriel."

"You wolves are really heartless." With narrowed eyes, Lesley's lighting lost its intensity as she found herself ensnared in a state of immobility. Having ventured forth with the sole purpose of eliminating Amelia, she now stood before her adversary, singularly, yet an inexplicable inability to act had taken hold of her.

With a narrowed gaze, Raven uttered his hushed words, despite their distance, Lesley heard him as if he was standing next to her. "She's bluffing. We should kill her now."

"I don't think we have much of a choice for the moment. I'm not going to gamble with Gabriel's life." Lesley whispered back, her gaze never wavering from Amelia.

"I understand your apprehension. However, I implore you to understand that you are fortunate to have encountered me, and not anyone else. Allow me to keep you safe."

"Keep us safe? That's a laugh. I really don't trust you to keep your word or even lift a finger to actually help. The only reason I'm not frying you to a crisp is because of Gabriel."

"Let's not be too hasty," Raven said, making sure Amelia could hear him. "There is no reason for us to fight."

"What are you doing?" Lesley whispered.

"Trust me, I have a plan." He whispered back.

"I fully agree." Amelia smiled, her tone being far brighter. "Follow me."

With a clenched jaw, Lesley felt drained from hearing the same repetitive statement. Despite the strong urge to retaliate, she knew that it was safer for Gabriel to avoid confrontation. "Stay vigilant," she whispered to Raven, who was trailing closely behind her. Reluctantly, Lesley followed Amelia.

"My father has agreed to grant Gabriel a knight hood should he pass a trail come dawn. He is to remain in the holding cells until dawn. Should someone go and rescue him prematurely he and his rescuers will be murdered."

"Though the message is well received, granting knighthoods to an outsider from beyond the great houses is an uncommon occurrence. What could have prompted them to honor him in such a way?" Raven inquired, expressing surprise at the decision.

"The cause behind their lineage can be attributed to the Fenrir house, which they belong to. Furthermore, they have genetic ties to the Silver Empire."

"That can't be true. You're lying. I am not a wolf!"

"No, you most certainly are not." Amelia's controlled facade wavered as venom laced her voice. "But you share our DNA, thus you can use the armor you have brazenly stolen on your escapade."

"Let's kill this bitch." In hushed tones, Lesley confided in Raven.

"You already know I'll follow your lead if that's what you really want. The threat upon Gabriel only halts my blade because of you."

Exhaling deeply, Lesley conveyed an air of exhaustion. Amelia's survival, fueled by rage, continued to haunt her. She chastised herself for missing the opportunity to eliminate Amelia when it was within her grasp. Now, despite his absence, Gabriel once again hindered her way forward.

Lesley's gaze shifted downward, fixating on Amelia's feet as they moved ahead of her. A vivid image formed in Lesley's mind—one where she set those feet ablaze, witnessing Amelia transform into an inferno. Lightning relentlessly struck her until nothing remained but a smoldering heap of ashes. Lesley released a soft breath through her nostrils, dispelling the imaginary scene. "We can't, not until we make sure Gabriel is safe."

Descending through the dimly lit corridors of the castle, the group's path was illuminated solely by the gentle glow of a nearby tree and a few strategically placed ceiling lamps. Amelia, taking charge, reached out and pushed open a concealed door, revealing the room beyond.

"You can rest here for the night. This was my handmaid's room, but it seems in my absence she has been given a new role."

Within the concealed chamber of the handmaiden, a world of lavish adornments unfolds, casting an aura of magnificent splendor. Rich fabrics drape elegantly from the walls, their sumptuous textures whispering secrets of bygone eras. Exquisite tapestries, adorned with intricate embroideries, depict tales of forgotten realms and heroic deeds. The air itself seems to shimmer with an ethereal glow, as if imbued with the essence of ancient enchantments. Gilded candelabras, adorned with flickering flames, cast a warm and inviting light, illuminating the chamber's opulent furnishings.

Despite her initial cynical reaction, Lesley couldn't deny the incredible beauty of the room. In fact, She found herself momentarily captivated by its charm, even entertaining the fleeting notion of making it her abode.

With a genuine-looking, warm smile, Raven uttered, "What a generous gesture." The authenticity of Raven's expression unsettled Lesley. "You had the same look on your face as well."

"You can join your brother in the morning if you wish to join the empire. You could become one of us as well."

Even though the room was opulent, there was an unsettling quality to it. Lesley scrutinized her surroundings and narrowed her gaze at Amelia. "Over my dead body."

"I surmised as much. Please stay the night at least. After Gabriel is knighted and formally blessed by Sol, we shall find something for you. Perhaps a small box in the middle of the ocean." Amelia slams the door shut and locks the door from the outside.

"I don't think these gems are real either." Raven tried to pick "Ah, an Illusion." Immediately, the room morphed into a compact holding cell, composed of silver metal and gray stone with no windows and tiny ventilation shafts. "We got tricked."

Lesley tries to conjure a glob of lighting, slamming it on the cold steel walls to no effect. "What the hell?!" She desperately tried to open the door and it didn't budge. The door melds into the wall and the door vanishes. "I knew we couldn't trust her!"

"We can't rule out that this is how she means to keep you safe." Raven shrugged, laying on the bed and tucking his hands behind his head.

"A small box in the middle of the ocean' did not sound like a threat to you?" Turning around, she assessed the room for vulnerabilities, her eyes narrowing as she did so. The only apparent weak spot was the air vents. She considered summoning a gale force, but hesitated, unsure if it would do anything more than simply circulate air through the vents.

"I always wanted to be a sea captain." With a carefree chuckle, he spoke. Lesley shot him a piercing glare, causing him to raise his hands in a gesture of surrender. "To clarify, I do not believe she holds any desire to harm you. It is possible that her previous statement expressing that sentiment was sincere."

"I guess we'll find out at dawn."

"We don't have to wait that long." Raven sniffed and rolled off the bed. Standing next to Lesley. With an irritated gaze fixed upon him, Lesley's arms crossed defensively across her chest, accompanied by an audible huff that expressed her annoyance. "Trusting me, as I advised, will now bear fruitful results. Our presence is undeniable, and no force can halt the inevitable outcome."

"How are we going to get out? Somehow we allowed ourselves to be imprisoned again."

"I believe that our runic gemstone is the answer."

Drawing the runic gemstone from her seemingly boundless bag, Lesley suddenly understood Raven's intentions. "We can use the gemstone to create a move through space and reappear in another location." A wicked grin stretched across her lips.

"Precisely. Reach out with your mind, think of where we will go next, find Gabriel."

Lesley felt as though she was reaching out with an unknown limb into the gem. It was a horrific feeling that she struggled to comprehend. It was as if her mind, body, and soul were intertwined in another plane of existence, one that was invisible to the naked eye. Suddenly, Gabriel appeared on the surface of the gemstone. He was alone in a holding cell.

"Remarkable!" she exclaimed, her voice tinged with excitement. As the unfamiliar sensation subsided, an inexplicable sense of expansion enveloped her being. It was as if she had transcended her mortal limitations, becoming an integral part of a greater, unseen force that continued to grow exponentially.

"Now bring us there."

Chapter Twenty-Four

Gabriel

The guards led Gabriel out of the throne room, down the halls. As he walked, he passed a tapestry depicting the kingdom being built around the great tree. The tree looked exactly the same, as if it had been frozen in time. About halfway down the hall, the mural changed to show the tree growing from the remains of an old battle. Gabriel assumed this was the Battle of the Darklings five thousand years ago, when the sapling was planted and blessed by the God Sol. The battle was Bloody, but the Darklings were defeated led by a warrior of light, with hair flowing like Shimmering blue fire that looks more like molten metal.

Gabriel was familiar with the tale of Cecil and the unnamed Void King, but this was the first time he had seen the Void King portrayed as a man with bird-like wings and a thousand shadowy hands. After the battle, the tree flourished, bathed in Sol's righteous light. The grand city of Lyndell developed alongside, atop, and around the towering tree. The tapestry served as a reflection of the city's growth and transformation over time. Upon further examination, it became evident that the tapestry was woven from a material resembling shifting grains of sand, which projected the images onto its surface.

A second, more intense stirring in his stomach since his arrival made him feel queasy. His skin became clammy and damp as he sensed an intangible force in the air attempting to draw his essence from him. Though subtle, the sensation was unmistakable.

"There it is once more," Father Lancaster stated plainly. Addressing the guards escorting Gabriel down the hallways, he commanded, "Halt!"

With a formal bow, Jennifer addressed Sir Gabriel. Celise, attempting to emulate her mother's actions, mirrored the gesture to the best of her ability.

Lancaster wrinkled his nose and inquired, "Oh, you know this knight?"

"Yes," Jennifer replied. "He saved my life when our home in Lightforge burned down."

"I see, I see," Father Lancaster responded, scratching his chin. "I am Father Lancaster, Head Cleric of Sol here in the temple." His gaze drifted away momentarily before returning to Gabriel.

"Father, we must take the prisoner to the Holding cells." The guard protested.

"Oh yes, I don't mean to interfere with your duty, Sir Charles, but this man has a look about him. Oh yes, where was I?"

James approaches them and sniffs the air, stepping in front of Jennifer and Celise. The guard reaches for their weapons and orders the big man to keep his distance.

"Don't worry Charles, they are with me. Jennifer is one of my apprentices, and this man is her husband. They mean no harm."

"Something about this tapestry feels very familiar. It's Story resonated with me."

"The story of Cecil, and his battle with the Void king. It's a classic tale. If it wasn't for Cecil, our world would have been lost to the void." Father Lancaster careful studies Gabriel Crest.

"I've always had a theory that he was transported rather than becoming the second Moon." Lancaster walks them back to the explosion that wipes away all the darkness. With a flourish, Father Lancaster brandishes a vine-entwined wooden wand, emanating a soft, ethereal glow. He gracefully wields the twig, tracing enigmatic patterns in the air above Gabriel.

"What are you doing?"

"Clearing the air." He continued waving the twig while walking around Gabriel.

"Through the masterful fusion of Sol's essence with the indomitable spirits of the wild, Jennifer and James have crafted a remarkable creation."

"According to the narrative, he possessed an exquisite countenance, complemented by rich, dark black hair. His striking appearance was further enhanced by piercing blue eyes and silvery irises that mirrored the phases of the moon. However, there was an underlying scent of the void that persistently lingered, a presence he grappled with until his cataclysmic act. This extraordinary event not only protected our realm from the encroaching darkness but also resulted in the creation of the second moon."

"I look like him?" Gabriel couldn't help but feel a swell of pride in Cecil's actions, a small smile tugging at the corners of his lips. Yet, the fleeting moment of contentment was abruptly shattered when Gabriel's thoughts turned to the tragic fates that befell Lord-Commander Cecil and his son. The realization that these two men were descendants of the same lineage as him struck him deeply, intensifying the impact of their loss.

"Look like him? No, no, I don't know. But you do smell like him. It is said he carried a power stench that was proof of his lingering corruption."

With Lancster persistently waving his wand, Gabriel observed a fragment of lifestone entwined among the tree roots. Confused by Lancster's earlier statement, Gabriel sniffed himself, attempting to comprehend the implied resemblance. He ran his hands down his body, trying to physically grasp his altered state.

"An imperceptible aroma, an aura only the tree of Lyndell can sense and eliminate, is present here. The key to keeping the void at bay has long been concealed within the mystical forces of Lifestone, wild spirits, Sol's energy, and the seedling Yggdrasil."

A palpable unease hung in the air, causing Gabriel to experience a sudden bout of nausea. His skin turned cold and clammy as he succumbed to the urge to vomit. A dark, viscous substance resembling soot erupted from his mouth, its texture akin to that of a starry night.

"Oh no. There it is, you have a void spirit in you. You must be purified."

Amidst the creation of a mysterious magic circle, Father Lancaster solemnly urged Jennifer and James to remain vigilant. Together, the duo combined their natural and divine magical abilities, bolstering the encasement's strength. During the darkest hour, Jennifer fervently sought solace from Sol. Within the sacred circle, Gabriel's viscous essence underwent a remarkable transformation, developing into fully-formed limbs and initiating a relentless assault.

The creature pounded forcefully against the circle's walls, emitting flashes of light as it struggled to break through. The dark, viscous residue emanating from Gabriel displayed extraordinary resilience and thickness.

The trio then reformed the ritual, successfully extracting and separating the creature from Gabriel. He expelled a greater quantity of the viscous substance, which emerged from his eyes, nose, ears, mouth, and even seeping from his pores. This substance coalesced into a humanoid man with warm, glowing eyes and a star-like pattern. As soon as it was separated from Gabriel, they promptly encased it in a separate magical cage, freeing Gabriel in the process.

Within the palace's dim illumination, the Void Knight's dark armor glinted menacingly. He relentlessly struck the encasement with wild abandon, accompanied by furious roars. Time and again, he raised his sword against the magical shield, his anger intensifying as the shield developed cracks and splintered.

As Gabriel leaped to his feet, his eyes expanded, and a newfound sense of lightness washed over him. It was as if the creature had always been a dormant aspect of his very being, deeply embedded within him throughout his entire life. There was an undeniable feeling of familiarity in the void knight's face, as if they shared a profound and ancient connection.

"This is the stench of Void." Father Lancaster says.

"What do we do now?" Jennifer asks.

"Now we kill it." James growled.

With a resounding shatter, the void knight annihilated the shield. Gripping his sword firmly, he prepared for the impending clash. The two valiant heroes charged forward, their paths converging in the heart of the room. The air crackled with deafening echoes of colliding steel.

Before the Void Knight could swing its massive, shadowed blade, James intercepted it. He gripped the lower part of the blade with his hands, which had transformed into burial claws, and roared fiercely. James pushed the giant blade back at the knight, but the void knight howled wildly and his strength grew exponentially, pushing the blade back towards James.

James's arms began to shake as he struggled to keep the blade from sliding forward into his flesh. He slid backwards on his heels. Jennifer leaped in with her mace raised high, but her arms were suddenly blocked by a radiant violet shield. With one swift movement, the void knight swung James into Jennifer, throwing them into the tapestry.

The void knight swung its massive two-handed weapon downward at Gabriel. Gabriel tried to block, but the mighty sword was blocked by a white shield around him. Jennifer had cast the shield around him, and then cast another enchantment to increase Gabriel's strength. Gabriel felt his flames grow in temperature, radiating holy flames around his form.

Gabriel charged forward, unleashing a flurry of attacks, each one leaving a trail of white flame in its wake. The two combatants clashed fiercely, their blades a blur of motion as they interwoven white and shadow flames. Gabriel prodded the knight defensives but was forced to retreat, barely able to keep up with his opponent's impossibly fast attacks. He dodged, blocked, and parried, all the while searching for an opening.

James and Jennifer form a circle around the knight, but the void knight's brute strength overpowers them. With each swing of its sword, it plows through them and summons a wave of darkness that pushes them closer together. With a swift strike, the knight's blade slices through another white shield, its edges scraping against the metal.

The guards formed up, but the void knight was too quick for them. He killed two of them in an instant, leaving Sir Charles with a pair of guards to fight with.

In unison, the guards fought back-to-back, each one protecting the other's blind spots. The void knight swung its sword, but the guards dodged its blows and landed their own. Gabriel sprang into action at the last second, blocking a killing blow and saving Charles' life. The two remaining guards lunged forward, their blades sinking deep into the knight's abdomen. The knight did not even flinch, its warm-colored eyes boring into Gabriel's soul.

"Magic infusion of wild and light. May be key to binding the unkillable."

James and Jennifer wasted no time in infusing the guards' weapons with magic, one with the light of sol and the other with the wild nature magic. The void knight roared in agony and blasted the three of them away with a surge of dark energy. James and Jennifer cast a spell, combining the two unexpected spells into one that bound the knight in place.

Gabriel drove his sword through the void knight's heart. The sword ignited with a ice-white flame, and the void knight screamed in agony as he burned from the inside out. Its screams turned into laughter as it stared into Gabriel's eyes and smiled.

With a surge of willpower, the knight began to radiate dark energy, breaking the binding spell. Suddenly, Celise leapt in placing her hands on Gabriel. His flames grew hotter, brighter burning and blasted the knight with a blast of Gabriel's radiant, ice-white flames. Gabriel's fiery ice-white aura stood in stark contrast to his vibrant blue eyes, which had transformed from their original brown hue. The void knight's body disintegrated into ash, which dissipated into nothingness.

"Yes, yes, my son. That is how you dispel darkness." Father Lancaster said, limping over to him. "You have raised a fine youngling in Celise."

Gabriel's eyes dropped and drifted to the left, then gradually moved to the right, his thoughts deeply engrossed in contemplation. The image of the void knight was forever etched into his memory—a haunting replica of his long-departed father. The weight of his father's death still burdened him. Despite the uncanny resemblance, Gabriel refused to believe this creature was his father; it was merely a deceptive illusion conjured by the void.

Gabriel's reverie was abruptly interrupted as James's large hand landed firmly on his shoulder, jolting him back to the present.

With wide eyes, Celise voiced her concern, "Are you okay?"

With a grateful pat on Celise's head, Gabriel expressed his gratitude. "Kiddo, I couldn't have done it without you," he said, acknowledging her contribution. Turning to the others, he extended his appreciation to the entire group. "I want to thank each and every one of you," Gabriel declared, recognizing the collective effort that had brought them success.

With a warm embrace, Jennifer greeted Gabriel. She expressed her relief and joy at seeing him safe.

Gabriel responded, attributing his safety to Jennifer's efforts.

Father Lancaster interjected, redirecting the gratitude towards Sol and the wild spirits. He bowed respectfully to James, who acknowledged with a grunt and a nod.

With a heavy sigh, Gabriel raised the Runic Sword to his face, observing the flames that danced along its edges before transforming back to a pristine white. He sheathed his sword and sighed once more, torn between relief and uncertainty. An ethereal lightness coursed through him, as though an immense burden had been lifted from his shoulders. His aura radiated with a brilliance and purity surpassing all prior experiences, yet he couldn't shake a subtle depletion of his spirit. Shifting uneasily, Gabriel voiced his doubt, "I'm not certain if it's truly vanquished."

"It's hard to say. Can one truly kill their inner demons?" Father Lancaster sighed.

"Is that what he was? A shadowed reflection of myself?"

"When it comes to the imagination of darkness, it could be anything. I know you hunger for answers, but I don't have them for you. It has been recently that I've come to realize the Truth of Lyndell."

Father raised the light-infused wooden wand of Lyndell. "This is a branch of the Great Tree of Lyndell. A fusion of Wild and Sol's magic. It drew the darkness out of you."

"Absolutely," Gabriel replied warmly, acknowledging the previous statement.

Father Lancaster, utterly captivated by the wand, repeatedly exclaimed his amazement. His gaze remained fixed on the wand as if he could not tear his eyes away from its captivating form.

After inspecting his hands, Gabriel extinguished the surrounding flames. With the darkness now expelled from his body, the world seemed much clearer. Gazing back at the tapestry, he comprehensively reviewed the complete story. From its beginning to its conclusion, Sol's presence permeated every part, even the void.

Amidst the ethereal glow of ice-white flames, a newfound sense of hope engulfed his being. A gentle smile tugged at the corners of his mouth as his thoughts wandered to Amelia. In that moment, he was reminded that not all scars originated from external injuries, some resided deep within the soul's secret chambers.

Jennifer grabbed Gabriel by the arm pulling him attention. "Before they take you away I have to let you know we encountered Lesley on the way here."

"She's alive, thank Sol." A sharp exhale escaped from his lips, giving him a fast sense of relief.

Jennifer shushes him and whispers. "The longer we were by her the more we realized that she carried a deep corruption within her. Far worse than what was found within you. We came up here to find her since we found an answer to her unique ailment."

Gabriel Clenched his jaw, but before he could respond A throng of guards appeared in the hall, surrounding the warriors.

Viktor emerged from the crowd, his sword drawn. He surveyed the room, his gaze lingering on James, then the two fallen guards. "What is the meaning of this?"

"A dark knight appeared and killed two of my men." Charles Suddenly grabbed Gabreil by the arm. "This Paladin and Father Lancasters compatriots fought and killed the void knight."

With a narrowed gaze, Viktor studied Gabriel. "What have you done?"

With a deep sigh, Gabriel revealed the truth. He bore within him a corruption that Father Lancaster and the others had worked to cleanse.

"I assure you my lord, he is thoroughly cleansed." Father Lancaster said with a nod.

Gabriel couldn't discern Viktor's thoughts as his expression remained an unyielding mask, concealing any emotions or intentions that lay beneath the surface. "Gabriel, King Marcus will present you with a Knight's Trial at the break of dawn. If you successfully complete it, you will receive Father Lancaster's blessings and be officially knighted into House Ascendant. However, failure will result in swift and certain death."

"Very well, I accept." He said, sure of himself and his path. He felt like a veil was lifted from his eyes, pure of his convictions.

"Your lack of agency in this situation is undeniable, captive." Viktor said with a wistful smile before turning to Charles. "It's essential to promptly escort Gabriel to the holding cells. Additionally, arrangements for the deceased must be made promptly."

Upon giving the command, Charles instructed the two surviving guards to take the fallen brothers to the infirmary. Meanwhile, he personally escorted Gabriel to the holding cells. Gabriel, with a meek nod, allowed Charles to lead him away. In his heart, he was resolute in his determination to prove his worth not only to Sol but to the entire kingdom of Silver Wolves. However, Gabriel was keenly aware that his path would be fraught with difficulties. He would have to muster all his strength and summon his courage to overcome the daunting challenges that awaited him.

When they were a safe distance away, Charles released his grip on Gabriel's arm and said, "Thank you for saving my life."

"I'm sure you would have done the same."

"I'm not sure I would have."

Chapter Twenty-Five

Gabriel

The wide-open door led them to the holding cells. It was a long row with a few open doorways, each barred with steel gates. Two guards stood facing the opposite wall. He watched them for a moment, then was escorted through the door. The holding cell was surprisingly pleasant, with a bed, a small toilet, and a sink with soap.

"Light's Blessing," Charles uttered as he closed the cell doors, leaving Gabriel behind.

Gabriel responded with a simple yet profound phrase, "Within his light." Each word was spoken not as a fitting reply but with genuine sincerity and deep-rooted meaning. Remarkably, even in his confinement, the words flowed effortlessly from his lips. Under the radiant sunlight, he experienced a sense of freedom, and his words resonated deeply with those who heard them, leaving a lasting impact.

Within the confines of his holding cell, Gabriel perched himself on the bunk, his gaze drawn to the resplendent glow of the twin moons illuminating the night sky through a diminutive, barred window. In light of his newly acquired knowledge about his fallen house, he couldn't resist the pull of a profound connection to Cecil the Redeemed. The notion stirred within him, contemplating the possibility that his own journey might lead him down a similar path of redemption and renewal.

Before him, in Gabriel's grip, rested the sheathed blade that had been passed down through countless generations of his lineage. It was a legacy, a connection to his ancestors, and the emotions it evoked within him were like nothing he had ever felt. It was akin to a fresh wound being reopened, still raw and painful. Each death he had witnessed, despite the numbness he had developed, now left him feeling vulnerable and weak. The deaths of Cecil and Lance, in particular, although necessary at the time, now weighed heavily on his conscience. Anxiety gripped his chest, prompting him to offer a prayer to Sol, seeking forgiveness.

In a surge of evident excitement, Lesley abruptly called out, "Gabriel!" Her piercing sapphire eyes bore signs of exhaustion, as if sleep had eluded her for several days.

"Lesley! You're really here!" Gabriel rose to his feet and reached through the bars to embrace her. They held each other close, and Gabriel could feel the stirrings of a dark storm brewing within her. Her body was abuzz with chaotic electricity.

"You knew?" she said, scrunching her face.

"In your absence, I struggled to comprehend the situation. However, a friend informed me of your presence. Upon seeing you, I noticed a decline in your well-being." Bearing unmistakable signs of exhaustion, Lesley displayed dark circles beneath her eyes.

"I'm more than well." She said with a mischievous grin. "Move back, I can blast this open."

"I have to stay here." Gabriel said without hesitation.

Lesley furrowed her brow, indicating her skepticism. With a determined expression, she summoned the ominous dark storm to her hand.

"In the morning, I must conquer a difficult challenge. After that, I will be honored with knighthood. We can create a new life for ourselves under the nurturing and favorable light of Sol."

"Are you buying into their bullshit?" Lesley clicked her teeth together. The lighting in her hand crackling and lashing outward into the bars.

"Lesley, your battle is over. You can finally rest. We can join our redeemed clan members in Sol's light."

Lesley squints at Gabriel, dismissing the energy ball with a dismissive wave of her hand. She then places her hands on her hips, adopting a challenging stance. "Our clan? Clan redeemed? Like Lance, Edward and Cecil?"

"It appears that they are descendants of Cecil as well."

"Screw them! We wouldn't be in this mess if it wasn't for them."

"Lesley, fighting will only make protecting you that much harder. Things have been strange in this new world but this could be the fresh start, filled with adventure, that we need. Being a Knight can't be that different from being a cop."

"Oh yeah I see you point, you both have shields. That's bullshit Gabriel. I'm not trying to move on and start over with these bastards. Look at you, look at where they put you. In prison."

"This is a formality, You don't know what you are talking about."

"It won't be long before they send someone down here to kill you. Like they did to Olivia."

Gabriel's guilt stirred within him, causing a heavy weight to settle in his chest. He shook his head in an attempt to dispel the negative emotions. "Lesley, I assure you that everything is going to be fine," he said, his voice steady and determined. "They wouldn't have left me armed if they intended to harm me."

"Of course they would. It's the thrill of the hunt. Wolves love to fight." She said through gritted teeth.

"So do you Lesley." he stated as he cocked his head forward, a frown forming on his face. Lesley's eyes widened in surprise, and she glanced at Raven before turning back to Gabriel, her eyes narrowing.

"Don't you dare try to turn this around on me. I'm nothing like them nor is this about me."

"It never is Lesley. Accountability has never been your strong suit. You summoned a storm and destroyed part of a major city. You then moved on to destroy an entire village of innocent people."

"Innocent?!" Lesley threw her hands in the air. "They lied and betrayed me, they were the enemy. They were wolves." She said, with exaggerated hand movements.

"They care for us in their own way. We should accept it. Let us follow the light of Sol and turn our backs on the darkness. The king will knight me. All I need to do is stay here and await their judgment."

"Do you even listen to yourself? You're indoctrinated." Lesley blinks and lets out a long, gusty breath, attempting to maintain her composure. "Gabriel. If you stay here you're going to die. You can either come with me or we will leave you here to your fate."

"Lesley, this is not indoctrination. Unless immediate action is taken, the impending darkness threatens to consume and obliterate our very existence." Gabriel extended his hands through the bars and grasped Lesley firmly by the shoulders.

In a swift and decisive motion, Lesley flung her arms outward, freeing herself from his grip. Raven arched an eyebrow, creased his brow, and folded his arms across his chest then watched Lesley with intense curiosity.

"I don't care about this world, its people, or what you think you say. We all saw some crazy things. The Silver Wolves are a stain on existence and they deserve to die." In a cold tone, her eyes transforming from a vivid blue to a steely gray hue, she spoke.

"Lesley, how could you say that? No one else has to die."

"Countless others must meet their end. I arrived here specifically to retrieve you. To spare you. Yet even you reject me. Once again."

"I'm not turning my back on you. I'm trying to keep you safe."

With an electrifying aura surrounding her, Lesley expressed her pent-up emotions. "I should have killed Amelia when I had the chance but I didn't want you to die."

"You were going to kill Amelia?" Gabriel gasped, his face a mask of abhorrence.

"Yeah, she used you as a deterrent. And it worked. But now I see you for who you really are: another wolf. You don't deserve that sword if you aren't willing to lift it. These monsters killed Olivia, Ripped us from our home. So, you wish to join them? Pretend you're one of them? Fucking pathetic!"

"No, Lesley, you are mistaken. I perceive the void's power enveloping you, cloaking the truth from your sight. The void that Cecil once rebelled against. Its influence now controls you, and I can witness the shadows encroaching upon you. Stay with me here. When morning arrives, we can embrace Sol's presence and initiate a fresh beginning."

With a sneer, Lesley twisted her face. "Very well, remain here and perish. Become the wolf you've always yearned to be. But if you dare to oppose me, I will not hesitate to act." Lesley let her words linger in the air.

Gabriel stared at Lesley in disbelief before reluctantly accepting her statement. "For you, I have sacrificed so much and have devoted myself to nurturing you into the woman you have become. However, for the first time, I fear that I have fallen short in this endeavor."

"I'm not going to dignify that with a response."

"I'm not going to give up on you."

With a firm jaw and focused gaze, Lesley reached into her bag. In one fluid motion, she tossed a vibrant teal worry stone toward Gabriel. As it landed in his hands, the stone emitted a brilliant light. "Meditate with it," Lesley instructed. "Perhaps it will help you find clarity, as it has for me."

"It's a worry stone," Lesley explained. "It will ease your tension before they come down here and try to kill you."

Gabriel rubbed the stone in his palm, feeling its familiar warmth spread through him. "This is a life stone," he said, recognizing its true nature. "There are natural caves made of this stone all around the world. They protect the world from Darklings."

In a welcoming manner, Raven approached Lesley with a kind smile and an affirmative nod. "Lesley, would you be so kind as to spare me a few moments of your valuable time?"

Lesley responded by taking a step back and crossing her arms across her chest. "He will not listen," she uttered in a tone of resignation.

With a gentle touch, Gabriel rolled the smooth stone between his fingers, allowing its calming energy to seep into his being. He took a deep breath through his nose, seeking solace in the act. His gaze shifted to Lesley, but her disinterest was palpable, offering no invitation for conversation. Undeterred, he redirected his attention to Raven, his voice tinged with curiosity. "Who are you?"

"I was like you once. Righteous and full of Justice."

"Is that so?" As curiosity piqued within him, Gabriel allowed the enigmatic individual to proceed with his narrative, eager to hear the mysterious words he had to offer.

"In this realm, I was once a celebrated warrior, blessed by Odin himself. My renown was great, but I won't dwell on the details. Suffice it to say, I was eventually betrayed by those who had pledged their loyalty to me."

With a furrowed brow and squinting eyes, Gabriel harbored a peculiar sense of where the narrative was headed. Yet, hesitant to make a premature leap, opting to ask a follow-up question. "In my culture, there is a saying that emphasizes the importance of paying attention to the minutiae, as the devil often resides in the details. Perhaps it would be beneficial for you to give them more consideration."

Raven smiles warmly keeping his tone cordial and friendly. "Lesley only wants to keep you safe. And there are only two things I know that will ease her mind. Kill you so you are not an obstacle."

With a distasteful gaze, Gabriel rested his hand on his sword's hilt as he regarded Raven. His attention shifted briefly to Lesley before returning to Raven. Before Gabriel could utter a word, Raven continued, acknowledging Gabriel's disapproval. He expressed his own dislike for the situation while emphasizing his fondness for Gabriel and Lesley. To resolve the matter, Raven proposed a solution, chuckling as he declared his intention to save Gabriel from his own actions.

"Save me from myself?" Gabriel echoed dully. "Is that some kind of joke?"

"It is, I feel like I heard this one from Amelia. It was when she told us that if she dies, so do you. Not in some abstract, philosophical sense, but as a practical and tangible act of self-preservation."

As Berenger's death weighed heavily on Gabriel's mind, he couldn't help but contemplate the circumstances surrounding his demise. Amelia's swift and ruthless decision to end his life once he had outlived his usefulness unsettled Gabriel.

Although Raven portrayed Amelia's actions as purely transactional, Gabriel believed there was more depth and strategic thinking behind her choices. He understood that Amelia had her unique way of navigating the world.

"Your eyes betray your doubts. The Void Kings' downfall was caused by the wolves' treachery, not darkness as they claim. The wolves will never keep agreements."

Gabriel's initial thrill dissipated as he turned his gaze from the sword back to Lesley, who was now surrounded by an unsettling, dark aura. The arrival of a man named Raven only served to heighten Gabriel's unease. Something about Raven's subtle presence reminded him of Akisu—an aura that seemed to demand trust and induce a profound sense of revulsion within him.

Gazing into Raven's eyes, he yearned for his words to illuminate Lesley's perspective as well. "They still chose darkness when they didn't have too. Being tested like that is exactly when they should have kept their faith in Sol."

"Indeed, the presence of choices is an undeniable truth. However, it's important to recognize that not all choices are created equal. Sometimes, the options available are inherently flawed, regardless of their alignment with light or darkness. Ultimately, both choices may prove unsatisfying, as neither truly cares about your well-being. Their only concern lies in securing what they desire. The choice I had was to become burned or freeze. So I chose the cold."

"That doesn't sound like a good argument, or even a choice. An excuse."

"It appears that we must agree to disagree on that point. I didn't expect you to become such a zealot of Sol in the little time you have been here in Terra. You think you see the whole picture but you are still in darkness."

"I can see fine."

"Your eyes were meant for darkness. When you see the truth, assuming you survive, I hope you will flock to me."

With a thoughtful gaze, Gabriel observed the intricate crest adorning his sword—a solitary, one-eyed wolf encircled by a circle of ravens. In that moment, the gravity of Raven's words and the significance of his decision weighed heavily upon him. "I didn't catch your name?"

"My friend calls me Raven."

"Do your Enemies call you Void King?"

"Cover your ears my dear." Lesley covered her ears with her hands, like a puppet. "I thought it might have been too risky to And one day they shall again?" Raven said with a coy laugh stepping back away from the holding cell. Talk to you directly, being an officer of the law." He said with a laugh.

"And here I thought Ravens were clever."

"Oh we are."

"Stay away from her." In a grand and theatrical gesture, he drew his sword from its sheath and forcefully swung it downward, causing it to strike the metal bars of his prison cell with a resounding clang.

"Careful now, the prisons here are something special." With a wave of his hands Lesley drops her hands to her sides.

"You're an idiot." Lesley says grimacing and letting her arms slide from her chest to her sides. "I hope you come to your senses before you join our parents."

As the pair turned the corner and disappeared into the shadows, Gabriel observed them with a growing sense of unease. Raven's words had instilled a deep conviction within him, unsettling his thoughts. Returning to his bed, Gabriel sat in contemplation, staring at the wall as he pondered Raven's revelations. To Berenger and the entire village of Stonewrath, their lives were deemed insignificant, mere sustenance for others.

However, unlike them, Gabriel possessed Sol's power coursing through his veins. Surely, they wouldn't simply discard such a valuable asset? With determination, Gabriel clenched the life stone tightly, summoning an intense flame. The radiant light of Sol filled him, casting an illuminating glow throughout the room. As Lesley had assured, his worries dissipated, replaced by a profound sense of euphoria.

Trapped within this predicament, he was rendered powerless to rescue his sister, regardless of his personal feelings on the matter. In the time being there was nothing to do but wait for morning.

Something rugged in his sense and his eyes went wide. He tossed his hand up and down in time to stop a garrote from slicing his throat. He groaned in pain, watching the garrote dig through his armor and into his hand. He flashed light from the life stone into his attacker's eyes, then he managed to flip his attacker over his shoulder.

"I'm surprised you noticed me." the assassin taunted with a hint of mockery.

Gabriel drew his runic sword, and the blade and his body were enveloped in a blazing aura of icey-white light. Gabriel and his opponent's blades clashed, the sound of metal ringing out through the air. Gabriel had the upper hand, parrying and countering with precision and force that the assassin could not match. Gabriel pressed his advantage, but he overextended and the assassin feinted and countered. The assassin struck Gabriel, knocking him to the ground. Gabriel's sword clattered away, and the assassin was on top of him pressing a dagger to his throat.

Gabriel felt the weight of his opponent pressing down on him, the dagger drawing closer to his throat. He pushed back with all his might, but his opponent was too strong. The dagger was being forced down. Gabriel knew he couldn't keep this up for much longer.

He still clutched the life stone in his hand. The stone began to glow, and a powerful force knocked the assassin backward into the far wall.

In a swift motion, Gabriel somersaulted backward, grasping his sword, and rose to his feet. However, his opponent wasted no time, charging toward him with a menacing swing of his own blade. Barely having a moment to react, Gabriel raised his sword, locking it against his adversaries and his together. The resounding echoes of their clashing steel reverberated through the air.

With every step back Gabriel took, the intensity of his light amplified exponentially. The assassin struggled to maintain his balance, completely overwhelmed by Gabriel's superior strength and speed. As his mask slipped off, the assassin's true identity was laid bare.

"You." As Lesley had warned, Gabriel spotted the man standing steadfastly beside the king. Realizing that his life was forfeit, Gabriel observed the assassin's unwavering grin as he continued his relentless assault. Gabriel understood the assassin's desperate resolve—he could neither retreat nor jeopardize his mission. Empathy for the man involuntarily welled up within Gabriel.

Seizing the opportunity presented by Gabriel's momentary lapse in defense, the assassin disarmed him. The runic sword soared through the air once more, leaving Gabriel defenseless with a knight's blade poised at his throat. "You don't have to do this," Gabriel pleaded, exerting all his strength to keep the blade at bay.

"Yes I do." With clenched teeth and an unyielding resolve, he steadily propelled the blade forward, inch by painstaking inch.

As the dagger neared its intended mark, Gabriel shoved his assailant off, propelling him backward with a blinding burst of light. Gasping for breath, Gabriel seized the fleeting opportunity. In one swift motion, he drew his sword and plunged it deep into the assassin's heart, ending the threat once and for all.

As Gabriel's breathing grew strained and the adrenaline waned, a new-found composure settled within him. Turning, he braced himself for Lesley, only to be confronted with an unanticipated sight. Standing before him was Amelia, her presence casting an unexpected presence.

"I see you've handled yourself well."

"So what's going on here? This guy was with your father and now he's trying to kill me?" Gabriel asked a ice-white humming on his body, reacting to his anger.

"Dorin, the king's left hand, is a tolerated warrior with no honor." She said eyes narrowed on the dead man.

"I'm assuming that is what I'd call an assassin."

"Indeed, Gabriel, he was an assassin. However, I have reason to suspect that a third party may be involved."

"A third party?" In a moment of thoughtful reflection, Gabriel accepted Raven's assertion of an inexplicable link to his identity. Holding the worry stone, his initial uncertainties gradually faded, replaced by a clarity that calmed his anxious mind. Steadily, he pushed back the encroaching darkness that threatened to cloud his thoughts and warp his judgment.

"Since your sister, along with an unscrupulous accomplice, confessed to wanting to end my life, I find it necessary to see how you are doing."

"So it's true? You used me to protect yourself?"

"Is it not for this that you have knights?"

Accepting his fate, Gabriel shrugged. The logic was sound, and his sense of duty as a Knight compelled him to protect his Queen with his life.

However, they had not reached their destination yet. "I thought I would only get that title if I passed your trails in the morning."

In a frigid vocal intonation, she offered him a reminder. "You did swear an Oath to me, remember?"

With a hint of skepticism, Gabriel arched an eyebrow in response, his smirk subtly revealing his doubts. Meanwhile, Amelia found the situation immensely amusing, unable to suppress her laughter. She covered her mouth and closed her eyes, heartily enjoying the moment. "Gabriel, you represent far more to me than a mere shield."

"Lesley was here and she told me that you would trade my life for yours."

A crease appeared on Amelia's forehead as she sheepishly admitted, "With a sense of trepidation, I must admit that I incarcerated Lesley and her companion in an unconventional holding cell situated multiple levels above the ground. Their successful evasion of this confinement leaves me thoroughly perplexed."

She flashed an uneasy, broad grin as she spoke. "Gabriel, I must clarify that I only informed her about the necessary actions to avert a fight. Their intention is to kill me, and I understand your desire to prevent harm coming to either of us."

"And you're not telling me what I want to hear now? Like you did with Berenger?"

"I can appreciate how you might draw parallels between the two situations, but I can assure you that they are not the same." Amelia extended her hand through the bars and caressed Gabriel's cheek. "I did not care about Berenger, but I do care about you. I'm not willing to dishonor this relationship with falsehood and deceit. It means too much to me." While speaking, she tenderly lowered her arm and massaged his arm with affection.

Determined to remain impartial, Gabriel allowed his gaze to meet hers, where a glimpse of honesty and truthfulness shone through her eyes. The scent and the familiar aura she exuded, a mesmerizing teal-like energy, reaffirmed her authenticity. As he held the pure life stone, his gaze delved deep into her soul, confirming the sincerity of her words.

"Now that that is clear, I have some really bad news for you."

Chapter Twenty-Six

Lesley

Within the labyrinthine corridors of the palaces, Lesley and Raven found a hidden sanctuary amidst the shadows. As the guard's footsteps echoed nearby, Lesley reached into her bag and retrieved the runic gemstone. Her eyes transfixed on the stone, she focused her thoughts, channeling her energy to discern Amelia's whereabouts. With each passing moment, her resolve to bring an end to Amelia's life intensified.

As the image cleared, Gabriel was revealed to be standing with the princess. Despite her mixed feelings, Lesley was relieved to find Gabriel alive. Although they spoke through the bars, their words were muffled and indistinct. Gabriel returned his sword to its sheath, and Lesley noticed a man's body lying on the floor. Realizing that Gabriel had been in danger, she felt gratitude for his survival.

With a hurl from Lesley's arm, the gemstone embarked on its trajectory. As it soared through the air, the ethereal image of Amelia and Gabriel locked in a loving embrace, dissolved into oblivion, obscured by the gemstone's inner mist. Lesley lowered herself, burying her face in her knees, as the gemstone hovered and returned to her.

"She's a monster, why can't he see that?" Feeling utterly perplexed, she found herself grappling with a sense of desperation.

"So let's finish this. Let's kill her."

Lesley lamented her missed opportunity with a sigh, expressing her awareness of the situation. She deeply regretted not taking advantage of the favorable situation when it was at her fingertips, recognizing that she had let a valuable chance slip away. "But they would have killed him."

"There is another way we can make sure he doesn't interfere." With an icy glare, Raven's gaze falls upon her. "Force him into the gemstone."

Lesley considered the proposal for a moment, but she was not keen on it. She didn't even like Gabriel in her room, so the idea of him being dropped into her pocket dimension was unappealing. "We don't know much about it. For all we know, we'd be dropping him into a swarm of monsters or spikes."

"He seems capable enough. I'm sure he'd survive."

"No, there are too many factors to consider," she said, gazing back into the stone. As Amelia and Gabriel indulged in a passionate kiss, Lesley's furrowed brow betrayed her discontent. Her thoughts, once again, were solely on the two of them. "She is doing this to piss me off. I know it."

Despite her longing to kill them both, a profound fear resided within her. She yearned to protect Gabriel from any potential harm. If Amelia's intention is to take Gabriel away from Lesley, then perhaps Lesley should reciprocate by doing the same thing. "We can make her pay by removing the heads of her family." she uttered her words, with a sinister grin.

"Lesley, we have others going after the rest of the royal family."

"I don't care!" With a resounding crackle of lightning, she retrieved the gemstone, summoning it back to her grasp. Lesley, her mind focused, extended her hyper-dimensional tendrils outward. In her quest to locate King Marcus, she closed her eyes and concentrated deeply. A vivid vision materialized before her—a silver-haired warrior engaged in an intense battle against a swarm of assassins. "Is this the guy?"

Raven curled his lip in disgust at the sight of the king, who was fending off the assassin. "Yes, that's King Marcus Ascendant," Raven said, narrowing his eyes. "It's clear we underestimated the old man."

"He looks incredibly powerful." In a flash of uncertainty, Lesley questioned her own capabilities.

"You currently possess the means to eliminate the king. With the guild's opportune attack, we have the chance to eliminate the king. Let's seize this moment to orchestrate his demise."

With determination in her eyes, Lesley extends her hand through the pulsating gemstone, causing a rift in space to open wide above the king. A portal forms, and a surge of dark lightning engulfs her as she descends from it. Her dramatic landing, accompanied by a thunderous explosion, sends shockwaves that push everyone back on their heels. Despite the force of the impact, the king remains steadfast, blocking her attack with unwavering resolve. In a swift move, Lesley leaps backward, unleashing bolts of lightning towards the king. With remarkable agility, he deflects and disperses the electrical assault, rendering her attack futile.

Marcus defensively raises his blade as he retorts, "An inflated number of assassins will not change the undeniable fact that your horde has already been defeated. Moreover, the arrival of two replacements for the fallen holds no significance."

As impending defeat loomed large, the weary assassins resorted to a bold and ingenious stratagem in a bid to outsmart the experienced ruler. Amidst the dramatic confrontation, furious bolts of lightning erupted from the ominous storm, relentlessly pummeling the king with unyielding force.

Raven and Lesley fought in tandem, pushing the king back from the assassins. Lesley fought from a distance, bombarding the king's defenses with lightning bolts. Raven weaved and dodged around the king, evading his attacks and striking back with her deadly blades. The king was powerful, but he was no match for the two assassins working together. They were relentless in their assault, driving the king back.

Marcus flooded the room with light, the radiance of Sol. He moved with impossible speed, slamming his shield into Raven and knocking him into the wall. Before Lesley could react, Marcus was on her, smashing through her dark shield. His sword cut through nothing but shadow.

Unsure of her abilities, Lesley used the gemstone to teleport a short distance. She then used the gemstone to forcibly take the strength of the guild members, filling herself with more strength. The guild members writhed in agony, but Lesley became far stronger.

As Marcus charged at her, Lesley defended herself using Lillyanna's dagger to parry his attacks. Behind her, the Runic Gemstones floated, gathering energy for a massive electrical blast. The king rushed her, knocking her back, creating an opportunity for Raven to swoop in and distract him. However, Lesley realized she still needed more practice to become a skilled fighter.

She notices the map on the marble floor, and feels the surge of energy flowing from it. She could feel the energy flowing through the Throne and into the king. Lesley came to realize that he had felt it the moment she entered the city. Lesley realized why they wanted all of their people to come into the cities. It wasn't to protect them but to leach their power from them.

Lesley teleported a short distance to the through and channeled the spiritual energy flowing within the pool. It was a sudden rush of energy. Her hair flowed upward and she levitated into the air propelled by the gale force.

"No, you don't know what you are doing!"

The king sprang and pushed Lesley away from the throne, severing her connection to the pool of power. Lesley was suddenly alight with lightning, her eyes glowing a deep thunderous blue. For the first time, the two fought evenly, Lesley fighting more like Raven, dual-wielding Lilltyanna's daggers. Her dark lightning clashed with Marcus' silver light. With a sudden surge of power, Marcus was knocked back, landing on the ground, groaning in pain.

Lesley lunges forward, both blades pointed downward, intent on killing her opponent. Viktor parries her attack with his bastard sword, stopping her in her tracks. He narrows his eyes at her. "You are quite strong."

"She has tapped into the tithe." Marcus says with labored breaths. "But something else is wrong, I feel weaker."

In a burst of radiant silver light, Viktor swung his bastard sword at Lesley. His swift movements proved difficult for Lesley to defend against, as most of his attacks bypassed her double daggers and struck her violet aura shield. The two engaged in a fierce exchange of blade and energy, neither one showing any signs of slowing down or weakening. Viktor struck Lesley with a powerful two-handed blow, forcing her to block with both daggers and her shield. The shield cracked under the force of the attack.

Lesley teleported backwards to create distance between herself and Viktor. She then unleashed a series of lightning strikes, but Viktor was able to navigate through them, taking a few hits.

Lesley attempted to draw power from the tithe pool, but Viktor fired a small blast, knocking her back. A moment later, he was on top of her, raining down strikes. In a flurry of teleportation, Lesley landed a dagger in Viktor's shoulder, which erupted in lightning. Viktor's arm went limp, and he began to breathe heavily.

Lesley assaulted Viktor with escalating might and velocity until she was beating him. She realized it wasn't her speed that was improving, but his speed that was decreasing. Viktors silver light dimmed, flickered and faded as he tried to defend himself with one hand. Taking full advantage Lesley fired a blast of electricity at the sending him socking back into the ground fell him to his knees.

Her strike to his abdomen was devastating. The lightning energy crackled through his body, and he fell to his knees. The blade slid back out, and the wound was partially cauterized, but blood spilled out freely.

"I told you little bird." Raven said, walking over to them with a slight limp. "You were magnificent."

"And you are a good thief." She replied with a cruel curled smile. "I suspect you had your hand in slowing them down." Raven smiled as equally cruel and winked.

King Marcus, his eyes widening in recognition, stared intently at Raven. A frigid expression settled upon Raven's face as her eyes narrowed, and she uttered the chilling words, "Your time has finally arrived."

Viktor shields his father with his body. "You have to kill me before you get to him."

"That's the plan." With remarkable power, Lesley conjures a tempestuous storm, contained within the expanse of her palm. "It's time for you to die."

In a valiant act of selflessness, Marcus channeled his remaining strength to confer newfound power upon Viktor. He positioned his hands on Viktor's back, shielding his son from harm. As Marcus's body transformed into shimmering silver particles of light, they intertwined with Viktor's aura, granting him an unprecedented surge of energy. "Your time is now, son. You need to ascend."

Marcus's intense glow temporarily blinded Lesley. When the light dissipated, only Viktor remained standing. His wounds had completely healed, and his silver hair cascaded around him like a luminous waterfall. A profound silver aura emanated from him, further enhancing his ethereal presence. "I have ascended at last!" He roared, "I am King." He narrowed his eyes and pointed his bastard sword at Lesley. "Now you die."

In a split second, Viktor pounced on Lesley, leaving her with little time to react. She valiantly defended herself, skillfully blocking the barrage of blows and bolts of light that he unleashed upon her. Her aura filtered most of the light, while Lillyanna's blades danced around desperately trying to keep the blows from landing. Lesley worked furiously to keep out of range of Viktors deadly bastard sword, making a series of short burst teleports.

Raven and Lesley once again assaulted Viktor, but this time, they were unable to get the upper hand. Viktor would not succumb to Raven's ability to steal his essence. The two danced around him like shadow and lighting, but they could not break through his guard.

Viktor was now faster and more powerful than either of them. Viktor broke through the violet shield, but before his blade could strike her flesh, he was knocked back. Viktor slid back on his heels, his momentum halted by a surge of energy.

"You don't know when to quit." Viktor said, his eyes narrowed.

Gabriel stood there equally lit a blaze with a pure white flame dancing around his body. "I'm not going to let you kill her."

Their auras were so bright Lesley had to squint to see what was going on. She had mixed feelings about Gabriel's sudden appearance. She was glad he came to help her fight.

Gabriel and Viktor blades clash, the sounds ringing throughout the throne room. Viktor's deep silver light mixes and blends with Gabriel's fiery white flames. The pair grew brighter and brighter, pushing each other to the brink.

Raven joined the fray, landing a double stab on Viktor's shoulder and forearm. Viktor howled in pain but swirled around, tossing Raven away. Seeing an opening, With a swift motion, Lesley lunged forward, aiming her blade at Viktor's chest. However, her attack was abruptly halted before reaching its target as Gabriel intervened, firmly grasping her arm to prevent any harm.

Lesley and Gabriel fought side by side, forcing Viktor onto the defensive. Their blades and auras worked in concert, flowing in a great circular motion.

Viktor continued his attack, undeterred. Gabriel stood between them again, creating openings for Lesley to finish Viktor off. But each time, Gabriel denied her.

In a moment of mounting frustration, Lesley directed a concentrated ball of lightning toward Viktor. However, Gabriel intervened, positioning himself between the two individuals. With a skillful display of power, Gabriel successfully dissipated the energy, causing it to harmlessly dissipate into nothingness. "Who's side are you on?!" Lesley yelled furiously. Thunder cracking with every word.

Viktor ceased his attack and taunted. "You'll have to kill me to save that witch."

With his arms outstretched, Gabriel firmly declared, "There is no need for further loss of life." He intervened, signaling to both parties to cease their conflict.

"No, that's where you are wrong." Lesley's fury manifested as a great storm, destroying parts of the building and throne. Lightning crashed, setting the great tree of Lyndell ablaze. "They all have to die!" The tree lighting ignites a ring of fire, setting the skyline ablaze with smoke blocking out the light covering the entire city in darkness.

Viktor renewed his assault on Lesley and unleashed a bolt of silver light. Gabriel stepped in front of her, dissipating the energy around him. Viktor continued to fire bolt after bolt, but Gabriel negated them all until he was within striking distance. The two duelists clashed swords again, sending waves of light with each strike.

Lesley grew frustrated tapping into the tithe again. She summed a sphere of lighting large enough to destroy the ceiling, The roof and stone pillars crumbled and were swept away in the increasing wind. With a downward wave of her hand she struck them both with lightning knocking them backward and convulse on the ruined marble floor. Across the floor, Gabriel's runic bastard sword slid to a halt before the throne.

Descending gracefully, Lesley collected it. "You don't deserve this sword!" She roared. With her open hand she summoned the sheath of the sword and little black hands reached out and attached it to her belt.

With the sword in hand Lesley could feel something darker lingering inside the blade. The runes lit up in deep colors of green, blue and red. Her eyes shifted from the deep thunderous blue to a deep warm light. She narrowed her eyes, tapping into the Tithe again. "It's time for all the wolves to die."

Chapter Twenty-Seven

Gabriel

Within the raging storm, Lyndell's tree burned intensely. Lesley, having absorbed strength for the tithe, could feel its energy stretching and sapping from the great cities. Even Gabriel sensed his own power pulsating away.

Seizing the opportunity of Gabriel's unarmed state, Viktor swung his sword relentlessly. However, each blow landed harmlessly against the teal aura emanating from the life stone around Gabriel's neck.

In a sudden flash of light, Gabriel experienced a vision of Sol communicating with him through the life stone. His eyes widened, and a pure white light radiated from them. The life stone pulsed outward, enveloping Gabriel in a protective field. From his hands emerged a sword of light, engulfed in his pure flames.

"What? The stone? How are you using it like that?"

In the midst of Gabriel's ongoing battle, the stone in his grasp undergoes a remarkable transformation. It morphs into a resplendent blade, composed entirely of pure light, amplifying his combat abilities. As time elapsed, Gabriel's prowess surpassed that of Viktors, with his strength and agility reaching unprecedented heights. Gabriel's speed outpaced his opponent, leaving Viktor struggling to keep up.

"How is this possible? I am the ascendant king!"

Amidst the chaotic storm, Gabriel and Darkwind engage in a fierce clash as the building around them erupts. Stone debris splinters and crashes, while their engines collide and swords ring, echoing through the maelstrom. Lesley, harnessing more power from the tithe, maneuvers amid the lightning strikes.

During their sword clash, Gabriel utilized the Life Stone's power to unleash a powerful, concussive blast of light. The blinding radiance disarmed Viktor and knocked him onto his back, leaving him defenseless. Before Viktor could recover, Gabriel positioned the sharp edge of his sword against Viktor's throat.

In a commanding tone, Viktor exhales heavily as he issues the order, "Do it!" The silver flamed crowing reverberates with an overwhelming sense of authority.

"Your people need their king." Gabriel said, his eyes full of empathy. "No one else has to die." He said, offering his hand to Viktor. "Besides, I'm still willing to bet your sister still wants her little brother."

Viktor's eyes dilated in shock, yet he swatted Gabriel's hand away, deftly rolling backward to his feet. "What the hell do you know?"

Fractures in reality manifested all around them, accompanied by the eerie crackling and buzzing of Darklings beyond the tears in space. These malevolent creatures eagerly awaited the opportunity to surge forth and invade their realm.

The tears in reality grew ever larger, unleashing an endless tide of Darklings. Gabriel and Viktor were forced to fight back to back, struggling to hold their own against the endless horde. Gabriel channeled the light of Sol, sealing as many rifts as he could, but for every one he closed, two more would tear open. The largest tears unleashed hulking goliaths, and the tide of darkness threatened to overwhelm them.

With unwavering determination, Gabriel and Viktor fought side by side, their weapons of choice contrasting starkly. Gabriel wielded a gleaming sword of light, expertly slicing through the ranks of approaching Darklings. Meanwhile, unleashed powerful blasts of silver energy and deadly strikes with his bastard sword, effortlessly knocking back groups of their adversaries. United they stood, their backs to each other, refusing to yield or falter in the face of adversity.

In the face of escalating adversity, Gabriel and Viktor found themselves pushed to their limits. As the tears in reality expanded and the onslaught of Darklings intensified, their determination remained unwavering. United in their purpose, they refused to surrender. Their relentless fight was driven by an unyielding commitment to protect the world from the encroaching darkness.

As the Darklings, one by one, succumbed to their fate, their bodies disintegrated into ashen remains at their feet. Undeterred by the insignificant size of their adversaries, the two warriors continued their relentless battle. The clash of their steel weapons and energy against the Darklings' shadowy void energy reverberated through the air. Gradually, the vibrant colors of the surroundings drained away, transforming the world into a grayscale landscape. Exertion took its toll as their breath came in ragged gasps, salty sweat stinging their eyes.

"I didn't think they were going to be how I died." Viktor grumbled in between breaths.

"I'm sorry." Gabriel said. "I couldn't do more."

Amidst the clash of steel and the echoes of laughter, Viktor's blade danced with deadly precision, slaying each challenger who dared to cross his path. Suddenly, a hulking monstrosity tore through the fabric of reality, charging straight towards them. Gabriel's eyes widened in alarm, yet he raised his own weapon to meet the impending assault.

As James landed in its path, he let out a ferocious roar, invoking the blessing of Artaois and Artio. He called upon their strength to protect them. His body underwent a remarkable transformation, becoming more beast-like than human. His furry form, adorned with wild paws that ripped and claimed, exuded a primal energy.

In a daring move, James intercepted the beast as it tore through the rift, proving himself to be an equal match. With a fierce roar, he valiantly hurled the beast back into the rift. Following his lead, Jennifer cast a powerful spell to seal it, ensuring its containment. With fiery cheers, Celise unleashed streams of flames from her hands, invoking the wild gods to join the battle. Sir Charles and his guards run through, his two knights still wielding the Light and Wild magic sword, entwining their magics to bind and slaying Darklings.

Jennifer evokes her own magic drawing upon the living flames of Loki and the radiant power of Sol. Further augmenting Celises flames. Together, they conjured an immense wave of fire that swept across the battlefield, annihilating most of the endless horde of small Darklings. Only the larger creatures remained, awaiting their fate at the hands of the remaining forces.

Amelia and Father Lancaster joined forces with additional paladins and clerics. Father Lancaster channeling magic through the Wand of Lyndell. They charged through the throne room, swinging their enchanted weapons wildly. They ripped through the Darklings and sealed more rifts. Briefly, the expanse revealed in the radiance of Sol, but the encroaching darkness, a relentless force, tore through the fabric of reality, extending its shadowy dominion.

Despite their effort they fought a losing battle against the endless horde of Darklings pouring through the rifts. Illuminated by the holy light, Lesley is seen floating above them, her clothing blending into the darkness like living shadows. Her eyes glow with a warm light.

"Eliminate her at once!" Viktor commands, surrounded by his loyal soldiers. In unison, they launch a relentless assault of energy blasts at the violet shield that shields her, but the shield deflects the attacks with ease.

With his radiant sword lowered, Gabriel's posture and expression exuded a sense of dejected sorrow. His unwavering gaze remained transfixed on Lesley, who stood at the epicenter of attention. She was illuminated amidst the clashing lightning and the ethereal violet shield that enveloped her.

In a swift and unexpected move, Lesley plunged into the midst of the wolves, unleashing her fury upon any within striking distance. However, her assault was met with resistance as her blade clashed against Gabriel's radiant sword of light, the two weapons entwined in a mesmerizing display of opposing forces. Light and darkness swirled in a captivating dance, devouring each other in their blessed collision. The clash resonated with crackling lightning, electrifying the atmosphere with its intensity.

"Why are you protecting them?!" In the resounding chambers of the throne room, Lesley's piercing shriek echoed, causing the air to tremble with its intensity.

In a surge of conflicting energies, Lesley unleashes a torrent of lightning, knocking Gabriel off his feet and into Amelia's arms. With a determined glint in her warm-hued eyes, Lesley lunges at Amelia, initiating a fierce confrontation. Side by side, Amelia and Gabriel valiantly defend themselves, struggling to repel Lesley's relentless assault. The tension escalates as the runic sword crackles with the reverberations of Lesley's thunderous strikes and electricity.

In a swift motion, Gabriel swung his sword towards Lesley, to be met with her deft parry and subsequent twirl. Lesley unleashed two daggers, catching Gabriel by surprise. The daggers shimmered in and out of existence, passing through him and finding their mark in Amelia's chest.

Amelia collapsed to her knees, tears streaming down her face as blood gushed from her wound and mouth. In a final, devastating blow, the daggers exploded in a burst of dark energy, taking Amelia's life along with them. The light faded from her eyes, and she slumped lifelessly to the ground.

Witnessing this tragedy, Viktor's eyes widened as he felt a surge of power coursing through him. With newfound determination, he lunged at Lesley. However, Lesley proved to be a formidable opponent, effortlessly dodging and parrying his wild attacks. She pushed him away from Gabriel, utilizing her violet shield to repel him further. Lesley takes to the air and lets out a dark and mocking laugh, reveling in her temporary advantage.

Drawing power from the tithe, more tears open, flooding the room with shadowed winged beasts. Circle around the warriors, dive bombing clerics and knights, ripping through them. Archers line up to take the beasts down, one by one they fall. But an endless supply of supplies flooded the room.

As Gabriel's sword of light clashed against Lesley's violet shield, its luminescent blade cracked the magical barrier. In the midst of a relentless onslaught by savage Darklings, Gabriel became entangled in a brutal battle. Dark, sharp claws and gnashing teeth tore viciously at his flesh as the Darklings attempted to dismember him.

Uniting with Viktor, they fought in perfect harmony. Their auras radiated a brilliant symphony of white and silver, forming an unbreakable bond. Together, they stood as a formidable force, unwavering against the relentless tide of darkness that sought to engulf them.

As Gabriel pivoted and sprang forth to renew his assault on Lesley, he was abruptly intercepted by Raven. The two engaged in a fierce clash, their bodies crashing heavily onto the marble floor, causing it to fracture. Raven rose to his feet, his magnificent wings of pure shadow unfurling, his piercing warm-hued eyes narrowing intently. His dual daggers radiated with an aura of dark magic, swirling and crackling with ominous power.

Gabriel stood up and swung his sword at the air in front of him. Raven stepped back to avoid the blow. Gabriel swung again, and their swords locked together as they clashed. They stared at each other, and Gabriel said, "You do have wings."

Raven said with a coy smile, "It's been a long time since I've felt them. We are so close now."

Raven's dagger extended in dark energy, stabbing Gabriel in the shoulders. Gabriel stepped back, the blades grazing his skin. Raven's daggers were more like a pair of scimitars, spinning and whirling, pushing Gabriel back. Raven shanked and extended the blades at will, poking and prodding Gabriel's defenses faster than he could block or parry. Each hit grazed and poked shallowly, a death by a thousand cuts.

Gabriel stepped backward to move out of the blades range, Raven mirrored his movement and added a spin with flare firing a dark bolt from a shadowed bow. Gabriel reacted by summoning his shield out of his arming, blocking the bolt, and pushing him backwards on his heel. Bolt after bolt landed on his defenses breaking and chipping away the shield until it was left half broken.

Gabriel reached out with his hand and the next bolt vanished into energy between his fingers. Gabriel moved forward trying to get back into range. Dissipating bolt after bolt until he was back in melee ranges. Gabriel sword of light in a flurry of blows, Raven returns to his daggers and scimitar combo spins and puts his blades to slam downward hard with a giant two handed sword of pure darkness.

Gabriel was forced to block the dark and light blades swirling against each other, both trying to consume the other. Gabriel gasped as he struggled to push the blade back. He filled the blade of light with more energy, causing it to grow larger and brighter. With a powerful blast, he blew Raven away. Raven hovered in the air for a moment before gliding back down to the floor unharmed.

Raven whistled, summoning a swarm of winged Darklings. They descended upon Gabriel, slashing and glowing as they dove-bombed him. Gabriel burned brighter as Jennifer cast an enchantment of holy light around him, creating an aura of radiant power that dealt damage to anything in its vicinity.

Celise further empowered the aura with her wild flames magic, extending its range and potency. With his flaming sword and aura, Gabriel tore through the winged beasts, slashing his two-handed sword across Raven's chest. A lingering radiant flame slash remained on Raven's armor as he vanished back into the shadows.

Lesley tore a hole in the fabric of space, revealing a circle of runic stones and new waves of Darklings and Void knights from more tears in reality.

Viktor rallied the troops, meeting the knights head on. His movements were like a vivid blur slicing through Darklings and void knights alike. He dodged and weaved through the enemy's attacks, his blade a blur of silver. With every swing, he cut down another foe. The Darklings and void knights were no match for his speed and skill.

Viktor's allies fought bravely alongside him, but they were outnumbered and outmatched. The tide of battle was turning against them. When it seemed like all hope was lost, Viktor unleashed a powerful attack. He channeled all of his energy into a single strike, and with a roar, he swung his blade. The attack cleaved through the enemy ranks, cutting down dozens of Darklings and void knights in a single blow.

Amelia lay on the ground, her face streaked with tears. Blood flowed freely from her mouth as she struggled to breathe. Gabriel rushed to her side, his ice-white aura merging with her teal one as he wrapped his fingers around hers.

"Fight on, Gabriel. I'm not dead yet." She said with a smile, a battle Medic rushed to her side. Gabriel recognizes her from the battle in Lightforge village. Lisa's deep teal healing aura surrounds Amelia in its light.

"That vile darkling attempted to murder my family, to extinguish us." Viktor bellowed, his silver radiance flaring balefully. "I will destroy her." Lesley deflected his strikes with her violet shield, and retaliated with her runic sword of darkness. Their weapons' silver and abyssal energies collided, sparking and flickering. The two combatants fought with such force that it appeared they could topple mountains.

Viktor unleashed a blast of silver energy that struck Lesley's shield. She walked forward through it, unfazed. She dashed forward, unleashing a flurry of dark attacks. Lightning clashed, and Viktor's sword flew from his hand. Lesley pierced Viktor's chest. Her warm-colored eyes narrowed as she pulled him closer to her relishing in his anguish and surprise. "Now, you're all dead."

"You will not have me, witch!" Viktor managed to cough up blood as Lesley lifted him into the air. "You left me an opening." With Viktor's hands on her stomach, Lesley received a powerful silver burst of energy. The resulting explosion sent Viktor flying backward, landing next to Amelia.

"What a pair we made." He said coughing up blood. "All the fighting. All the sacrifices that seem so important."

As the explosion's fury diminished, Lesley emerged unscathed from behind her shimmering purple shield. Her burgeoning tempest manifested as dark clouds that unleashed a barrage of lightning in all directions. Her energy pulsed through the ranks of guards, lights, and clergymen, affecting countless individuals.

"It was all for nothing. I couldn't stop her." Amidst his laughter, Viktor convulsed, expelling more blood from his mouth.

In a weak motion, Amelia nodded her head, ejecting a spray of her own blood from her mouth. "You were always a pain in the ass little brother." She said, reaching out to him.

As Viktor grasped her hand, the gravity of his injuries began to ease as his blood seeped onto the floor. His face grew ghostly pale, reflecting the pallor of death. "I'm sorry for everything."

Amidst a desperate plea, Lisa's voice quivers, "Someone, please help! The anguish in her eyes overflows with tears, torn between the impossible choices before her.

In a single motion, Lesley dove downward and landed amidst the center of the runic stones. She unleashed her fury upon Lisa, enveloping her in a vibrant violet shield and propelling her backward, away from the royals. With a grim determination, Lesley uttered, "You will save neither."

Her gaze unwavering, Lesley kept her attention fixed on the two royals as their blood spilled forth. A dark smile spread across her face as she spoke, "This is the moment, isn't it?"

Raven dropped out of the shadows into the center of the circle, his eyes narrowing in a smile. "It will all be over soon. Use the runic gemstone, the same as before. However, focus on me."

Lesley gazed intently into the gemstone, her eyes widening. She looked up at Raven, who placed a gentle hand on her shoulders and kissed her forehead. She stared at Gabriel with a look of regret, then the vortex appeared and swallowed them both. The gateway lingered, it's dark tendrils warping and distorting reality around it.

"I'm going to die." Viktor's cold eyes, brimming with tears, betray his inner turmoil.

"Hold on. We can reconcile this." Amelia said her emerald eyes filled with despair.

"No, sister," Viktor said. "You were right all along. You have always been the one to lead us, and now you will live on, ascendant." Exerting his final strength, Viktor bestowed his power upon Amelia. The silvery light suffused her body. "This was not my intended fate. Live,"

Witnessing the profound and selfless sacrifice that Viktor made for his sister, Gabriel found himself rendered unable to speak, his emotions frozen in numbness. His gaze fell to his own hands, and a haunting question emerged within him—was a similar act of sacrifice necessary for him to save his Lesley?

Amelia lifted her gaze to meet Gabriel's, her luminous emerald eyes ablaze with a mix of sorrow and newfound clarity. Her blonde locks cascaded like a silver flame and crown, accentuating her radiant beauty.

With a tone filled with emotion, Amelia acknowledged, "I now possess a deeper understanding, akin to the wisdom our father and Viktor have acquired. A connection to Sol, Ascendant. This level of clairvoyance was not something I had foreseen."

"It all looks so foolish now." Amelia looked over at Viktors, his body turning into silver particles and flowing into her. "I did not want this. Not like this." She said tears were rolling down her face. Amelia's wounds healed and she inhaled deeply. "Go, save her." Amelia said, touching Gabriels face.

"I don't know if I can."

"Only you can. It is imperative that you proceed with great urgency." With glistening emerald eyes, Amelia's tears began to well up. "Go, now."

As Gabriel observed the escalating turmoil, a torrent of doubts engulfed him. His gaze alternated between the whirling, turbulent vortex and the steadfast figure of Amelia, amidst the chaotic battle surrounding them.

"Go! We will hold the throne room! Stop the youngling." Father Lancaster yells unleashing a hailstorm of elemental magics with his Lyndell wand.

With a radiant glow, Celise and Jennifer channeled their remarkable power into James' bear. In response to their efforts, the bear underwent a remarkable transformation, expanding to an immense size. With newfound strength, James valiantly defended against the relentless Darklings, effortlessly swatting them away. He possessed the remarkable ability to tear apart their rifts, completely eliminating their presence from reality.

"Jennifer, assist me with the princess," Lancaster bellowed, shifting his focus to Amelia. The two of them channeled their healing light into her.

Amidst the relentless onslaught of Darklings, Gabriel valiantly fought, only to be halted by a colossal darkling resembling a small mountain. James stepped in, grappling with the creature and creating a path forward.

As Gabriel glanced back, he caught Amelia's warm smile. He reached out, allowing the tendrils of darkness to encase his fingers. A familiar warmth coursed through him, and his peripheral vision illuminated with silvery light and dark tendrils. However, a sudden, piercing cold bite jolted his skin.

Chapter Twenty-Eight

Lesley

In the shadowy depths of a concealed network of tunnels, Lesley emerges. Fearlessly, she traverses the unlit passageways, effortlessly descending into tunnels that have remained untouched for eons. With nimble steps, she embarks on a daring descent along colossal tree roots. "Where am I?"

"This hidden chamber under the tree of Lyndell."

"What a fascinating ability," Lesley had remarked, uncertain how she had perceived the enigmatic figure before her. Despite Raven's tangible presence, his appearance had resembled pure shadow, a mesmerizing blend of solidity and shifting darkness that seemed to have flickered in and out of perception.

With a cunning grin, he spoke. "It will make more sense once we reach the bottom."

As they ventured deeper into the tunnels, they finally arrived at the bazaar room, encountering an overgrown door in their path. The state of the room appeared even more deteriorated compared to Lesley's previous memory of it. However, she wondered if it was possible that she had merely dreamt of its former condition, as the distinction between reality and illusion began to blur.

With a determined effort, Lesley forced the door open, revealing a haunting sight. The tree's roots protruded ominously through the decaying wood. Inside, they encountered a man in a state of advanced decay, bound and concealed beneath a thick tangle of roots.

Without a moment's hesitation, Lesley began hacking at the roots, but she soon found herself pinned down by an ancient, wooden creature resembling a tree. She struggled against its relentless grip, feeling its malevolent force attempting to drain her strength. With a surge of determination, she tore through the roots and unleashed her fury upon the creature's flesh.

However, the tree's resilience proved formidable. It rapidly regenerated, pushing Lesley back with its overpowering force and pinning her arms against the wall. She hung there, seemingly helpless.

But Raven, ever vigilant, sprang into action. With his daggers gleaming, he skillfully attacked the creature's back, exploiting its vulnerabilities. The Trent retaliated by summoning more roots to ensnare Raven, yet he proved elusive, slipping through the shadows and avoiding capture. With a swift invocation, Raven conjured a formidable shadowy blade upon his daggers and resumed his assault on the tenacious tree, hacking away with unwavering determination.

With the Luminescent gemstone in hand, Lesley conjured a protective shield to repel the advancing creature. Though the shield successfully halted the creature's progress, the tenacious roots of the creature latched onto it, draining its energy. As the shield flickered and weakened, Lesley dismissed it, only to find herself face-to-face with the persistent creature once more.

Determined to fight back, Lesley engaged the Trent in a fierce swordplay battle. However, the overwhelming number of the creature's limbs proved to be a formidable challenge. One by one, the relentless limbs entangled and pinned her against the wall, leaving her vulnerable and exposed. The moldy maw of the creature loomed closer, its chilling breath sending shivers down her spine as it hungered to consume her spirit.

"We have come too far to fail." Emerging from the shadows, Olivia bestowed a divine benediction upon the gathering. In the midst of the encroaching darkness, Lesley's radiance intensified, causing an inversion of the surrounding light. Unleashing a torrent of luminous energy, Lesley's cry reverberated through the air. As lightning crackled and thunder roared, she unleashed her storm-empowered runic blade upon the Trent, engulfing it in a fiery embrace.

With each swing, Lesley's sword rhythmically sliced through the wood, an exhausting display of relentless chopping. Her aching arm and perspiring forehead told the story of her exertion. Finally, she halted, inhaling sharply as she surveyed the lifeless heap of timber with a mix of satisfaction and contempt. A final, deliberate tap of her foot served as a confirmation of its defeat.

As Lesley chopped away at the unyielding tree roots, a sense of uncertainty hung heavy in the air. Despite her reservations, an irresistible force compelled her to persist. Raven's desire for something in this place had become her unwavering motivation, overshadowing any doubts she may have had.

The empowered runic blade splintered the wood with each swing, more exhilarating than the last. She was so close, a wide grin spreading across her face. She filled the blade with surging power, splintering the wood deeper. When it was deep enough, she placed her hands on the wood and pulled apart, summoning a deep darkness from within.

Beneath her strength, the wood splintered, exposing a man encased in the roots of the tree. Withered and old, his bones radiated power. The great tree was both his prison and his jailer. Lesley reached out and grasped his bony hand, absorbing the power of the forgotten dark avatar. More than power flowed into her; she felt a presence. Darkness swirling around her vision.

"Is this what we came down here for? A corpse."

"Not any corpse, my corpse." With a tender touch, Raven caressed the corpse's cheek, his gaze shifting to Lesley. His eyes flashed a vibrant orange hue, and the world around them underwent a remarkable transformation. The grayscale surroundings melted away, transitioning seamlessly into an immersive darkness. "Witness."

Amidst the shadowy embrace of darkness, her gaze fell upon a solitary figure. A king, unyielding in his regal position on the throne, exuded an aura of strength unmatched by any in the realm. However, when treachery struck him in the form of the four wolf clans, he sought refuge in the embrace of the dark goddess, yearning for the power to exact revenge upon his former comrades.

In the void's abyss, he conjured his malevolent power, a dark star exuding corruption. Ancient, writhing tendrils surged from the shadowy depths, infusing him with their malevolent essence. His eyes emanated an eerie orange glow, while his skin darkened to an abyssal hue, absorbing the surrounding light. From the emptiness emerged a suit of ignited black armor, enshrouding his form. The Void King stood once more, his dominion over darkness unyielding.

With his sinister dark magic, the Void King forged the Tithe Pool, a formidable force capable of extracting the life essence from his subjects and amassing it within a colossal crystal known as the Aura Catalyst. Utilizing the Aura Catalyst, the Void King mercilessly drained the essence of all except those who remained staunchly loyal. These abyssal paladins served as conduits, channeling the essence of Oblivion, a realm untouched by light, and wielding it as a potent weapon in the Void King's sinister dominion known as the Voidguard.

In the aftermath, the once flourishing kingdoms were reduced to desolate wastelands, stripped of vitality and overrun by mindless creatures birthed from the depths of the abyss.

Leading his clan, the Void King launched a brutal attack on the Wolves, annihilating their numbers mercilessly. However, as he neared victory, a treacherous act awaited him. His loyal lieutenant, Cecil, betrayed him, wielding the combined might of Sol and the Yggdrasil druids. Overwhelmed, the king was imprisoned deep within the tree's roots by Cecil. Over time, the tree absorbed his power, succumbing to the darkness that consumed him.

With the passage of time, the disparate wolf clans unified under The Silver Wolves' Banner, led by Sol, and the Wolves of Sköll, who would later become the Ascendant Avatars of Sol. Imprisoned within the isolated confines of his tree, the enfeebled Void King was compelled to witness the growth and transformation of his betrayers. Over time, he managed to harness his ethereal essence, enabling him to manifest a shadowy projection of his being. Inhabiting a dual existence, both within and beyond the tree's embrace, he diligently plotted his ultimate revenge.

Through strategic manipulation, he adeptly established a revered guild. With masterful control, he commanded the dreams of the Wolves, harnessing their power for devastating conflicts. Meticulously, he constructed four grand cities, artfully aligned in a mystical circle called the Tithe. This sacred domain served as a spiritual tax for the King of Lyndell, granting him and his Kingsguard, along with any deserving warriors, an infusion of power and strength.

Lesley observed Raven's ethereal manifestation, noting a profound shift in his appearance. Raven's skin had darkened, and his eyes glowed with an eerie dull orange hue. The abysmal aura surrounding him seemed more potent than ever before. "Now you see." In a chilling gaze, Raven's essence harmonized once more with the Void King, a manifestation of pure darkness. Its eye sockets ignited, casting a gentle glow. "Cecil imprisoned me and forced me to live as a nameless shade. The eyes, the thoughts and memory of a great king."

"Having arrived, let us unleash the might of the Aura Catalyst, eradicating the treacherous wolves from the surface of Terra. Once this is accomplished, we shall extend our dominance over the entirety of reality in Oblivion's name."

"No, you cannot absorb me!" As darkness encroached, Lesley's weakening body succumbed to its relentless grasp. Her muscles protested vehemently as she fought to break free, unleashing a mighty roar while pulling back her arms. But the persistent roots, already draining her life force, showed no mercy. Her mind grew numb, and the edges of her vision dissolved into darkness, igniting an unprecedented primal fear and terror.

In a final, desperate bid for freedom, Lesley swung her sword arm down, only to be ensnared by the swift roots behind her. They yanked her arm backward, lifting her off her feet. A fierce roar erupted from her lips as she battled against the inescapable clutches of her captors.

As the runic gemstone flew out of the bag, Lesley was enveloped in a runic shield of crystal. The dark energy of the runic gemstone pulsed, and the shield moved from her hand and enlarged, severing the roots, and encasing her. She smiled as she floated in the center, wind and thunder picking up speed. The gemstone itself became the shield, and Lesley felt emboldened, lifting the Runic Sword in one hand. "I should have known, I can't trust anyone."

"You can trust in me, Lesley. I meant it when I said you were important to me." The intricate entanglement of roots enveloped and encased the shield, inadvertently reinforcing its strength instead of compromising its integrity. Lesley's eyes widened as she recognized that the shield, intended to protect her, had transformed into a confining prison. With renewed determination, she pounded on the shield using the hilt of her sword.

"But it was foolish of you to think you can use my own weapons against me." Raven said his voice twinged in sorrow. His spirit floats over to Lesley, his warm colored eyes narrowing as he grabs her chin. Raven summons the symbiote-like suit, lifting Lesley into the air. Transforming into many little hands, wrapping around her like a cocoon.

In a solemn and deliberate motion, Raven stretched out his hand, aiming to make contact with the concealed cocoon. The surrounding air was charged with an intense and turbulent energy, emitting a crackling sound as particles of dark blue light refracted and scattered. The dark green braziers that encircled them emanated a deep and foreboding crackling noise, adding to the ominous atmosphere.

From his wooden throne, the deceased Void King emerges. Lyndell's roots rupture and fracture in defense as he ascends, breaking free from their grasp. The corpse's eyes flutter open, casting a warm glow upon the chamber. His flesh undergoes a remarkable transformation, morphing into living shadows as it engulfs the cocoon of darkness, consuming it entirely. Abruptly, the room plunges into complete darkness.

In the enveloping darkness, the Void King's voice resonated with a thunderous proclamation, "Lesley, do not resist. Your worth extends far beyond being a mere soul destined for consumption. You have been instrumental in my reunion with Oblivion."

Lesley couldn't see but she could hear her presence, Olivia's voice. "This is the path I have set before you," Olivia's voice echoed, vanishing as the world around her dissipated in a wave of darkness, transforming into nothingness. Lesley curled into a fetal position, stretching her limbs as she floated in the endless dark. In the distance, a small red orb hung dimly.

As the orb drew nearer, it grew brighter. Suddenly, an endless number of eyes appeared, all snapping open. Lesley realized they were eyes—or at least something like them. A swirl of dark colors formed into an image of a woman, like the one Lesley had seen so many times before in her dreams and visions. "You shall have all the stars in the sky, little one. Eternity awaits, open your eyes and see what binds us."

Lesley looked down at the runic blade in her hand, feeling its weight. A dark green mist swirls with the red lights to a fine point. It shines brightly and explodes into fine shimmering star dust. A tall dark and beautiful woman walks into view molding out of the shadows. Her wrists were shackled with chains that hummed with power. She puts out her arms, wrist up, as if to present the chains. "Free us." She said this time a little more motherly. "Together."

The Void King appeared before her once more, his body cloaked in darkness, his tendrils encircling and embracing Lesley. The sensation was comforting, like a warm hug or a father's embrace. Accompanied by Raven, Lesley believed in their combined strength to triumph over their foes and avenge themselves on the wolves. However, an unsettling sensation gripped her as she felt her spirit weakening.

At that pivotal moment, she discerned an unmistakable connection between herself, Gabriel, and Raven. Adorning the Void King's armor was a familiar crest—a menacing, one-eyed wolf crowned by a circle of soaring ravens. This newfound revelation ignited a tempest within her soul.

The once-enigmatic Void King stood unveiled, no different from the rest, merely another wolf in the pack destined, and he had, to betray her.

As Olivia's gaze pierced into the depths of his warm-hued eyes, a sudden surge of power coursed through her veins, accompanied by an unsettling sensation of shadowy tendrils twisting ominously. As Olivia's fingers lightly brushed against her cheek, her smile warped into an unsettling and malevolent expression.

Within the encompassing shroud of darkness, The Void King's eyes flickered, illuminating briefly before dimming once more. A soundless scream emanated from his lips, piercing the heavy silence. The Void King's destiny was now unalterably sealed. He joined the ranks of the fallen, becoming merely another lifeless wolf, reduced to a mere fraction of his former self, while Lesley consumed an abyss of unending darkness within her.

"Together." With a firm grip, Lesley wielded the blade using both hands and brought it crashing down with great force. The shackles shattered, disintegrating into a brilliant, blinding stardust. Regaining clarity, Lesley's gaze locked onto Gabriel's imposing figure. His sword acted as an impenetrable barrier, deflecting her own weapon.

Bathed in the radiant glow of a sword's light, she discovered herself once again beneath the shade of the grand tree. Her own blade found itself blocked by a shimmering blade of pure light. Despite her great dread and reluctance to take the life of Gabriel, she understood the dire necessity that she faced. Liberation was an unattainable dream unless the wolves were eliminated—every last one of them.

Chapter Twenty-Nine

Gabriel

Through the portal, Gabriel found himself in a deep, rooted cavern. The pathways seemed violently alive, trembling and causing deep tremors. The details of the area around him were notably lacking in color, an unnatural grayscale, like his home before he was teleported away through the vortex.

He took a deep gulp and pressed forward holding the life stone up. It wasn't long before he felt like he was being encroached upon. He sensed movement in the corner of his eyes but when he looked there was nothing there. Pure terror edged on his heightened sense. The life stone was his only anchor that kept his growing anxiety in check. This was a familiar sensation but multiplied and much worse than before.

He thought about what he was going to find at the end of the tunnel. Some sort of dark avatar, bound by the tree. That's where Lesley was headed. He doubted that she knew what she was getting into, fumbling around in the dark. Gabriel started to doubt himself as well. Did he know what he was getting into?

He pushed the thought aside when he heard the distinctive growl of Darklings. A sound he wasn't too eager to hear again. He kept moving forward keeping the light of Sol channeling through the life stone. If there were Darklings down here he hoped that the light would keep them at bay.

He found a carved spiral staircase leading downward. It looked endless and he leaned over the hole, trying to gauge its depths. He felt a tendril wrap around his foot. He didn't hesitate to summon a sword of light and swung down. He stopped himself before striking. His eyes went wide as he realized it was Lesley. She is childlike and has eyes full of wonder. Gabriel kneeled down and patted her on the head.

Approaching the child, he affectionately greets her with a warm, "Hey there, kiddo." In his casual attire of jeans and a t-shirt, he gently kneels down, carefully lifting her from the concrete surface of the playground. Examining her injury, he notices her scraped knee, which is bleeding slightly.

"Gabriel, the other kids were picking on me."

"Were they now? Why would anyone pick on a cute baby girl like yourself?" He said, pinching her little cheeks.

"They said it was your fault."

In a gentle and amiable tone, he inquired, "What was my fault?"

"That I don't have parents."

Gabriel tilted his head in contemplation, struggling to find the right words. Conflicted within, he hesitated to reveal the truth to her, yet a sense of guilt gnawed at his conscience. The inner turmoil he experienced was palpable. A dark laughter erupted, transporting him back to the dark innards of the tree of Lyndell.

As the life stone's pull yanked him abruptly back to reality, he gulped down air, his sword cleaving through the shadowy creature that had taken the form of Lesley. The illusion, uncomfortably lifelike, weighed on his mind. However, there was no time for second-guessing. He continued, descending the spiral staircase. The walls, crafted from intertwining roots, resembled wriggling snakes. The Sol tree, infected by the encroaching darkness, succumbed to corruption.

He was suddenly attacked by the roots, he sliced through them like thick jungle vines. They endlessly blocked his path, regrew the more he sliced.

But he moved fast. Making slow progress forward, the closer he got the darker the vines became until they were true tendrils of the void. He pushed forward, summoning the light of sol, and its radiant flames. The tendrils faded allowing him to pass.

Endless hordes of Darklings soon assaulted him, and he cut through them. They were led by a creature that forced them to move forward. It was a knight of pure darkness, wielding a sword and shield. Gabriel cut through them as well.

"Kinslayer." It said in a harsh tone. The two knights clashed, Gabriel desperately keeping his flank clear not allowing the Darklings to surround him. Gabriel felt the dark creatures whisper, chattering, nonsense into his mind.

In a swift maneuver, Gabriel deflected the knight's blade, feinting to create an opening. Capitalizing on the knight's vulnerability, Gabriel launched a counterattack, delivering a decisive slash that cleanly severed the knight's head from its body. The Void Knight disappeared like a shadow fading in the light. But he still had the smaller creatures to deal with. He pushed them back with his sword of light, picking them off one by one until they were all vanquished.

During a brief instance. Gabriel's upward glance revealed his father in a ghostly form, mocking him from a distance. Sensing an urgent tug at his shirt, Gabriel's instincts kicked into high gear. With lightning-fast reflexes, he pivoted on his heels, drawing his blazing sword of light in a swift arc. The illuminated blade left a stream of light as it moved through the air, mere inches from Lesley's face. Gabriel's gaze softened as he assumed a sitting position.

Gabriel and Lesley were comfortably nestled on the plush cushions of the couch. The soft, warm blanket wrapped around them like a comforting embrace, adding to the cozy ambiance of the living room.

In the comfort of Lesley's lap, she gently turned her head towards him. Her gaze met his, revealing a subtle transformation wrought by the passage of time. Her voice carried a mix of curiosity and concern as she inquired, "What has become of our parents?"

With a heavy sigh and a frown, Gabriel expressed his discontent. "Lesley, I'll tell you when you are older."

"Is that a promise?" She questioned, her voice thick with sleep and a yawn escaping her lips.

Gabriel studied her soft face, his gaze lingering on the tiny scar on her face. "I do." But Gabriel knew that never came to pass. He never kept his promise and she never got the truth. He never had the heart to tell her, even the lie he told everyone else. Resting her head on Gabriel's lap, she continued to watch the movie, her eyes drooping until she eventually succumbed to slumber.

In the enveloping darkness, Lesley's resonant voice echoed with a haunting reminder, "But you never did."

The void knight gabbed Gabriel by the back of the head, tossing him off the couch into the wooden cavern wall. The knight leapt onto Gabriel wrapping his cold armored hands around his throat squeezing the life out of him. Upon seeing the Void Knight's countenance, Gabriel was overcome with astonishment, as it bore a striking resemblance to that of his own father.

Gabriel shoved the knight's arms away, planted his knee between them, and pushed him off. Gabriel came to his senses and unleashed a beam of radiant light, annihilating the knight. He looked around wildly, panting, rubbing his sore throat.

He continued down the corridor of darkness until he found a room with six pillars and several braziers burning with dark blue flames. There was a ruined doorway that someone had hacked through. He assumed that it was Lesley, who had ripped the door open with his sword. In a fleeting moment, he briefly shook his head as he held her accountable for recklessly using their cherished family heirloom to break down the door.

Amidst the crackling brilliance of lightning, Gabriel finds himself ensnared by the encroaching darkness. Thunder crashes menacingly, its reverberations echoing through the room. An oppressive void engulfs him, leaving him stranded and isolated within its boundless expanse. "You were always that way." In the enveloping darkness, Lesley's voice reverberated, devoid of any physical form.

In that instant, Gabriel blinked, and to his astonishment, she materialized right in front of him. Standing before him was a freshman in high school, clad in her brand-new black and red school uniform, complete with a bag slung casually over her shoulder. "I'm sorry, I'm trying to protect you."

"I don't need you to protect me, tell me the truth. What happened to our parents?" Her voice, once vibrant, now exhibited signs of strain, while her eyes, once lively, appeared sunken and detached from the present. Down her cheeks, tears cascaded, smudging her ebony eyeliner.

With a heavy heart, Gabriel averted his gaze downward and to the left, releasing a deep sigh. He yearned to shield himself from the haunting memories of the past, and dreaded the prospect of revealing the truth to her. "I'll tell you when."

"You're older." With a voice devoid of emotion, Lesley concluded his sentence, conveying a sense of profound disappointment. "Have you ever thought of the possibility that I might not be here? That You or I could die at any moment and then the truth will never be told?"

Gabriel wished that the truth would never come to light. He knew she was right, but he still couldn't tell her. An abrupt, sharp intake of breath brought him back to reality as he was about to speak. He discovered he was paralyzed and being dragged forward through the door by mysterious, tentacle-like hands. Amidst the commotion, he could hear the cries of a young girl. Suddenly, Lesley appeared in his line of sight.

In the darkness, Lesley knelt alone, her tears flowing freely. Gabriel's throat constricted as he watched her, feeling the dryness spreading within him. He watched her for a moment, a flash of lighting inverting the shadows and faded back to black. "I didn't want to burden you."

"That's bullshit." With her head snapped upward, her face contorted in anger and her eyes reddened from crying, she displayed a striking image of distress. "You were sparing yourself."

"I don't know what you want me to say."

"The truth, tell me the truth!" Another flash of lightning dramatically altered the darkness into their parents' room.

This sudden change caused Gabriel to gasp in surprise, his eyes widening in astonishment. His throat constricted, and his heart momentarily skipped a beat, gripped by a surge of trepidation. With a gulp, Gabriel watched as the shadowy figures of their parents emerged from the darkness and entered the room.

"Mom and dad were killed by a burglar." Lowering his head and furrowing his brow, he averted his gaze from the unfolding events before him. The weight of witnessing this moment in time bore heavily upon his spirit, stirring a deep-seated reluctance within him.

A silhouette of a man with a gun walks through the entrance pistol raised firing twice. Their father was instantly dead but their mother sputtered blood for a second before succumbing to her wounds. The man spun around and fired rapidly after a sudden noise in the hallway. He was then shot in the head into the bodies of their parents.

"Stop lying, stop lying to yourself!" Lesley's disembodied voice screamed, her warm colored eyes sneering at him through the two large windows.

Gabriel was dumbfounded; he was at a loss for words. He did not want to revisit that moment. He sat there on the ground for a long time. He took a deep breath and closed his eyes. He prayed for strength, guidance, and patience—anything that would help him through this situation. But all he heard was silence.

"That's not what happened." Trembling, Lesley's bodiless voice resonated, its chilling tone piercing Gabriel's mind. He could sense her relentless probing, an agonizing sensation as if invisible claws were slicing through his skull, desperately trying to infiltrate his very thoughts.

When Gabriel opened his eyes he found himself standing in the hallway of their home. He was facing the master bedroom, Their parents fighting in front of him. His father was wrestling with a burglar, their mom standing nearby. Gabriel picks up a pistol off the floor and fires two shots into the bedroom. He moved forward and his parents were dead, killed by his hand.

Gabriel looked down and saw a burglar begging for his life on his hands and knees. Gabriel narrowed his eyes coldly and shot the burglar in the head. Gabriel wiped the gun clean of his fingerprints then placed the gun in the dead burglar's hand. He fired a few more rounds at the door, the sound of a waving baby echoing through the halls.

Gabriel raced into the room where the crying was coming from and found Lesley crying in her crib. Gabriel noticed her bleeding cheek, which was grazed by a bullet. In his frantic attempt to frame a burglar for murder he almost killed Lesley. Gabriel picked up Lesley and cried with her. Tears rolled down his face as reality caught up to him. "It was a mistake, I'm sorry." The scene fades into the shadows leaving Lesley and Gabriel standing among the bodies of their parents in the master bedroom.

Lesley touched the little scar on her face with her finger. "So that's where I got this." She let her finger slide down her cheek and then let her arm drop to her side, her eyes narrowing.

"I was trying to protect them." A crushing weight pressed upon Gabriel's chest, a fusion of physical and emotional agony that emanated from within. The sensation of guilt was an inescapable force, binding him to the ground, like an abyss weaving endless tendrils of darkness around him.

"You were only trying to protect yourself." With a sudden, eerie appearance, Lesley emerged in the window and floated down to the floor. Despite the warmth of her eyes, a cold and disdainful sneer was etched across her face. Her determined steps carried her over the lifeless bodies of her parents, as she made her way towards Gabriel.

Gabriel attempted to avert his gaze, but was unable to tear his eyes away from the blood-soaked carpets. Perspiration beaded on his brow, and his breathing became labored. "No, no, no," he muttered, shutting his eyes and swaying back and forth. The nightmare had taken a toll on his mind.

With a commanding cry of "Open your eyes!", Lesley's voice rang out, accompanied by the ominous crackle of black lightning that surged around her.

Gabriel's knees buckled beneath the burden of his guilt held upright by the tendrils of darkness, the dark truth of his life. His throat was dry. He had dreaded this moment for the past seventeen years, and now that it was here, he didn't know what to say.

As Gabriel opened his eyes, he was met with the sight of warm-hued eyes peering at him through the windows, a sneer on their face that mirrored Lesley's own expression. The light cast by these eyes seemed to darken Lesley's features, giving her the appearance of a living shadow.

The life stone's radiance illuminated Lesley's warm colored eyes, the black lightning within them shifting to blue in the flashes of light. "You shouldn't have betrayed them," Lesley said, kicking Gabriel in the chest. He fell through the carpet and into a vast pool of darkness. The lights around him faded as he thrashed around, feeling like he was drowning in an ocean. He could feel Lesley's pain intensely.

Gabriel swam with all his might, the Life Stone's light pulsing around him. Then he closed his eyes and prayed to Sol. He grew still as he sank into the void. Suddenly, a burst of light shot from his body and he was back in the master bedroom. "I'm sorry you had to find out this way."

The bodies on the floor varnish. "No, you're sorry I had to find out."

Lesley laughed, turning to the dresser. A portrait of their parents sat next to a child's finger painting labeled "Lesley's first painting." Their father looked much like Gabriel, with a strong jaw, raven black hair, and piercing blue eyes. Their mother had long, dirty blond hair, hazel eyes, and a genuine, warm smile.

"I was trying to protect you."

"Protect me?" In a moment of mirth, Lesley's laughter echoed, while a lone tear gently glided away from the corner of her eye. "You've only kept me in the dark."

"I'm so sorry baby girl."

Lesley wiped the tears from her eyes. "You are and that's okay," she said, smiling, as a living shadow enveloped her, a pair of dark wings emerged from her back, spreading out in a display of power. Black lightning crackled and danced around her, filling the room with an eerie glow. Her voice, now deeper and more resonant, reverberated within the shadows, leaving an undeniable presence. "Knowing. Finally knowing the truth gives me the strength to do what I need to."

Lesley lunged at him, tearing through the walls and beyond. Gabriel felt as though he were being ripped through the tree then he was falling. He landed on his hands and knees, crying out in pain. When he opened his eyes, he saw Lesley floating above him, the Runic sword in one hand and the violet gemstone in the other. Her eyes were a warm color, and her aura shifted in and out of reality, looking like a collection of small hands. She was like a Valkyrie of pure darkness. "That you were always a monstrous wolf."

Behind her, the Tree of Sol, which normally shone with a bright white light, was now dimmed as it burned in shadowflame. The flames danced and flickered, casting eerie shadows on the ground. The air was thick with the smell of smoke and ash. The tree was being consumed by the flames, and it was only a matter of time before it was completely destroyed.

"Now all the wolves will end." Within the shroud of darkness, Lesley's silent fury burned like a hidden flame. The booming echo of her voice reverberated through Gabriel's chest, creating an intense sensation of pressure.

Drawing her strength from the spirit tithe, Lesley harnesses the collective power of the wolves, their spirits swirling around her. The intensity of their energy is palpable, coursing through her veins and granting her immense spiritual might.

As Lesley unleashes her powers, Gabriel bears witness to the writhing agony of the people caught within her spell. Their anguish fills the air, a testament to the potency of Lesley's magic.

Amidst the chaos, Lesley calls forth a tempest of unparalleled fury, enveloping the entire city in its wrath. Dark clouds gather, unleashing torrents of rain that cascade down upon the land. Yet, the Great Tree of Lyndell, a symbol of resilience, continues to burn defiantly, its shadowflame impervious to the deluge.

Raising his gaze towards Lesley, Gabriel summoned the resplendent Sword of Light. "Don't let her channel the tithe!" Gabriel yells, shooting bolts of firing ice-white flames crashing on Lesley's violet shield.

Father Lancaster waves the wand of Lyndell and chants. "O Spirits of the Wind, in the name of Sol, grant his sword the gift of flight."

Gabriel, suspended in midair by his magic, leaps into the air and breaks Lesley's shield. His sword of light burns through the shield, cutting her flesh shallowly. Gabriel's attack was enough to disrupt Lesley's channeling from the spirit tithe. They dueled in the air, but Gabriel was outmatched by Lesley's superior magical power. He was knocked back to the ground, dazed and injured.

Lesley unleashes an extraordinary surge of energy, aiming it directly at Gabriel. With swift reflexes, Gabriel nimbly dodges the forceful attack, causing him to lose his footing momentarily. Lesley, capitalizing on this lapse, unleashes an unrelenting barrage of powerful blows, each subsequent strike eclipsing the preceding one in intensity. Overwhelmed by the relentless onslaught, Gabriel finds himself defenseless and is mercilessly beaten to the ground.

James leaps after Lesley with Jennifer and Celise on his giant back. He grips her in his mouth, his giant maw crashing around the violet shield. Lesley expands by dislodging James' jaw and freeing herself.

As the giant beast roared in pain, Jennifer screamed. "James!"

"You cannot stop me. All reality is mine to claim!" Lesley rips open several new tears in reality, spilling forth Legions of Darklings fought alongside void knights spilling forth from the tears in reality. The last of the wolves, cleric, paladins and fighters met them in combat. The sounds of battle rang around the city. But the heart of the battle raged right here in the throne room.

Within a radiant blaze of light, Jennifer called forth Sol's light and repaired James' shattered jaw. The massive bearman let out a thunderous roar and fearlessly plunged back into the midst of the conflict. With unparalleled strength, he tore through the countless forces of darkness, leaving a path of destruction in his wake. Jennifer, wearing a satisfied smile, focused her energy on bolstering the surrounding troops, granting them increased vigor and fortitude.

Jennifer and Father Lancaster used Sol's light and spiritual enchantments to keep the troops standing and fighting. They mended rift after rift, but the tears kept opening. They weakened and removed great tears in reality.

Celise controlled fire as if it were an extension of her own body. Her Sol-enhanced white flames burned through the Darklings, large and small.

Gabriel knew they were being overwhelmed. They would eventually be worn down and defeated. He looked past Lesley and through the dark storm that was ravaging the city. He could see the twin moons of Terra, glowing brighter than ever before. He detected their vigorous energy, seemingly beckoning him. This reminded him of the potent energy Cecil had summoned in the Holding Cells.

Gabriel stretched out his hand, entwining his energy with that of the moon of Cecil, establishing a connection. Next, the silvery moon of Mani began to glow, imbuing Gabriel with its power. He reached out to the life stone clutched in his fist, which emanated protective power. From the ground, Gabriel's figure ascended, his blade of light pulsating with a magnificent fusion of white, silver, and blue and teal energy. The radiant spectacle emerged as the rotating energy particles merged, creating a breathtaking sight—a radiant, pure white light.

Lesley unleashed a torrent of dark lightning towards her opponent, only to see it dissipate against the protective barrier. Undeterred, she charged forward, her own blade drawn, meeting Gabriel head-on. In a thunderous clash of steel and energy, their blades collided, sending sparks flying through the air as they engaged in an intense battle for dominance.

Gabriel pushed Lesley back, evading her blade. He sidestepped her counterattack, but she deflected his attack. The two continued to trade blows, neither one able to gain an advantage. Their movements were like the yin-yang symbol, swirling in a dance of death. The air was filled with the sound of clashing steel and the smell of sweat.

Gabriel saw his chance and took it. His blade sliced through Lesley's defenses, and she cried out in pain. She fell to her knees, her blade clattering to the ground. Gabriel stood over her, his blade raised. "Yield."

Lesley looked up at him, her eyes filled with rage. "You'll have to kill me!"

Gabriel lowered his blade and helped Lesley to her feet. "Please don't make me do this."

Lesley's stern face softened into a smile. "Thank you," she said, gazing up with gentle eyes. "It was an honor to have dueled with you." Then, with a sardonic smirk, her warm-hued eyes narrowed as her hands gripped the wolf-hilted sword.

"Don't." With a sincere gaze, Gabriel implored fervently, his furrowed brow underscoring the intensity of his plea.

Lesley struck out with her wolf-hilt sword. Gabriel parried the blow and thrust his blade through her chest. Gabriel's eyes went wide, and dismissed the blade of light. He was stunned by his own reactions. "No, no, no! I didn't mean I didn't want this. I'm so sorry baby girl." Gabriel tried to hold her up As Lesley attempted to push him away.

She looked up at him with hatred in her eyes growing still in his arms. "I knew you had it in you wolf." Gabriel's lap and the floor were stained with her blood as the shadows that enveloped her body ebbed in and out of reality.

Overcome with sorrow, he began to weep. The loss of his parents wracked him, and he felt responsible for it. The rifts sealed, the battle waned, and the Darklings and void knights were defeated. The storm abated, unveiling the twin moons, Cecil and Mani. The blue and silver light of the moons shone through the night sky.

As blood gushed from her abdominal wound, Lesley struggled to stand, but her eyelids grew heavy, and her body surrendered to weakness. Meanwhile, Father Lancaster conjured a magical circle that bound Lesley and Gabriel, enclosing them. Within the circle, Lesley thrashed and fought, but Gabriel held her firmly in place. The roots of the tree, as if alive, tore through the ground and entwined themselves around both of them, further securing their imprisonment.

Gabriel closed his eyes and began to pray. He drew in a deep breath and fed the flames, causing them to grow larger and brighter. He exhaled, stoking the fire until it burned hot and strong. Gabriel's body began to emit an intense flame glow, and waves of fiery light erupted all over it. He places one hand on Lesley's forehead and another on her navel. The light stone explodes in a brilliant teal light covering them both in its light.

James raised his massive arms to the sky, as spiritual particles flowed in from all around them. The particles were blue, green, and red in color, representing the wild spirits. The spirits mingled with the energies from the life stone and the flames of Sol Gabriel's channeled power. With heads bowed, the priests, clerics, and guards prayed fervently, lending their strength to Gabriel.

"Sol, I implore you to banish Lesley from the darkness," Gabriel beseeched. The twin moons and the sun spiraled their energy downward, bathing Gabriel in fiery light and granting him immense power. Gabriel extended his hand, drawing upon the Tithe's energy from the ground. The surrounding area became enveloped in a brilliant white light.

Within Lesley, the darkness battled to remain, its black aura swirling around the radiant light, attempting to envelop it. Her dark wing extended and twisted backward, burning away, as her warm-hued eyes reverted to a deep sapphire blue. The violet aura encompassing her shattered and burst into fragments, expelled by the brilliant light. Her black lightning transformed back to a natural blue, protesting with crackling. The intense pulsating flash of light resembled a blinding bomb, forcing Gabriel to involuntarily close his eyes, temporarily blinding him.

As the magical light of the spell began to dissipate, Gabriel's gaze met Lesley's. Her wounds were miraculously healed, and the invasive tree roots gradually receded into the ground. Lesley's breathing slowed and deepened, indicating a state of tranquility and recovery. Engulfed in shimmering white flames of Sol, his body radiated light, driving away the lingering darkness. As the darkness waned gradually, dissipating into the air like ashes, Lesley's normal state was restored, and she lay on the ground.

With tears pooling in her sapphire eyes, Lesley gazed at Gabriel. Following a prolonged silence, she ended it by saying, "I don't believe I could ever forgive you." While adrenaline surged through her body, causing it to tremble, she composed herself by sitting up and gazing at her own knees. "You should have told me."

"I couldn't." He said with a pause. "If I did it would have made it too real, especially the consciences." Gabriel brushed Lesley's hair out of her face. "You were right. I was only protecting myself, and I wasn't there for you when you needed me the most. I'm deeply sorry for that. But I'm here now, and you'll never get rid of me."

"We have to do something," Celise's words jolted Gabriel, bringing him back to the present. Despair washed over him as the tree continued to burn in the clutches of the shadow flames. "We can't stand here and watch it burn." In the flickering light of the flames, Jennifer knelt alongside Celise, their figures elongated. Before them towered the grand tree, engulfed in flames and shrouded in shadows ignited by the dancing fire.

"I know," Jennifer said. "But what can we do? My healing magic isn't strong enough to put out the flames."

"Mommy, I can do this." With her arms extended skyward, a taut expression indicating strain, Celise's words reverberated through the air. After taking a deep breath and gathering her focus, Celise channeled her flame magic, releasing a potent beam toward the shadow flames.

"I'm always by your side, my love." Jennifer closed her eyes and focused her mind. She held her arms and placed her hands on her heart as warm radiant light channels out of her intermingling with Celise's Fire magic. In unison, Celise and Jennifer directed their resplendent energy into the tree. With Celise's precise control over the magic and Jennifer's healing touch, they infused the tree with a restorative force. As their magic flowed, the tree's vitality was gradually restored, reversing the damage caused by the flames. From the tree, an ethereal glow bathed its surroundings in a gentle light, and the flickering flames gradually subsided, leaving a sense of serenity. However, dread persisted, warping the shadows and intensifying their strength, reigniting the lingering darkness that grew and spread.

"It's not working!" Celise said. "We can't do this alone!"

With a reassuring tone, Father Lancaster gently placed his hand on her shoulder, comforting her with the words, "You are never alone, my child." United in their efforts, Father Lancaster, James, Amelia, Gabriel, and every resident of the city poured their hearts and souls into assisting the tree. Despite their collective energy flowing from the tithe into the tree, the flames stubbornly persisted.

Lesley's eyes were a stormy gray, and lightning crackled around her palm. With a single gesture, she released the lighting fixture from her grasp, propelling it into the heavens. In response to her command, a tranquil storm materialized above the city, sending torrents of rain cascading down. In unison, they worked together, nurturing and mending the ancient tree. The persistent flames eventually diminished, yielding to the brilliant illumination emanating from the Great Tree's revived splendor.

Father Lancaster raised his hands. "Radiant Sol, I implore you to bestow your luminous blessing upon Lyndell's heart. May your brilliance shine with unwavering intensity, warming the hearts of all who behold its splendor." As the flickering light of Sol on the tree intensified, enveloping the scene in an extraordinary brilliance, Father Lancaster's heart swelled with a sense of awe. He fell to his knees, his eyes fixed upon the miraculous transformation, a warm smile of contentment spreading across his face.

Exhausted, Celise and Jennifer collapsed to the ground. James, shifted back to his regular, human form, silently knelt down behind them and enveloped them both in his warm embrace, wordlessly expressing his affection for his family.

"We could have been like that." Lesley said, watching the family comfort each other. Lesley said, her hand over her chest where the sword of light had pierced her flash. "Mom and dad died…"

Gabriel, his eyes filled with tears, uttered, "…Because of me."

"I never got to know them." She traced her fingers where the wound was. "You killed them. Then you killed me." She said, with a dark laugh. "But I don't feel angry anymore. Anger replaced by a profound serenity that borders on numbness. It feels as though a significant part of me has been detached." A crackle of dark lightning flashed between her fingers. "Leaving a void within."

With a deep breath, Gabriel observed the dark lightning around Lesley morph into a pure void energy. A shadowy, purple energy expanded, enveloping his sight completely then vanished without a trace.

With an expression of uncertainty, Lesley inquired, "What have you done to me?"

In a moment that stretched interminably, Gabriel folded Lesley in a warm embrace. A wave of emotions washed over him as he contemplated how his younger sister had become much more than just a sibling—she had also become his daughter in many ways. The shame of his past mistakes, the guilt of his inability to protect his parents, weighed heavily on his heart. But amidst the darkness, he found solace in his ability to safeguard Lesley, a reminder of a love that transcended the boundaries of blood. "I believe I saved you," he whispered in her ear.

In response, Lesley leaned in, her eyes fluttering closed as she rested her head upon his chest. With a gentle touch, she clasped his hand, uttering softly, "I hope so."

Epilogue – Gabriel

As months passed, the people of Lyndell grieved for their fallen king and prince, along with countless others lost throughout the realm. Over time, the palace's grandeur was meticulously restored. The mighty tree of Lyndell healed, yet scars from the epic battle remained. Within the grand throne room, a magnificent ceremony unfolded as citizens assembled to bestow blessings and the honorable title of knighthood upon a new paladin of Sol. United in tribute, they gathered to mourn, bless, and crown their beloved Queen in a splendid and awe-inspiring display.

Father Lancaster raised his hands to the sky, calling upon the light of Sol to bless Gabriel. A bright light shone down from the heavens, bathing Gabriel in its radiance. Father Lancaster spoke a few words in a language that Gabriel did not understand, but he felt the power of the blessing coursing through his body.

After kneeling before Amelia, Gabriel officially became a Paladin of Sol, a dedicated warrior sworn to protect the light of the sun. With this newfound title came a profound sense of pride and honor, but he was also well aware of the significant challenges that awaited him in his new role.

Amelia, attired in an exquisite white and silver dress, drew a magnificent sword embellished with an intricate design depicting a wolf chasing the sun. With this sword, she bestowed upon Gabriel the honor of knighthood.

The Lord-commanders gave speeches in honor of the new Queen, and they pledged their loyalty to her. They also spoke of the importance of unity among the clans, and they vowed to work together to ensure the safety and prosperity of their people. In a grand display of optimism for the kingdom's future, the coronation ceremony symbolized a new era. Moreover, the coronation was an extravagant event characterized by copious amounts of food, beverages, and music. Amelia sat on a throne at the center of the festivities, and he received the adulation of the crowd.

Edward bestowed upon Gabriel Cecil's sword and shield, ensuring Cecil's death in battle. He had done what he thought was right at the time. The giant wolf shield felt too unwieldy at first, but with some adjustment, it became comfortable hanging from his arm. Gabriel felt awkward carrying the shield, it taking on his radiant fiery white light. It felt like yesterday this shield tried to rip his head off and here he was wielding it.

Cecil and Lance had perished at Lesley's hand, and he had no doubt that Edward was aware of this. Yet, here he was, presenting the shield—one that should rightfully be his to wield—to Gabriel. "I am honored to carry this artifact. But why give it to me?"

Edward glances away for a moment, then meets Gabriel's gaze. "You've shown great courage wielding Sol's light in defense of the realm. Against all odds you purified the essence of void out of your sister, a feat never known to be a possibility. You would honor the memory of my father, and our clan by wielding the Shield of Cerberus." Edward said with a bow. "With it you can defend our new Queen and nation."

Gabriel was moved beyonds words by Edward. He couldn't help but to smile. Composing himself, "Thank you, I will honor you on this day."

"The honor is mine, Sir Gabriel." Edwards bows in return. Edward turns and rejoins the festivities, a new song and drinks flowing freely on the tongues of the joyous people. Amelia officially assumed the crown, and the crowd erupted in applause. The new monarch had been greatly anticipated, and his ascension to the throne was met with great enthusiasm.

"I sincerely hope you do not have any objections to my taking Gabriel from you." With a mischievous grin lighting up her face, Amelia spoke. Gabriel couldn't help but smile broadly as her radiant glow mesmerized him.

With a simultaneous bow and salute, Edward respectfully greeted, "Your Majesty."

Amelia's hair flowing with vibrant silver light had led Gabriel around the room, introducing him to many new faces. From left to right she had walked with him, spending a few minutes with each member.

Three lords of the Yggdrasil, sat in the far left of the table. Bjord, Lief, and Fjordlyn. In the center were the three Lord-commanders—Frederick, of Sarum; Sara, of Dinard; and William, of Bremen and Edward of Sarum. As they journeyed onward, they happened upon a knight named Kain the Kingguard, a familiar face to Gabriel from a previous encounter. With narrowed eyes, Kain acknowledged Gabriel with a respectful nod. On the far right of the Table, King Malik and his wife Rea of the Shattered Swords, followed by King Amaterasu of Emerald Empire and his son Prince Takasago.

Amidst the bustling party, Gabriel found himself gravitating towards the peripheries, while Amelia engaged with the royal families and lords. Leaning against a wall, he wore a contented smile as he observed the unfolding festivities before him. Gabriel derived a profound sense of pride from his role as a protector, standing ready to serve and safeguard individuals in their moments of vulnerability.

With a coy smile playing on her lips, Amelia inquired, "You don't intend on surreptitiously departing, do you?" The fire in her emerald eyes matched the brilliance of her new, silvery flowing locks. Gabriel understood that accustomed to the presence of a living flame would be a necessity. Its unreality was jarring, but attractive.

"No, I was having a hard time adjusting. I feel like I can't stand still."

"You have the heart of a warrior. If all goes well, you should be more than equipped to be the best copsmen you can be."

A smile crept across Gabriel's face at the utterance of the term. Its absurdity remained unchanged since the initial time he had encountered it.

As the celebrations die down. Gabriel is approached by James, Jennifer, and their daughter, Celise. "It is time we take our leave. We still have a journey ahead of us."

"It was an honor to fight by your side." James takes Gabriel's extended hand and shakes it. "It will be missed."

"If you are ever near Snowfall Village you are always welcomed." Jennifer added.

"We will be traveling with the Lords of Yggdrasil. Come dawn, or whenever the wine is gone. Whichever comes first."

"There is no shortage of wine in my Kingdom." Amelia says with a smile.

Torn on what to do next, Gabriel had one certainty: Amelia. With a vision of a radiant future alongside her on Terra, he had no immediate plans to return to Earth. However, he was aware of the potential conflict with the darkness that loomed over Earth.

As Gabriel's mind wandered, he couldn't help but think of his younger sister, the sight of her forming a sorrowful frown on his face. He empathized with her desire for solitude, recognizing her need to grieve and find solace in her own way. Despite his protective instincts and desire to be there for her, he honored her request to be alone for the first time, respecting her newfound independence.

Epilogue – Lesley

In the heart of the smoldering crater that once bore the name Moonbright, Lesley finds herself seated, consumed by grief. With a profound sense of reverence, she establishes a shrine dedicated to the lost village, a testament to the memories and lives forever etched in its history.

"Such a lovely tune from my childhood." With a prayerful tilt of his head, Edwin's eyes fluttered open once more.

With her gaze fixed on the shrine, Lesley remained engrossed, seemingly anticipating the arrival of the visitor. A tear gently trickled down her cheek as she spoke. "You must be Edwin."

"I am. My mother used to hum that to me? Did you know her?"

Without sparing him even a glance, Lesley could sense the underlying malevolent intent hidden within his words. Regret glistened within her eyes as she finally admitted, "I did, and I do."

With a focused gaze, Edwin's eyes constrict. "You are the darkstorm correct?"

Lesley chose to disregard Edwin's question, "She missed you, you know." As she spoke, she engaged in a peculiar action, placing her hands in the charred dirt and splaying it around.

Edwin drew his sword, and pointed the blade at Lesley. "I've come here to avenge her."

"If there was one thing I've learned, Sol, is in all. Good in every aspect of life, But Void is also us all. It's easy to see them in great opposition but that's not always the case. There are many things that are attracted to the dark, but that doesn't mean they are evil. Attracted to the dark." With her eyes now open, Lesley got to her feet and turned to face Edward. "But I can't let you kill me."

"Well said." A disembodied voice said.

For the very first time, Lesley recognized the voice as belonging to her mother, Olivia. Above their heads, the runic gemstone soared, distorting the air around them. The village miraculously reverted to its original state, and they discovered themselves inside Lillyanna's frozen residence. Time was suspended in a dark explosion on the verge of eruption, capturing a battle that had nearly reached its conclusion. Lillyanna was frozen in time, desperately defending her family from Lesley's imminent attack.

Witnessing her own distorted self, consumed by rage, filled Lesley with deep remorse. She realized she was on the brink of annihilating everyone in the village.

"What is this?" Edwin inquired, his voice breaking the eerie silence that had settled over the motionless village. As he opened his mouth to continue speaking, an invisible force halted him, freezing him in time alongside the other villagers.

With an unwavering tone and a renewed sense of purpose, Lesley declared her words, letting her voice carry the weight of her convictions. It was as if she was being guided by an invisible light through the fabric of time itself, possessed with a profound understanding of what the future held. "We are here to save them."

With a swift glance upward, Lesley's gaze settled upon her distorted reflection, contorted with fury. From her core, a cataclysmic outburst of void energy and electricity erupted, threatening to obliterate everything within the village's boundaries. However, a flicker of movement caught her attention as she turned her head. Olivia stood mere steps away, observing Lesley's actions, seemingly unfazed by the frozen temporal realm. A subtle smile graced Olivia's lips as she gracefully approached.

"You are not my mother. But you use her face, her voice. Who are you?"

"I am the void, the darkness, the shadowed one," Olivia declared, her arms spread wide walking down the stairs moving through people and objects as if they weren't there.

"You mourn them, you wish this mistake to be undone. And it can be. Olivia took Lesley's hands and pulled her away from the shackles that had appeared on their wrists. "Invisible companions, always present."

"This is your one chance to break free, all you have to do is wish for it."

With a swift and cautious motion, Lesley retracted, reminiscent of a wounded puppy's flinch. Her eyes scanned her surroundings, seeking assurance. As she took in the familiar scene, a relieved sigh escaped her lips. Turning to Olivia, Lesley's gaze met hers, and in those eyes, she beheld an enchanting cosmos. Stars, suns, moons, planets, and endless realities intertwined, creating a captivating multiverse. "What are you?

"Before the multiverse existed, I was already in being; at the end of all things, I patiently await. I am the void, the very essence that separates life from death and death from rebirth, the boundary between heaven and hell. My true form surpasses all mortal perception, transcending mere physical form, shape, and substance. This body, this realm, and all beings within it originate from me."

Lesley was utterly captivated, completely lost in the mesmerizing depths of Olivia's warm eyes. The intensity of the allure made the idea of breaking eye contact or shifting her gaze away seem utterly inconceivable. It was as if she was witnessing a continuous cycle of infinite realities colliding, fading, and then rejuvenating endlessly.

As Olivia's form gradually faded away, Lesley found herself isolated in a solitary moment, frozen in time. The surrounding chaos had come to a standstill, leaving her immersed in a chilling stillness. "I am Oblivion." Her disembodied voice echoed in her mind.

In a resounding snap, the shackles began to disintegrate, dissolving into nothingness. The pulsating energy of the gem's essence served as a conduit, propelling them back to the present, restoring the natural order of time. Lillyanna's eyes expanded in a dawning revelation as she anxiously surveyed her surroundings. Lesley enveloped Lillyanna in a tender embrace, a world of unspoken emotions evident in her softened expression.

With Edwin's support, Alphonse and his Grandfather found themselves steadied on their feet once more. As they beheld their meticulously reconstructed dwelling, a sense of awe washed over them as it was magically transported to the present. In this extraordinary moment, the entire village was reborn, a testament to the rejuvenation of its former glory.

"Please forgive me." An ethereal emptiness engulfs Lesley's hair, causing it to dance in the unseen currents of the void.

Made in United States
North Haven, CT
02 June 2024